The Huguenot

*To Grace Flanagan,
a nurse of extraordinary
attentiveness who brings
joy into the sick room.*

Flight From Terror

*God Bless You!
Dolly Charmaine*

DeForce

Force, D.C.
The Huguenot: Flight From Terror: a novel /
D.C. Force

ISBN 978-1-7339762-0-6
eISBN 978-1-7339762-1-3

Published in the United States of America

Book Cover Design by
The Book Cover Whisperer:
ProfessionalBookCoverDesign.com

Front Cover: The Huguenot Cross

The Huguenot

Flight From Terror

By

D.C. Force

iv

Other books by D.C. Force

Family: a Century of Blood and Tears

(Huguenot Series)

The Huguenot: Flight From Terror

The Huguenot II: Building the Dream
(summer of 2019)

The Tower of Constance
an ebook Novella
(autumn of 2019)

The Huguenot and The Heathen
(winter 2019)

The Heathen II: The Prodigal Son Returns
(proposed release in 2020)

This series is dedicated to all the men,
women, and children throughout history
who have suffered severely and cruelly
because of their sincere and non-political
beliefs in and love for
our lord, Jesus Christ.

Contains scenes not appropriate

for those under the age of 18.

"Persecution is not wrong because it is cruel,
but cruel because it is wrong"
__Richard Whately

"If we let things terrify us, life will not be worth living."
__Seneca

Prologue

The South of France – 1625

It was as if the infant in Isabeau Charte's womb had some premonition of the monstrous things to come. It rolled, gained leverage and gave a kick that sent percussive waves to the inner backbone of its mother. Isabeau awoke and her eyes popped open as she moved to adjust the child in her belly. The cozy bed-chamber was bathed brightly in stark moonlight.

Outside the casement windows of the neatly kept two-story stone dwelling, their little hamlet was quiet and still. Inside she only heard the soft snoring of her husband Paul, retired Captain of the King's Regiment. She smiled. Many wives complained of their husband's snoring but to her it was a lullaby reassuring her that he was home now for the rest of their lives. He had given twenty-five years in service to his king, more than enough. The prime of his youth, the best years of his manhood gladly sacrificed to follow the call of duty and fealty to his sovereign. Surely no one, not king nor God, could ask for more.

Isabeau moved restlessly in the warm featherbed and slowly stroked her belly. This child Paul would know from its very birth, this one they would share the memories of together, and this one would be the blessing of their old age. And if their eldest was already stretching toward his adulthood, at least the others would share some of their childhood years with their revered father.

Was that a sound she heard between Paul's breaths?

Isabeau adjusted her position again and threw the coverlet off. The miracle of another child filled her with such ebullient joy but it also made her very warm. She had been concerned that she had grown too old to conceive again. Auguste was already seventeen and studying in La Rochelle. Doubtless, in a few more years they would be grandparents but God had given her another chance to have the daughter for which she longed. Not that she would love the babe any less if she had another son, she quickly assured both the child and the Almighty; as long as the babe was healthy, that was the only truly important thing.

She and Paul had been granted four healthy sons over the years despite the lengthy separations they had endured. Each one was a special source of fierce pride. Gabriel, their active fifteen year old wanted to be a soldier like his pa-pa; Lucien, her musician of ten played the *violino* like an angel at services each Sunday; little Pierre, almost seven, was always about some fanciful mischief but was so gifted in his letters that it was impossible to be harsh with him. And, of course,

Auguste, their eldest, their first born, *may God keep him from all harm in his stay away from home;* he was a serious student.

The faint sound grew louder than Paul's breathing but was not as yet identifiable.

She listened intently. The moment she realized it was the sound of horse hooves, she felt fingers of fear grip her heart and constrict her chest. *Auguste!* Something had happened! A messenger. No! She strained to hear. It was more than one horse. It was beginning to sound like a stampede of the animals and it had set distant dogs to barking.

"Paul," she shook her husband. "Paul, awake, awake! Someone comes! Something must be wrong!"

Paul Charte was instantly alert. Years of discipline allowed him to shake sleep from himself like one shakes dewdrops from a fresh head of cabbage. His attention was already focused and assessing as he bound from the bed in the singular unstopped movement of a man half his age. He was at the slightly opened window just as a half dozen horsemen reined to a halt on the cobblestones below.

"Paul Charte!" a sonorous voice called out amidst the clatter of iron clad horse hooves. From each point of the compass, watchdogs could be heard barking in the distance adding to the dissonance.

"Who in the devil..?" Paul breathed low, his eyes narrowing on the riders.

"Is this the house of Captain Paul Charte?"

By then two of the riders had dismounted and were pounding vigorously upon the thick oak door below.

"What is it you want?" Paul called back in a level guarded tone from the window overhead. "Do you seek to wake the dead?"

"We seek Captain Paul Charte," a voice replied.

"I am he, so you have found me. Now lower your voices before you awake the entire village." Paul spoke authoritatively. He was a man used to commanding others.

"Paul Charte...?" "Is it him?" "There … see him..?" "I see him."

"If you are Captain Charte, come out immediately!" The continued clatter of restless hooves on cobblestones combined with the horses snorting wind and the loud voices created a raucous din shattering the stillness of only brief minutes before.

"In the name of God, keep your voices down," Paul replied at the window. "Not a captain any longer. What is it you want?"

"We must speak with you on the king's business!" another voice came back in no quieter a tone.

"I will come out; one moment. But lower your voices or my neighbors will have my head tomorrow." Paul gestured and turned back into the chamber almost bumping into Isabeau.

"Who are they?" she asked sucking in her breath.

"Isabeau," Paul's hand grazed her shoulder and gently took her arm. "Get back into bed, my dearest. I will go and find out what these noisemakers want." His voice was soothing.

"You do not think… Auguste…?"

"No. No-no, they sound like soldiers. Doubtless it has something to do with my old command. They just cannot accept that I have no obligations to the military any longer," he sighed. "My resignation was accepted. I am a free man. Soldiers forget their manners and the civilities of normal life. These clods forget they are no longer in a barracks encampment."

"Paul Charte, come down in the name of the King," a voice from outside demanded again.

"Come, now… to bed, to bed," Paul coaxed his wife. "I must go down before they awaken everyone in the entire valley… if they have not done so already." And with that, the retired captain left his wife and to the beat of fists pounding upon his front door, he descended the stairs to the hall below. More concerned with stopping the commotion than with ceremony, he was still barefooted and clad only in his nightshirt. Moonlight flooding in from the high windows made navigation easy within the darkened home. He caught sight of Joseph, their aged servant, coming from the back of the house with a candle.

"Master… I am sorry…" the old man shuffled stiffly, his arthritic hips and knees paining him. "I move as quickly as the Lord makes possible…"

"Never mind, Joseph, go back to your warm bed, I will take care of this," Paul assured the white-haired old man. But the elderly retainer did not turn back. Instead, he continued slowly onward holding the candle up for light, following his master. Distracted, Paul was at the front door of his home within seconds and throwing off the crossbeam. "Has no one among you any sense of decorum? Someone is going to hear about this outrageous…" he began gruffly as he pulled open the heavy front door and stepped out to face his unwanted and noisy visitors.

Almost immediately he found himself seized by each arm. "Wh… what is the meaning of this? Unhand me at once!" he demanded in a voice of such authority that the youngest and least experienced member of the group almost released his left arm. The more seasoned and sadistic fellow on Paul's right chose to respond by rendering a blow to his head with the butt of a pistol. The assault caught Paul completely by surprise so used was he to the respect and discipline of his regiment. He staggered, momentarily dazed, and struggled to keep his footing.

Joseph moved feebly to his master's defense but was easily knocked aside. He fell, the candle flying out upon the stones, its small flame expiring. One of the men kicked out viciously at the fallen servant and landed such a fierce blow to his head that Joseph remained senselessly still.

"You have no protectors now, heretic!" The dark man still on horseback spat out the last word with venom.

Paul heard something in that voice that triggered a memory, an unpleasant recollection floating just beyond his grasp as his head began to throb. He stiffened as a name came to him. "Trebideau? Trebideau is that you, you bastard son of a syphilitic whore? What ill wind has brought you to my doorstep? Step down from that horse and face me like a man; do not hide in the shadows like a mangy cur!"

"The fine Huguenot *ex*-captain is no longer in a position to give orders," the voice sneered. "And I come to repay old debts."

"How dare you come to my house and in the middle of the night, pretending business for the Crown. You got exactly what you deserved and I would do it again. You were never officer material. Go back to whatever hole has been hiding you."

"Enough! You are no longer protected by your commission from the king. You are a fool, Charte. Do you not realize that when you resigned, you became just another ordinary heretic? Your entire family could disappear and no one will even care."

"You leave my family out of this!" Paul strained against his captors' hold on him.

"I think we have a nest of heretics here," the ominous voice stated calmly, "but I am a reasonable man. Do you wish to abjure your heretic ways, Charte?"

"What? Have you found your like among the priests, Trebideau?" Paul asked in disgust.

"In the name of the king and the Holy Roman Church, I ask you publicly if you wish to abjure?" Trebideau demanded, raising his voice.

Paul spit toward the rider. "That is all you will get from me!"

Trebideau nodded and the four men standing around Paul began to strike him. Isabeau was watching the altercation from the window above.

"Stop! Please stop! Mercy! For the love of God!" She screamed out and left the bedchamber as quickly as her swollen girth allowed. Surely she could move these men to pity, she thought wildly as she made her way down the staircase. She could hear rapid thuds and strangled groans, the sounds of a merciless beating. As able as her husband was, he was only one against many. Who were these devils? What had they to do with her Paul? She must beg for his life before it is too late.

"Ma-ma?" It was fifteen year old Gabriel, his fair blond hair tousled from sleep. "What is it, Ma-ma? What is happening?"

"*Je ne sais pas,* I know not," she gasped not stopping to look back at the youth. "Stay inside and mind your brothers." As she raced to the door, she saw beyond the threshold to the white of Paul's nightshirt covering a crumpled mass upon the courtyard stones while four men continued to rain heavy blows downward with the butts of their muskets. The leader remained calmly seated upon his horse and the sixth man held tightly to the reins of the nervous animals disturbed by the unmistakable iron smell of fresh blood.

"Stop! Stop, I beg you!" Isabeau screamed out again, panic destroying her self-control. By the light of the moon she could see black spots spreading all over the pale nightshirt and she knew with a sickening certainty that it was her husband's blood. "*Mon Dieu! Mon Dieu!* What have you done?! Paul? Paul?" She fell on her knees beside her husband's form and spoke toward the apparent leader who was still on horseback. "Have mercy… please, mercy, I beg of you."

"Close your mouth, slut!"

Isabeau felt a rough hand jerk her back to her feet. "Only one thing her kind is good for…" her assailant looked toward the seated rider. Perceiving a nod of consent, he rent the thin linen shift down the front exposing Isabeau's heavy breasts and swollen belly.

"The bitch is breeding!" exclaimed another as the moonlight reflected off her protruding abdomen.

"Just what we need. Another Huguenot bastard on the way!" a contemptuous voice came from behind as her arms were restrained to arrest her flaying nails. She felt other iron-hard hands pull her around. She was surrounded with nowhere to go and she could not move.

"We can soon fix that," said the first, looking to the dark triangle below her belly, "but before we do, she can do us a service, think you not?"

Isabeau felt herself being half pushed and half carried down onto the small flower bed. She was on the ground, her shift ripped completely asunder, weight falling on her. There was a scream. Had it come from her? She felt the pricking of flower stems upon her neck, her back, her skin registered the cool of the ground, the damp of dew. The distinctive almost astringent smell of marigolds replaced the heavy smell of blood in her nostrils. She struggled for leverage. Her hands had lost all feeling so tightly were her wrists being squeezed as someone held them high, pulling her shoulders upward. The skin of her legs burned as the flesh was twisted in a steely grip against her struggles. She tried to resist but she could not. She did not have the strength and she thought of her baby. Better to lose her honor than their child. She gave up suddenly and let her legs be spread wide. She tried to look to Paul. Her anxiety and fears blocking all sensation of the penetration taking place below. She could catch only glimpses of him and he lay so deathly still. Isabeau closed her eyes against the moonlight and her shame, tears streaming from her eyes. *Please dear God, Lord Christ, please, let it be over soon.*

"Ma-ma?!' Gabriel's cry brought her back to her surroundings.

"Go back…" she cried out to warn him but it was too late. The brave child, armed with his father's saber, rushed to her rescue only to have his arm sliced from his body in a movement so swift he did not realize what had happened until he tripped upon his own limb lying upon the ground at his feet. Briefly, he felt the warmth of his blood as it drained down his side. In shock, the lad's large gray eyes grew larger as he looked to his severed limb, the fingers of his hand still wrapped tightly around the saber's handle as it lay on the pavement in front of him. He could still feel the saber in his hand but he could not move it. He fell to the ground in a swoon where he was left to die, his life ebbing from him in gushing spurts timed to the beat of his heart.

Isabeau closed her eyes again. She blocked out all thoughts of Gabriel, all thoughts of Paul, all thoughts of the rape. A primal sense of self-preservation came over her as she thought only of her unborn child; she must protect this new life. She must submit and survive for its sake. It was the one thought to which she could still cling.

Excited by the violence and dry friction of her body, the man grunting over her made an early end of it as he gave out a gut-wrenching groan. The next was upon her, laughing as she squirmed to push his weight off her belly. The child was kicking erratically as though it also was trying to rid its mother of her attackers. Isabeau stifled her sobs and let the second stranger enter her without a struggle, his way made slick by the emissions of the first.

"The bitch is starting to enjoy it!" he gritted out then lapsed into a rhythmic grunting as he took his pleasure. "Who is next?" he invited when he finally withdrew and grabbed at his breeches to hoist them. Isabeau did not even try to move as the third took up his position in a failing effort to prove his manhood to his companions. He grunted in pretense, his flesh grown soft, and finished his charade in a matter of seconds.

"There, that is what they are good for," he said with heightened braggadocio, quickly moving off. "Now you, Galère."

"No names!" snapped one of the group.

"Sorry..." the third responded instantly.

"Now, the Huguenot slut knows my name," growled the one called Galère. "Oh, well, no matter," he grinned and grabbing Isabeau's thick, silken hair he wrenched back her head and sliced her throat from ear to ear.

Isabeau felt a burn as though the blade was hot and then the soothing warmth of her own blood. Her breathing sounded like winds whistling in a cavern. *I am going to die,* she thought with acceptance. And with that knowledge she grew calm. It was a better world they would find with the Lord. *Paul, you must wait for me*, she tried to say but the words never came out and black folded in on her consciousness before she could hear the next words.

"Get the whelps inside," ordered the leader from his horse. "There are three more."

Immediately four soldiers went into the house seeking the other children. After a ransacking hunt through the premises, the two younger boys were found cowering under a bed in the attic, an old nurse standing a feeble guard.

"Step aside old woman!"

"No-no! Leave the babies alone!" she cried, "May God curse your wicked sou..." A powerful fist halted her speech and she was knocked to the floor. The swipe of a saber ensured she would never rise again.

Beneath the bed, Lucien and Pierre clung so tightly to each other that it took only one saber thrust to pierce both their hearts.

As the marauding group reassembled outside, some quiet had returned to the scene.

"Did you find them all?" asked Trebideau in a low voice.

"Only two, plus this one," Galère said, kicking at the fallen boy.

"I want all four!" Trebideau snarled in frustration. "I want his bloodline wiped out forever! Where are the servants?"

"Dead," came a proud reply.

"Idiot! The dead cannot be questioned," seethed the leader.

"I will give you a fourth," Galère responded and with gorilla-like movements he reached down and slit Isabeau's belly open like he was gutting a fish. He ripped out the infant nestled inside. Holding up the wet and perfect little body in one hand, he laughed as it twitched and trembled. Spying a garden stake near the wall, he spiked the child upon it and drove the stake into the small patch of earth at Isabeau's head. The last death throes caused the stake to quiver in the air. "A bouquet!" Galère laughed coarsely and wiped his bloodied hands on a strip of Isabeau's torn shift. He hoped Trebideau was pleased.

"Heretic swine," Trebideau looked down upon the body of Charte. "Make certain he is dead."

The youngest hovered over the body, then drove his sword directly into the fallen man's chest. "He is dead."

"I am satisfied," Trebideau said after several long moments of consideration. "Let us go."

They lost no time in mounting their animals and urging them back the way they had come. Again, there was the clatter of twelve pairs of iron hooves hitting the cobblestones until they hit the dirt road leaving the village. The dogs renewed the intensity of their barking. The sound lasted a long time as the retreating horsemen faded off into the distance.

They were gone and the last echoes vanished with them.

Nothing stirred, nothing moved, and the dogs again grew quiet. There was only an occasional bark now.

The cold and emotionless moon continued to light the scene. In black and gray starkness the bodies, which only minutes before had been animated with living souls, now were but empty bloody husks of discarded flesh and bone without breath, without life, the blood growing cold as it mingled with the earth.

After several long minutes, the shutters of the window on the house to the right opened very cautiously. Then the second story window of the house on the left opened slowly. Across the road a door swung open. And another. A door down the way. Slowly the neighbors emerged and, carrying lanterns, they cautiously approached the grim gray scene of carnage in front of the Charte home. They were shocked into utter silence, floating as ghosts around the grisly tableau until one woman burst out weeping.

Paul and Isabeau had been such fine people voices whispered, good neighbors, a lovely family. God-loving, Christ-loving people. A model family. They were martyrs now, gone to receive their rewards in a better life. And could not any one of them expect the same if they were not extremely careful, the voices continued to murmur? The authorities would do nothing. The murder of a Huguenot was no murder at all. It was merely an extermination. The children? What of the children? Such good-looking, polite children. Such innocents. They saw the infant suspended on the stake and several became sick, falling to their knees and retching violently. An elderly woman pulled the little body free and wrapped it in her shawl before her own tears blinded her. It was a girl, the daughter Isabeau Charte had wanted so badly.

They were living in murderous times but none could recall having seen such obscene and brutal cruelty before. This went beyond sanity. The work of madmen, they told each other.

Madame Isabeau's mutilated body was horrifying to behold; someone covered it hastily with a blanket but the expression upon her finely featured face was one of incomprehensible peace.

The cobblestones were sticky and slick with blood. What was left of Captain Charte was beyond recognition. Gabriel's fingers were gently pried from the saber hilt and his arm tenderly placed with his young body. Only old Joseph was found to still be breathing but very weakly.

What of the other children?

Soon their bodies were also found. Shrouds were quickly made. The bodies were covered. A cart was brought. They must be buried in all haste, secretly, so the authorities could not defile their graves.

As dawn was about to break, a quiet gathering was bowed in prayer over the new grave at the edge of a clearing in the forest. The pastor gave a final blessing and urged everyone to hurry home before daylight came. The family had been laid to rest together, the site would remain unmarked.

"Someone must go to New Rochelle and take the news to Auguste," the pastor said half to himself as he led the way back to the hamlet. "He has family, I believe, in the north. He must go there and never come back here again." Various sounds of agreement riffled through those within hearing.

"I will carry the unhappy tidings myself," the pastor said with resignation, closing his lips tightly against the unpleasantness of his task. There were times, God forgive him, when deep in his heart he would much rather take up a saber against these foes than pray for their souls' forgiveness. He would sooner see their souls burn in Hell.

Almost immediately the pastor felt a tide of shame wash over him. *Forgive me, Lord. That is wrong. You have called me to be a shepherd to these people, not an avenging angel. If you could forgive all that was done unto you, how can I not do the same in your name? But strengthen my resolve, I pray, for it is so hard to turn the other cheek when I see your faithful children so terribly abused.*

Chapter 1

Northern France – 1684

The old man sat in a sturdy chair upon which wheels had been attached for easier mobility. His silk dressing gown, old and showing wear, enveloped his shrinking figure. With the addition of a shawl draped over his fragile shoulders, his small gray head resembled that of a turtle trying to emerge from its shell. Another shawl laid across his lap and bony legs as he basked in the warmth of the summer sunshine. A young man sat attentively on a bench near him listening to stories he had heard many times before.

"It was open season on Huguenots," the elder went on, his thin voice raspy with age. "It had been so ever since Good King Henry's wedding when the soldiers and the Roman Catholic clergy decided to slaughter all the unarmed Huguenots who had come to Paris for the occasion. We know it now as the Saint Bartholomew's Day Massacre and that viperous daughter of Satan was behind it, that Medici woman! Within a week thousands of them died just in the city alone. *Henri Quatre* himself escaped by making promises to convert to Catholicism."

"I know, *Grand-père*… 'Paris is worth a Mass' is that not what he said?" nodded the younger man stretching his well-shaped legs out in front of him. He marveled that his grandfather could stand to wear so many layers of clothing and shawls while sitting in the heat of the sun. As for himself, Jacques-Jean had left his waistcoat and cassock indoors and was enjoying the warm breezes in the informal comfort of just his linen shirt and breeches.

"You have no idea what it was like in those days," the old man said almost as an accusation. "Over 100,000 Protestants were killed within a week," he wheezed slightly. "One week! Men, women, children all fell in heaps before the mobs and the bloodthirsty troops. No one in their grasp was spared. Bodies were left tangled within the corners of public buildings, corpses sprawled on stairways. The rivers were so filled with the carnage that for months, no one would eat the fish. In the valley of the Loire, wolves would come down from the hills to feed upon the decaying flesh of our countrymen. And small massacres continued on and on, through the countryside wherever *might* had the advantage over the defenseless."

"*Oui-oui, Grand-père,* but that was so long ago and since Good King Henry signed the Edict of Nantes, all Huguenots have had the same protections as any

Catholic citizen of France. The slaughters have ended, it is long over." Jacques-Jean knew his grandfather had not even been born when the War of Religions had started although it had continued through many years of his childhood.

The old man looked sharply at his grandson. "Not so long ago," he waggled a finger just barely visible from within a huge cuff. "Not so long ago. Forget not my sainted mother and father, your great-grandparents, Jacques-Jean. They were part of the ongoing slaughter... as were my three brothers and my poor unborn sister."

Jacques-Jean's handsome young face grew more sober. "*Oui, Grand-père,*" he nodded respectfully.

"I hope some day to meet her in Paradise... my sister," the old man muttered softly.

"Do you think she will have grown up?"

The old man looked at his grandson and smiled indulgently. "Do the ancient writings not tell us the Lord God created all souls at the same time? That means all souls are the same age, we just wait to serve our time on earth and just as our Lord came as an innocent babe, we all must come as innocent babes, remembering nothing of what was before... but would God in His mercy allow us to remain in the form of inept babes through all eternity?"

Jacques-Jean said nothing; deep thoughts on religion seemed an elder person's sphere. His grandfather had grown silent. The young man could only guess what thoughts were running through the old man's mind.

"Private vengeance was often the main motive," Auguste spoke out suddenly. "No one can convince me that battle-hardened soldiers give much thought to what church their comrade attends or *if* he attends. No. It was a convenient way to exact revenge and take from your neighbor that which you envied and for which you lusted." The old man coughed and took a swallow of wine from the glass setting upon a small table to his side. "I will never forget the day our village *pasteur* arrived at my school. He had set upon the journey as soon as he had laid my family to rest and he requested a private room where we could talk. No one else knew exactly why he had come.

"He tried to spare me the gory details but I would not believe him. I could not believe him. My entire family gone?! Wiped out in a single, random evening? Not from the plague mind you, which might be considered the will of God but by human hands? Who could believe such a thing? It was beyond my comprehension." The old man paused again. For some moments he was lost in his own memories.

"I thought it was the most tasteless of macabre jokes. For a moment I thought I must be dreaming and at any second I would awake from the nightmare. Finally, he told me how my unborn sister had been wrenched from my mother's womb to be impaled upon a garden stake and at last I knew it had to be true." The elder man shook his head slowly, a tear glistening in the corner of his eye. "No one could say such a thing, no one could dream such a thing... unless it was true."

"It is beyond words," nodded his grandson who never failed to be moved by the story but whose compassion also saw the events as being so distant in time that they had little relevance to his life for he was only nineteen and sixty years was many lifetimes ago in his mind.

Jacques-Jean enjoyed visiting his grandfather but wished the old man would not dwell so on the horrors of the past. They were brutal times, of this there was no doubt, but it was ancient history. Now, the 17th century was rapidly hurtling toward an end and they lived in a different age. A new modern century was advancing toward them. Philosophies were changing. New worlds beckoned the adventurous. Advances were being made in medicine and science. It all made the times of his grandfather's youth seem very ancient and barbaric indeed. What purpose was served in dredging up old memories of horrors one could do nothing about? It only served to foment continuing personal upset. Better to forgive and forget as the Bible taught and enjoy life, was it not? Louis XIV was king now and it was an enlightened era filled with gaiety and pleasures.

"*Oui-oui…* beyond words," the old man nodded an echo, his wrinkled face reflecting all the old anguish. "Only two short years after I left La Rochelle, Richelieu and Louis XIII had the town besieged. They starved out half the Huguenot population. Half! While the other half dined on rats and dogs... even their own flesh! It is an irony to me that because of my family's tragic misfortune, I escaped it all."

Jacques-Jean said nothing.

"I have lived my life knowing I live because my family was murdered and because I live your mother was born and because she lives you were born. Think on that, boy. Think on the debts we owe the past. You exist because your great-grandparents were murdered!"

Jacques-Jean was not certain what he thought of that. Perhaps it was true, but might not his grandfather have been one who survived eating dogs or rats in La Rochelle? Might he not have escaped to the north anyway? Might not he have still met his wife... oh, what good was wandering down such odd paths of thinking? Was it not the kind of twisted reasoning that had Italian families stabbing each other in alleyways for generations?

"*Grand-père*, you are letting it upset you again," the young man cautioned. He sat quietly and politely as his grandfather lapsed into another melancholic, ruminating silence.

Auguste Charte had been a youth on the cusp of manhood when his family had been obliterated. With the hot blood of youth, he had desired above all else to seek revenge but cooler minds had prevailed in sending him to his father's brother in the northern part of France where his father's enemies could not find him. It also got him away from those who advocated open rebellion. And in truth, had he not been grateful in the end? It was against his bookish nature to wield a sword. He had no skill in fighting. He was good with a ledger not a pistol. It was his brother Gabriel who had been born to be a soldier, a fighter, a warrior. If Gabriel had been a little older, had escaped the murderous visit, Gabriel would have exacted revenge for the family, Auguste had no doubt of that.

Instead, Auguste accepted his fate and was educated to be an estate clerk. In time he lived a respectable and rather protected life at the behest of the *Duc du Pouvoir*. But even now, in his secret heart of hearts, Auguste thought himself a very unworthy son and brother; a shameful coward for never seeking out his family's slayers and avenging their brutal deaths. The rancor he bore his family's murderers was well deserved but as he saw his end approaching he wondered. Did he not have just as much rancor for himself?

"Jacques-Jean," Auguste said suddenly with a strange sense of urgency, "it is *not* over. I worry for your mother. She is alone. She will have no one to seek protection from when I am no longer here. There are rumblings if you know how to listen. Like the gathering of the clouds at the horizon before the winds send the storm to encompass you. I worry for you, too, my boy. Be warned, be warned. It is not over and you are all that is left to carry on our bloodline. Our king has become too insulated and too ill advised. His mistress wants the blood of every Huguenot. The enemy is creeping, creeping to the door."

"*Grand-père*, you worry too much," Jacques-Jean said soothingly and gave his grandfather a very charming smile full of positive youthful optimism. "Nothing is going to happen, and never fear, upon my honor I shall always watch over *ma mère*."

A few days later Auguste died quietly in his bed and Jacques-Jean was forever grateful that he had made the time to visit when he did. He would miss the old man, the only father figure around when Jacques-Jean had been a small child.

Chapter 2

1685

A shaft of sunlight made its way passed the window's edge and streaked into the upper chamber of the small cottage; it hit Jacques-Jean in the eye as he lay in a troubled sleep in his mistress' bed. The peace of the French countryside, streaked with its watercolor pastels of spring, was deceptive as the unseasonable heat was incongruently oppressive but it was the sound of the pigeons, restless in their nest under the eaves, which had broken into the young gentleman's dreams. He jerked awake and, upon opening his eyes, immediately blinked as an involuntary scowl marked his handsome face. His pounding heart found relief in the realization that he was awake, that he had only been dreaming.

He quickly moved out of the sunbeam's reach and threw off the limp linen sheet with irritation. Now that his pulse had slowed and his breathing had steadied he was infused with a vague anger at being overly warm. He felt stifled, smothered. No wonder he was sweating so profusely. It was small wonder he was having bad dreams, he told himself. It had hardly been a refreshing slumber and that realization made him frown again.

The dream... he could not remember it anymore, it had flown out of his grasp and retreated into the darkness that belongs to the land of slumber. It had been nothing but fantasy, he was certain. But the pigeons were real enough, shifting and fluttering and making deep throaty noises in soft tremulous coos. He focused his irritation on them.

Had he not told Bertrell to clean out that filthy nest so close to the bedchamber window? One could not open the window for a simple breath of air without contending with feathers and noises and bird droppings. It was disgusting. His mood was not improving as he recalled that he had, in fact, specifically told the dim-witted servant just that. He was sure of it. He remembered the oaf had grunted and shuffled away. Shuffled like a sack of meal that had grown legs. Why Celimene persisted in keeping that worthless dullard around was beyond reason.

With his right hand he pushed golden curls from his face. Stray hairs clung to his sweaty brow and caught on the soft stubble which had appeared on his jaw overnight. He gave a habitual and absentminded stroke to his small, silky moustache. It was still early in the day but already the air had a heavy, moist, tangible feeling. It was much too hot for a healthy spring, everyone said so.

As the young man purposefully stretched his athletic body trying to rid it of the residue of tension created by his dream, his skin and chest hair glistened with a thin layer of perspiration. Well formed muscles, supple and smooth, moved beneath taut skin. The muscles purposely tensed more tightly, bunched and relaxed. The light snoring of his mistress stopped as she stirred beside him with a tiny sigh. He looked over at her and all remaining irritation melted away.

Masses of chestnut curls tumbled about her pretty head and spilled over her pillows. Her mouth, generous to a fault, had a hint of a smile as though she was dreaming of something amusing. He knew the teeth behind those full lips were straight, white, and well spaced. Even at seventeen it was a wonder to possess as perfect a set of teeth as hers. In all his twenty years he could remember seeing no other woman with a smile to compare to his beautiful Celimene. But that was only one of her treasures.

He smiled to himself as his gaze dropped to her flawless breasts exposed in perfect symmetry above the sheet. What magnificent creatures, women, he thought indulgently. Incredibly soft, infinitely tender, one delightful curve after another, yet certainly capable of a peculiar tensile strength that defied visible explanation. They tasted at once sweet and salty. They could look so cool yet contain such molten heat. Appearing frail enough to be crushed under a single blow and evoking the lenient consideration due their fragile forms, yet they could beguile, hypnotize and mesmerize a mighty giant or cut a man to the quick with one well-placed withering glance.

He chuckled aloud. It was already too warm to think of strenuous activity and he was hungry. As if in response to this thought, his belly echoed a rumbling growl. He sat up and gingerly swung his legs over the edge of the bed. The air had a mildly cooling effect as perspiration evaporated from his warm body. He went to the dressing screen and took aim at the slops pail housed there.

"Celimene, *ma fleur de cœur*," he called out in a rich resonating voice, "come my heart's flower, it is time to rise and fetch me something to eat." The smell of fresh urine rose up from the slops pail to mingle with the other aromas in the small bedchamber. Through the partially opened window drifted the musky, earthy scents of the neighboring farm animals laced with the subtle but unmistakable fragrance of spring grasses. The cheerful little flowers blooming at the window box added their own sweetness to mingle with the rather pungent inner smells of human living: sweat, sex, and alcohol.

Taking a deep breath he sucked his lungs full to capacity and stretched his body once again before grabbing a towel resting on the washstand. He dipped it quickly in the washbasin as he poured water from the pitcher and rubbed vigorously over his torso, neck, and under his arms. Feeling refreshed, he padded barefooted over the waxed planking of the floor back to the bedside.

"Celimene, my sleepy one, get up, get up. I am going to die of hunger and who will you bring into your bed to replace me, huh? Have you grown tired of me so quickly?" His voice held the trace of a good-natured chuckle and he pulled the sheet completely from the bed and watched Celimene respond by turning and burying her head under the pillows. He eyed her plump bottom and gave it a playful smack at which she turned back, took a long languid stretch and smiled.

"*Bon jour, ma chérie*," he said with a little grin as she opened her eyes to him. Celimene, her dark blue eyes only half open, stretched her arms out and waited for him to fill her embrace.

"Never, never will I grow tired of you," she murmured in his ear as he bent over her and kissed her soft fresh cheek.

"You are truly the most adorable of treasures but if I die of starvation how will I ever be able to show you again how much I do adore you?"

"Oh, JJ, you are impossible," she sighed, her fingers tracing lightly over his muscled back and down over the now crisp hairs of his arm. "How can you be so hungry for mere food? It is early still." Her voice was a throaty whisper. The warm morning air had a decidedly different effect upon the young woman and it was not food she was craving. Undulating her hips with intended provocation, she looked at him invitingly. Her gaze traveled from his smiling face to his chest. With growing overt sensuality, her eyes took on the attitude of a caress so palpable he could almost physically feel her touch run over his abdominal muscles until eventually she was boldly gazing upon his prominent male appendage. She took a long moment to look upon him appreciatively, watching him visibly react. She reached out her practiced hand to stroke him teasingly, lightly but persistently.

"Woman, how brazen you are!" A feigned expression of shock played over his lean, well-proportioned face, his gray eyes now reflecting her playful mood. "It is broad daylight!" He pretended to be scandalized. "Have you no shame?! No modesty?! God and all His creatures are watching you!"

"Perhaps that makes it even better, no?" she giggled softly as she watched him continue to react, swell, rise, and harden under her touch.

"You are a witch," he sighed, then took in a sudden gasp of air. "I had no other thought but to feed my hollow belly." His arched brows knit in mock surrender. "You are insatiable, *ma chérie*, and I am very glad that you are mine."

Slowly her legs parted in a familiar invitation as she arched upward, reaching out to wrap her arms around him and draw him down over her as her legs made him her prisoner. Jacques-Jean had, for the moment, forgotten completely both his empty stomach and the heat.

It was close to eleven o'clock when the young man finally bid good-day to his amorous young mistress still rosy from their lovemaking and now contentedly curled up in sleepy repose amidst the tangled sprawl of bedding. He smiled as he pulled on his boots, draped his jabot around his neck, and jammed on his hat. She had every reason to be exhausted, he thought to himself with more than a hint of self-satisfaction. Taking his waistcoat and rapier filled scabbard in one hand, he gave the well rounded bottom presenting itself to him a final pat before exiting the room.

He slipped on his sleeveless waistcoat as he tread lightly down the stairs and fastened on his sword belt, freeing his hands. Scrounging cold chicken from the larder, he grabbed a breast in one hand and took a hunk of day-old bread in the other. It would have to do he shrugged and began to eat without sitting down.

He strode out of the cottage, chewing as he went to the barn. Bertrell was nowhere to be found. Of course! Jacques-Jean would have to saddle his own horse. The food disappeared at amazing speed, verifying his famished state. When the last scrap of chicken was in his mouth, he tossed the bones aside and paused briefly to wipe his hands and mouth fastidiously with his handkerchief. Stroking his moustache to assure himself no remnant crumbs clung to the hairs, he set about preparing his horse.

Leaving the cozy, low roofed little cottage behind, he headed toward the village on a narrow dusty road. He had no pressing business but still a gentleman must make it a point to keep himself informed. These were changing times they lived in.

What was the future to bring, he pondered? From beneath his hat he squinted slightly in the light of the full radiant sun. The sky was absolutely cloudless and a dazzling deep blue, but the breeze was not enough to move the tree limbs already heavy with their leaves. The birds hidden within those leaves gave out a cacophony of chatter that lent itself to the impression that their number was in the hundreds as the young rider and horse trotted undaunted beneath them.

Jacques-Jean continued in his thoughts. He was a gentleman by birth but with little to no means. Fate had dealt him a sad hand, he sighed while still retaining a smile. It was not self-pity, just realistic assessment. To be the bastard son of a duke could be quite respectable, if one was the first son, bastard or not, or the only son, but to be the third bastard son of a man who already had legitimate sons was to be... nothing.

At that moment his glance fell upon a peasant in a nearby field occupied in planting the prepared soil, back bent in weary toil, bare arms as brown as the earth itself with a wet kerchief upon his head to deflect the sun's heat. The young aristocratic offspring reconsidered from beneath the broad brim of his plumed hat. *Well, almost nothing,* he corrected himself, although admittedly blood ties to nobility no matter from which side of the blanket did give a certain advantage in social standing.

The former *Duc du Pouvoir,* had found much pleasure and amusement with the lively eyed and intelligent young daughter of his resident clerk and stores keeper, Auguste Charte. The duke had been in his late fifties, recently widowed and disconcertingly faced with a strong sense of his own mortality. It had pleased him to settle down and begin taking his confessions and penance seriously, and to be faithful to just one mistress. He chose the modest and reverent girl who had a soft laugh, haunting beauty, and a gift for appreciating the simple things in country life. When her baby was born, the old man was properly proud and basked in the admiration of his peers that he should yet father such a fair son, fat cheeked, strong limbed, and glowing pink with perfect health.

Perhaps because she never asked anything of him, the aging duke favored the young madonna with the provision of a modestly adequate pension in his will and the endowment of a sturdy little cottage of her own. And so, when he died somewhat suddenly of heart failure two months after Jacques-Jean's third birthday, mother and child were not in poor circumstances.

Jean-Andre, legitimate and first born son of the old man, inherited the estates. He was a self-absorbed and spoilt young fellow bent toward tyranny and cruelty. Fortunately for all who were dependent upon the ducal lands, the new duke did not live long. After a drunken and sadistic tirade on the village one night, Jean-Andre met a fitting end when his horse threw him over a sty and landed him head first into a pile of sheep dung. He well might have survived if directly beneath the dung had not lay a sizable formation of solid rock. Two days later the new duke was dead, never having regained consciousness.

And so the ducal title passed to the next legitimate son, Jean-Philippe, a thoughtful and serious fellow who valued books and paintings more than the amusements of wine, women, and song. The new young duke had an honest regard for the lands which had unexpectedly become his duty to manage just as it had become his obligation to look after and provide for all the people who made their living on those lands. It was a heavy and sobering responsibility to fall upon the slight shoulders of a callow youth only just out of his teens. And there had seemed to Jacques-Jean to always be an aura of sadness about the young duke. Jean-Philippe was only twenty when the estates passed to him but, of course, to the very small boy, the new duke had seemed quite old. Old enough to be his father, as old as his own mother, although, Jacques-Jean mused, his mother would never seem old to him.

The present *Duc du Pouvoir*, however, had always appeared almost elderly. It was perhaps his stoop, or the slow careful way he always did everything. The conservative rather antiquated cut of his clothing certainly added to the illusion. And then there was his quiet pensive manner, more suited to a monk than a young lord.

Duke Jean-Philippe had always demonstrated an appropriate amount of respect toward Jacques-Jean's mother. He had nodded his head in acknowledgment of her when, by chance, they met at the festivals or in passing through the village on market day. And in time, he had paid a personal visit to her tidy cottage. Jacques-Jean remembered that day well.

The duke arrived on a dapple gray horse rigged out with a magnificently hand-tooled, black Spanish leather saddle trimmed in the most intricately wrought silver. Jacques-Jean was a boy of twelve at the time and very impressed by such things.

He remembered his mother flushing pink from the edge of her modest neckline to the roots of the hair above her smooth forehead as she received her unexpected guest although his manner was meant to put her at ease. The duke had gestured for her to be seated; then, he himself had sat lightly on the edge of the damask covered couch in her small salon. Jacques-Jean had stood close to his mother; he recalled her faint scent. She always smelled like summer flowers.

"Madame," the twenty-nine year old duke had begun after clearing his throat. "Your young son is growing up very quickly and I have come to ask your permission to give my half-brother a place at my table." The words had come out slowly with deliberate care. "As the son of my father and the grandson of my esteemed clerk, I wish to see him educated as a gentleman. It is fitting that he should not be ignorant..."

"*Pardonnez-moi! Monsieur le Duc*," his mother had dared to interrupt while her face turned very pink again. "Jacques-Jean already knows how to read as well as write. I, myself, though only a woman, have taught him as I was taught by my own ma-ma."

"Forgive me, Madame Charte, of course, I meant no insult," he had said most earnestly, looking strangely uncomfortable but quite handsome in his dark blue velvet knee breeches and matching jerkin. "Please excuse my regrettable choice of words. I only meant it is fitting he should learn more advanced studies," he paused for a moment. "Latin, philosophy, also... fencing and hunting. I know your father has been unwell for some time and I would consider it a favor if you would grant me the privilege of contributing to your son's education."

There was, for one brief moment, a look that passed over the duke's face that the boy had not understood. Yet, it made an impression on him. Even today, as Jacques-Jean rode relaxed, letting the horse set its own pace, he remembered that look. It had said the duke really meant it when he said it would be "a favor" to him. And so Jacques-Jean had moved into the chateau.

For the most part it had been a very happy time. The duke had no children of his own, although a match had been made for him soon after his elder brother had died. Gossip said his wife had brought forth one stillborn child and since, had remained barren. Jacques-Jean ate at the duke's table, took lessons with the sons of the estate's more highly esteemed employees, and had private lessons of his own in fencing and dancing. The duke himself took the young lad riding and hunting. Jacques-Jean never felt his half-brother much enjoyed those ventures. Later, the youth realized it was the hunting itself that the pensive nobleman had no taste for, yet he made a point to go out anyway. Why? Just to spend time with his half-brother was Jacques-Jean's only answer, to set an example and to lend encouragement in the acquisition of such skills.

Duke Jean-Philippe was really a very kind and unselfish man, Jacques-Jean concluded, something of a rarity within the titled nobility of France. Perhaps a rarity within the nobility of any country, he pondered. And the youth grew quite proud of his quietly studious half-brother.

As the years went by, Jacques-Jean visited his mother and grandfather often but it had become different. He no longer felt that his mother's cottage was his home. The chateau had become his home and his mother's house was where he was now the guest.

There was only one point on which Jacques-Jean did not blend into the ducal household. His mother had raised him from the cradle in Calvinistic Protestantism, reading the Bible for himself, rejecting the graven images and papal rule of the Roman Catholic Church, and thus, he could not accept his half-brother's religion. Jean-Philippe respected the young lad's choice and Jacques-Jean had not been required to attend mass with the rest of the household. Instead, he went always to services in the village, sitting next to his mother in the pew-box his grandfather's uncle had established for the family, and enjoying the warmth of her appreciative smile.

Now, at the age of twenty in this spring of the year 1685, Jacques-Jean was in all ways the portrait of a young country gentleman. His blond curls and clear gray eyes were a masculine copy of his mother and his slightly arched aristocratic nose showed a marked likeness to his father's side of the family. He had the easy graces and manner of a young lord. He hunted well, fenced with an engaging style, and carried himself with an air of *noblesse oblige* that made him appear much taller than his actual height which was average. And it was with this self-controlled yet aloofness of carriage that he now dismounted from his horse and entered the local tavern.

It was dark and cool within the small stone building. Jacques-Jean paused for a moment just inside the doorway to allow his eyes time to adjust to the dimmer light. The brilliance of the outdoors was now reduced to only a few shafts of light sneaking through the small windows in the thick stone walls.

"Jacques-Jean, *mon ami*, over here," he heard a voice call out to him. The voice was familiar and he moved toward it, slowly at first. As his eyes adapted to the dimness he could see more clearly the table in the corner where three young men sat over glasses of wine. Two he recognized as his close friends, but the third fellow sitting between them was not familiar to him.

"Come, come, sit, sit, we have been expecting you for some time. We had almost given up hope. That enchanting mistress of yours must have had you chained to the bedpost, eh?" The deep raucous laughter unmistakably identified the speaker as Richard Bonchance, Jacques-Jean's closest friend. He was an angular young man, obviously the tallest of the group but lacking the easy grace of movement possessed by his best friend. "Ahh-ha, we should all have jailers such as she, my friends," he grinned as he turned his dark, bushy head to the other two, "she could turn a stay in the Bastille into paradise, eh, Jacques?"

"I come when I want, I go when I want" Jacques-Jean replied with a slow easy shrug, smiling a bit smugly at the envy Celimene could invoke from other men. "The significant point is... *when* do I want, eh?" He added with good humor as he took hold of the empty chair thrust toward him. He acknowledged the others with a nod, then he turned to speak directly to Richard. "Besides, what are you talking about? The sun has not yet reached its zenith!"

"At least for another moment or two you can say that," Richard bantered back, then he gestured to the stocky, clean shaven young stranger seated beside him. "Let me introduce you to Denis Dufee, whom I have just learned will soon be taking marriage vows with my little cousin, Madeleine Mouri, which makes him my cousin now as well. As small children, we all played together each summer when Denis came to the country with his mother to visit. Denis, this escapee from the bedchamber is my closest friend, Jacques-Jean Charte."

Dufee stood. He was dressed very conservatively like a mercantile man. His simple linen shirt was devoid of lace but had a linen band tied neatly about his throat and his sleeveless tunic and pantaloons were of brown jersey. His hair was cut close to his head at the sides while the back was tied snugly with a brown ribbon at the nape of his neck. The two young men exchanged respectful bows of greeting, then both were re-seated.

"Denis has just come from Paris," Richard continued more quietly, "everything is astir there it would seem. Go on, Denis, continue. Jacques-Jean is to be as trusted as I."

Dufee spoke softly. "There really is not that much more to say. In appearance all is quiet. The Court abandoned the Louvre several years ago when Louis moved all the nobles to Versailles. One hears nothing coming out of Versailles. Of course, being at le Académie des Sciences is very much being in a world apart. We stick to the Latin quarter and read Plato and argue the theories of Descartes and Pascal; we discuss the Englishman Newton's work. We are not particularly concerned with politics... or religion. But at night in the taverns there is talk. Rumors spread through the shadows like steam coming off boiling water. Who knows how they start or where they come from but is there ever smoke without a fire? Can there be steam without heat? Some say we will see another St. Bartholomew's Day," he said. "Some say it will be worse. That it will stretch far into the provinces. That there will be many arrested, imprisoned. Lands seized. Le Roi Soleil is choosing to look the other way while the cry goes out to eradicate the Huguenots." Dufee's voice had dropped to little more than a whisper.

"Our king may look the other way but can anyone believe these things happen without his approval?" The question was posed by the fourth young man whose rich if well-worn costume betrayed his noble standing. Thomas du Vaille, second son of the third highest ranking nobleman in the province, was a Catholic by birth. His loyal friendship with the others had bridged the gap of common prejudices.

"How could they?" he answered his own question. "The Edict of Nantes established by his grandfather promises tolerance. But Louis promises nothing; he wants all France to be united in one religion. On the one hand, he promotes reason and logic, the tolerance of artistic freedom, and the international exchange of ideas, but the Church... there is a much different point of view, n'est-ce pas? It never accepted the Edict. And no matter which side you speak for, the other will passionately despise you. Louis needs money and the Church is inclined to be very generous... if it gets its own way. But our king wants the affection of his people, as well. So, he makes it difficult to tell where he stands."

"Louis stands only for Louis," Richard added darkly.

"Hush," Dufee spoke quickly, glancing around. "Men have gone to the Bastille and the gallows for far less than such words," he cautioned. Nervously looking about again he decided to say something positive in case anyone was eavesdropping. "We cannot forget that there is much going on in our country that is very good. Louis has made us world leaders. A nation to be respected and reckoned with. Look how his policies in the New World have expanded our holdings. The trading companies had such a narrow view. Believe me, I know. And look how all the courts of Europe try to imitate us and our beloved sovereign. Their courts all speak our language; they all seek our knowledge..."

"They all receive our countrymen who have fled for their lives!" Du Vaille interrupted. The passion of the moment was quickly set aside as Marie, the little serving wench, approached the foursome.

"M'lord, I bring you a goblet... is there anything else you would like?" the young girl asked with a smile that uncovered a slightly chipped tooth. She leaned in closely, setting the pewter goblet in front of Jacques-Jean; she draped her arm easily across his chair back. Her sweat-stained linen blouse opened so widely at the neckline that it served as little more than sleeves while the soiled kerchief around her grime-streaked neck had twisted askew, exposing a good deal of her young breasts thrust up by her corselet. Unabashedly, she stroked back a few strings of greasy hair and coyly tucked them up under her cap. Not knowing her actual birthday, the girl marked the years with the calendar and had only recently passed her fourteenth new year. But she, like many, had been forced to grow up too quickly.

"I require nothing more at the moment, but *merci*," Jacques-Jean replied politely and with a wink gave her a small coin. It was understood that since the wine was already paid for, the coin was for her alone to do with as she wished.

"*Merci*, m'lord," she cried out softly with delighted appreciation mixed with affection for the familiar young gallant; then, she left the group to their discussion.

Like any temperate Frenchman, Jacques-Jean would never think of drinking plain water unless he wanted an ague. However, Jacques-Jean Charte was not a drunkard. He drank his wine well-watered at breakfast, usually well-watered at lunch, and enjoyed it in the evening at full strength but chiefly in moderation. When he did get drunk, which was rare, it was with purposeful intent. Now he poured wine and water into his goblet.

For a time, the four young men sat silently around the heavy black oak table, each deep in his thoughts. It was growing busier in the tavern as more travelers stopped in for some respite from the mid-day heat. Marie's coarse childish laughter could be heard as she bantered with a couple of soldiers sitting on the far side of the room.

"I fear for us, my friends," Richard finally spoke quietly. "It is not healthy these days to be a Huguenot."

Du Vaille nodded sympathetically.

Jacques-Jean gave Richard a smile. At the moment, his friend reminded him of his departed grandfather. "Richard, you worry too much," he responded calmly, stroking his small moustache. "Have you forgotten the true objective of the Church leaders? They cannot line their coffers with the small allowance of a bastard son. You have nothing of value, *mon ami*, you are quite safe. I have nothing of value and so, I am safe as well. Even the cottage of my mistress is owned by my half-brother and ours to enjoy through his generosity alone. To arrest us and confiscate our horses would hardly be worth the Church Council's time."

Du Vaille snorted in humorless agreement.

"And what of your mother?" persisted Richard.

"Ah, *ma mère*," Jacques-Jean said carefully, mindful that women who are to be respected were not openly discussed in a public tavern with too much familiarity. "A beautiful and charming lady, is she not? But quite penniless. Her home, in fact, belongs to *le duc's* estates and shall revert back upon her death. Her pension, although adequate for her needs, comes again from the cash box of *le duc*. She received only a small monetary inheritance when my grandfather died and she has no other assets. I think my mother is quite safe as well," he concluded with a small smile of ironic acceptance as he lifted his goblet to his lips.

"My family, on the other hand," said Dufee very seriously, "does have something to lose and the threat is very real."

"I have told Richard," du Vaille said thoughtfully, "it would be better for us if we were to try our luck in the New World. What have we here, I ask you?" He looked pointedly at Richard and Jacques-Jean.

"You have position here," offered Jacques-Jean.

"Let us be very honest," du Vaille quirked a dark brow. "My brother Arnaud is healthy and young and has already sired two healthy sons. When our father dies, may God keep and preserve him," he added quickly, crossing himself, "the family holdings go to Arnaud who shall pass them on to his oldest son. And so, what of me? My prospects are so poor despite my family name I cannot even make a decent match for marriage!"

"It is true, it is true" grunted Richard morosely, "that is the way of it. There is not enough land to be had. Our forefathers fought for their sovereign and received gratuitous land grants. Our great-grandfathers received divided portions, and now, everyone fights to keep what is his intact. And I, like you, *bon ami*," he nodded toward Jacques-Jean, a note of bitterness creeping into his voice, "am a noble bastard. What real prospects do we have in this stale and used up place? We have been educated to have the tastes of our betters who never will let us forget they are our betters."

"There are many untried opportunities in the New World," spoke Dufee with soft encouragement. "A man with nothing can go there and become a veritable prince."

"Oh, *oui*, it is that easy?" Jacques-Jean asked with gracious humor masking his sarcasm.

"Not easy," Dufee responded quite seriously, "many have also died for trying. But it is possible. I have heard so many stories..."

"Ah, stories!" Jacques-Jean interrupted with an exaggerated sigh, more polite than a scoff. "*Mon ami*, one can always hear stories. The Spaniards, hah... they thought they would find cities built of gold and silver. Easily amassing fortunes beyond their wildest dreams."

"And so they did in the southern Americas," put in du Vaille.

"But not in the northern America," continued Jacques-Jean."And Ponce de Léon? He hunted for the fountain of youth and disappeared for his efforts." He poured himself more wine and added water.

"But the English were more pragmatic," Dufee continued undeterred, "they sought land for farming and raising families. They set down roots. Now, since they have gained the New Netherlands from the Dutch, the English own the majority of the accessible eastern coast of the northern continent. I speak not of fortune hunters, *mes amies*, but the real fortune to be had that comes from owning land and trading goods. England's James II was just crowned a few weeks ago and I heard that in his address he encouraged colonization in the New World.

"My father now owns three ships that do nothing but go back and forth across the ocean to the New World and he is in the process of building a fourth. Often he has the captains come for dinner when they arrive back in port, and I have heard such marvelous tales. But they are real stories, testimonies, my friends, not fantasies."

Dufee had their full interest again and paused for a moment enjoying the attention. He took a sip from his goblet and set it back upon the table top with exaggerated care.

"Where do these ships go?" Thomas du Vaille asked with genuine curiosity.

"One goes always to Acadia, to the north, in the late spring and again in late summer. It travels up the river *Saint Laurent*, deep inland, and comes back with the most magnificent furs you have ever seen. Nowhere in all of Europe can you find furs like these, so thick and soft, like a cloud from God's own Heaven. The natives sell them for beads and simple trinkets. And many of our countrymen run traps themselves and grow very prosperous in the business of trapping and trading," he nodded knowingly, and took another sip of wine before continuing. "When seasonal storms turn fierce and the rivers begin to ice up, this same ship joins the second in the tropical waters of the south. There are many island ports, and the sugarcane plantations flourish. The natives are not nearly so fearsome as in the Brazils… let the Portuguese have those jungles, eh?

"And the third?" Richard asked.

"The third ship finds port within the English colonies... when we are not at war. But my father has our ships fly our own private flag which is much better for business anyway. The English colonies can never get enough of our goods and they have fine hardwoods to trade and tobacco."

Denis' serious plump features became very animated as he continued for some time keeping the other three amused and spellbound retelling the stories he had heard from the sea captains. Stories of planters and sugar plantations, rum trafficking, the growing settlements, trading posts and Indian natives, the fortunes made and lost, the misfortunes and dangers, but mostly, the opportunity and *hope* of the New World.

"The land is so bountiful and there are so few people. It is just there for the taking," Dufee gestured, reaching out and grabbing the air with his fist, "to farm, to plant. We bring back skins and furs, sugar, molasses, copra, lumber… that is true gold. And to them we bring cloth, tools, utensils, goods of all kinds. They are people who need everything we have here. Is not our furniture the most beautiful in the world? Do we not make the very best wine? And through our trading contacts can we not supply the most beautiful fabrics, the finest laces, the most intricately worked silver, crystal, not to mention weapons...?"

"Enough, enough," Richard raised his hands in a mock gesture of surrender and laughed, "spoken like a true merchant, cousin. So... tell us, Denis, why does your father send you to *le Académie*? Does a merchant need to study philosophy?"

Du Vaille had just refilled his goblet and cried out dramatically, "I drink therefore I am!"

The young men laughed easily. Dufee shrugged, going back to Richard's question.

"This I do for Henri," he said, pointing his thumb at himself and giving a small sheepish smile. "I know my father wants me to work with him. I am to carry on the family business. It is more exciting than anything else I can imagine. I truly like it. But I wanted to study other things as well. I willingly agreed to follow in his footsteps, I asked only to be allowed to go to *le Académie* first, and so my father agreed. For is not all knowledge valuable?"

The question hung in the still quiet of the now empty tavern as though suspended by the thickening humidity. Each young man silently considered his own answer. None noticed that Marie had found a place in the corner not far from them where she had been mesmerized listening to their every word.

The afternoon shadows had grown long when the four took their leave of each other and stepped outdoors into the late afternoon heat. Jacques-Jean decided to head to his mother's cottage. With a tinge of guilt he realized it had been three days since he had last seen her, and that was only at church services. He had ample time now, he reasoned; he would stop by for a visit before supper began at the chateau.

Jacques-Jean let his horse walk, not pushing the beast to any speed in the still afternoon heat. As they moved along, the young man removed his lace jabot from around his neck and stuffed it into the deep pocket of his sleeveless waistcoat. From his seated position, he slipped out of the waistcoat itself, laying it across the saddle in front of him.

His full sleeved, linen shirt was clinging to his damp skin. With his lace kerchief he mopped his brow and scratched his chin stubble. He made a mental note; he must have the chateau barber shave him again. He liked to be smoothly shaven especially in the heat. Never in his twenty years could he remember such weather at this time of the year. It was, perhaps, a very bad sign for the summer to come, he mused. Finally, he loosened the ties which gathered his shirt closely to his neck so that it fell open more comfortably. As he crossed the meadow to his mother's cottage, he could feel a tiny breeze and the air hitting his moist clothing had a cooling effect that was reviving.

To say his mother lived in a cottage was true but there were many kinds of cottages in the French countryside. A peasant's cottage was little more than a hut, sometimes having a small loft gained by use of a ladder whereas the cottage into which he had been able to move his Celimene had a pleasant little upstairs under its sloped roof. Hélène, on the other hand, lived in a spacious home comprised of two full stories and an attic, with pleasant gardens in the rear. It was still considered a *cottage* being nowhere near the size of a manor house but very fitting for a ducal favorite such as a mistress raising ducal offspring.

Jacques-Jean resisted the temptation to prod his horse to hurry in order to more quickly gain the cool shadows of a small copse of trees separating him from his mother's home. In good time, man and horse entered the quiet stand of elms and walnuts and the young rider was aware of a mixture of melodious birds singing and calling high in the tree tops. Other than bird sound, there was no evidence of any other wildlife. The twittering above turned almost to irritated scolding. Jacques-Jean laughed aloud at the thought of the disturbance he had created within the secret world of the birds and in response a group of them took flight from the trees and soared up into the blue.

By the time Jacques-Jean reached the small footpath leading to his mother's front door, he felt mildly refreshed. His sweat dampen clothing had dried somewhat and he slid down from his saddle without ceremony. A series of strides brought him to the entrance where he simultaneously rapped, opened the door, and called out.

"Mère? C'est moi!"

Turning into the salon, he was shocked to see his young mother reclining on her couch, a compress to her brow.

"Ma-ma, what is it? What is wrong? Are you ill?" Jacques-Jean instantly was beside her on one knee.

Hélène Charte looked up at him and smiled weakly. "It is nothing, *mon fils*, just the heat, but it is so good to see you."

"How long have you been ill?"

"I am not ill... really..."

"You look quite pale, Ma-ma," he observed anxiously.

"JJ, when have I ever not looked pale?" she replied with brave humor knowing full well her alabaster skin tones never contained a great deal color. "I just felt a little dizzy and decided to lie down. It is the heat." Her words sounded convincing but the drawn look about her mouth was saying something else.

Despite the humidity which was wringing sweat from the stones, Hélène's skin looked as dry as parchment. Jacques-Jean put his hand to her cheek and felt radiating heat.

"Ma-ma!" he exclaimed, "You have a fever! You should not be alone. What if I had not happened by?"

"No, please, be not so concerned."

"But of course I am concerned," Jacques-Jean's worry made him exclaim more forcefully than he intended. "I shall stay and care for you and have no argument about it."

"I have been more than blessed to have you as a son," she said with an accepting sigh full of appreciation. Noticing his cast off bits of clothing, she added in a mother's way, "JJ, please make yourself more comfortable... put your things over there. Eva will come, in the morning... to take the laundry... Find yourself fresh linen in your old room … and something cool to drink. The food has all been put into the spring house where it is cooler... the cupboards in the cook shed... are bare, I am afraid," she tried to give a little laugh. "Lisa now comes over... every day to help with the evening chores... she will fetch the meal... I will be fine, I just needed... to rest a moment... but, perhaps… we can play some cards..." Hélène was breathing in short, shallow breaths, and this, too, alarmed her son. He had never before known his mother to be ill.

"Sh-sh, Mama, you are supposed to be resting, now lie quietly and I will take care of everything. I am going to the spring house to bring more cool water for your towels. This has grown as warm as soup." He picked up the basin on the small table beside her and strode out quickly glad to have some action to take.

By the time he returned, she had lapsed into delirium. Her skin was as hot as embers and Jacques-Jean kept changing the towels on her head. He paced back and forth to the door looking for Lisa, the farm girl from down the lane. At last he saw her coming slowly up the road and he ran outside the cottage to meet her.

"Lisa, can you ride a horse?" he called to her as he rushed toward her with his horse in tow.

"*Oui*, monsieur," the girl replied timidly. Hearing the tension in his voice, she sensed something was wrong with Madame Charte and quickened her pace.

"Good! My mother is very ill and she must have a physician. Go into the village at once! Take my horse. Find *le physicien* and send him here. Then, go to the chateau to tell *le duc* that madame is ill and we have great need of Gussie. And get back here as fast as you can!" As he spoke, he lifted the girl up into the saddle. Her eyes growing big at his words. She, too, had never known madame to be ill.

"*Oui, monsieur.*"

"*Bon*, now what did I tell you?" Jacques asked her gravely.

"To go to the village and fetch *le physicien*, monsieur," she replied quickly.

"And?" he prodded.

"And then I must ride to the chateau and ask for... for..." she stumbled.

"For Gussie," he stated strongly.

"Gussie, *oui*, monsieur, Gussie," she repeated.

"Now go quickly!" he cried and smacked the horse soundly on its rump. Now was the time to demand speed of the animal who lurched forward as if sensing the human distress. Without a sound, it took off at a lope with the young girl clinging to its back, both of her hands buried in its mane.

Jacques-Jean watched horse and girl disappear down the road to the village and he returned to the sitting room inside. He bent over the couch and picked up his mother as easily as one might pick up an infant. She was completely limp now and unaware. Carrying her up to her bedroom, he laid her gently upon her bed and loosened the laces on her bodice. Flinging the window shutters on one side of the room open and opening the doors wide to the small balcony, he could feel a merciful evening breeze flow through the stuffy room.

Returning to his mother's bedside, Jacques-Jean gingerly slipped her tight bodice off over her head while drawing the equally heavy sleeves from her arms. Next, he removed her heavy silk skirts. Remembering from the time he was a small child, he easily found a light linen bedgown in one of the drawers of her dressing chest. He slipped it modestly over her head and shoulders. Averting his eyes he struggled with removing her stays and half tore her delicate chemise. The young man was not to be faulted. He was very familiar with the feminine garments of the day but undressing his mistress and undressing his mother were two very different tasks.

Pulling the bedgown farther down, he removed the bulky petticoats from beneath. Sweating lightly with distress as much as activity, he gently smoothed the garment below her knees. *There,* he thought to himself hopefully, *she will be much cooler now, more comfortable.*

He went back down the stairs to fetch the basin. Returning to his mother's side, he continued putting cold compresses on her brow and wrists while waiting for someone to arrive.

Chapter 3

B ehind the tavern in a roughly hewn lean-to, Marie scrubbed the pots, crockery, mugs, and pewter goblets from the day's crowd. The purpose of the raw timbered structure was to provide covering overhead in inclement weather and little more. To the side of the lean-to a small fire burned under a large old cauldron which had been handed down from mother to daughter or daughter-in-law for several generations. The vessel was too heavy to transport with ease and had sat in much the very same spot for many years. The tavernkeeper's wife had died childless; there was no one to pass the ancient cauldron to now, and mysteriously, it had begun to show signs of rust and deterioration. From this aging cauldron, Marie dipped scalding water with a large, long handled dipper in order to rinse the bowls she had just scoured clean.

As she worked over her buckets, she could feel the sweat rolling down her back and tickling through her scalp to emerge on her face and find its way in rivulets down to her chin. She was alone at her work. The tavernkeeper had given her instructions concerning the tasks he expected to be completed when he arose from his afternoon nap to prepare for the evening crowd. And so Marie toiled on. She dare not complain. She was fortunate to have a place to sleep and food to fill her belly. It had not always been so.

Almost two years ago, Marie had come to the tavern to beg a crust of bread. The tavernkeeper's wife, Anoui, had taken pity on the frightened awkward girl, heavy with child, and had offered her a place to stay. Within the month, Marie had given birth but her small son had been too frail and sickly. They did all they knew how but the babe would not suckle and did not survive.

Marie herself fell into a fever, her breasts engorged and heavy with milk. They ached and were extremely painful to the touch. Anoui gave her cold packs and compresses while the news traveled around the district quickly. By the second day, a tenant farmer from the neighboring valley arrived at the tavern with a small infant in his arms. His wife had just died in childbirth and he agreed to make payment for Marie's shelter for the next six months if she would keep his son and wet nurse the child. Marie agreed without hesitation and taking the crying infant into her arms, she instinctively shoved one sensitive nipple into its greedy little mouth, feeling at first pain and then relief as the baby clamped on eagerly and began to drain her breast.

Baby Bo-Bo, she had called him. She liked that, it suited him much better than...? She had already forgotten whatever it was his father had said he had named him. Probably "Louis" after the king as her oldest brother had been named, or perhaps "Léon" after the *comte* who owned the valley acreage the farmer planted.

"My Bo-Bo," she would coo to the babe "you are not a stuffy aristocrat, no-no-no, and you do not look like a weary, long faced saint, no-no-no, you are my little Bo-Bo." And with gentle pokes to his sides, she would draw a toothless grin from his round little face. Anoui watched the bonding develop and tried to warn the girl that she must not become so attached. Marie dismissed the older woman's concerns. But in truth, the young girl realized she was thinking of Bo-Bo more and more as though he were her very own son. And his bright eyes recognized her as his mother. It was the first time in her young life that she had ever felt such need and love. It made her feel good and secure.

Time passed quickly and six months became ten and still Bo-Bo stayed on. The arrangement agreed with everyone. Soon the toddler was pulling himself upright, then walking, then chasing the ducklings and worrying the chickens to death. His father came every month to check on his progress. The farmer was proud of his son's growth and pleased that Marie's milk was proving to be so nourishing. Although the rugged man was awkward in handling the babe, it was obvious that he cared deeply for his little son. As things were, however, what could a man in his position do, alone on a farm with too much work, one half grown child and no woman? How could he possibly take care of a small baby as well? So he was pleased that Marie seemed content to continue keeping the child for the small remuneration the poor farmer could barely afford.

In the shade of the lean-to, Marie sloshed water over the mugs and wiped her face with her worn apron. *Those were happy days*, she thought sadly, *those were the happiest days of my life. I had a little family for a little while*. Anoui was like the mother she had lost when she was almost too young to remember. Baby Bo-Bo made her forget she had lost her own child. Even the tavernkeeper could be caught every now and then with a smile sneaking across his usually grim face when Bo-Bo was being particularly adorable. Then with a swiftness that is life itself everything changed.

It began very late in the autumn. The weather started out mildly enough and everyone thought it would be an easy winter. Then, it began to rain. The temperatures grew colder but still it would not freeze. The rain continued, day after day, constant, bone-chilling rain that turned every inch of exposed earth into mud. The dirt floors of the poorest huts became spongy with the cold dampness. The cooking and heating fires would not burn well because there was no truly dry wood to be found. The peat fires even under the best of conditions put out as much smoke as heat and filled the huts with a stinging acidic vapor that made everyone's eyes water and throats burn. The villagers began to grow fearful and increasingly superstitious. Almost everyone had a runny nose or sniffles by Saint Nicholas Day and coughing drowned out the mass on Christmas Day. They wore garlands of garlic and asafetida bags filled with raw onions and bitter herbs. Charms were sought from the village wise woman while the stories circulated: who had the flux, who had the fever sweats, and who had died.

The tenant farmer arrived unexpectedly one day and told Marie he was taking his son home to stay.

"I am most grateful for all you have done, but it is time he is weaned from his wet nurse," said the large man, rain dripping from his clothing. "He is a boy now, not an infant."

"Truly he is only a baby still," Marie said, struggling with the tears coming to her eyes as a feeling of despair crept over her.

"He will be two years soon." The farmer realized he did not sound convincing even to himself and paused a moment before confessing the truth. "I am a-feared. If he stays here... he could die. Everyday more are stricken. There is too much sickness in this valley. It is for the child's own good. My son must live."

"I know you are right," Marie forced an agreeable attitude. "It is best. It is best for his health. Very well, take him to your cottage and tend him well all winter, he is a good boy, a very good boy... such a sweet, good boy." She patted his pudgy little leg as his father held him. "By the time it is spring he will be helping you to plant. He likes a little song at bedtime and he will eat most everything except turnip greens." She forced a small smile at the minor imperfection, blinking back her tears. "Will you ever bring him back to visit?"

"Of course," replied the farmer as he watched Marie gather the child's belongings, but they both knew it was not likely that the farmer would have time or reason to come back to the village except perhaps for fairs and festivals when he could trade his crops. And that would be a busy time with none to spare for useless visiting.

The child cried as his father carried him out to the wagon and put him under a tallow treated canvas, trying to keep the wiggling bundle warm and dry.

"Ma-Ma... MA-MA!"

Marie heard the cries coming from the small wagon and she thought her heart would tear in two as she dug her fingers into the door frame forcing herself not to fly out into the rain and grab the child back to her bosom.

Anoui stayed up late that night consoling the desolate girl whose room without Baby Bo-Bo now appeared to her as empty and cold as a prison cell.

"What is the point, Anoui, what is it all for? Life is so dark and miserable, why are we born?" Her tears flowed, unchecked by any pretense of pride. She was, at that moment, just a thirteen year old child. "From as far back as I can remember, everything has been death, drudgery, and losing the people I love most," she wailed. "Does God intend for people like me to only have happiness in small flashes as short lived as lightning?"

"We learn to be strong," the older woman said quietly. "The Almighty gives us our rewards in Heaven."

"Why must we wait for Heaven?" Marie cried. "It is not fair," she sobbed. "It is not fair. Louise was about my age when our mother died. I remember Ma-ma was in the bed and called us all around her. Her voice was always so soft and quiet. Like rose petals, Ma-ma's voice was always soothing and gentle. '*This is your new brother*,' she had said, '*God has sent him to us and now the Lord is calling me to be with Him. I want you to love each other and care for each other... especially your new little brother*.' I was three and did not understand it at all; she made it sound as if they were trading places. I remember looking at the scrawny new baby, all red and blotchy, and thinking... '*no wonder God does not want him, he is so ugly, but we do not want him either. I already have two brothers, I do not need a third, I want my ma-ma*.' I wanted to give him back.

"I did not understand why she had to die. Ma-ma told us Louise was to be our mother from then on and Louis, the oldest boy, was to help her."

Marie had lain with her head in Anoui's lap and as her sobbing subsided she had started to babble, talking about her whole family. Going on and on, dragging up memory after memory. Things she had kept locked away in her heart for a long time.

Marie paused to take stock of what kettles were left to be cleaned. She was almost finished and needed to gather the linens to be washed before she went back inside to sweep out the tavern for supper.

What a lot they had been, she shook her head to herself with a wiry smile as she spread the linens out on the rope line to dry, and how much she missed them all even now. How wonderful it would be to gather together again even if for only one afternoon. Maybe that was what Heaven was like, she mused to herself, but Heaven was supposed to be for only the very good. Well, her mother would certainly be there. The woman had been a saint. Surely God knew that.

Marie remembered little of her mother except that she was a very gentle, patient presence. And that she had always been able to calm their father who had a very volatile temper. She had bore seven healthy children, four girls and three boys, and had one child die at birth, and one miscarry. Louise had been the first born and had taken after their mother. She had the same sweet and gentle nature, but she could not control their father's temper like Mother had.

Louise took tender care of the baby their mother had named Guillaume but who they all called "Shu-shu." She kept the house and watched over them all until suddenly one night just before her twentieth birthday, Louise doubled over from severe pains in her right side. She lay in agony with fever and pain for five or six days. None of the home remedies the local midwife tried did any good. And suddenly, Louise was dead. Gone from their lives forever just like Ma-ma.

Louis was the second born, a bright and spirited boy who at thirteen years of age did not need to do much to raise his father's anger. When he was younger his mother had saved him many times from a beating at his father's hands but soon after her death he received a severe and brutal one and ran away from home. No one had heard from him since and Marie did not blame him for going although she had always hoped that he would come back.

Juliette was the next child that had lived. She was ten at their mother's death and when their brother ran away she was expected to watch over Annette who was only seven, Armand who was almost five and Marie who was just three. Unfortunately for them, Juliette had a temper like their father. Annie, Mandy, and Marie received a goodly share of slaps and pinches from their older sister but thanks to Louise's watchfulness, it had been nothing too severe.

With Louise's sudden death, the household again changed drastically. Their father began drinking even more and was often gone for days. Juliette, at sixteen, wanted a home of her own, not to be keeping her father's house, and her frustrations did little to improve her moods and temper. It fell upon Armand, who was now eleven and no longer answered to *Mandy*, and thirteen year old Annette to do much of the field work while nine year old Marie and six year old Shu-Shu helped Juliette with the animals and the house.

Juliette grew more bitter as time went on. She saw no hope for her own future. No one had expressed any interest in marriage with her although she was a comely girl with rich dark curls, a flawless complexion, and flashing dark eyes. But she had no dowry and her face and hands had both grown hard. And so it was that when she found her barely twelve year old baby sister in the barn with a pretty young boy from some wandering troupe of players, Juliette had become so angry she had lost all self-control, picked up a length of board, and set upon them both. It had been a mad scramble of naked bodies, flying clothing, curses, and screams.

The agile fellow, although handicapped by the tangle of clothes, managed to defend himself and disarm Juliette but not before she had landed a glancing blow on Marie, chipping her tooth and causing her mouth to bleed profusely. Once Juliette caught sight of the blood and realized what she had done, her anger quickly subsided. The lad grabbed his clothing and ran away without a word, his pale, naked buttocks being the last either of the girls saw of him. Marie was left to face their father alone.

For some reason Juliette never told their father. Marie lived with the anxiety of their father's homecoming and when he finally arrived, Juliette remained silent. Five months later, however, none of Marie's clothing fit her properly. One night, when her father gazed up from his bottle and took a long, hard look at his youngest daughter standing before the fire, their eyes met and he knew. He started up at her and, more out of fear for the child she carried than for herself, she bolted out of the cottage door and into the dark cover of the woods beyond, knowing she never dare go back.

From that time on, Marie had not seen any of them. For a while she had cried incessantly, telling herself if Louise were alive she would help her, if Louis were there he would help her, if Ma-ma were alive Marie would be safe. Then, she stopped crying and took to the road, begging a little, stealing a little, scratching up barely enough food to remain alive until she ended up in this village, begging bread from the kind and childless Anoui.

Marie emptied the last bucket of dirty water over near the vegetable patch. With the weather so hot, the plants could use the extra water. She made certain the herb garden received a goodly share. Too dry a heat would spoil their potency. As she walked back into the dark of the tavern, she recalled again the winter just passed.

After that single night when Baby Bo-Bo had departed, Anoui did not allow Marie to indulge in any more tears. "You must learn to go on," the older woman had told her over and over again, "Never give up hope. It is the most precious gift we have." Being a practical person, Anoui knew there was work to be done. Much sickness was lurking and a sad spirit was more likely to fall victim.

But it was Anoui who was the next victim. Between violent vomiting and watery stools, the woman was sapped of all strength in less than a week. She could not eat. Nothing, not even water, would stay down. Her skin began to hang loosely on her face. Marie kept cold cloths on the older woman's searingly hot forehead, but her fever would not break despite a potent concoction the mid-wife had brought over made of lemon grass, hibiscus flower, chamomile, and a few other very nasty tasting things she would not identify. Anoui's eyes burned so hot they were red, filled with blood shot veins. Her tongue was swollen and blackish. By the morning of the twelfth day, it was over.

Marie felt as though she had lost her mother again. But there was no time to cry once the earth covered Anoui's shriveled body. Now Bouchet, the tavern-keeper, expected Marie to do everything the older woman had been doing as well as her own work. And so, life and struggle continued.

Marie paused for a moment to catch her breath and mop her brow with her forearm, with the edge of her apron she blotted deep into her young cleavage. Where was her life going, she asked herself? She knew things could not stay as they were now. Her small cache of savings had not grown since Baby Bo-Bo had left except for the occasional coin she received from a friendly customer such as the young gallant, Jacques-Jean Charte.

The tavernkeeper had given her some of his wife's old clothing but... in truth, she was beginning to feel very uncomfortable whenever she was alone with him. He said little. He was a gruff, abrasive man but there were times lately when she caught him staring at her with a hard glint in his eye. It was different when his wife had been alive. His looks had pierced through her as if she was not there. Now, she knew he looked at her with lust.

She thought about the things she had overheard in the tavern that afternoon. The New World. It must be a frighteningly savage place but also an exciting place. The young men had talked of it being a place of opportunity. Did that mean opportunity for women as well? Was it possible for a girl who worked very hard to gain something of her very own? Did she not work very hard already, everyday - day after day? But it got her nothing save today's roof over her head and today's meal. In her present circumstance her life held no hope for the future that she could see. Had not Anoui taught her hope was a precious thing? Hope kept one going onward, but one had to have something in which to hope. And the young gentlemen had talked of the *hope* in the New World.

Chapter 4

The ugly, shapeless parasite was satiated, gorged with blood and easily prodded off of its host. With consummate concentration, the dour faced physician held this last leech ever so gently with a blunt pincer-like tool and conveyed it into a jar to join its kind. It was the third time the physician and his jar of loathsome assistants had been out to see Hélène, the third time he had strategically placed their kind on the insides of her wrists and elbows, the tender flesh behind her ears, over the veins in her neck. And it was the third time the noxious appearing worms had plumped themselves up, fat and full, by sucking in her warm, red blood. Now, with a great sense of his own importance, the physician gravely packed the leeches back into the black leather satchel he had brought to the house with him. He was satisfied that he was doing good. Hélène was lucid again. That she would have been lucid without this procedure was a thought that never occurred to him.

"I shall be back tomorrow, but she is looking better," he said abruptly to Jacques-Jean. "We can be grateful the heat has lifted. Now, do not let her chill. Try to get some soup in her and give her these powders."

"*Oui, monsieur, merci*," Jacques-Jean accepted the packets mechanically and walked to the bedroom door with the older man. "Lisa, please see *le Monsieur Physicien* out," Jacques-Jean called to the young girl who had been living at the house since Hélène's collapse. Lisa came to the foot of the stairs and waited to open the front door for the departing physician.

Back at his mother's bedside, Jacques-Jean adjusted the shawl about Hélène's shoulders and took a long look at her. The pale blonde hair, streaked ever so lightly with silver giving it a gilded appearance, lay spread across the white pillows. Her skin was almost as white as her pillows, sheets, and bedgown. If it were not for the coloring of the shawl, one could almost lose sight of the human being lying there. She looked so tiny, as if she could drown in the bedding itself. He saw her trembling finger twitch and her eye lids fluttered. Intuitively, he knew she was calling to him. He bent low over the bed, his ear close to her lips.

"JJ... I beg you... do not allow him... to do it again." Her voice was so weak he could barely hear her, but the look in her large gray eyes was full of fear.

"Very well, Ma-ma, I promise. You have seen the last of the physician's leeches. Gussie never believed in them... but your fever is gone," he added, trying to convince himself that his mother's ordeal with the disgusting creatures had been of some benefit.

Just then Augustine opened the door and brought in a pungently inviting bowl of herbal broth. Setting the tray down on a small polished table near the bed, her eyes quickly surveyed the room.

"I see someone has closed up all the windows again," she said dryly and immediately went to the farthest windows on the south side of the room and opened them enough to admit a warm but fresh breeze. The room itself did not smell like a sickroom. Augustine insisted that all the bed linens be changed daily and had personally bed-bathed madame with rose water and herbs every morning and again each night. The woman knew the stimulation of the accompanying massage was itself a tonic.

Affectionately known as "Gussie" by the family, Augustine had a reputation within the household of the chateau that inspired awe from some, fear from others, and a veritable deification from a few. In hushed tones she was called a *mysticité*, a healer of supernatural powers. Many whispered of the special talents she had inherited from her dark Gallic ancestors practiced in such arts. She would have been in charge of the nursery if the duke and duchess had children, but as things stood, her broader duties centered on maintaining good health everywhere on the estates.

It was difficult to tell Augustine's age. Her face had no wrinkles and always held a placidly serene appearance no matter the circumstances of the moment. Her black eyes were full of life and sparkle. Her carriage was so perfectly balanced and fluid that small children had been known to stand watch at the bottom of the staircase to catch a glimpse beneath her skirt hem to see if her feet really met with the floor or, as rumor insisted, just floated above it. At first glance, one would almost mistake her for a girl of twenty but for a thick full head of pure white hair that was done up in one huge braid that wrapped round and round her head.

"Madame needs to drink this, please." Augustine always spoke with the utmost of formal politeness but her patients knew better than to argue with her. She carefully held one spoonful of broth to Hélène's lips, guiding it down her throat and followed it with another and another in a rhythmical pattern, pausing only to allow her patient to breathe.

"Madame has been leeched too much," she added with an unmistakable tone of condemnation. "One should not dabble where one has no wisdom." She had said everything of importance to say for the moment and silently continued her task.

Jacques-Jean watched, suddenly remembered the packets. "Here," he stretched out his hand to the older woman, "he said to give her these."

Augustine took the packets and held them to her nose. She sniffed briefly, almost imperceptibly lifted her nose to look down at them and slipped them quietly into a large pocket in her skirt. Jacques-Jean did not bother to ask what she thought of the medication, he already knew. She would probably throw it out with the slops.

After the bowl of broth had been emptied, she announced that madame must sleep and ushered Jacques-Jean from the room. He waited until the door was closed before speaking.

"Gussie, is she going to be well?" he asked, seeking reassurance, his round gray eyes betraying his fear and his youth.

"Madame is very weak," the woman said in a level voice, "too weak. Even your physician should have realized she should not have been leeched as well as bled. If he steals more of her blood, I am certain she will have no strength left to live. But if you keep that man away from her, I am just as certain she can recover. She is strong and still young. I will work with her."

"*Merci*, Gussie," Jacques-Jean said with quiet sincerity. He felt guilty and yet, relieved. Augustine had a competent strength about her that allowed one to relinquish all concerns, turning them over to her with complete trust.

"Monsieur Jacques, if I may be so bold," she observed after a discreet sniff, "it would do you much good to freshen up with a rosewater toilette, take a change of clothes and lie down for an hour or two." And she added, as though there were no question of his agreement to her suggestion, "I will send Lisa with the hot water."

Jacques-Jean nodded and gladly did as Augustine suggested. He almost staggered as he went to his old bedroom. He stripped out of the clothes he had been wearing for several days straight, sponged off and stretched out on his old childhood bed. For the first time in four days, he slept soundly, so soundly that he did not awaken until early the next morning.

Dressed in the fresh breeches and clean shirt which had mysteriously appeared in his room along with a pair of slippers, he immediately made his way to his mother's bedroom where he found Augustine sitting in a chair pulled close to the four poster bed. The gauzy bed curtains were pulled almost closed but through a small opening, Jacques-Jean could see Hélène quietly sleeping. A faint color was returning to her cheeks! Augustine rose from the chair as soon as she saw him and walked into the hall motioning him to follow.

"I have been spooning my broth into her every two hours, Monsieur Jacques. As you saw, her color is beginning to return. There is a root about which my mother taught me, it helps to build back the blood – but he must not be allowed to take anymore of hers!" she warned sternly.

"I promise to talk to the physician." Jacques-Jean nodded contritely, and felt the need to add an apology. "I am sorry, Gussie, I should have known you were all my mother needed. If it had been me, if I was the one ill, I would not have had a second thought but to let you alone attend me but this is Ma-ma! I have never seen her ill before in my life, and I admit – I panicked. I would have called upon the Devil himself to see what he could do for her. Can you forgive me?"

Jacques-Jean looked so handsomely appealing in his earnestness, Augustine was placated and a small smile flickered about her lips. "*Would have?* Monsieur Jacques, you did call in the Devil – *Monsieur le Physicien* is the Devil." She said it so matter-of-factly that Jacques-Jean had to laugh.

With the aid of her little donkey and cart, Eva, the village laundress, delivered the fresh laundry on schedule that morning. She inquired as to Madame Charte's health before she left with another load. She was very glad to hear the madame was doing better for two reasons. First, she genuinely liked the petite lady whose linens she had been caring for ever since Hélène and her son had been installed into the cottage upon the old duke's death. And secondly, the workload had increased tenfold under Augustine's cleanliness campaign and it was fatiguing the aging laundress. She did her job well, however, no matter the load. Everything was always returned sweet smelling, spotless, and pressed.

Young Lisa had done such a commendable job delivering messages on horseback that Jacques-Jean also sent her to Celimene to inform her of events. Lisa returned with a basket full of fruit breads, some small cheeses, and a jar of strawberry preserves which Celimene sent with her best wishes for Hélène's speedy recovery.

Hélène was growing stronger each day. It was now almost two weeks since she had taken ill and she was sitting up on the small divan in her bedroom, having just finished her breakfast. The doors to the small balcony were wide open and a delightfully light breeze floated through the room.

Hélène wore a loose linen bedgown and silk shawl. Her back rested against a cushion of satin pillows braced against one end of the divan which rose up to form an ornate side arm. A soft, light throw lay in her lap. With her feet pulled up daintily under the throw there was ample room for a visitor to have a seat at the far end.

"*Entrée, entrée,*" she beckoned when she saw her son's smiling face peering through the partially opened door. His expression was one of honest happiness at seeing his mother up and looking much stronger.

"Good morning, Ma-ma, it is wonderful to see you looking so much like yourself again," he greeted cheerfully and bent toward her, brushing a kiss upon her cheek. "And see what a dashing figure your son cuts in the tailor's latest creation? Thank you, Ma-ma, it was most thoughtful but it really is not necessary for you to buy me clothing," he added almost sternly. "I receive sufficient allowance from *le duc* to dress properly."

"I know, I know, but I wanted to... and, yes, you do look very dashing, very handsome," she smiled proudly, her attention diverted for a moment. "The colors suit you."

He grinned and preened just a trifle like a magnificent young cock justifiably proud of its plumage. He struck a pose in a new suit of rust brocade with a waistcoat of peach silk. The light summer wool breeches were cut tighter in the leg as was the growing fashion. The outfit had arrived from the tailor the day before, a present from his mother arranged for long before she had taken ill.

"I love the brocade pattern, JJ, it is full of life, just like you," she smiled.

He returned her smile and pushed the topic of clothes from his mind. He actually was less concerned about what he wore than was thought fashionably proper amidst the aristocracy. It was one reason he knew he would be bored to tears at court.

"I have spoken with Lisa," Jacques-Jean said mildly, "and she is going to stay here from now on. I insist. She is a bright girl; I think she will make a very able maid and companion to you. You need someone to be with you, Ma-ma... all the time, not just for a short moment in the mornings and evenings. You used to have a housekeeper."

"She died..."

"And a cook."

"Who is there to cook for?"

"And a full-time gardener..."

"He still comes twice a week."

"You should have someone here all the time, Ma-ma."

"As you wish, JJ," she sighed, "I suppose you are right." Hélène gave her son a small amiable smile. She appreciated his concern for her.

"Of course, I am right. I shudder to think what might have happened if I had not stopped by that first evening. Or worse, I ask myself - if I should have come by earlier, might you have been saved such distress?"

"No distress, JJ, you could not save me from a fever, please..." Hélène waved aside the conversation. Deeply focused on her own thoughts, she hoped and prayed her son's regard and concern for her might never be altered. As if gathering her strength she continued much more seriously. "JJ... I..." she halted for a moment.

"What is it, Ma-ma, are you in pain?" he asked most tenderly.

"*Oui*, but of a different kind. I mean, oh, *mon fils, mon fils*, I have something I must tell you and I am afraid it is not very easy for me to begin. Please sit down." She gestured graciously to the divan beside her.

"Is it so serious?" he asked lightly, his handsome face cast in a relaxed almost teasing smile, his gray eyes attentive.

"*Oui*." She motioned again for him to sit by her. He removed his new coat, carefully laying it aside, and took a seat at her feet on the end of the divan. He grasped her small hand affectionately in his. She began to speak slowly, her eyes on their hands at the edge of her lap.

"I have a very troubled heart, JJ. I have something to tell you, something I know I should have told you long, long before now. But the longer I waited, you see, the harder it became to approach the subject. I kept telling myself, someday, someday... *someday*.

"Being so ill has made me realize that I could have died without that *someday* ever coming. That would be very wrong." She paused and took a breath stealing a glance up into her son's face which was attentive but expressionless. "I might have left things unsaid which must be told. I know it is very wrong that I have waited so long." She paused again to steady her voice, realizing it held a nervous tremor.

"Ma-ma, if it is so upsetting to you, please, it has waited this long, it can wait until you are stronger," he tried to ease her.

"No, JJ, I might have been standing before God on Judgment Day trying to explain why having sinned I had not the courage to at least set the record straight for my own son. I thank God He has given me another chance to do so. Now listen... and please," the next came in almost a whisper, "forgive me." She looked up now into his eyes. "I cannot rest until I... I can only start by saying I love you more than my own life. No mother has loved her child more than I love you. JJ, you must know this."

"Of course, Ma-ma, I do know this," he reassured her, patting her hand.

"If I have done some hurt to you by keeping this a secret for so long, I can only beg you to please forgive me. We expect our parents to be wise but they are, after all, just people, full of human weaknesses and not always so wise." She could not look in his face any longer and turned slightly away.

"When I was very young I made some terrible mistakes... terrible mistakes... but I was very young, you see, and young people are often very foolish," Hélène paused for another moment, gathering the strength to continue.

"When I was very young," she began again, "I fell in love with a young boy, a boy barely seventeen who said he loved me with all his heart. We were both so young, so innocent, so inexperienced in love and I could not help myself. He was so compelling in a quiet, tender, intense way and I found myself overwhelmed by his brooding passion. Then, *le duc* took notice of me, and at almost the same hour that I suspected I was with child, the old man proposed that I should become his mistress.

"As you know being the mistress of a *duc* is a very honorable position. My young mind was flooded with questions and doubts and fears. I had no mother from whom to seek counsel, I had to make my decision quickly... whether it was better for me and my child to be the mistress and bastard of a *duc* or to be the wife and legitimate child of a young boy who had nothing, a boy not yet out of his teens who could ill afford a family, a boy whose very livelihood would eventually depend on the generosity of a monster of an elder brother.

"But God has punished me for not being true to my heart, and not being true to your father, your *real* father. No, that is not fair. It is not true," she corrected herself with a small shake of her head. "God has not punished me, I have punished myself. My choice has punished me. How was I ever to know things would turn out as they did?" Hélène's thoughts had turned inward and she was quiet for a moment.

"My *real* father? Ma-ma, whatever are you saying? Are you telling me the old *duc* was not my father?" Jacques-Jean's voice betrayed his surprise. His mother shook her head. "But , who....?"

"*Le duc*, my son, *le duc!* It is life's irony. Do you not see? I turned my back on his love to go to his father, passed his son off as his half-brother and he ended up being *le duc*, after all," Hélène's voice broke into a sob. "I am so ashamed. You must believe me when I say I did not do it for money. Money never meant anything to me. I had no idea the old *duc* would give me a cottage and an annuity for life. I did it for you. Whether I was to bear a son or a daughter, I knew being the offspring of a *duc* was of some consequence. Oh, JJ, please, please do not hate me."

"Hush, Ma-ma, never," he took her hands again and drew her closer. "There, there, be calm. Am I hearing correctly? *Le duc* is Jean-Philippe... so you are saying Jean-Philippe is really my father?" He stared at her intently while she nodded her head, then he put his arms around her. "Does Jean-Philippe know that I am his son, Ma-ma?"

Hélène shrugged her small shoulders within her son's embrace. "We have never spoken of it but I think he knows it to be so. No one else knew of our love affair so no one else could have guessed. But Jean-Philippe knows you were born quite short of the nine month anniversary of my first going to the old *duc's* bed and the old *duc* was no longer a virile man. For him to father a baby at all would have been a great surprise - to father one so quickly, nothing short of a miracle."

"My father is... alive!" Jacques-Jean contemplated the full meaning of the words. "Jean-Philippe is my father! But Ma-ma, this is wonderful! Now I understand the special interest he has always shown me. I cannot believe you two have not spoken of this... not once in all these years?"

"Are you forgetting my shame?" she retorted quickly, pulling away as a tear rolled down her pale, smooth cheek. "I loved your father deeply as I believe he loved me... yet I went to his father's bed. Truly, Jean-Philippe must despise me. I crushed his heart and denied him his own son. I can hardly look him in the eye, even today after all this time. It has been my great sin that I cast away his love."

Jacques-Jean gathered his mother into his arms again bestowing a comforting embrace and offering soothing words as he held her. "Hush, Ma-ma, hush, you must rest now… and relax. Everything will be well. I promise you. Life is full of mistakes, is it not?. You were not the first young girl to break a man's heart and you will not be the last. Now calm yourself, please. You punish yourself far more than you deserve, far too much." Hélène took comfort from him and after a deep breath, she pat his arm as he held her. "What did my father say when you told him you had accepted *le duc's* proposal?"

"We never had a chance to talk. Jean-Philippe was gone suddenly, disappeared. I was alone with the realization that I carried his baby and the old *duc* made his proposal. It all happened so quickly. It was only later that I learned Jean-Philippe had been sent to another vineyard to stay with them and study something about leaf molds, I believe. And when he finally returned I had made my decision and there was no going back."

At that moment there was a tap at the door, it opened and Augustine returned to her post directing Jacques-Jean to leave.

"I am sorry, Monsieur Jacques, but it is time for madame's toilette, and then we shall have a very short stroll in the garden."

"Very well, Gussie, I leave her in your good hands," Jacques-Jean replied as he stood up and leaned over to kiss his mother's forehead. "I need to go now, Mama, I shall return before sundown. Perhaps we can sup together this evening?" Hélène knew he would talk to Jean-Philippe and said nothing as she nodded a weak agreement.

As soon as Jacques-Jean left the room, Augustine set about preparing Hélène's toilette silently, sensing that she was deep in her own thoughts. Going to the side cupboard, Augustine withdrew a very large pan and set it down in the center of the room. Next, she brought out towels and perfumed soap and a large copper wash basin. A knock on the door announced Lisa's arrival with a large bucket of fresh warm water. The young girl could barely carry the full bucket but Augustine took it from her with ease and shut the bedroom door again.

"We are ready, madame," she announced quietly, and Hélène stood. Augustine helped the slender woman remove her light linen gown. Completely naked and without self-consciousness, Hélène stepped into the middle of the shallow pan. With a wet sponge and fragrant soap, Augustine quickly but gently lathered Hélène's firm body. Carefully, the older woman used a porcelain pitcher to pour a slow sheet of clear, warm water down around Hélène's shoulders rinsing away all the little bubbles clinging to her pale, smooth skin. Another pitcher full was poured slowly around her waist. Before Hélène could begin shivering, Augustine wrapped the tiny frame in towels and guided her to sit at the dressing table. With gentle yet powerful hands, she rubbed Hélène's limbs briskly with the towel to aid circulation.

"It is still too soon, madame, to be concerned with full accoutrements. A fresh bedgown and a light peignoir are best, I think."

Hélène nodded her approval as she allowed herself to be dressed.

Her linen bedgown embroidered with tiny multicolored flowers peeped out from under the peignoir wrapped snugly around her as she sat quietly before the dressing table watching their reflections in the mirror. She was remembering the last time Augustine had cared for her. The old duke had sent the woman to watch over a very pregnant Hélène in her chambers within the chateau. The young girl had trusted Augustine instantly, and when labor began Hélène had no fears. She did exactly as the older woman told her and Jacques-Jean had been born almost easily.

Augustine brushed the long, pale blonde hair until it shined and wrapped it up into a simple chignon.

"A touch of rouge, madame, may make you feel better," she suggested tactfully.

"You are right. I look so pale." Hélène reached for her rouge powder and small puff. "Tell me, Gussie, how is the *duchesse* these days?"

"Well, madame."

"I hear she does beautiful needlework…"

"*Oui*, madame."

"and plays the harpsichord charmingly…"

"*Oui*, madame."

"Does she like my son?" As soon as the question left her mouth, Hélène regretted having asked it. "I am sorry," she gasped, "I do not know what made me ask that, it is a stupid question. Please forget the words were even spoken." She stole a furtive look in the mirror at Augustine's expression. It was as placid and inscrutable as ever.

"Please tell the *duc et duchesse* that I am most grateful for your care," Hélène finally said with sincerity, "and their generosity in sending you, but I do think it is time I let you return to your duties at the chateau. I am sure you are very missed."

"As madame wishes, if you are feeling so well tomorrow, I shall take my leave. And now our walk, madame," she said, taking Hélène's arm and guiding her down the cottage staircase and out the garden doors.

On a swift horse the ride from Hélène's cottage to the chateau was a short one. Jacques-Jean's mind raced with a hundred thoughts as he urged his horse on. *So*, he contemplated, *Ma-ma and Jean-Philippe were lovers*. He had never even suspected but as he considered the fact, it explained so much. The looks. The strange tension between them. It also explained Jean-Philippe's interest in Jacques' welfare. The young man laughed aloud. Last week he thought he was nothing, a mere bastard half-brother, but today? Today, he was the one and only son of the current *Duc du Pouvoir*. Life was amazing! Absolutely amazing! And Celimene was now the mistress of an heir. Jacques-Jean laughed aloud again as he envisioned the passion such news would inspire in his beautiful, long limbed darling.

The day was magnificent. Huge, billowy clouds like ships with full sails dotted the upside down ocean of the deep blue sky. The air was much lighter than it had been for weeks, the breezes were refreshing, and the sunlight was bright and just comfortably warm. Jacques-Jean imagined he heard the birds singing but the sound of his horse's hooves upon the road was too loud for him to hear much of anything else.

A stable boy took Jacques-Jean's horse as he leapt down from his saddle and took the stairs, two at a time, up to the huge iron bound front doors. A smaller door, cut into the larger one was used for entering and exiting in inclement weather and at night. But during the day when the weather was pleasant, the immense twin doors stood wide open to circulate the air and admit the breezes. A second set of equally large doors carved out of fine golden oak stood open at the top of a shorter set of inner stone steps. These doors opened into the large main hall of the chateau.

The white Italian marble floors echoed the sound of Jacques-Jean's heels as he approached the large curved inner staircase. A downstairs servant told him the duke was in his upstairs study.

As Jacques-Jean strode up the long staircase, he became more hesitant on broaching the subject with Jean-Philippe. Surely the duke knew but why had he never said anything? What if he did not know? He must, at least, suspect, must he not? But why had he never pursued the facts himself? Still, one's parentage was not a subject a man could ignore once it had been brought out into the open. Jacques-Jean told himself he could not set this news aside and, two or four years later say *Oh, yes, by the way, a while back my mother told me you were my father, I assumed you knew*. No, that would be absurd, this was much too important.

He had reached the door of the duke's study and after a brief final pause he knocked lightly only to be suddenly overwhelmed with the thought that perhaps the duke did not want to acknowledge him as his son or his heir.

"*Entrée!*" spoke the voice from within and Jacques-Jean opened the door. "Ah, Jacques, it is you. Come in, sit. How is your mother feeling?" The duke was seated at his finely carved desk and set aside the bulky old manuscript he had been studying. He wore his usual garb, a pair of dark knee breeches with dark stockings and a jersey tunic over his soft linen shirt trimmed sparingly with lace around the old-fashioned collar.

"M'lord, she is doing much better, thank you. But I hate to think what might have happened without Gussie. She is quite *fantastique*."

"*Oui*, I can remember several illnesses Augustine nursed me through. And oddly enough, I can remember my mother saying the exact same thing. It gives one pause. I have never had the audacity to ask Augustine how old she is." He gave a small laugh. "I remember once, as a young boy, I did ask her how long she had been a healer and she replied rather enigmatically, '*ever since I knew what needed to be done*.'" After a pause he added thoughtfully, "Well, anyway, I am most pleased to hear Madame Hélène is again feeling well."

"*Oui*." Did he detect a certain sentimentality when Jean-Philippe referred to Madame Hélène? "*Merci*. After all the deaths this winter, I must admit it was quite frightening to see her so ill. It gave us both a terrible scare." Jacques-Jean was aware of feeling uncomfortably warm but he could not stop now, he told himself. "As... a matter of fact, Ma-ma was so shocked by her own frailty that she was pressed to make a confession to me," Jacques-Jean paused, watching the duke intently.

"A confession?" the older man puzzled.

"*Oui*, something that she admitted should have been said years ago but out of her overwhelming sense of guilt and shame she could never bring up the subject."

"I cannot imagine your mother having done anything for which to feel so much guilt or shame," the duke replied evenly.

Jacques-Jean watched his father's facial expression carefully, trying to detect any trace, any hint of an indication that the duke knew what Hélène had confessed. There was nothing.

"I, too, sir, could not imagine what my dear mother could have done that would weigh so heavily upon her conscience." Jacques-Jean paused again trying to find the right words. "She told me that when she was very young she did something very foolish which she has regretted all these years."

Jean-Philippe's face remained expressionless while he listened to Jacques-Jean with singular attention.

"It seems she was very much in love with a young man who she said also loved her but she...to quote her...'*cast away his love*.'" Jacques-Jean saw it now, like the shadow that moves over the ground when a cloud comes between the earth and the sun. He detected a shadow passing over the duke's countenance. "But worse than the love she threw away, she grieves most deeply that all these years she has denied him the knowledge that he, in fact, fathered her son."

The air within the study suddenly grew very still and quiet. The only sound to be heard was the ticking of the small porcelain clock on the fireplace mantel and a faint dog bark from the far end of the courtyard. Neither man moved a single muscle. Jacques-Jean felt as though time had stopped, life had frozen, all except for the beating of his heart which he could feel within his chest. He could say no more, he awaited the duke to say something, anything. At last, Jacques-Jean heard the duke's voice.

"You are saying my father was not your father?" the words were measured.

"Sir, I am saying I have just been told that you, m'lord, are in fact my father."

The duke slowly pushed back his chair and stood without a word. He walked to the window, his hands clasped behind his back, his shoulders slightly stooped. He peered through the curtains, apparently staring at something but his eyes were unfocused; he saw nothing. His concentration was all on the past. After a few moments, he turned to Jacques-Jean with great self-control.

"I have always loved you as a son because you were *her* son. Now, I am proud to call you my own," he rasped in almost a whisper.

Jacques-Jean rose from his chair and stepped into his father's embrace.

Marie heard the rap at the door of her little room. She lay very still, almost afraid to breathe. Her eyes were closed, her ears straining for every sound. It was the fourth night Bouchet had come to her door. She pretended to be sound asleep but she heard him try the latch which she had taken the pains to tie off securely. Tomorrow he would say nothing, he would watch her and ask how she had slept and she would reply that she had been exhausted and had slept deeply. But she knew what he wanted and she was frightened.

She was a nobody, she thought to herself, as she lay in the dark. A tear formed in her eye. She had no one, she belonged nowhere, but she was not a *nothing*. She was a person. She had feelings. She had dreams. She wanted more from life; she was trying to make her own way. And he treated her as if she was of no more consequence than a kettle in his kitchen.

He had started touching her. At first, it was a pat, almost a bump, as if to move her out of his way although there was always room enough to pass. Yesterday, he had pinched her buttocks and laughed. Today, when she had returned from the hen house, her hands carefully gripping her apron full of fresh eggs, he had come up behind her and actually put his hand under her skirts and tried to grab her between her thighs. She had tried to pretend nothing had happened as she deftly slipped away from him. She did not know what else to do. If she acknowledged him, she could not ignore the circumstance; she would have to face him. What would he do tomorrow?

Marie knew it was only a matter of time. Now that Anoui was gone, he wanted Marie to do *all* the things his wife had done but she did not want to play his wife. She was not a virgin and he knew that. Perhaps he thought she had been with many men. Perhaps he thought she would agree to lie with anyone. But that was not true. She had been only a child when she and the young boy from the traveling troop had... and it had happened so quickly. He had been so young himself, so tender and sweet... he had touched her down there and pressed his hips against hers. She had not even understood what he was doing to her, he had been small and she had barely felt him. He had groaned deeply and then, Juliette had been there shouting and... Marie had had no idea that a baby would come of it.

In the darkness, the girl shuddered. She would have to make a choice: sleep with Bouchet or leave. But where could she go? She heard his footsteps as he shuffled away from her door.

The duke had sent word ahead to Hélène that he was planning to visit her cottage. It was two days since Augustine had returned to the chateau and Hélène felt quite like her usual self again except for the cloud of butterflies that kept dancing about in her stomach. Lisa helped her to dress that morning. Hélène chose a pale lilac frock that she had most recently ordered to be made up according to what one heard was the fashion at the Court of *Louis Quatorze*. The neckline, edged in a very wide snowy white collar of heavy Belgium lace, dropped low and off her slight and softly rounded shoulders. The snugly fitting bodice accented her tiny waistline as the over-skirt pulled back in front by plump bows displayed a silver silk taffeta underskirt. Hélène had chosen the colors because they were a compliment to her soft coloring. With Lisa's help, her hair was arranged in small rings of curls which cascaded from high off either side of her head over her ears.

"Madame is very beautiful," Lisa said shyly, her eyes wide with admiration.

"Thank you, Lisa, but tell me truly, do I look like I have been ill?" Hélène asked anxiously as she patted more powder on her nose and smoothed it over her cheeks.

"No, madame, not at all," replied the girl earnestly.

"Just a little crème rouge now for my cheeks… and my lips and… I am finished." Hélène paused still staring into the mirror.

"Madame, I am so nervous. To receive a *duc* in your home is such an honor, and I am only a peasant girl; I am afraid I will not know the proper thing to say or do."

Hélène looked at the serving girl and smiled sympathetically.

"Lisa, I am so sorry. Please, forgive me. I have been so involved in my own preparation, I never thought about your feelings. But you will be fine," she spoke encouragingly, "just do as you always do. You should curtsy when he first arrives and pay attention to what you are asked. You have been doing a splendid job here for me. *Le duc* is a rather quiet man, he does not hold to the fancy airs of the Court, it will not be difficult to serve him." Hélène stood and spontaneously gave the girl an affectionate squeeze on the arm before walking down to the small salon.

The older woman did not want the young girl to see how her own stomach was a mass of nerves. It had been years since Jean-Philippe had last been to the country cottage. That was when Hélène had allowed for his son to move into the chateau with him. She had thought he had known. Now she knew for certain that he knew. Jacques-Jean had spoken to him. What exactly did she expect Jean-Philippe to say? One moment she looked forward to his coming like a young maiden awaiting her swain. The next moment she was filled with dread, fearing the recriminations he might heap upon her for what she had done to him.

No, Jean-Philippe was not like that, she told herself. He had never shown her the slightest contempt for what she had done when she had become his father's mistress. His heart was too good, too generous for that. He was too kind and caring. He had had no security to offer her. Hélène began to relive the memories of their romance over twenty years ago and found passion stirring within her once again.

At last, the duke arrived. With knees trembling and voice shaking, poor little Lisa answered the door. She dropped an awkward curtsy and ushered Jean-Philippe into the salon where Hélène was waiting. She was poised graciously to receive him.

He had a small moustache now and there was a bit of silver in the hair at his temples. But he still looked much as he always had. His clothes were austerely conservative, old fashioned some would say, and yet he was so pensively handsome.

"May I offer you some refreshment, m'lord?" Hélène asked graciously after she dropped a deep curtsy, hoping he did not notice the slight quake in her voice.

"Nothing, *merci*."

With that, Hélène excused Lisa who was more than happy to escape to the safe familiarity of the cooking pantry. The sound of the girl's quick departure left a silence in the room. For a long moment Jean-Philippe looked intently at his first and only love and then he spoke.

"You are looking very well, Hélène."

"*Merci*, m'lord," she replied simply, modestly casting her gaze downward.

"It is quite unbelievable," he went on in a tone of mild disbelief. "I came here fully expecting to find a wan and sickly creature and here you are... looking more beautiful than ever, if that is even possible." It was a casual compliment, like so many one might hear fall glibly from the lips of any gentleman but it held special meaning for Hélène. Jean-Philippe had never been a courtly flatterer and he had spoken with serious sincerity.

"M'lord, you are very kind," she replied softly. They stood, each extremely conscious of the other's presence. The silent seconds ticked by until the atmosphere grew awkward. "Please... be seated, m'lord, forgive me for not offering sooner..." the words rushed from her in embarrassment.

He waved aside the apology. "It is nothing... I am satisfied to stand for a moment," he added, then had a sudden thought. "But perhaps you wish to sit. You are still weak?"

"No-no, I am quite well now."

"Jacques said you were very ill," he said softly in almost a question.

She started to deny it, but thought better of it. She had been very ill, it was what prompted her to confess to her son. There was no sense in lying about it.

"*Oui*," she said simply.

"Very ill," he repeated. "Despite how well you look. You gave everyone quite a fright," he said looking at her intently as she cast her eyes down again. "You gave *me* a fright as well."

"M'lord?" she looked up again in puzzlement.

"Am I never to be *Jean-Philippe* to you again?" It sounded almost like a cry choking up out of his throat and her eyes were riveted on his face. He added quickly, "Jacques has told me... is it true? He is *my* son?"

"It is true," she nodded and diverted her eyes again from his scrutinizing gaze.

"You never told me." Was there a trace of anguish in his voice, or was it accusation? She could not tell.

"I always thought you knew... and that you must hate me for it." He looked at her with hurt and sadness in his eyes but said nothing. "When you came to my home and asked to take JJ to the chateau to live, I was certain you knew. I even had a fear that somehow you would take my son away from me and turn him against me to punish me for what I had done to you."

"Oh, Hélène," her name came out in a long anguished sigh. "I could never wish to hurt you. No, I did not know. I suppose it never entered my mind that you could have left me knowing you were carrying my child." The words were spoken candidly, without malice, but they stung her to the bone. "If only you had told me, Hélène," the words came wrenching from within, "you would have been my *duchesse!*"

"Please, do not hate me, Jean-Philippe. I was a foolish, foolish girl who thought she was doing the best thing for our child. Perhaps I thought when your father died, we could be lovers again. I do not know. Not a single day has passed that I have not regretted my decision. My happiness ended. I have spent the past twenty years without a man's love, and the past eight years alone. That has been my punishment. I could not bear it if you now hated me as well."

He stepped toward her, drawn irresistibly to be near her. His arms longed to hold her once again, caress her, feel the warmth of her kisses, kisses that still lived in his memory. He took her hand in his, brought it to his lips, and smelled her scent. She looked like a fragile crystal angel but she was warm and soft.

"Oh, *ma chérie*, I could not hate you though you broke my heart. I have never stopped loving you. If only you had not stopped loving me. You are and always will be the love of my life, the only one to whom I have ever given my heart. My poor wife, may God forgive me, deserved better. I could not foster enough interest to get her with child."

Hélène was drawn by an invisible force to be closer to him, her trembling fingers traced lightly over his cheek. How many years since she had been permitted this intimacy? Her fingers went on touching him, his brow, his jaw, then, boldly she caressed his lips.

"Jean-Philippe, *mon amour, mon cœur*, I never ever stopped loving you. Is that what you thought? Of course, you did. What else? I acted so heartlessly but I thought... You were not here when I realized I was with child... oh, my love, how could I have been so stupid?"

His eyes were full of a sad longing which as her words registered was replaced by passion. She was quivering, standing so close to him. Suddenly, the years melted away and they became very young lovers again, thirsting for each other's embrace. For a long while they held each other, feeling their hearts beat in unison and being consumed by a burning desire.

At last, he picked her up in his arms, drawing her into his body. She was gossamer light and clung to him as he carried her up to her bedchamber. Drunk with the heady wine of mutual passion, desire, and love, they spent the next hours making up for twenty lost years.

⚜

It was late and the last customers had just left the tavern. Marie hurriedly carried the abandoned tankards to the kitchen. She brought a bucket, brush, and rag back out to the main room and began to scrub down the table tops just vacated. She was very aware of her employer and could not wait to finish so she could escape for the night to the safety of her room.

Bouchet walked heavily to the thick planked front door and opened it. He extinguished the candles in the lanterns that hung outside on either side of the entrance. He moved back inside and closed the door, dropping the bar in its place. He saw the girl working in a frenzy. He had already decided that she was not going to get away from him this night.

Every evening it was his routine to tip the chairs and benches up onto the tables and sweep and sometimes scrub down the floor. Marie planned to finish with the table tops before he had completed his task so she could slip out as she had been doing. She had just wiped off the last table and turned to leave. Startled, she dropped the bucket on the floor as she ran right into Bouchet who had quietly crept up behind her.

She gasped and looking up at his face, her own face went white. He did not need to say a thing. She knew and she began to shake her head.

"No... please, monsieur, no, no, please." It came out in almost a whimper for he had grasped her wrist in a vice-like grip. He said nothing but a mirthless smile played upon his lips as he bent in closing the distance to her mouth. She was neatly pinioned against the table.

She could smell the stench of garlic and rotting teeth on his breath and struggled, trying to evade his kiss. In desperation she gripped the wooden brush tightly in her free hand and wheeling it with all her strength she attempted to hit him. It was a mistake. He saw it coming, easily ripped it from her grasp and let it drop to the floor. In retaliation, he delivered a stunning blow to her head with his huge meaty hand.

Marie felt the blow with a crack that rattled the teeth in her gums and sent darts of pain shooting through her head to her eye and ear. She was momentarily stunned and almost lost consciousness as strange light bursts danced before her eyes. She hardly felt it when he threw her onto the table. His voice sounded as if coming from a great distance.

"Do not play the innocent with me, you little slut! You came here with some man's seed growing in your belly. I see you with the others, you like to tease."

His hands yanked her skirts up and out of his way. He pushed her legs apart and stood between them. Before she could gain back control of her arms, both were pinned against her chest by one hand pushing down on her. She could barely draw breath.

"I feed you, I shelter you... I have a right..." he was panting now, his free hand fumbling fiercely with his own laces.

Marie felt a burning pain as he thrust into her with his bloated member. She winced and cried out but there was no one to hear her and he only laughed. She could not fight him, he was too strong. In response to her struggle he simply leaned more heavily upon her until she thought her ribs would crack. She had to endure. She willed herself to relax to make it easier on herself but she could not. It would not take long, she told herself it would be over soon. She must endure. Every stroke was a searing burn against her tender flesh and she bit her lip to keep from screaming. She could taste her own blood in her mouth. She could hear his labored breathing, like an animal with each exhale fanning her face with fetid air. She would endure. Her eyes were clenched shut until a final harsh thrust sent such a lightning bolt of pain through her body she opened her eyes with a gasp and saw a black curtain begin to draw up around her but she did not pass out completely.

Bouchet was sweating profusely. He shuddered and with short repeated jabs he ejaculated in a series of snorting grunts. Then he was still. He had been a fool to wait this long, he thought to himself taking a deep breath. He withdrew looking triumphantly at the flesh he had just violated, very pink in its nest of curls. She was here for the taking. She had no protector and there was no reason he should not have her whenever he pleased he assured himself as he pulled up his britches.

Marie lay like a limp bird whose wings had been broken. Bouchet sneered, licked his dry lips, and moved off to get a tankard of ale. Slowly she lifted herself to her elbow, and struggled to sit up. Gingerly, she slid off the table top, her skirts falling back down over her nakedness. She felt bow-legged as she began to walk across the room.

Bouchet was watching her over the tankard as he swallowed. He saw her cheek beginning to change colors where he had struck her.

"Marie!" He barked. She stopped. "Where do you think you are going?" She turned toward him, her eyes averted. "Did I say you could leave?!" He heard her utter a small sound. "Get back over here!" She shrank from him involuntarily. "I told you to come here!" he commanded and she moved slowly toward him, stopping just out of arms' reach.

Bouchet emptied the tankard deliberately and wiped his mouth with his sleeve. He had just robbed her of all dignity and it empowered him absolutely. He felt the power and pushed his advantage over the small female standing broken before him. He set down the tankard and lumbered toward her.

"Look at me!" he commanded sharply. She looked up at him quickly and avoided his eyes, dropping her gaze to his whiskered chin as he glared down at her. "No more games from you unless you want more of this," he threatened and tapped her swelling cheek with just enough force to make her wince. "Understand?!" She nodded quickly, submission in her eyes. "Good!" He belched loudly. He deliberately grabbed hold of her ill fitting bodice and with a ripping tug on the rotting fabric, he exposed both round young breasts. He took hold and squeezed them, pinching her flesh between his forefingers and thumbs, wanting to leave her black and blue in reprisal for all the time she had made him wait. "It has been a long time," he said ominously, "and I am not yet through with you."

Marie tried not to cry.

Chapter 5

C elimene avoided the full force of the summer sun whenever she could. It was how she kept her skin milky fair and soft as a babe's. The last thing she wanted was freckles like the peasant girls or to grow old with the criss-cross wrinkles of the peasant women. No, that she would not have ever if she could help it, she told herself. But now the day's sun was low in the trees and the long shadows it cast provided ample shade for a ride along her favorite path close to the river.

As she rode the beautiful bay Jacques-Jean had presented her with on her eighteenth birthday, she thought of all the changes of the past few months. Her lover was now the sole heir of the duke! As such, Jacques-Jean's allowance had been increased greatly. His father had also provided him with a personal servant who attended him everywhere; well, she smiled to herself, *almost* everywhere. And he now had responsibilities involving the administration of the estate. He had explained to her that in this way he would become familiar with everything that was going on. To pay for itself, the estate needed to be managed wisely he had learned. And this management was part of the excuse Jean-Philippe made for stay-ing away from Versailles.

Celimene understood all this although she had no idea why anyone would want to stay away from the glitter, glamour, and entertainments that surrounded the king. Perhaps some day she could persuade Jacques-Jean to take her there. But for now she accepted that all these changes meant she saw less of him. Even so, he had insisted she have a full-time housekeeper-cook so they could entertain prop-erly with little fetes. And often times of late, she would play hostess to his small group of intimate friends.

Celimene was in a very happy mood thinking on this fortuitous turn of events in her life and she laughed lightly to herself as she rode the winding trail. Bertrell was still around to JJ's dismay but she had a soft spot of pity in her heart for the big dummy. And he was very loyal to her and did all the rough and dirty work around the cottage, asking for nothing except his food. He slept in the small barn which he now shared with her newly acquired horse. And she had to give him clothes when she saw his wearing thin or he would soon walk naked and never notice.

Her own wardrobe now included several fancy dresses that required an atten-dant's help in donning with intricate underpinnings and lacings down the back. No longer did she wear only the simple garb of a country girl which could be put on easily by oneself. Today she had changed her costume twice already, and when she returned from her ride, she would change out of her beautiful claret riding habit into yet another gown. It was grand!

The path had opened onto a meadow and Celimene urged the horse to a quicker pace. She was a charming sight and she knew it. She could picture herself as an onlooker might see her – a colorful streak of red on the shiny bay. Her chestnut curls bouncing under the tidy veiled hat trimmed with stiff pheasant feathers. The rich red folds of her skirt draped perfectly over the horse's flank as she rode sidesaddle, as every proper lady rides.

There was just a tantalizing bit of snowy white lace petticoat exposed by the force of the rush of air against her red and white striped silk underskirt. Her carefully tailored jacket, aping the gentleman's style but without the bulk of its male counterpart, was fitted trimly to her ripe curves and straight shoulders showing them to advantage she knew, while the crisp white lace jabot at her neck set off the lovely features of her face. Her riding gloves of the softest pigskin were dyed dove gray to match her charming hat and soft leather boots.

Her boots! Celimene smiled again broadly. She loved her boots. Custom-made just for her and smoothly hugging her toes, they made her feet look so small and dainty. One little foot could be seen dwarfed in the stirrup. And in her hand she held a small riding crop which she carried only for effect.

The young rider knew that she would turn the head of any gentleman who should see her. That was not vanity, she told herself, simply accurate assessment. What nature had given her is what she had to work with in getting on in life. And along with a lovely body of ample curves and a delicate face, nature had given Celimene an artistic sense for putting together color and style to its best advantage. She smiled again. And through these unique gifts and graces, she complimented herself, she was now the mistress of a future duke! Life was indeed *very* grand!

In short time, horse and rider crossed the meadow and the young woman reigned in the animal and slowed it back to a walk. They both needed to cool down. Celimene let the horse pick its way through the trees and back to the river where it sought a way down to the water's edge to slake its thirst.

It was while they stood quietly, the horse engaged in a long drink, that Celimene heard a distinctly human sound coming from nearby. Straining to hear, she recognized what she thought to be the sound of weeping. When the horse's thirst was satisfied, it blew and whinnied as she nudged it on in the direction of those sounds. The horse walked on several more yards picking its way over the rocky embankment and Celimene spied something. Two steps more and her keen eyes discerned what appeared to be a torn skirt sticking out from behind a tree on the other bank.

Cautiously she walked the horse through the stream and circled around to the other side of a huge elm. Sitting at the tree's base she saw a dirty, grimy little heap with stringy snarled hair and very ill-fitting clothes.

"What is wrong, girl?" she asked, not unkindly. "Are you hurt?"

Marie was startled to hear another voice. She looked up and saw Celimene's bright blue eyes peering down at her.

"No, m'... m'lady," she answered obediently with a hiccup.

"Are you lost?"

Marie shook her head.

"What is your name?" Celimene asked.

"Marie," she replied, wiping quickly at her tears.

"Where are you from, Marie?"

"Nowhere, m'lady."

"You must come from somewhere," Celimene smiled. "Where is your family?"

"I have no family."

"But where do you live?"

"At the tavern in the village, m'lady."

"And why do you weep so?" There was something warm and gentle in Celimene's voice that reminded Marie of her sister, Louise. Marie could not control her emotions and began to weep again. "Come, come now, you can tell me," Celimene coaxed, "perhaps I can help. I do have friends of influence," she added a little proudly.

"F...For... g...give me, m..m'lady, I am so m..miserable I kn...know not what to do."

Celimene decided to dismount and landed on the ground with agile grace. She walked up to the girl. The little ragamuffin did not appear deformed and was not unpleasant looking under all that grime but she needed a very hot and soapy bath and her clothing simply begged to be burned.

"You cannot sit here crying," Celimene said firmly. The girl looked so lost and totally friendless, it stirred Celimene to pity. "Come, come along. You must come home with me," she announced resolutely and Marie got to her feet without argument.

Guiding her horse to a fallen log, Celimene easily re-seated herself upon her steed and beckoned Marie to climb on behind her. It pained the beauty to have the girl sit so close to her. Marie reeked of sour sweat, burnt grease, and stale cooked foods: of fish, cabbage, onions, and garlic, and Celimene's riding outfit was so new. But there was no other way. She would not force the little creature to walk while she rode, besides she did not have the patience to walk the horse all the way back home. It would take forever. And so together, they took off riding in the direction of the cottage at an easy pace.

Celimene had a large round tub she used for bathing. It was one of the things Jacques-Jean found amusingly attractive about her. To submerse the entire body in water was not a common practice in their society. The common belief was that it opened the pores and rendered a person subject to invasion from the plague but Celimene disputed the truth of this belief. She had never been ill or threatened by plague so she pooh-poohed those notions and claimed that quite to the contrary, a hot bath by a warm fire made her feel very good indeed.

When the two returned to the cottage, Celimene called to Bertrell and told him to quickly fetch water for a bath. She announced to Cook that they would need lots of hot water while Cook's mouth fell open at the sight of Marie tagging along behind Celimene.

That task in process, Celimene went to her bedroom, and Marie, still following wordlessly, stood in the doorway. Without any self-consciousness the vigorous beauty doffed her rich garments down to her shift refusing to wear more for she might get splashed with water. She shook her new riding habit vigorously lest any unwanted "guests" had jumped into it from off her riding companion and she hung it where it could air out. Minutes later they were back in the kitchen where a screen had been set up to provide a degree of privacy.

"Off with those rags," Celimene gestured with a touch of impatience as she tied on a large apron. Marie tugged off her clothing letting the filthy garments drop to the floor. She had to take a step up on a small stool to raise her leg over the edge of the tub and when she did, Celimene could not help but notice the black and blue marks on her arms, her thighs, her buttocks, even her small young breasts.

As Marie slipped into the tub of steaming water, the cook picked up the discarded clothing on the point of a stick and threw them into the fire. Marie began to utter a protest but Celimene cut her off with a smile. "Good riddance!" she exclaimed not unkindly as she lathered Marie down with strong soap and added an unguent comprised mostly of yarrow, sure to repel lice. "I do not doubt that you were not the only one living in those clothes. Let Cook burn them, I will give you others." Celimene looked down at the water and was horrified to see it had turned a muddy hue, covered with scum.

"Out, out," the older girl cried softly and made Marie stand shivering with only a small towel clutched around her while Bertrell came in unmindful of anything but his mistress. He emptied the tub and filled it up again. The second scrubbing proved to be the charm and Marie finally emerged pink and clean.

Next Celimene gave her a set of fresh clothing. Although Celimene was taller and had a more robust figure, still the castoff garments fit Marie much better than anything she had worn for a very long time. She dressed quickly and sat silently as Celimene tried to comb through the tangle of matted hair. It was a sadly snarled mess and although the older girl attempted to be gentle she could tell she was hurting the other by the grimaces that played across Marie's young face.

At last in frustration, Celimene took a shears and trimmed the heavy hair so it barely fell to the tops of Marie's shoulders. Now able to get a comb through it, the young beauty combed it thoroughly pulling out the occasional louse body as she went. Trimming again to even the length, she doused Marie's hair with strong vinegar and combed it carefully until Celimene was sure no nits remained. Finally, she brushed and brushed until the hair began to dry. With a small satin ribbon of bright yellow, she tied the loose curls back behind the girl's ears.

By the time they were finished, Marie had heard a stern but friendly lecture on the sins of allowing oneself to become so dirty and the virtues of regular bathing. She was given a spare brush and a directive to never go to bed without brushing her hair one hundred strokes without fail.

At last Celimene led Marie back into the bedroom to stand before a full-length mirror.

"Now, look. *Voila*! Who is this?" Celimene exclaimed brightly.

Marie looked and saw someone she had never seen before looking back at her. It was the first time ever that she had seen herself like this, in a good mirror and full length. All her life Marie had only seen her reflection dimly, perhaps in the water or distorted in a shiny pot, or by bits in a piece of broken mirror, or darkly in a pane of distorted window glass. She liked the image she now saw. She almost looked pretty, she thought. Celimene had tied the strong strings of the shift's neckline up closely as befit a modest maid. The dark corselet further covered her, holding her breasts close as it also held her skirt and shift in place and nipped in the material around her small waist. She noticed for the first time and with surprise that her hair was streaked with soft golden highlights as it rippled down.

"So...what do you think?" Celimene smiled at her own handiwork. "The world looks not so bad now, eh?"

Marie stared in the mirror.

"Mademoiselle, what do you call the color of my eyes?"

"You goose. You know not the color of your own eyes?"

"They are not blue. They are not brown, not like I have seen on others."

"No, they are what is called hazel. Quite beautiful, you know, with golden flecks."

She should have been pleased but Marie's expression changed and hot tears began coursing down her cheeks again. She had suddenly thought of what awaited her back at the tavern.

Over soothing cups of tea in the quiet of sunset, Marie poured out her heart to the first friendly female face she had seen since Anoui had died. She told Celimene about her family, her baby, Anoui and Bo-Bo, and finally, about Bouchet. With great shame she confessed that he had finally raped her. And ever since, under the threat of a beating, he expected her in his bed regularly before she could retire to her own little room. It had become one of her duties around the tavern. She had tried to numb herself to it, she said, grateful that it was not every night but one evening not long ago, after he had told her to go up and ready herself, she had heard voices in the hall as she lie waiting for him. Bouchet had opened the bedroom door and she had been shocked to see one of the soldiers that often came to the tavern, follow him in.

"Here is a friend, Marie," Bouchet said with a hard smirk, "and I want you to be nice to him. He needs a little comfort so far from home. So do as he wishes."

After taking coins from the soldier, Bouchet admonished him to take care with a reminder that he had no use for a pregnant serving girl. With a coarse laugh Bouchet had left the room, shutting the door behind him.

Unable to look Celimene in the eye, Marie confessed that Bouchet always had someone for her *to be nice to* now and sometimes he watched and took his own pleasure with her after. Often he hurt her for no other reason than he enjoyed it, even if it was not a full fledged beating. She could not bear it anymore, she told Celimene, and so, without any plan, Marie had run away.

Late that evening, with Marie safely asleep in the kitchen, Celimene told Jacques-Jean the girl's story.

"JJ, I cannot send the child back to that. There is little of her body that is not covered in ugly bruises," Celimene said as she brushed out her cloud of silky brunette hair. "Her life has been so *tragique*. She has nothing, no one to help her. That monster has taken the worst kind of advantage of her. He is worse than a pimp. He has made her a *putain*, but she gets nothing from it. I intend to keep her as my maid. I need someone now to help me with my toilette, to assist with my laces, and do my hair. It is not seemly that the cook should do it. Besides, Cook likes to go home at night."

"Very well, my darling, if that is what you wish, why not?" he agreed easily. "The girl certainly cleaned up nicely and I have always liked the child."

"There is just one thing, JJ, a favor," Celimene turned to him and flashed her most dazzling smile. "Would you go with Marie to the tavern so she can collect her possessions?"

"What possessions?" he laughed. "The girl has nothing you would want brought into this house."

"Except for one thing. It seems she does have a small cache of coins, her life's savings. She should have it and the tavernkeeper certainly owes her more than that."

"Are you suggesting I should go give him a sound thrashing?" he asked in amusement.

"That would be very nice, *mon chère*, and justly deserved but of no real value to the poor thing. No, I was thinking more along the lines of some deserved compensation, her share so to speak. That would be of more real value to her." The seductress glided over to the bed where he was waiting for her.

"Is it too much to ask?" she murmured as she began to kiss his fingers. He could feel her soft velvety tongue in the palm of his hand. She began sucking his fingers slowly in a most erotic suggestion.

"Anything you want," he agreed carelessly before he sought her eagerly with his mouth.

The next morning, Jacques-Jean rose early. He was a man with responsibilities now he thought to himself with understandable pride. He no longer had the option to sleep the day away. Cook had his breakfast ready in the kitchen and as he ate he spoke to Marie.

"Mademoiselle Celimene has told me you would like to stay here and serve her," Jacques-Jean began easily.

She nodded in reply standing shyly by the hearth.

"And I believe you have some personal belongings you wish to pick up from the tavern, *oui*? So, I will ride with you to Monsieur Bouchet's where we will tell him that he shall not be seeing you anymore, and we shall collect your things."

Marie said nothing but he could see nervous fear in her eyes.

"Worry not, *ma petite*, you will be quite safe," he added with calm reassurance. "Can you ride?"

She bobbed a quick nod, afraid to disappoint.

Jacques-Jean had Bertrell saddle the bay for Marie to ride. Once their business at the tavern was complete, she could return to the cottage on her own while he continued on to the chateau, he told her. With Jacques-Jean's assistance, Marie bravely climbed up on the horse, straddling it like a man. Her heart was beating wildly. She felt the large animal move beneath her. She was terrified. She must control it, she thought. She must ride on her own but she wasn't sure how. The animal, however, recognized the smell of Celimene's soaps and proved gentle. Without much effort it fell in behind Jacques-Jean's steed. All she had to do was hold on.

This early in the morning, the tavern was always deserted but Bouchet was in the back trying to get things in order for the day's business to come. As Jacques-Jean and Marie approached the rear of the building, they could hear the tavern-keeper swearing and muttering to himself amidst the clatter of utensils.

When Bouchet saw Marie he was speechless for just a moment, so taken back by her changed appearance. It also surprised him to see her with the young aristocrat. Almost immediately he began to calculate how much more money he could get for her favors and at the same instant he grew more angry thinking of all the money he had not made because she had not looked like this before.

"Where have you been, girl?" he snarled in accusation. "You left me stranded last night with a mess of work and no help. I have a good mind to…"

"Monsieur Bouchet," Jacques-Jean interrupted, "Mademoiselle Marie is no longer in your employ. She has come to collect her things."

"She cannot leave!" Bouchet exploded, his unshaven face twisting in anger.

"And why is that?" Jacques-Jean asked with purposeful hauteur as he dismounted and rested his hand nonchalantly but not insignificantly on the handle of his rapier. "Are you saying she is under contract to you? Do you own her? Is she your daughter or your wife that you can speak for her? No, monsieur, I think not. She is free to choose where to work and she is now in my employ." He glanced at the girl. "Go, Marie, get your things and we shall leave."

"The ungrateful slut!" Bouchet snarled. "I took her in when no one else would have her!"

"That is not exactly true, is it?" Jacques-Jean continued to speak in a dry, mild, almost affable fashion. "I believe it was your good wife who took Marie in and since, she has more than earned her keep. Yes, much more. In fact, I believe most recently you have forced her into a business partnership wherein she gave all the services and you shared none of the earnings." Jacques-Jean stepped in closer to face Bouchet's bulging eyes and sweating brow. His voice suddenly lost all of its apparent good humor.

"I believe you owe the young lady a tidy sum for all of her extra efforts. I am certain it is simply an oversight on your part so I shall give you the opportunity to set accounts straight before we leave. I suggest a purse, a substantial purse, Monsieur Bouchet, to rectify this omission."

"Are you mad?" Bouchet sputtered, "She worked in exchange for her keep. I owe her nothing!"

"You owe her, monsieur, for special favors done beyond those commonly due from a servant girl. Or would you prefer my blade?"

The tavernkeeper blinked, his face was purple with rage and the veins stood out on his temples but he was no swordsman and no match for the young gentleman.

"All right," he hissed, and went inside to his moneybox where he took out a small purse.

"One opportunity," Jacques-Jean stated with emphasis as he watched attentively.

Bouchet took another purse, twice in size and threw it at the young aristocrat who caught it and threw it back with such force it stung the tavernkeeper's meaty hand.

"No, no, no, it is to the lady you owe this, not me," the nobleman explained with calm, exaggerated politeness.

Marie had returned from her old room and was standing to the side. Before Bouchet could throw the purse at her, Jacques-Jean clucked his tongue and said with an admonishing wave of his finger, "Mind your manners now and hand it to her nicely, *s'il vous plait*."

Bouchet snarled again and thrust the grime stained purse into Marie's hand.

"Good. Now, please be advised," Jacques-Jean spoke with cold politeness, "I never want to hear that you have come near this girl again. *Adieu*, monsieur."

Bouchet was so livid his eyes blurred as he watched the pair leave his door and ride away. Jacques-Jean had made his first real enemy.

Chapter 6

Along with the brisk autumn air came news of a coming visitor. Pierre-Jean Glaze, *Comte du Marshe*, fop extraordinaire, favorite of the Court, and son of the old *Duc du Pouvoir* by an early mistress, sent word of his expected arrival at his father's old estates. In the estate office, Jean-Philippe received the news with reservation.

"What on earth could be bringing him here?" Jean-Philippe mused to his son. "From what I have heard, it would take something extraordinary to pull him away from court. He enjoys the favors of the king's brother as well as other favorites and relishes dazzling in his own spotlight. He never has been enthusiastic to mingle with such as us whom he considers simple country boors."

"I had almost forgotten about Pierre," Jacques-Jean replied lightly. "It has been so many years since I have heard his name." He set aside a ledger he had been studying and stretched. "I remember being told he was simply an older, illegitimate half-brother."

"An illegitimate uncle as it turns out," Jean-Philippe replied with a small smile. "I understand he has done quite well for himself, considering. I am afraid my father was much less inclined to bestow paternal affection upon his children in those days. Pierre-Jean was born a few years after I, in the midst of father's other off-spring, legitimate and else-wise. His mother was only one of many at the time, and realizing she held no special power over Pa-pa, she decided to go to Paris. I do not believe they ever saw each other again. I suppose it was through her industry that Pierre-Jean was introduced to court society. He must have fit in very well since he has spent years at Versailles on Louis' generosity. He had a *vicountcy* bestowed upon him some years ago, now he is a full *comte*. He is also known to be a voracious gambler, and a very lucky one at that."

"Does he have a family?"

"It is hard to say, I have only heard rumors…" Jean-Philippe paused.

"Rumors?" Jacques-Jean responded with an amused smile and arched brow.

"He could have a family tucked away that we have not heard of, although it is probably not likely. It has been said that his popularity at court comes from his many male… benefactors."

"You mean lovers?" Jacques-Jean looked at his father, who shrugged. Jacques-Jean roared with laughter. "Then, it is even more curious that he should come to the country; best he remain at court where such things are better tolerated."

Jean-Philippe sighed and nodded.

"It strikes me Pa-pa that we have an extraordinary number of *Jeans* in our immediate family," Jacques-Jean mused.

"Did your mother never tell you?"

"Tell me what?" the younger man asked, a trifle leery of any more hidden family secrets.

"My father was not an evil man," Jean-Philippe replied evenly. "Certainly compared to many he was quite decent although no saint by any means. But he was a very vain man. Still, vanity is a sin shared by many, is it not?" he asked just as Jacques-Jean looked into the gilt mirror on the wall to assess his own reflection. "Even you have a little I think."

Jacques-Jean flushed and smiled. "Guilty."

"A little is perhaps a good thing, it accounts for a feeling of self-worth, eh?" his father returned the smile and nodded. "But as I was saying - my father was vain, vain enough to insist on all his children being named after him. His legitimate ones were *Jean* or *Jeanne* first. His illegitimate ones had *Jean* or *Jeanne* second. Sometimes I think it was how he kept us straight in his mind."

The arrival of the count into the rural province was a spectacle of such grand scale it was worthy of comparison to one of the theatrical productions made famous by Louis XIV's Court at Versailles. Unlike anything the locals could recall in their lifetime, mouths gaped, children ran shouting for their parents, dogs set to barking and, in general, all regular activity halted for a considerable time. The time it took to gawk as his train passed by, the time it took to discuss what had been seen, and finally, the time it took to describe to any and every soul who had the misfortune of not being a first hand witness. The count was not a man to pass by unnoticed.

His traveling party consisted of an ostentatious parade which set the dried leaves at the side of the road spinning and rustling in the little gusts of wind it created. First came the mounted pipers followed by no less than six pair of mounted fore-guard. A gilded carriage, resplendent with an elaborate design imitating but not actually being an official ducal crest, was drawn by six beautifully matched horses. Two footmen clung to the carriage. A second, plainer carriage followed in which rode the count's personal servants and luggage while four more pair of mounted livery pranced smartly in the rear.

Down the long drive leading to the chateau, the parade came strutting along at a practiced pace, halting in front of the huge wrought iron entrance. Allowing adequate time for an audience to assemble, the carriage sat gleaming in the sunlight, lavender window shades drawn tightly shut. Finally, with a perfect sense of theatrical timing, the door opened and the count himself stepped out.

As he emerged from the plushly appointed interior, the first thing seen was the huge, bobbing, pink and magenta plumes atop his widely brimmed hat of vibrant fuchsia. He wore an enormous black periwig which made him appear a full half foot taller and dwarfed his heavily powdered, clean shaven face. His cheeks and lips were brightly rouged, his eyelids tinted blue, and a small, heart-shaped, black beauty patch adorned his left cheekbone.

Ruffle upon ruffle of lace cascaded down his chest over a bright orchid brocade waistcoat which buttoned to the knees but flared from the waist to allow adequate room to walk. His rich velvet jacket and tight breeches were of the same vibrant fuchsia as his hat. The huge jacket cuffs, matching the orchid brocade, hung only to mid forearm while billowing white shirt sleeves, cuffed in multiple rows of fine lace, stuck out a fashionable half forearm's length from beneath.

The jacket body was also cut trim to the waist and flared over the waistcoat to stop one inch below it, just passed his knees. Triple rows of gold buttons alternating with tiny bows ran lengthwise down either side of the front opening while bows and ribbon loops also trimmed the large pockets. More ribbon loops accented his knees at the close fitting cuffs of his breeches above pale pink silk stockings and intricately wrought black leather shoes, each trimmed with a gigantic silver buckle and a bright red high heel.

He stood for a moment, towering above the crowd, one gloved hand resting, elbow askew, upon his waist, and the other holding the top of a thin, ebony black, silver-tipped walking stick with more bows trimming its stem. He struck a fashionable pose while surveying his reception party with an air of disdainful tolerance that curled his upper lip ever so slightly. As a gentleman of the Court it was almost a duty, his posture seemed to say, to give the country bumpkins a good view for he was, beyond a doubt, the epitome of *haute couture.*

Just then Jean-Philippe and his wife arrived at their own front entrance.

"Welcome, Pierre-Jean," Jean-Philippe said cordially. "Were you expecting to be accosted by a band of robbers that you felt the need to bring an army with you?"

"One can never be too careful," was the strained reply and the fop bowed grandly to his half-brother and his wife.

Dinner that evening was a very formal affair in *du Marshe's* honor. Jean-Philippe had given extensive instructions to his major domo, feeling a bit piqued into showing his outrageous houseguest that those who choose to live within the peace of the countryside are not savages devoid of all refinement. The cook had been forewarned to spare no effort, to double the kitchen staff, to dig deeply into the chateau recipe book for special delicacies and to mind the sauces personally. The duke had gone to his wine cellars to personally select the accompanying wines for each course himself.

The duchess, a sallow, nervous, bird-like little woman, was not accustomed to such entertaining and felt completely ill at ease although she tried her very best to be gracious for her husband's sake. She blushed and stammered and had the unfortunate habit of repeating herself incessantly when she did speak. Knowing this, but unable to stop herself, she instead chose to speak as little as possible and prayed unceasingly that she would not succumb to hiccups.

Jacques-Jean proudly brought Celimene to the chateau that evening. The young woman was glowing with excitement, relishing the opportunity to dress in her finest and to be seen by someone from the Court. Her effervescence drew even the count's eyes, so attractive was her high color and so honest was her unabashed enjoyment. Her eyes danced and sparkled, reflecting the hundreds of candles lighting the chateau.

Hélène had hesitated before accepting her invitation. Jean-Philippe wanted his heart's love there but neither of them had the poor taste, so common in court circles, to flaunt their renewed love affair under the nose of the duchess. Finally, persuaded that she was being invited solely as the mother of Jacques-Jean, and would be treated publicly only in this reference, Hélène agreed to accept and arrived looking delicate yet regal in her pale beauty. She could not deny a curiosity regarding the newly arrived houseguest and whatever stories he might tell of the king's court. And she had been assured that the duchess knew nothing of Hélène's relationship with Jean-Philippe.

The duke's aging sister, Jeanne-Charlotte, sent her regrets; her husband was bedridden, the note said, and doing too poorly for her to accept any social invitations. But younger sister, Jeanne-Éléonore, her husband the *Comte du Tullielle*, and their eldest daughter arrived fashionably late and decked out in their grandest attire which was still conservative in comparison to the *Comte du Marshe*. At Jacques-Jean's request, Richard Bonchance had been invited. And since his mistress lacked both proper clothing and social graces, he cheerfully came alone rounding out the little dinner party to ten.

The evening was going very well. If the *Comte du Marshe* lacked personable warmth, he certainly was amusing. He had dozens of stories to tell and people to describe and his wit was needle sharp. The duke's other guests enjoyed watching and listening and did not seem to mind at all that *du Marshe* monopolized the dinner conversation the entire evening. And since the count liked nothing better than to be in the spotlight with an appreciative audience, to that extent, he, too, was enjoying himself.

After almost three hours of food, wine, and stories, the duke announced that they would move to the salon and have brandy. The chateau's salon was an exquisite room with expansive windows opening out onto meticulously kept gardens. For the occasion, the garden had been adorned with paper lanterns glowing with candlelight in the now dark evening. In uncountable numbers, the lanterns lit up the gardens adding an illusion of fantasy just beyond the salon.

The guests buzzed with a mixture of sighs, cries, and exclamations. The ladies could suppress neither their delight nor their surprise. The duchess beamed rather shamefully in overt pride at the ingenuity of her husband. Was he not the most inventive of men, she whispered to Hélène who was speechless in momentary wonderment. A walk through the transformed gardens beckoned and even *du Marshe* had to admit that although such displays were rather common at Versailles he had never seen a garden quite so elegantly charming in its more modest proportions.

Refreshed and cooled by the sojourn outdoors, everyone made their way back into the salon. A harpsichord sat prominently to one side and there were three exquisitely furnished conversation circles established before two magnificently mantled fireplaces, one at each end of the long inner wall. The women gravitated into their own circle of conversation at one end of the salon while the servants served delicate cordials and confections. The men lit small pipes of tobacco which they savored with their cognac as they stood and sat near the second fireplace at the other end of the salon. Pierre, alone, declined the tobacco in favor of his pearl inlaid snuff box. Eventually, their conversation turned to politics.

"Is the Court aware of the stories coming out of the southern provinces?" Richard asked at last, unable to stay away from the subject any longer.

"Pray, what stories are those?" Pierre replied evasively in his thin voice cultivated to be a half octave higher than the others.

"Surely you know our minister of war, Louvoir, has declared that all soldiers are to be billeted by Huguenot families exclusively," Richard continued. "And now, not only are they spied upon while enduring all the expenses but they are being harassed without mercy."

"The Huguenots do not contribute to the Church of State so they are required to make their contribution elsewhere; I see nothing terrible in that," Pierre replied casually, appearing more interested in studying the firelight through his brandy glass.

"They were making such contributions before, with more equity," insisted Richard. "But now, the expenses amount to punishment for being a Protestant. That is not what the Edict of Nantes promises. But worse, we hear stories of gross deeds, an increase in rapes, beatings…"

"We have heard nothing of the kind," Pierre cut him off with a dismissive flip of his wrist, "and I would venture to say they are nothing more than vicious, ugly rumors started by incessant trouble mongers."

"You cannot deny there has been a very real and threatening push by the Church to cancel all Protestant rights," Richard persisted.

"Rights? What rights? My dear fellow," Pierre sniffed slightly, "Huguenots are outlaws of the Church. It is not my opinion that outlaws have rights."

"Is that the feeling of the entire Court?" Jean-Philippe asked quietly.

Pierre looked at the duke and smiled. "Oh, do not misunderstand, brothers dear, we all have a little Huguenot or two we feel near and dear to," Pierre condescendingly reached over and pinched Jacques-Jean's smooth tan cheek. It was an act the young man found scarcely tolerable and he pulled back from the count's grasp with a stern look.

"But France and her king," continued *du Marshe* without seeming to notice, "are a country and monarch loyal to the Holy Mother Church. We do not want or need to have outlaws running our country, schooling our children, holding office, or sitting in our government. And power comes from owning property, so it makes good sense that Huguenots should be limited in their personal holdings. For a country to be strong, it must be united in all ways. That is exactly how our most gracious sovereign feels. All of our people should return to the true Church for the sake of stability."

"Stability!" Jacques-Jean felt his temper rising. "Come now, Pierre, do you really believe hundreds of thousands of Frenchmen are simply going to roll over and give up their beliefs or else give up all standing and rights within their communities? How far do they intend to push things? And what comes next, another inquisition?"

Pierre looked sharply at Jacques-Jean, one eyebrow arched high. "If I were you, my dear boy, I would become a good and loyal little Catholic immediately," he said with glib hauteur and just a hint of something sinister in his voice.

"Indeed!" *Du Tullielle* shook his head and tried to ease the tension, "Come, come, gentlemen, it is not that bad. We have always had our ups and downs, but the French temperament is, nonetheless, basically tolerant."

"Tell that to those who died on St. Bartholomew's Day," retorted Jacques-Jean.

"An unfortunate page in history," responded *du Tullielle* in a fluster, "but I cannot believe we would ever stoop to the same dark levels as the Spaniards."

"*Henri Quatre* was not too proud to embrace the Church," Pierre sallied and *du Tullielle* laughed nervously.

"'Paris is well worth a Mass,'" *du Tullielle* echoed bobbing his head in agreement.

Jacques-Jean thought of his grandfather's warning and joined Richard in a scowl aimed at his aunt's husband. Jean-Philippe gave his brother-in-law a disquieting look.

"Well, I for one," yawned Pierre affectedly, while patting his mouth with a bejeweled hand, "find the whole subject an immense bore." With that he stood with the graceful elegance of a dancer and strolled over to the group of ladies.

"M'lady," he flourished an exaggerated bow, balancing gracefully upon his left leg with his right leg extended stiff-kneed out before him. He extended his hand to the duchess, "I have it from excellent sources that you are a splendid harpsichordist, and so I have come to beg you to honor us with a melody."

The duchess flushed and stammered slightly, his attentions had taken her so by surprise she was actually caught short of breath.

"Please, please, dearest lady," he continued to coax in sugary politeness, "we all await your favor. Is it not said that music soothes the savage heart? Pray do not deny us this simple request for it seems we have need of soothing."

The duchess's face turned as red as the ribbons and bows on *du Marshe's* jacket but it was obvious that she was also quite pleased. With a little bob of her head, she accepted his hand and he escorted her grandly and with a great flourish to the tiny bench in front of the instrument. With a small, beatific smile he pulled the bench out for her himself and she took her seat upon the heavily embroidered cushion, adjusting her skirts modestly. She wiggled a bit, put her foot to the pedals and her hands in position. Then she adjusted the bench again, just a trifle.

The dinner party drew attentively around with a hush of anticipation. The duchess paused for a moment seeming to go somewhere within herself and with complete concentration she brought her hands up, poised her fingers over the keys, and began to play. As soon as the first notes of *Le Roi Danse* by her favorite composer Jean-Batiste Lully rang out, she lost all timidity and was completely and quite amazingly transformed.

A compelling spell rose up from the keyboard and wound its way through the assemblage, ensnaring the audience and holding them in rapt attention. The mousey little woman grew bold in stature, playing as though only she and the instrument existed, her fingers flying gracefully over the keys, her total concentration turned inward. She completely forgot her spellbound audience and played enchantingly without reserve, her body swaying with the music, her breathing matching the tempo.

It was absolute magic and a very pleasant end to the evening. The undercurrents of tension, hostility, envy, and greed had gone, or were, at least, no longer visible. All were soothed and uplifted by the captivating melodies which filled the chateau.

The next day Pierre slept until noon as was his custom, then rang for his breakfast to be served to him in bed. After a painstaking toilette, he was dressed just as gloriously as the day before but in a completely different ensemble. Now he strutted in shades of peacock blue and yellow-green complete with a powder blue wig, making him look like an exotic bird as he met with Jean-Philippe in his study.

"What is it that you would like to talk about, Pierre?" the duke began cordially, stifling the impulse to laugh as he offered his blue haired guest a chair. "I somehow felt you must have some specific purpose for making so long a journey to visit us."

"Oh, my dearest Philippe, is it not enough that I should wish to see my family again?" cloyed the fop, knitting his carefully plucked brows and pulling his rouged lips into a little pout. Jean-Philippe sat soberly, saying nothing in response. After a long moment *du Marshe* relaxed his pout into a slow smile. "Well, of course, you are right; there is something I do wish to discuss with you. And it does have to do with family affairs, something we all have an interest in serving. It has been on my mind, *mon frère*, that you have no children, and at this stage in life, I would not be expecting your dear little wife to suddenly grow fruitful, *n'est-ce pas?*"

Jean-Philippe felt himself tense.

"Jean-Andre," continued *du Marshe* smoothly, glancing at his manicured nails before seeking the snuff box in his pocket, "had the decency not to leave any chips from his block, sister Marguerite died leaving only a daughter, and Charlotte has no children." He paused to take a pinch of snuff. "I would assume if anything should happen to you... not that I expect anything would, dear brother... but we never do know about these things, do we?" he gushed before giving forth a soft sneeze. With a snowy white lace handkerchief he patted his nose in satisfaction. "Where was I? Oh, yes, as I was saying... it would seem the family estates must pass to our nephew Henri-Richard, Éléonore's son. I would, therefore, like to offer my services as executor, as it were, if that unfortunate situation should arise before the child comes into his majority.

"As you know," he added a bit smugly, "I do have excellent connections with the Court and should do my very best, as one of *le Pouvoir*, to further the best interests of our family. *Du Tullielle* has never impressed me as the brightest of fellows," he added bitingly. "I certainly would not trust *my* estate to his management. He is not even blood."

Jean-Philippe was so taken back by the audacity of the posturing peacock sitting before him that he failed to interrupt Pierre immediately. He drew a breath and spoke. "I regret that you are laboring under a false assumption, Pierre," he said not smiling only by sheer willpower. "You have not been fully informed. I do have a son."

The words halted the dandy in mid-gesture. His watery blue eyes opened wide and his jaw went slack.

"You do?" he sucked in a breath, almost a gasp and then exhaled, gaining control and giving a broad lascivious grin. "Not legitimate, of course... a bastard? Well, well, well, belated congratulations, *mon frère*." The practiced courtier carefully held his facial expression, never wavering, never betraying his denigrating astonishment. *Who would have guessed you had the balls?* he thought. Aloud he continued moderately, "But, of course, that does not change my proposition at all. In fact, it makes my services even more necessary. The child will need help and guidance, in the event..."

"I regret again, Pierre," Jean-Philippe felt his lip twitch despite his efforts, "you still do not understand. Jacques-Jean is my son. If anything should happen to me, he is quite grown do you not agree? But I do thank you for your considerate offer."

"Jacques-Jean?!" The count was momentarily flustered and completely surprised. "But I thought our father...? You are saying it was you? He is yours? Hélène and you?" He recovered with another lewd grin. "Well, my dear Jean-Philippe, you do surprise," he oozed lazily. "And all the while Pa-pa thought the boy was his!" He gave a bellowing laugh in honest appreciation for the deception played on the old duke. "That is rich, just too perfect... it serves the old *roué* right."

"I have no desire to embarrass my wife, so it is not widely known," Jean-Philippe stated quietly and added pointedly, "except by those who need to know."

"Well, well, it would seem my concerns for the family holdings were unnecessary," *du Marshe's* tone had become a trifle stilted. "Quite a dashing young gallant, your Jacques-Jean. Has a good head for business beneath all those pretty curls, I have no doubt. Part of his Huguenot heritage, I am sure. Well," he took a deep breath, "and so, I regret to say, I do have pressing obligations calling me back to Paris. As much as I would like to enjoy your gracious hospitality further, I am afraid it is quite impossible," he said smoothly but managed to convey that his meaning was just the opposite. "Please extend my farewells to your dear wife, she is a marvel at the harpsichord," he rose from the chair. He took one step and turned suddenly. "Tell me, *mon frère*," his smile had gone nasty, "do you still plow that little heretic field after all this time?"

Jean-Philippe stiffened.

"Ah, well, a prick knows no religion. I fully understand," and he grabbed his crotch in a gesture he knew Jean-Philippe would find both rude and coarse, "my own has become quite the heathen these days. But what can one do? And now, I shall bid you *au revoir*." With a courtly bow oozing mockery and a great sense of self-importance, Pierre-Jean Glaze, *Comte du Marshe*, swept out of the room leaving one small blue-green feather from his hat floating slowly to the floor.

Later that day, Jacques-Jean went to his father's study to ask if the true purpose of Pierre's visit had been discovered.

"*Oui*," nodded Jean-Philippe with sober pensiveness, looking up from his work with a frown, "It would seem that pompous jackass has aspirations of getting his hands on our duchy."

Jacques-Jean looked at his father with raised eyebrows and the older man told him briefly about his last conversation with *du Marshe*. "Make no mistake, under that silly foppish facade is an intelligent and cold blooded schemer. There was a look in his eye when he left that made my blood run cold. But I must admit, this has made me realize I have neglected my duty," he added as he laid aside his quill.

"In what way, Pa-pa?"

"It is not too soon to begin giving consideration to securing the line," Jean-Philippe said in his slow but firm manner. "I have been remiss for not giving this thought sooner. We need to find a wife for you, *mon fils*, and get you settled with an heir."

The younger man said nothing at first but gave a quick amiable smile, refusing to take the thought of marriage too seriously; he was, after all, only twenty.

"You know how these things are," Jean-Philippe continued, looking his son in the eye without humor. "You are now an heir of the aristocracy, Jacques, and so a marriage will be arranged."

"As one was arranged for you, sir?" Jacques-Jean countered, suddenly feeling apprehension rising in his stomach.

"*Oui*, as one was arranged for me," Jean-Philippe nodded with a mild frown.

Jacques-Jean's expression went from disbelieving shock to belief and dismay and then suddenly, to anger. "But…"

"I know what you are thinking; you are thinking what of your mother and me..."

Jacques-Jean had indeed just been thinking that his mother had said she had made a choice but one of the possible choices had been marriage to a second son. That would not have been an arranged marriage. So, why must he accept an arranged marriage?

"As a second son," Jean-Philippe continued, seeming to read his son's thoughts, "I might have eloped and gone unscathed. I might have been forgiven the impetuousness of such a love match. After all, as a second son I had little else to live for. And do not forget your mother through her mother has claim to noble blood herself; it is distant but valid. There was for a small time the possibility that we might have..." his voice drifted with his thoughts, as he once again felt the deep frustration of the wasted lonely years when he and Hélène might have had a very happy home and several children if they had married. With self-discipline, Jean-Philippe refocused on the practical matters at hand and continued almost sternly.

"However, once Jean-Andre died and I became heir, the matter was out of my hands. Marriage within the aristocracy is a matter of business. And as with any business, the lawyers are always looking for the best advantage. Uniting houses and fortunes and producing heirs is the primary objective. It is necessary for the continuation of the lines and securing family fortunes for posterity. This is nothing you do not already know, Jacques. Love is the least important sentiment in a marriage contract."

In agitation, Jacques-Jean arose from the chair he had been sitting in and went to the tall window of the study to gaze blindly out over the lawns below. This was something that had never occurred to him. He had not been raised with the expectation of an arranged marriage and he now chafed at the very thought of someone else determining to whom he would be wed. Images arose of two fat, pale, and balding lawyers, wigs askew, sitting across from each other at a table spread thick with foolscap pages. Pages upon which they wrote as they argued an intricate marriage contract defining whom he should marry and plant his seed in like a stud horse. The whole idea fueled a growing fire of resentment in him.

"Of course," Jean-Philippe continued more gently, "every effort will be made to find a pleasant and attractive girl for whom you can feel real affection. In time, who knows... love may grow. It is not unheard of. Once you have a bond, and children are always a bond, you may find the rewards quite satisfactory." He could see the veins at his son's temples throbbing as Jacques-Jean turned back toward his father with a snort of displeasure.

"I cannot believe you of all people are saying this! Are you trying to tell me your marriage has been *satisfactory*?" Jacques-Jean added stiffly, "*m' lord.*"

The older man reacted as if he had been slapped in the face but he kept his voice level and firm. "We are not speaking of me now, but, yes, I have tried to do my duty and I expect my son to do the same." After a moment his expression changed to one of conciliation. "We are allowed to have our mistresses, Jacques. One might even say," he shrugged slightly, "it is expected. You need not live without love."

Jacques-Jean moved restlessly back to his chair but he could not sit, his mood and his look had become very dark and agitated.

"I did not realize you hold such a passion for your young mistress," Jean-Philippe said softly.

"Celimene?" The younger man looked at his father with mild surprise and shook his head. "No, Celimene is a beautiful creature and she amuses me... we amuse each other... but I have never considered her as a *wife*. No, you misunderstand; it is the principle of the matter. If I am to marry, it is a life long bond and I refuse to be bound for life in a tepid relationship!" The blood was rising in his cheeks. "I want my heart to be in my home, not in a mistress' cottage as yours is!"

"I understand," Jean-Philippe replied softly. "Believe me, I do understand. But let us try to look on the bright side, Jacques. If you have not yet fallen in love, your heart is free. Why might you not give it to one of the many young ladies who will be suitable? Why is it not possible for us to find a love match for you among the right families? You must remember, we have much to offer and are in a very good bargaining position. Your wife will be a *duchesse* and her son by you will be the future *duc!* In addition, our estates are without debt, we gained the Fuquay lands through my marriage and two very fashionable houses in Paris. And Jacques, I promise, we will not let the lawyers have the final say. I will keep you actively involved in the selection of your bride. It is entirely possible that we can satisfy both the lawyers and your heart," Jean-Philippe said with growing optimism.

"*Oui, oui,* our duchy and holdings will satisfy the lawyers which will satisfy the fathers. And you, *mon fils,* are young, healthy, handsome, charming. You will surely satisfy the daughters. I daresay we can quite literally take our pick, and I cannot imagine that the one you choose will not fall in love with you. You need only apply yourself to the task," Jean-Philippe said confidently.

"You forget one thing, Pa-pa," the young man spoke in a calmer voice, almost amused at his father's efforts to make the prospect sound so benign.

"What is that?"

"I am a Huguenot."

Jean-Philippe waved the idea aside with a gesture. "The fact that you will be a *duc* and therefore your son will be a *duc*, will far outweigh the fact that you are not a Catholic," the older man said with complete confidence. "Although you will undoubtedly be required to promise that all issue from the marriage be raised Catholic," he shrugged. "This is a small matter."

Jacques-Jean considered and chose to say nothing more. The longer he thought on the subject, the more he was beginning to feel that, to the contrary, this may prove, in fact, to be a very large matter.

Chapter 7

François Michel Le Tellier, *Marquis de Louvoir*, the king's Minister of War, sought his own brand of persecution with a vengeance. It was not enough that he had seen to it that only Huguenot families were forced to suffer the expense and inconvenience of housing and feeding the armies, but now these citizens' personal property was subject to confiscation, plunder, and destruction. As political opinion strengthened, *Louvoir* grew even more bold in his directives. Belligerence and cruel behavior was not only overlooked but actually encouraged within the ranks. The word was out. Anything, save murder itself, was acceptable.

Resentment was growing against the Huguenots who comprised a substantial portion of the bourgeoisie. Considered materialistic and crass by the disdainful nobles, they were, nonetheless, envied for their lucrative, capitalistic business successes and accumulating assets. Huguenot numbers were growing despite prejudice and animosity. And because of this same animosity they were becoming ever more clannish, feeding the fires of further suspicions, resentment, and anger.

The country's ongoing conflicts with Protestant England and the Netherlands gave rise to further distrust and concerns involving the national loyalties of France's Protestants. In addition to the jealousies of the nobles, France's citizenry as a whole grew increasingly suspicious and hostile. The Church, on the other hand, had its own motives for stamping out those it labeled *heretics* and continuing its crusade to convert all to Catholicism. The Church wanted the tithes and offerings, the purchase of indulgences and masses, and the control.

Between three seething camps of prejudice, Huguenots were being squeezed with growing harshness. More and more were leaving the country despite efforts to deny such efforts. And many more, who were less zealous in principle and more amenable to adaptation, made a pretense of converting.

The family of the ship merchant, Ives Dufee, fell into the latter category. Being a practical and pragmatic man, shrewd in business and pliable in the winds of political storms, he had built a sizable fortune in cargo hauling and trading. Was it so difficult, he rationalized to himself, to go down on one's knees before the crucifix and accept communion just because the priest said the wafer was the body of Christ? Any sane and rational man knew it was a wafer, and allowing the priest his fantasy was almost an act of charity, brotherly love and understanding, compassion for the blind, Christ-like forgiveness for those who knew not what they did. Yes, Ives told his wife and sons, God alone knew what was truly in each man's heart, and God would understand.

Stories flew back and forth across the provinces relating horrifying tales as

Huguenot families were being harassed unmercifully by the soldiers they were forced to billet. These soldiers were now referred to as the *Dragonnade* and persecutions were capricious. Some victims were only made to dance until they dropped from sheer exhaustion while others were forced to hang their feet over fires until the bottoms were burnt to blisters. Still others were maliciously tortured with candle flame. Men had the hairs of their beards viciously pulled out leaving ripped skin and bloody sores, while others were forced to hold hot coals in their hands. It was not uncommon for Huguenot women to be seized and stripped naked in public just to be ridiculed, insulted, and humiliated by those who passed by while the rape of young women had become an all-to-common offense.

One gloomy overcast day the viciousness of the times in which they all lived came quite tangibly into Hélène's life in the person of a cousin from her mother's side of the family. Hélène heard the creaking wheels of a large wagon as it rolled to a stop before her cottage door. Curious and not used to many visitors, she went to the window to see who it could be. Alighting slowly from the rough bench seat of a sturdy if worn and paint bare wagon was Pernelle Donné, her older cousin. The two had played together as children before Pernelle had married a simple craftsman and moved to the neighboring province. But it was more than distance which had come to separate them. Pernelle had not approved of Hélène's decision to become the old duke's mistress and their relationship became strained as life took them in two very different directions. Now, after so many years with only the most meager of communications between them, Pernelle stood at Hélène's front door dressed in somber dark clothing and a rain cape.

"Pernelle? Is that you?" Hélène asked with mild hesitation. The woman only vaguely resembled the cousin of her youth and for a brief moment Hélène was not certain. The face was still thin and angular but it had taken on a pinched look, the mouth at one time quick to smile had gone sour, the lively eyes had turned somber, and she now looked much older than her years. But a jerky nod assured Hélène she was not mistaken. After momentary shock, Hélène smiled at the nervous figure. "What a pleasant surprise," she said graciously, sounding less than sincere to her own ears. She could not help but wonder what could possibly have brought this estranged cousin to her door so unexpectedly.

"Hélène," the older woman acknowledged and then looked squarely into the beautiful face of her younger cousin. The dark circles around Pernelle's eyes were obvious. "Forgive me. I present a terrible sight, I know, and I have no right to be here, unannounced and uninvited..."

"Do not be silly, Pernelle. You are family. Please, come in, come in."

The woman advanced no further. "In truth, I did not know where else to go. Who else to turn to…"

"But what has happened, Pernelle? Come in, please," Hélène insisted and took the woman's arm, guiding her through the front door and into the small salon. "Sit. Please. Compose yourself. We will have some tea," Hélène added amiably as she turned to go to the little bell cord which would summon Lisa from the back.

"No," the older woman reached out a hand to catch hold of Hélène's sleeve and keep her from moving. "There is no time. I must get back to..." suddenly Pernelle burst out in tears. "It is my daughter, my little Genevieve," she sobbed.

"What has happened?" Hélène asked as she eased her cousin down onto the settee and took a seat beside her. Instinctively, Hélène took hold of the older woman's hand. It was cold and calloused.

"*Louvoir's* men... the Dragonnade, they came. Genevieve had just been delivered and was still recuperating, her infant only three days old. They forced their way into the house."

"Forced? The soldiers? But how...?"

"They do whatever they want, there is no stopping them."

"Why?"

"No reason, no reason at all, it was just something for them to do." Pernelle put her hand to her brow as if physically checking her growing hysteria. She looked at Hélène with tightly held composure and continued as dispassionately as she was able. "They dragged my daughter from her bed. I think the only reason they did not rape her was because she was still passing blood and wore a clout. So, they tied her to her own bedpost and stripped her of her clothing and modesty like a common *putain*. But that was not enough..." her voice cracked. "Next they took Étienne, my tiny grandson... barely three days old. And they... they tossed him through the air... like a rag doll, a puppet!"

Hélène gasped in shock, horrified at the image.

"They devised a game, you see. To drop the infant from high in the air, letting him fall toward the floor and catching him just before he might dash his little brains out." Pernelle's voice had grown hard with the hatred she felt. "Over and over they did this, pushing my daughter to the very edge of madness as she watched her precious new born being dropped repeatedly to within inches of his death, his head wobbling as though to fall off his shoulders. The poor little mite. He was screaming in terror. But the louder he screamed, the more the soldiers laughed. The more Genevieve cried and begged their mercy, the more amused they were. Her milk let down. With her baby crying, her milk flowed like a river to the floor, and they laughed and jeered and mocked the poor girl. They held tiny Étienne, screaming and clutching out for his ma-ma, they held him to her pap as if to let him suckle. Genevieve strained to reach her infant. They pulled him away and threw him around again. She begged them to stop. With every toss she was certain he would slip through their hands, that his little body would be left like a fresh egg smashed upon the floor. She begged as she stood helplessly bound to the bedpost unable to do anything to help her child. Unable to comfort him, rescue him. Unable to fight for him or protect him. As a mother, can you imagine her terror? Can you? She begged them and all they would do is spit in her mouth every time she opened it."

"*Mon Dieu!* Pernelle! *Mon Dieu!* How is the baby? Where is Genevieve now?"

"They live," she replied with an unfocused look in her eyes. "By the grace of our Lord. The soldiers tired of their savage sport and left. They grew bored with the horror they had inflicted. They grew bored with the shame and humiliation they heaped upon my daughter. Can you imagine? They grew BORED! The terror and torture these *brave* men could inflict on a helpless little infant no longer served to amuse them! After they had driven a defenseless young mother beyond the limits of sanity, what more could they do? They grew tired of it all and simply moved on, by then they had drunk all the wine in the house and sought spirits of which my daughter had none."

Hélène felt tears of compassion and anger welling up in her own eyes as she listened. Dear Lord in Heaven, what was this madness? Grown men torturing a small baby? Molesting a new mother? Where had honor gone? It seemed unimaginable and yet it brought to mind vividly the story her father used to tell of her grandparents and their horrible end. Only today, some four or five generations later, they seemed reluctant to actually murder. But the soldiers of France who were supposed to fight for and defend the country were terrorizing it or more correctly, they were terrorizing the Huguenot portion of it. It was a nightmare mocking the image to which the leaders of the country aspired to set before the world. Innocent civilians, trapped in their own homes, unable to defend themselves. Who was to stop this terrible thing?

"When the soldiers finally left," Pernelle continued, her voice grown hoarse, "the neighbors ran to the sounds of the screams and found Genevieve. They rescued her and Étienne and sent for me. I have been staying with them ever since. Physically, she is unharmed but..." the older woman twisted her own skirts, "her mind... her mind has become very... fragile. She lives with a morbid fear. Every sound gives her panic, her eyes go wild, her breathing comes in gasps. She grabs the baby and runs to the wardrobe to hide. She has no peace even in sleep. Her sleep is riddled with nightmares.

"Léon came home late that day from market. The poor man blames himself for not being there to protect his family. There is blood in his eye, and he is ready to kill. But what good would it do my Genevieve if her husband dies trying to defend his family's honor? What good would it do? What good would it do?" Pernelle asked repeatedly, desperately as she sank into an exhausted silence.

"Oh, Pernelle, I am so sorry," Hélène said and tried to put her arms around her cousin to comfort her. But the older woman pulled away. To Hélène it felt like an accusation. "What can I do?" Hélène asked quickly, earnestly. "What can I do to help? Please tell me."

"My daughter has Catholic neighbors, Cousin, good people who do not approve of *Louvoir's* policies or his Dragonnade. They have composed a formal complaint, a formal protest to which they all are signing their names but it would mean a great deal if someone of high rank would sponsor it and carry it to the Court. I know it was the old *duc* to whom you were… close," her voice trailed off in momentary embarrassment. "But do you think you could persuade the young *duc* to champion our protest? He is your son's half-brother, after all, and Genevieve is your son's second cousin."

Hélène looked at Pernelle and nodded her head. There was no need to say anything more, and there was no need to explain her real relationship with the current duke. Hélène vowed that she would take the matter to Jean-Philippe. He, too, she assured her cousin, did not approve of *Louvoir's* policies.

When Hélène saw Jean-Philippe late that afternoon she told him of her cousin's unexpected visit and shared her tale of civil terrorism. When she had finished she had no need to ask any favor of him, he offered to carry the petition to Versailles if her cousin would entrust him with the task.

"This is a shameful disgrace to every honest gentleman of France," he said with calm strength of character. He rose from her bed to pace slowly back and forth in front of the fire. "As one of the nobility, it is my duty to speak to my sovereign. I will take the petition and advise him of all that I know. I will let him see the proof for himself of what his subjects are enduring. I cannot believe Louis knows the extent to which the Marquis has allowed his men to go." He returned to settle himself against the bed pillows and take Hélène comfortably into his arms. "Louis may be spoiled and self-indulgent, but he loves France as much as his own life and has a keen sense of her honor. It is his honor as well, after all, the two cannot be separated. He is an intelligent man. He will see the wrong in this, but more importantly, he will see the lack of wisdom in all of this persecution."

"Oh, *mon chéri,*" Hélène sighed sadly, snuggling into the loose folds of Jean-Philippe's soft shirt and feeling the warmth of his chest beneath, "I hope you are right. I so hope you are right."

Hélène sent word to Pernelle and in due course the petition arrived bound in red satin ribbons. It bore over one hundred signatures of freemen, Huguenots and Catholics alike, all men who deplored "the hostile and denigrating actions of an unconstrained body of men-at-arms against an unarmed civilian population." It cited the case of one young mother, an honest law abiding subject, Madame Genevieve Venue and her three day old infant, and their day of unexpected, unprovoked, and inhumanly insensitive harassment at the hands of members of the French military.

As much as he disliked dancing attendance at Versailles, Jean-Philippe willingly set about the task of bringing the petition to the Court. He accepted the mission even though he knew he was also bringing attention to his own lengthy absences. Foregoing the comforts of a carriage in favor of speed, he rode on horseback taking only his valet and the master of horse with him.

The journey through the countryside was made in good time, with only one night at an inn. The second night, fresh horses were hired and the trio continued to ride, until just hours before dawn they arrived at the gates of Paris. Immediately, the nobleman went to his townhouse and roused the servants who kept his property for him. Sleepy and surprised, they rushed about to make a good showing of themselves: drawing off the dust covers; fetching hot water; bringing up refreshment from the wine cellar. The kitchen became a beehive of activity with the cook scolding and supervising the start of fresh bread for breakfast while the duke caught a few hours of much needed sleep.

Jean-Philippe rose in the late morning, ate sparingly to the cook's dismay and proceeded to dress carefully in fresh garments for his visit to Versailles. From a tall cupboard he bid his valet bring out a neatly kept periwig.

"When in Rome…" he sighed and sat down dutifully allowing his own hair to be wrapped up tidily after which the heavy wig was fitted carefully upon his head. The hair of the wig was a natural brown and fell down passed his shoulders in neat rows of tightly made sausage curls. Jean-Philippe looked at himself in the mirror and grimaced.

"It suits you, m'lord," his valet remarked with dignified approval as he made a few adjustments to the curls cascading down his master's back.

"Hmmm, well, I can endure what I must. In an hour it will be hot and itchy, I have no doubt. But I can hardly go into court company without it, can I, Jules? His Majesty is very fashion conscious and it would not do to offend him."

The servant nodded his head agreeably.

Sometime later Jean-Philippe sat astride his horse looking a foot taller with a dark blue, three cornered hat modestly trimmed with soft light blue plumage atop his cascading periwig. The light feathers floated in the air as the horse crisply trotted along. The nobleman sat erect and straight in his saddle. His dark blue coat and breeches of silk velvet were impeccably tailored, if somewhat conservative. There was a notable absence of the ribbon loop trim the dandies sported, but one heard that the king himself had grown more conservative since his rumored marriage to the *Marquise de Maintenon* and the growth of his off-spring.

The sun was high in the sky as Jean-Philippe and his two servants approached Versailles, the residential palace outside Paris. It was common knowledge that *Louis Quatorze* was never available before midday. He kept long hours staying up late into the night and was, therefore, a late morning riser. Only those under special invitation were allowed in his presence as he broke his fast and embarked on his lengthy toilette during which he was washed and shaved and dressed for the day. Louis lived in the most opulent of apartments, surrounded with immeasurable wealth and doting, fawning minions, but he was impoverished of that simplest of resources generally allotted the meanest of peasants for the taking: *privacy*. Jean-Philippe knew better than to even try to infiltrate this more intimate time which was still anything but private, and sought instead to be put on a list to be announced at His Majesty's open court in the afternoon.

The grounds of the palace were even more spectacular than Jean-Philippe remembered them. They seemed to have grown, as had the palace itself which stood gleaming in the brilliant sunlight. Meticulously kept lawns and bushes clipped in perfect symmetry graced the entry road and pathways. Fountains of spectacular design and marble statuary of the finest artistry filled visages in every direction. Gaily dressed beauties in softly billowing muslins accompanied by gentlemen in silks and satins could be seen on a far lawn occupied in a game of lawn ball. Intermittent sounds of their laughter rippled softly through the air. Farther on, a game of Blind Man's Bluff was in progress while little blackamoor pages stood close at hand in attendance with refreshments. In a separate quiet garden a small group of children played while surrounded by somberly dressed females who were undoubtedly their nannies and nurses. On the other side of the palace an area of construction was in evidence, expansions were obviously being made although, Jean-Philippe noted, small trees and hedge bushes had been placed strategically to create a screen to shield the eye from the meanest and ugliest aspects of the construction site.

Most of the aristocrats who had once lived in Paris and danced attendance at the Court in the Louvre now lived at Versailles at the king's pleasure. Louis distrusted his nobility and chose to hold them close where he could keep a paternal eye on them. And if they valued their standing at court, their positions, and the king's favor, they really could not leave without Louis' consent. For the nobility, Versailles was a golden cage.

Most wanted to be there for this was where everything happened, the seat of government, where Louis decided the law. This was where society showed off for one another, where deals were struck, where fortunes were increased, where advantageous marriage matches were made. And the king did throw lavish entertainments and wonderful feasts for his "captives." But Jean-Philippe had never enjoyed living in Paris, never enjoyed the Court. He had been brought up in the country and never wished to live anywhere else. He was an exception who personally ran his large estate and his sovereign had begrudgingly accepted this. Jean-Philippe had always lived quietly and did not have a reputation for intriguing.

It was a beautiful palace, a point of pride for any Frenchman if only... *If only*, Jean-Philippe thought grimly, it were not true that a short ride away honest French citizens were being robbed blind and treated without any respect or dignity simply because of the way they wanted to worship the Almighty.

"Politics!" he snorted under his breath as he reined in his horse and continued at a gentle walk. Politics and money, not religious zeal, was at the root of it all. Was it not always so?

When the duke announced himself to the outer gatekeepers and told them he was there to see His Majesty, they let him and his attendants through with a cursory glance. Three solitary riders hardly represented any major threat. But when Jean-Philippe approached the inner guard of the palace grounds, he was halted and his conservative attire and meager attendants scrutinized. While one soldier held the horse's bridle, a lackey was dispatched in haste. Suddenly, a middle-aged man of perhaps forty-five appeared, wearing a well-fitted suit of brown satin brocade encrusted with gold embroidery and yards of rich lace. Upon his head he wore a stiff black periwig and his face was clean shaven but unpowdered.

"Do I have the honor of addressing *le Duc du Pouvoir*?" he rasped in a voice that sounded scarred by some old strain or injury but which did not conceal a faint sarcasm.

Jean-Philippe drew himself up to full height and gave a short nod.

"If you would be so kind *Monsieur le Duc* as to dismount and follow me," the rasping man invited while raising an eyebrow.

"And who might you be?" Jean-Philippe queried while remaining seated upon his mount.

"Ahh, I am only your humble servant, monsieur, but m'lord requests an audience with you."

"And who might your lord be?"

"Monsieur Boyette, Chief Secretary to His Majesty's Chief of Security."

Jean-Philippe did not understand why the Chief of Security for the King would need a word with him but he shrugged and decided to dismount without any further delay. His horse was held by a sallow cheeked youth in uniform. With a nod to his own servants that said *wait here*, Jean-Philippe followed the man in brown satin into a small ante room at the side of the palace.

It was a cool room receiving no heat from the sun until late in the day. The lower half of the wall was marble as was the floor. A singular painting of the king hung upon thick golden cords from hooks at the molding near the high ceiling. The two tall, thin windows gracing either side of the door gave sufficient light and no candles or lamps were necessary until sunset. Jean-Philippe ignored the singular chair, a surprisingly small piece devoid of any cushioning upholstery.

He stood waiting with his escort and after a moment, a head wearing a very pink periwig matching pink rouged cheeks, bobbed out from behind the door, glittering brown eyes fringed with long black lashes stared for a few silent seconds at Jean-Philippe and the head disappeared again. Jean-Philippe looked at his escort who offered no explanation. At last the door opened again, this time by a little black boy in the courtly uniform of a page, and a female voice called from within.

"*Entrée, s'il vous plait.*"

Jean-Philippe walked with dignity into the chamber and was met by a man of such dissipated appearance it was difficult to judge his age. Swathed in satins, laces and brocades of the highest fashion and finest quality, bedecked with a huge periwig of glossy black, with hands and clothing encrusted in jewels, he was himself, however, of a sickly, unhealthy, and putrid appearance. As he sat behind a gilded desk, his rouged and tightly pursed lips hid unnaturally red gums and yellowed teeth. His eyes, evidencing some liver ailment, appeared yellow in their lusterless bloodshot orbs, and the skin beneath them bagged heavily. His nose, always of strong Gallic dimensions, had grown meaty and bulbous and was heavily powdered in an effort to hide a myriad of broken veins that bespoke of hefty indulgences. His cheeks dipped hollowly into heavy jowls while teeth and eyes looked all the more yellow for being contrasted against all the white powder.

Jean-Philippe took in his host, careful not to show by facial expression any disapproving judgment. He glanced about the room looking for the woman he had heard but saw no one. A moment passed and his host opened his mouth to speak. With startled surprise, Jean-Philippe realized the high, breathy, effeminate voice was the same as the one he had heard moments ago and had assumed to have belonged to a female.

"So you are *le Duc du Pouvoir* I am told, come to pay us a visit," lisped the creature. For wont of collecting his wits, Jean-Philippe failed to respond immediately and only hoped his shock was not written on his face. "And to what do we owe this visit from a man whom I have been told does not choose to grace our Majesty often with his company?"

"I am afraid you have me at a disadvantage, monsieur. I do not recall that we have formally met," Jean-Philippe sidestepped the question while standing in front of the desk. No chair had been offered.

"I am Antoine François René, *Marquis du Broche*, and Assistant to the Under Secretary to the Chief Secretary of the Minister of Security for his Majesty, *Louis Quatorze*, King of France and all her holdings," the voice pronounced with great self-importance and a hand was extended in a thoroughly feminine gesture as though expecting Jean-Philippe to kiss it.

The duke ignored the hand and gave a slight bow. "So now, what business is it that you, monsieur, believe you have with me? I was told a Monsieur Boyette wished to speak with me."

"It is my duty to assist in screening all visitors to Versailles. Our Majesty is very busy and his time is most valuable. No one sees him without an expressed invitation." The rouged lips were stretched so thin and tight they almost disappeared altogether.

"No one?" Jean-Philippe frowned implying that ranking nobility must surely be an exception.

"No one, *Monsieur le Duc*, not even long absented *ducs*."

"I have business with my king. How would you suggest I request an invitation?"

"Ah, that is where I may help. As I requested before, state your business with His Majesty."

"It is... of a rather delicate nature." Jean-Philippe suffered a glower. "Personal... for the king's ears only."

"There is nothing personal in the life of our king, not even his daily shit nor the frequency with which he beds his latest *aime*. You are wasting my time," came the clipped stinging reply.

"Are you telling me that I may not request to see my own sovereign without giving you an explanation? I think not." Jean-Philippe lost his temper at last. "I want to see your superior."

If looks could kill, Jean-Philippe knew he would have been dead before his body hit the marble floor. One long nailed, be-ringed hand snatched across the desk top at a bell. The sound of the bell immediately brought two men-at-arms and Jean-Philippe was escorted out of the office. Astonished, surprised, and frustratingly bewildered, he found himself very quickly outside the gates.

"I demand to see my sovereign," Jean-Philippe stated emphatically.

"You can demand all you wish," replied a heavy-jawed guard, "unless the Chief of Security passes you on, you will see no one."

"This is outrageous; I was not permitted to see the Chief of Security. I am *le Duc du Pouvoir*, not some peasant to be left in the dust of the road. I demand to see your Chief of Security right now."

"He left early this morning on a special matter. Try again tomorrow." And with that the gates clanked shut in Jean-Philippe's face.

Once the sting and mortification of the insult had subsided, Jean-Philippe had difficulty believing the reality of what had just happened. He was a duke, the highest rank in the land outside of the royal family, a nobleman, an aristocrat, and he had just been expelled like pig dung from the palace. Who were these petty demigods who dared to act with such effrontery and with such authority? Had things really changed this much?

As Jean-Philippe, followed by his servants, allowed his horse to walk slowly along the roadway, he thought of an old friend. The Granvilles had been friends with the Pouvoirs for generations, and Jean-Philippe had heard that *Comte Gautier Granville*, the aging head of the family, now lived in Paris, close to his physicians. Perhaps Granville could explain how matters were and offer some advice for, in truth, Jean-Philippe was at a loss. He nudged his horse and with a word to his servants encouraging them to keep pace, they rode to the Granville manor house just outside the city.

The old count was not well but he received Jean-Philippe into his private sitting room where he sat before a fire despite the mildness of the day. Bundled in a silk dressing gown covering a long silk nightshirt and layered over with a colorful blanket, the withered body of the count seemed very small indeed in the immense, high backed, old chair he chose to sit in. A fur lined silk cap was pulled down over his balding head like a medieval coif and one hand gripped at the blanket while the other, heavily weighted by a large jeweled ring, waved about in gesture.

"Forgive an old man for not rising but these legs no longer hold me. Ah, Jean-Philippe, you are a sight for these old eyes, *mon fils*." The old man waved Jean-Philippe into the room and as he did the reflections of light bouncing off the huge diamond on his finger danced about the walls and gleamed upon the rich wood paneling. "Let me look at you now... stand in the light, there," the old man ordered.

"Hmmm," was all he muttered for a moment, pausing in assessment. "You still remind me of your mother, although you have your father's nose and chin. I think it is the eyes, yes, definitely. You have her eyes. That is your good fortune." He grinned displaying several gaps where teeth had been. Those teeth remaining were stained brown by the years and by chocolate. "It looks as though life is treating you well, Jean-Philippe."

"*Monsieur le Comte*," Jean-Philippe bowed in respect for although he outranked the old man, age did warrant its own entitlement. "my cherished friend, I thank you for receiving me on such short notice. I regret that you have been challenged by health concerns. I hope my visit is not too taxing?"

"Nonsense, your visit will be the bright spot of my week... perhaps, the whole month. Have a seat, dear boy, sit down, sit down. Now, that is better. Bernard," he addressed a servant standing motionless to the side, "pour my guest a glass of cognac. Or would you like it in chocolate?" he asked the younger man, who shook his head politely. "And one for me as well, in my chocolate... then leave us."

The elderly retainer served them, his footsteps muffled by the thick Turkey carpeting underfoot. He poured a generous glass of cognac for the duke, then filled a small delicate porcelain cup a third full before replacing the stopper. From a matching porcelain pot he poured a deep brown liquid into the cup, filling it close to the rim. After placing the cup within the count's reach, the servant silently turned and left, pulling the door closed behind him.

"Oh, lad," the old man continued, "you do bring back memories. I so miss the happy times I spent as your pa-pa's guest. A beautiful estate as I recall, lovely countryside, fine vineyards, and such a treat to get away from...." pin points of light continued to dance about the room as he waved his scrawny hand toward the window in a gesture that left one to finish the sentence for one's self. To get away from what? The Court, the king, the intrigue, the gossip, the spies, the duties, or the stench and crowds of the city? Or perhaps all of these and more.

"I live a very quiet life these days even here at the threshold of intrigue." He picked up his cup and saucer and bending slightly over the cup drew in the pungent, hot liquid with an indelicate slurp. "Ah," he grinned again. "This is the thing I will miss the most when I die. I had many pleasures when I was a youth, now I have only one and if the physicians had their way they would take this one away from me as well," he grunted.

Jean-Philippe smiled faintly in reply and sipped his own cognac.

"But tell me, *mon fils*, what pries you away from that lovely country abode and brings you to this cesspool of humanity?" An indelicate fart punctuated this last and Jean-Philippe politely ignored it.

"I came seeking an audience with His Majesty," he explained setting his glass down. "You can imagine my surprise when I found myself being interrogated like some common peasant by an upstart subordinate who looks like he is dying of the English pox. And when I refused to humor this simpering fop, the ass actually had me removed from the palace grounds."

The old man grinned impishly. "Ah, now, you must know better than that. One does not simply *arrive* these days and get an appointment with the king. There are palms to be greased and arses to be kissed and cocks to be sucked if one is to get an audience with our king today," he snorted. "Or is it hands to be kissed and arses to be greased? That might make more sense, eh?" he wheezed in what passed for laughter and fell into a fit of coughing that left him gasping for air but undaunted. "You look in fine shape, Jean-Philippe," he continued at last, "if your derrière is firm and tight, you should be able to get anything you want at court." Another snorting wheeze of laughter ended in another coughing spell.

Jean-Philippe looked puzzled and shocked. "Surely our king does not…"

"No-no," interrupted the count, his mirth hardening into disgust, "our sovereign is very conservative and moral by comparison. He is quite the picture of domesticity these days, I hear, with his mistress turned wife and his children. And he never has been carnally interested in any save the females of the Court. Indeed, he does not approve. Do not ask me how it happened, damned if I know. But I would look to his brother, the grand *Monsieur*. However it came to be, there is a power structure orbiting our Sun that is filled with the damned sodomites. They pray upon the fresh young faces and soon ensnare them into their poisoned world of corruption, Italian sex, and unnatural lusts where blackmail is easy. Make no mistake, Louis does not approve the behavior even from his own brother. But they have become a formidable barrier, you may be sure."

Jean-Philippe's face was a blank but his stomach tightened. After a few silent moments, he spoke. "I carry a petition from His Majesty's subjects out in the province. There are dishonorable things going on out there that you would not believe we have lived to see. Our king must be advised of what is happening."

The old count looked up. "There are dishonorable things going on right here and no one can advise the king. What kind of things do you speak of, *mon fils*?"

"Perhaps it is better you do not know," Jean-Philippe answered evasively.

"I have no need for you to try to protect me. *Bon Dieu!* I am dying, Jean-Philippe! I will be lucky to make it through this winter. Do you think I could dare to speak out so rashly if it were not so? What is it, my boy?"

"Are you aware of the persecution of the Huguenots?"

"*Les Huguenots?*" the old man asked blankly, registering only curiosity.

"*Oui.* The injustices being heaped upon these citizens is nothing short of criminal and most inhuman. I cannot believe the king is aware of what is going on and someone needs to advise him. I have a petition signed by over a hundred loyal subjects begging the king to investigate the excesses of violence and civil terrorism being enacted upon his loyal subjects by members of his own troops." Jean-Philippe proceeded to relay the story of Genevieve Venue.

"Hmmmm," the old man said pensively after Jean-Philippe had finished. "You are right, of course, it is a terrible thing, the barbarism of the old days all over again. *C'est triste*," he shook his head slowly. "But again, if the matter was to be brought up formally, and *Louvoir* put on the spot... I can just hear what he would say.

"*Boys will be boys, your Majesty, and after all what did they do that was so terrible, eh? They teased a girl. Boys have been teasing girls since the beginning of time, n'est-ce pas? They removed her clothing? Yes, well, can we really blame any Frenchman with blood in his veins for that? Do not your courtiers attempt to do the same to attractive young women right here in the alcoves of your own salons? It did not hurt her to display her charms, eh? They did not rape her, did they? And her infant, was it hurt? No. Was a single hair on its little head injured? No. So, it cried a little, do not all babies cry? An excellent exercise for the lungs, is it not? And mothers get hysterical. But no one was hurt and so, what was the harm? After all your Majesty, do you not need your soldiers' good will for your next campaign? And while they are waiting upon your Majesty's pleasure, awaiting that next campaign, can you really fault them for getting a little bored and enjoying some sport? You need your men-at-arms, your Majesty, and you do not wish to turn them against you by punishing such a relatively harmless boyish prank.*"

Jean-Philippe looked stunned. For a few moments the room was completely silent save for the sound of the crackling fire.

"You must forgive me, *mon fils*," the count wheezed softly. "I only play the devil's advocate. And truthfully, if there are excesses, Louis prefers not to know about them. And as long as there is doubt, he can ignore them."

"But... there *have* been rapes, and beatings, not just beatings but out and out torture..."

"Prove it! Rumors, nothing more. What proofs have you? Have you personally seen this?"

"No."

"Do you have witnesses? Do you have sound unimpeachable *Catholic* witnesses to swear to these accusations? Do you have so much as two good stalwart men to swear to having personally seen these crimes being committed? Men who would not falter under *Louvoir's* scrutiny of their own homes, families, business dealings, finances, and loved ones?"

"The Huguenots can speak for themselves," Jean-Philippe retorted, "they need only be invited..."

"The Huguenots are disenfranchised, *mon fils*, they might as well not exist. Our sovereign's current wife has a passionate hatred for them. Such a pious Christian lady filled with the milk of human kindness, *n'est-ce pas*? No-no... they will not be suffered to speak on their own behalf for no one would accept a word they said. Traitors! Malefactors! Libertines! Disloyals! These are only some of the more polite names they are being called."

"But this petition is not just signed by Huguenots, Gautier; it has been signed by many Catholics as well. Good honest people," Jean-Philippe argued, "people who are willing to stand up and be numbered."

The old count shook his head sadly, the fur of his cap rubbing against his thin hunched shoulders. "People who had best pray *Louvoir* never reads this petition."

"It must be possible to get this to the king," Jean-Philippe insisted.

"No, dear boy, I am afraid it is not. *Louvoir* has his own men firmly entrenched everywhere. Nothing gets to Louis that does not go through *Louvoir's* hands first. Nothing. I am telling you the truth. Absolutely nothing."

"I will write to the king."

"The letter will never reach him. You will receive a summons, go through another interrogation. And until they learn what you want you will not gain way... and once they learn what you have, they will most assuredly never allow you in but they will confiscate it."

Jean-Philippe felt the frustration as he tensed. It rose within him like a thick bubble causing his muscles to ache, then he gave way to reason and the bubble seemed to burst with a sigh of acceptance. He now realized that to surrender the petition into Louvoir's hands would undoubtedly do more harm than good. It had all been for nothing. He shut his eyes and nodded his head briefly in understanding.

From his position of power, Louvoir turned an unconcerned and deaf ear to all complaints only making very certain none ever reached the ear of the king. While *Louis Quatorze* was playing croquet at garden parties, importing orange trees to Versailles and planning foreign strategies, his soldiers continued to grab whatever they took a fancy to from their unwilling Protestant hosts, including their daughters' virginity. While the Sun King was hosting lavish theatricals and dallying with court beauties, the armies of France, leaving havoc in their wake within their own country, tried to invent new, non-fatal indecencies to heap upon the luckless Huguenots.

Jean-Philippe was wise enough to now harbor grave concerns for his son.

Chapter 8

*L*e Roi Soleil, France's magnificent Sun King, being somewhat isolated from realities, was eventually convinced by his ministers and advisers and second wife that the actual number of unconverted Huguenots existing in France was not even worth counting and thus, the Edict of Nantes signed by his grandfather and guaranteeing tolerance and equal citizenry was no longer relevant. And so it came to be that in October of 1685 at the *Palais de Fontainebleau*, King Louis

XIV signed a document to be known as the Edict of Fontainebleau which rescinded the Edict of Nantes.

With that pen stroke came the power to close all Huguenot schools, for, it would seem, there were no Huguenot children to warrant them. And to remove all Huguenots from public office, for how could they represent a Catholic constituency? It was further commanded that all newly born children be baptized into "the true faith," which was only asking that every good and presumed Catholic parent do his duty. And all children by order of the State were to be taught in Catholic schools and learn their Catholic catechism.

The Protestant churches were pushed underground when their buildings were confiscated, buildings considered of no use to a non-existent congregation. By order of the king everyone of age was to attend mass and give confession to the local priests who were charged with keeping a wary eye on compliance. Small metal tokens were dispensed as proof of one's attendance, tokens which were to be carried at all times and produced upon demand of the authorities.

It was declared punishable by a sentence of life as a galley slave for any Huguenot male to seek to emigrate out of France. Even so, thousands fled in secret. England, Germany, Scandinavia, and the Netherlands enthusiastically welcomed the Huguenots with their resources and talents, both of which added much to their newly adopted countries. And the New World offered opportunity as well. Many *émigrés* also welcomed the opportunity to fight against Louis' armies and volunteered to join the ranks of their new countrymen on the battlefields.

The little congregation to which Hélène had belonged since childhood could no longer meet openly. Their church building had been taken by the Crown and auctioned. The new Catholic owner used it as a stable and the pew box established for the family by Jacques-Jean's grandfather's uncle was now a horse stall smelling of piss and manure.

Every Sunday the shrinking membership was forced to meet secretly in a different place - someone's home or barn or cellar. Every week after services, they shared news and took note of the latest absences.

Hélène realized that some of their members had dropped away due to pure fear and she could not condemn them. How would she feel, she asked herself, without the security of her own personal protector in the person of the duke? It was safer for many families to quietly study the Bible and worship in the privacy of their own homes with curtains drawn. Others of their members and lifelong friends had simply disappeared mysteriously. The optimists said they had escaped the country; the pessimists speculated which prison or galley might now hold them.

At first, there had been an eerie but oddly romantic feeling about their circumstances as though they were all walking in the footsteps of the early Christian martyrs, driven to meet in secret, flirting with a final confrontation with the lions of Rome. Like a child's game played out by those who are touched by madness or just insulated from any real brush with *Louvoir's* power.

But now, fear dominated the thoughts of most every Huguenot man and woman still remaining in France. They had become a target which could not defend itself. They were not allowed to fight back.

Jacques-Jean still carried the warmth of Celimene's embraces with him as he rode through the chill of the late autumn night. He disliked leaving her warm bed so long before daybreak but it had become his habit to ride by his mother's cottage and then go on to the chateau. He could see the cottage now in the moonlight. It stood peacefully quiet, two elms standing like sentinels on each side, with the neatly trimmed hedges defining the small garden. No doubt Hélène and Lisa were fast asleep within. All was well. It was foolishness perhaps, he thought to himself, no one would dare to harm his mother. No one would dare to come onto the duke's own estate to make mischief against someone under his protection but still, it eased Jacques-Jean's mind to see for himself.

As the aristocratic heir approached the chateau he could see light coming from the windows of the duke's private rooms, high on the second floor. The rider had no need to urge his horse onward. The animal knew where a warm stall and fresh hay awaited. Rider and horse trotted around to the side yard near the stables and close to the kitchen garden. Sliding quickly from the saddle, Jacques-Jean gave his horse over to the sleepy stable boy who was by now used to the young noble's wee-hour arrivals. A lantern burned at the door post although the brightness of the moon made it unnecessary.

Jacques-Jean let himself in through the servant's entrance at the kitchens. Taking the stone stairs two at a time up to the main floor, he traversed a short hall to find the main staircase and continued upward. At the next landing he turned down the corridor toward his father's apartments. It concerned him to discover his father up this late. The thick Turkey carpeting cushioned his steps in the dimly lit hallway while the guttering candles in the wall sconces caused disquieting shadows to dance upon the walls. He reached the door to his father's study just as Jean-Philippe himself opened it.

"Come in, Jacques, I have been waiting for your return," the older man said gravely as he moved back into the warm room toward his chair, his face looking drawn and anxious.

"What is it, Pa-pa?"

"Sit down, *mon fils.*"

Jacques-Jean obeyed, sitting immediately in a guest chair close to the large desk. In typical fashion, the duke continued slowly, choosing his words with care.

"I received a letter late this evening from a very good friend of mine in Paris. *Comte Granville* says the *Duc de la Force* was summoned to Versailles where our king is reported to have had a lengthy conversation with him regarding his religious *attitudes.*"

"Religious atti... he is a Huguenot, is he not?" Jacques-Jean responded, a frown wrinkling the high brow beneath his thick mane of curls.

"*Oui*, the only member of Louis' Court reported to be so. He is also an old man in poor health who suffers from dropsy, not much of a threat to our country or the crown, eh? However, my friend writes, *la Force* has been taken to the Bastille and is under lock and key. Louis is said to have sent his own priest to counsel with *le duc*, to instruct him on the errors of his thinking." Jean-Philippe paused waiting for the significance of his words to sink in. "Jacques, this is very serious. It means not even a noble is safe. And I regret to say that is not the worst of it. Your uncle, the *Comte du Marshe,* has been drawing attention to us I am afraid. To you, more specifically, and it is only a matter of time. Granville is not an alarmist. I believe him when he says a *lettre de caché* is being drawn up to authorize your arrest."

"*My* arrest?!" Jacques-Jean started, suddenly sitting very upright at the edge of his chair.

"*Oui.*"

"On what charge?!"

"Does it really matter?" Jean-Philippe looked intently at his son. "Besides, Jacques, a *lettre de caché* need make no charge. It is simply an order for imprisonment on the authority of the king." The young man looked at his father in shock, the blood draining from his face. "I have never asked you this before," spoke the duke, "but I feel it is my duty to ask you now. Are your beliefs so strong you would go to prison rather than change them?"

The question, having been said, stood before Jacques-Jean in a strangely tangible way. It was like a mirror he was being asked to look into which did not reflect his face but his soul. In the quiet hush of the pre-dawn hour, the young man rose from his chair and moved closer to the fire. His body was suddenly cold, so cold he was numb, but a calm was settling over him.

"Sir," he spoke at last, "I must confess I never believed it would come to this. And I can honestly say, until this moment, I have never considered the choice but... I believe what I believe. I cannot dis-believe what I believe to be true. I am doubtless a sinner and have much for which to repent, but I feel my relationship is directly with God through Christ our Savior and I could never accept the hypocrisy of myself if I pretended to convert to Rome's way of thinking. I know in my heart I cannot accept papal dominance nor papal doctrine and I can never believe the communion wafer actually becomes the body of Christ... but I have no desire to be a martyr either."

The older man studied his son's face. Jean-Philippe never claimed to understand what he considered the fanaticism of the Protestant movement but he respected it. He walked over to Jacques-Jean and reaching out, he clapped his hands upon his son's shoulders.

"An honest reply, Jacques. I do not want you to become a martyr either. I can see no choice but to flee. I do not really believe a sudden conversion would help you anyway. *Du Marshe's* motives have nothing to do with religion. If he could, I know he would discredit me as well." Jean-Philippe went to the side table, picked up a crystal decanter and poured some brandy out into a glass. He gave it to his son. "But, we must accept that, at present, it is impossible for you to remain here or be my heir. The powers that be will not allow it."

Jacques-Jean thought for a moment. "And so, I am now what I was before, m'lord," he shrugged, "nothing less, but more than that I have been blessed to have known my own true father and for that I am very grateful."

"Not *m'lord*. Heir or not, you are still my son, something for which I am both proud and very grateful. And that no one can ever change."

Unfallen tears glistened in both their eyes. Jean-Philippe knew he was about to lose his son, possibly forever.

Jacques-Jean went back to his chair but could not sit. He held the brandy glass in both hands and found himself looking at it with the eye of someone who is viewing things for the last time. Consciously soaking up each detail, he looked over at his father, a slightly built but quietly strong man, only in his late thirties. When would he see him again? The library table with its curiously detailed carvings on its thick legs had seemed so much larger when he had first come to the chateau. He studied the huge, high backed winged chair his father always sat in with its softly crinkled leather covering. The room decor. The dark, silk damask wall covering. The paintings. The folds of thick draperies at the windows. The rows and rows of leather-bound books, smelling always just slightly musty. His heart was telling him these memories were all he would have to take with him and he might very well never see any of these things again.

After a few moments, Jean-Philippe spoke thoughtfully. "We must devise a plan. I can give you money, that is no problem. You will need to be very generous in your bribes. Undoubtedly, there will be a tempting reward posted for you."

"What of my mother?" Jacques-Jean asked suddenly, startling realization passing into his eyes that he would not just be leaving his mother behind, but leaving her to the same evil dangers. "I cannot just leave her on her own."

"I will always watch over your mother, Jacques; you know that. But I believe she is in no real danger. Certainly Pierre has no reason to persecute her. She lives a quiet life... but perhaps the choice to go or to stay should more properly be left up to her," he added in quiet contemplation. "I think she would be the first to see that her presence would only slow you down. You, after all, are the one being sought. It is you they wish to throw into prison."

Suddenly the sound of splintering crystal reflected Jacques-Jean's shattering composure. In a burst of anger he had thrown his glass violently into the fireplace where it lay in a myriad of pieces.

"It is so wrong!" he rasped in frustration. "Who are we hurting? We wish no one harm! I remember the story my grandfather used to tell of the ghoulish murder of his parents, my great-grandparents. I was so callow. So naive. I thought it ancient history and best forgotten but he warned me, he said it was not over, that it was going to happen again. What is wrong with our king?!" Jacques-Jean nearly shouted and his father stood close to demand his obedience.

"Jacques, get hold of your anger! It will do you no good. It would kill your mother if anything happened to you. Better we hear that you are safe in a Protestant country than lost in the bowels of the Bastille or worse."

Jacques-Jean had never seen his father so adamant and commanding and it cooled his temper. "I am sorry, Pa-pa, of course, you are right."

Jean-Philippe brushed his apology aside with a gesture. "You would hardly be a man if it did not raise your bile but as a wise man you must control that ire, never let anger control you. Now," he shifted back to the topic of concern, "if you start in the cover of dusk and ride north to the border, you should get there sometime before the end of the next day. Say your good-byes today, but discreetly, very discreetly. The fewer who know you are leaving the better."

"Pa-pa, wait. Is that not exactly what they will expect? And does the Dragonnade not have guards posted all along the roads leading to our borders with the Protestant countries? It is a long ride to the border. I have no contacts to hide me along the way if I should run into a patrol."

"But what else...?

"What if instead I rode right into Paris, right into the belly of the beast? The *gen d'armes* would hardly expect me to do that, would they?"

"You cannot stay in my houses; they will almost certainly be watching for you there. What would you do in Paris?"

"Get passage on a ship going to the New World," Jacques-Jean replied with resolve.

As soon as dawn neared, Jacques-Jean dispatched a message to Richard Bonchance to meet him at Celimene's cottage as quickly as possible. He had changed to fresh clothing and had one of his father's horses saddled. First, he rode to his mother. It was not going to be easy to tell her. Perhaps Jean-Philippe was right. She was not in danger; she led an unobtrusive life on the duke's estate and the duke was her only regular visitor except for Jacques-Jean himself. It would only make her more conspicuous and subject to real danger to take flight with him. And he was leery of Lisa. She seemed a decent girl but what could one really know anymore. She was from a staunch Catholic farm family and he could not allow her to know the situation.

Jacques-Jean went quietly into his mother's cottage just as the sky began to turn a leaden gray. Noiselessly he climbed the stairs to her bedroom avoiding the squeaky third step from the top. He could hear Lisa faintly singing to herself in the back of the cottage. Doubtless she was beginning the daily breakfast preparations. He entered his mother's room and quietly closed the door behind him. Tiptoeing up to her bedside, he went down on one knee and gently shook her shoulder.

"Ma-ma?" he whispered.

"JJ?" Hélène recognized her son's voice before she was even fully awake. "Wh..what is it?" Hélène opened her eyes and immediately propped herself up on her elbow. In the faint dawn light she could just make out her son's form. "What brings you here so early? Something is wrong...?!"

"Ma-ma...shhh, I do not want Lisa to hear us."

Hélène was sitting up in bed now, completely awake, her long, thick mane of pale blonde hair draping about her shoulder in a loose braid as she pulled the neck of her heavy, long-sleeved cotton bedgown close against the morning chill.

"Pa-pa has had news from Paris. The *Comte du Marshe* is using his influence at the Court to have me arrested."

Even in the predawn light, a look of disbelief and shock could be detected on Hélène's smooth face.

"We are Huguenots, Ma-ma," he whispered simply, "that is not a wise thing to be in France today. Pa-pa knows I must flee and is going to help me but I am concerned about leaving you."

"JJ!" The anguished gasp from Hélène's throat said everything. She had only just found a state of contentment, her son had a future, her old love had returned to her. Now, everything was coming apart. "But where will you go?" she whispered.

"I must leave the country..." he could not bear to suggest that it might be forever, "at least until things calm down once again. As with everything, Ma-ma, it comes, it goes. Someday, I am sure things will again be sane in France for those who do not choose to follow Rome. But I am concerned about leaving you behind with things as they are."

"Oh, JJ," she could not help the tears as they began flowing down her cheeks, hot and fast. Her heart was beating wildly in her chest as her arms went out to him and she cradled his head in her embrace.

After a few moments, he knew she must stop or she would become too distraught to control herself.

"Please, Ma-ma, we do not have time for tears. You must calm yourself... please? You must do it for me. Pa-pa does not believe that you are in any real danger. He has pledged he will protect you always and..."

"I care not for myself," in a whisper she cut in sharply, disdainful of any concern for her own well being. "But you, why are they doing this to you?" she asked with a mother's inability to fathom the persecution of her young.

He shrugged. "Ma-ma, I will write when I am safe. You must promise me that if Pa-pa asks you to move into the safety of the chateau, you will do so. He will not ask it unless he feels you may be in real danger. I could never forgive myself if I left you behind and anything happened to you."

"*Oui, oui*, JJ, I will be well," she said dismissively. "It is you who must take care for yourself. I will be fine," she insisted but suddenly knowing she was not being truthful. She was trying to exude a brave appearance while realizing fullwell that to lose her only child could be a mortal wound to her being.

"Promise you will heed Pa-pa's advice?"

"I promise."

"Ma-ma, the fewer people who know that I am leaving, the better. I think it would be wisest for you to go on about your day exactly as usual, as if you know nothing. But I could not leave, Ma-ma, without seeing you. *Je t'aime, ma mère.*"

Hélène stifled a sob. "As I love you, *mon chéri*... oh, my dear, sweet God, please bless my son and keep him safe," she said as a prayerful blessing. Hélène consoled herself with the hopeful thought that it could not be for long. Affairs would be straightened out and her son would be allowed to come home to his birthright. Surely the world would not stay mad, could not stay mad forever.

Jacques-Jean kissed his mother lingeringly on both cheeks and then on both hands. "Remember, Ma-ma," he spoke in hushed tones as he stood up and backed lightly toward the door, "for me... you must be calm and act as if it is just an ordinary day." He put his finger to his lips, and silently opened the door and slipped soundlessly back down the stairs avoiding the squeaky third step.

Marie saw Richard Bonchance approaching the cottage on his steed. She had been alerted by Jacques-Jean's personal servant to expect them both.

"Monsieur, *entrée, s'il vous plais*," she said sweetly, dropping a little curtsy as she had recently been taught to do. During the past months with Celimene, Marie had learned much. She was gaining a sense of self-respect she had never had before, and a belief that life did have something to offer her after all. Now, dressed in clean, fresh clothes topped with a snowy white apron, she escorted Richard into the tiny salon.

"M'lord has not arrived yet, but we are expecting him," she smiled pleasantly, her voice gently modulated.

"*Merci*, Marie," Richard replied with a wink that brought a blush to her cheek. "You are looking very well this day, as pretty as one of the meadow flowers." Her cheeks reddened further. "Life here with Mademoiselle seems to agree with you."

"It is so much better than the tavern, monsieur," Marie acknowledged softly.

"Ah, I have no doubt of that. Bouchet is a harsh taskmaster, and stingy with every sou."

"*Oui*, monsieur," Marie agreed, quietly wondering how much the tall man knew of her last days at the tavern. It made her uncomfortable. She wanted to forget those days forever. Suddenly craving the shelter of the kitchen, she began backing from the room.

"Please give Mademoiselle Celimene my greetings," Richard spoke amiably, a friendly smile upon his angular face.

"She is not awake yet, monsieur, and m'lord's message said not to wake her until after he arrived."

Just then they both heard a horse gallop to a stop at the front of the cottage.

Marie went back to the door and opened it wide to admit the familiar figure of the handsome young lord. Marie's expression took on a look of adoration.

"Marie, have Bertrell look after the horse, please," Jacques-Jean said quickly, barely seeing her and removing his riding gloves as he strode into the cottage. "The animal has been ridden hard and should be walked for a time."

"*Oui*, monsieur," she responded promptly with a curtsy and left the cottage.

"Richard," Jacques-Jean addressed his friend without pause as he entered the small salon, quickly shutting the door behind both of them.

"Your message was so urgent," Richard responded with a nodded greeting. "What has happened?"

"I have been informed that a *lettre de caché* is coming with my name on it," Jacques-Jean said abruptly in a low voice.

"No...!" Richard protested in shock. He knew very well that people could and did disappear into the Bastille for no more reason than a perceived slight if their enemy was powerful enough. Some were eventually released if the king's mercy could be prevailed upon. Husbands of pretty wives had the best chance of release. If their wives presented themselves to the king to beg for his mercy and if they willingly let Louis under their skirts, then chances were good all would be forgiven. But others rotted away for the rest of their lives, rarely to be seen by friends or family again.

"I am afraid it is true."

Richard had a quick mind and instantly surmised that his friend's sudden good fortune as the Huguenot heir of a Catholic duke was not to be tolerated in the current political climate. "What are you going to do?" he asked.

"I must leave the country," Jacques-Jean said bluntly and went on to tell Bonchance the details. He concluded by explaining his hope to try to get to America and asked if Richard thought his cousin by marriage, Denis Dufee, could be persuaded to help.

"I am very sorry for you, *mon ami*," Richard said thoughtfully as he helped himself to a glass of cognac. He offered to pour one for Jacques-Jean, who declined with a shake of his head and poured out some wine instead, adding water to it. "Because you are your father's heir, I had very much hoped things would work out for you here. But I cannot say I am really surprised. To have a Protestant bastard inherit a duchy? Never would they allow it. Not when they have declared all Huguenot marriages null and void and all issue from those marriages, illegitimate. But even *la Force*? I did not think Louis would go that far - throwing his own nobleman into the Bastille over a religious difference? I would have thought by now we were more enlightened than that. These are sad days for France," Richard sighed darkly, "and I think there are far sadder days to come. It brings back everything your grandfather used to tell us... remember?" Jacques-Jean looked to his friend and nodded. "Personally, I see no reason to be around to watch the tragedy unfold. I have long been thinking of going to the New World myself. I want to go with you, Jacques. I am certain Denis will help us. We shall be partners in a bold new adventure... that is, if you want a partner?" Richard looked at his friend and extended both his hands outward at his sides as if presenting himself for consideration.

Without hesitation, Jacques-Jean held his own hand out to Richard in an invitation. The other grasped it and the two men embraced with easy brotherly affection.

"Are you certain?"

"Very certain," replied Richard.

"Leaving everyone and everything I love behind shall be the greatest hardship I have ever had to face, but this exile will be more bearable if I have one *bon ami* to share it with. I shall be honored to have you as a partner in such an adventure," the young nobleman responded with intense sincerity.

It was decided that the two should rendezvous back at Celimene's that evening at sunset and Richard left to take care of his last business and preparations. There was no need for Jacques-Jean to caution the use of discretion. Richard knew exactly what was at stake.

Now, thought the fair-haired nobleman to himself as his friend rode off, *now to tell the sweet Celimene.*

Celimene reacted exactly as Jacques-Jean had expected. First, she was shocked, then angry, then she wept the most beautiful tears and begged to follow him "to the ends of the earth." He firmly rejected the very idea. He knew his exquisite darling better than she knew herself at times. She was a beautiful, soft and sensual creature of civilization and comfort, and was not meant to endure the uncertainty and perils of a new world. And he was in no position to support a mistress. At last, they comforted each other by making love through the middle of the day with the energy of futile desperation.

Jacques-Jean was determined that, if nothing else, his lovely young mistress would not easily forget him. With impending danger acting as an aphrodisiac, they sought repeated satisfaction from each other's flesh in a strange, wild abandonment they had never experienced before. There was an edge to their repeated ecstasies, an edge created by the imminence of great peril. He all but drown himself in her pliant flesh and she was strung tightly, breathlessly defying the world to interrupt them during the unending waves of mindlessness. Finally, totally exhausted, weak, spent, soaking wet with sweat, they lay entwined upon the rumpled bed, sated but still breathing in each other's scent as if it was a kind of magical protection to suspend time and danger.

There was no doubt in Celimene's mind that she would never have another lover to equal Jacques-Jean but there was also no doubt in her mind that she would soon have to have another lover. Damn politics, she thought as sleep began to overcome her, why did it have to affect her love life? His sweet young body, his youthful endurance, his extraordinary ability to satisfy her so completely, the comfortable way he knew her and yet always knew how to surprise her, these were not going to be easy to find packaged altogether in another man. And to find them all in another ducal heir? *Pas possible*! Her next lover might be fat and easily winded or old, ugly, and too quick to grow soft... or perhaps all of these together. She only knew he must be very rich and have a title for she was going to move upward not backwards.

She did love Jacques-Jean in her own fashion. He was so handsome it almost made one weep and incredibly charming, generous, and good to her. He had never mistreated her. But now that the tears were over, she had to admit to herself if to no one else, that she was grateful he had wisely refused to consider her plea to go with him. Hardships did have a way of erasing romance and strangling *amore*.

It was late afternoon when Jacques-Jean left his sensuous Celimene in her bedchamber bidding her to slumber and assuring her he would return later that evening. He was anxious to be on his way back to the chateau. Rapidly descending the staircase, he strode with great purpose toward the cottage entrance, and had almost reached it when he heard a small voice.

"M'lord," Marie called out quickly. He stopped and took a step back toward the girl. "I heard, m'lord, I know, and I want to go with you."

"What are you saying?" He confronted her sternly, fingering the wide curled brim of the hat he held in his hand.

"You are leaving for the New World," she replied in a hushed voice. "I overheard. Please, m'lord, I beg you. I, too, want to go. I have some money saved; take me with you, please?"

"Marie, do you realize what you are asking? We are not just going to take a long journey. If you heard, you know I am now a hunted man. If I am caught, it will be most unpleasant for anyone who is caught with me. In fact, it could be extremely dangerous."

"I understand the risks but I have my reasons, m'lord. I have nothing here but the life of a servant. M'lady has been very kind to me, please do not misunderstand. She has been a wonderful benefactress and I am not ungrateful but I want something of my own. I want a chance to be something more than a servant... is that so wrong?"

"No... no, of course not." Jacques-Jean now looked at the girl as though seeing a person for the first time. "It will be very difficult, as well as dangerous. And you have never been to sea, I wager. If we make it that far, we could all be drown in a shipwreck, or be swept overboard in a storm. You could get sick in the new land. Wild animals could attack you... or the native savages. It is an untamed, wild and fearsome wilderness. Here, at least, you have the comfort of what is familiar."

"I have heard much about it, monsieur, and I have made up my mind. I want to go. Please take me with you, I beg you." In a final desperate attempt to gain his agreement, she added, lowering her eyes, "I... I will do anything you want of me, m'lord, anything you... desire."

Jacques-Jean understood what she meant and shook his head. "That is not necessary, Marie. You do not have to act the *putain* to make your way." He paused and looked long at the girl, assessing her anew. "You appear bright... if you are that determined," he finally shrugged slightly, "I guess I cannot stop you from coming along."

"Oh, m'lord, *merci! Merci beaucoup!*" she burst out with joy. On impulse she grabbed his hand and kissed it repeatedly. "You shall not regret it, m'lord, I promise. I promise. I shall not get in the way. I will get ready now."

"Marie, remember to say nothing to anyone except Mademoiselle Celimene," he warned, "no one!"

"*Oui*, m'lord," she said quickly with a curtsy and hurried to her room at the back of the house.

Jacques-Jean's personal servant had been sent on an errand guaranteed to keep him away for two days. It was the only way to keep him from growing suspicious of his master's activities. Although a trusted member of the duke's household, the lad was also a Catholic and best kept ignorant of things as they were unfolding. At the chateau, Jacques-Jean had packed for himself what little he could put into his saddlebags. A simple but sturdy suit of clothing in addition to the multiple layers he was going to wear, several pairs of stockings plus several changes of linen, a few articles of grooming, a miniature of his mother and one of his father. These last were the most important items except for the purses of gold Jean-Philippe had brought to him, and the small, leather-bound Bible published by Calvin, written in French, and given to him by his mother.

The duke was waiting in his shirt sleeves and jerkin at the small side door to say a quiet good-bye. On impulse, he took a heavy, gold signet ring bearing the *Pouvoir* coat of arms from his finger and put it onto Jacques-Jean's own finger.

"The world can have its opinion, and the world may have its way, but as far as I am concerned you remain my only true heir," he said roughly, emotion evident in his voice. "I hope, *mon fils*, someday you can return to claim your birthright. May God and the Blessed Virgin watch over you, and keep you from all harm. Write when you are safe."

"I will, Pa-pa."

For a moment they looked at each other, then, they embraced. Neither said another word as Jacques-Jean agilely mounted his horse and urged it down the long entry path. It was only after the horse could no longer be heard in the dusky distance that Jean-Philippe, in solitude, collapsed down onto the stone step and quietly wept into his hands.

Bouchet was in the back of the tavern when he heard the approach of many horses. He still had not found anyone to replace Marie. He was unwilling to offer a fair wage and except for the services of the lame village boy who came over to do chores every evening, Bouchet was forced to do everything himself. His temper and the tavern grew more foul by the day. He walked heavily into the main room and saw twelve brightly uniformed figures walking through his door.

"Wine and bread, tavernkeeper, and some cheese and meat," ordered one of them. Bouchet guessed by the man's swagger and more elaborate dress that the speaker was the officer in charge. It was confirmed when he added, "My men have ridden a long way and are hungry."

Bouchet grunted and set out pewter goblets and wine first. These were enthusiastically acknowledged by the men as they took seats around several tables. Bouchet went into the back room to find the bread he had baked fresh the day before. He brought out three large loaves and set them on the bare and greasy tabletops. Within minutes he had served up a kind of stew and, if it was not the tastiest of cuisine, it was hot and filling.

After the officer had eaten his portion and noticed that his men were about finished as well, he called to Bouchet.

"Tavernkeeper? Here!" He threw a leather purse which Bouchet deftly caught. About to count out the coins due to him he was halted when he heard the officer say, "Keep the whole thing... in exchange for the food and a little information."

He had Bouchet's complete attention.

"Do you know the *Duc du Pouvoir?*" the officer asked directly.

Bouchet's narrow greedy eyes opened wider and his mouth twitched. So it was trouble for the grand duke, he thought, inwardly smirking.

"*Oui*, everyone around here knows *le duc*. He is lord of this land." Bouchet kept his voice calm and even.

"And you also know *le duc's* bastard son?"

Bouchet frowned in puzzlement. "You mean the old *duc's* bastard? *Oui*."

"The one called Jacques-Jean Charte."

"*Oui*."

"Does he come here often?"

"Not anymore. He has a mistress cottaged beyond the village perhaps half a league or so," he gestured in the direction of the road that led to Celimene's. "If he is not at the chateau, he is usually whoring with her."

After Bouchet had given a more detailed description of Jacques-Jean as well as the cottage and its location, the officer stood and adjusted his sword.

"Montpellier," he commanded, "take three men and go to this cottage, the rest of us will go on to the chateau."

"What do you want him for?" Bouchet could not keep himself from asking as he fingered the purse of coins. In an oily, subservient manner he added, "I know it is none of my business but..."

"You are quite correct," the officer responded. "It is none of your business. Best be glad of it and keep it that way," he added sharply, staring at the tavernkeeper. Bouchet lowered his gaze to the ground as the men left the tavern.

Outside, the *gen d'armes* wasted no time mounting their horses. They split into two groups as directed and rode off in separate directions. The lieutenant took his men on toward the chateau while Sergeant Montpellier led the way along the road toward Celimene's cottage with his three men close behind.

Bertrell was not totally oblivious to the circumstances around him although Jacques-Jean considered him too slow witted to comprehend much. Bertrell himself knew he was slow witted but he allowed people to think him more thickheaded than he really was because it was much easier than trying to keep up with everything the world expected of one. But he had caught snatches of conversation and knew something was afoot. The young lord was in fear of the authorities. Why exactly, Bertrell did not know. What the heart of the trouble was he did not understand, but he understood trouble well enough.

He had no particular liking for the young lord but the half-wit worshiped the ground beneath Celimene's small delicate feet. He would lay down his life for her, die for her, do anything within his powers of comprehension to make her happy. She was fond of the young lord and therefore, Bertrell looked to the young noble's interests as well.

When Bertrell saw a flock of birds suddenly rise like a cloud from a small copse of trees on the horizon, he stared into the dusk and detected the horsemen pounding down the road. It was the horsemen that had frightened the birds and somewhere in the slow mental processes of his brain, Bertrell connected this hard riding group with danger to the young lord. And if the lord was in danger, Bertrell's mistress would be unhappy. Bertrell ran faster than he had ever run before in his life. Bursting into the little kitchen, he saw Marie and began to gesture before he could get the words out of his mouth.

"Th..there...," he pointed, hopping from one foot to another.

"What is it, Bertrell? What?" Marie tried to see into the growing darkness.

"Horses! Men coming!"

"Oh, *Mon Dieu*!" she gasped and ran into the main part of the cottage. "Monsieurs! Monsieurs! Bertrell has seen a group of men coming on horseback," she cried out.

Celimene, Richard and Jacques-Jean looked at each other. Richard had only just arrived a minute before. They were ready to leave but leaving now would be a mistake.

"Quick, Marie, take the horses out to the barn, tell Bertrell to unsaddle and stall them," Jacques-Jean ordered.

"No, wait... we cannot both hide and one needs a horse," Richard interjected. "Marie, tell Bertrell to put up one horse, leave the other out front where it is." Turning to Jacques-Jean as Marie hurried out, Richard rapidly began to take off his clothing.

"Trust me, my friend. They must find something or they will be suspicious. Best they find what we want them to find. Celimene, pour two glasses of wine, drink a little so it is on your breath. Here, give me a glass." Richard had taken off his jacket and waistcoat, and opened his shirt to expose a chest covered with thick black curls.

"My boots," he exclaimed and quickly Jacques-Jean helped him remove them. Richard rumpled his hair and grabbing Celimene, gave her several hard, fast kisses which brought the color to her cheeks and neck.

Jacques-Jean realized what his friend was doing. "And where do I go?" he asked.

"*Mon ami*, there is no safe place here you can hide except one," Richard answered. They could hear the horses approaching the cottage and Celimene could feel her heart begin to pound like a hammer in her chest. "Get down on all fours, quickly," he commanded his friend. Pulling Celimene over, Richard lifted her huge, voluminous petticoats and skirts, and dropped them over Jacques-Jean.

"Your chair, mademoiselle," Richard smiled and handed her back her glass. "No gentleman would dare to ask a lady to move from her seat."

When Marie escorted the *gen d'armes* into the little salon, the picture they saw was that of a ravishing young woman and her lover caught in the midst of foreplay before retiring to the more intimate pleasures of the bedroom.

"Are you Jacques-Jean Charte?" the Sergeant asked abruptly.

"Richard Bonchance," Richard replied with a slightly drunken grin, "and you?"

"I am Sergeant Montpellier," the sergeant bowed slightly, not immune to the sight of Celimene's ripe and glowing beauty. "I am sorry to interrupt your evening, mademoiselle, but I am looking for Monsieur Jacques-Jean Charte, son of the *Duc du Pouvoir*. Has he been here this evening?"

"How do you do, Sergeant?" Celimene willed herself to purr pleasantly and to extend her hand. "He was here earlier, this afternoon, but he has long since left."

The sergeant bent to kiss Celimene's soft, small hand, his gaze taking in her round, creamy, flawless shoulders before he peered appreciatively at her plump young breasts, the nipples of which were only just covered by her strained bodice. They threatened to spring out at any second. Quite the fickle beauty, he thought to himself with amusement, forgetting to breathe as he stared in anticipation of seeing those hidden nipples so very close to being exposed.

"I hope you will understand that we must search the premises, mademoiselle," he said when he found his breath again. "I have an order for Charte's arrest."

"Arrest!" Celimene opened her eyes wide making them round and hoped she sounded properly surprised. "But what has he done, *mon sergent*?"

"That is not my concern, mademoiselle," the tall man smiled warmly, "nor should it be yours." He turned and dispatched his men. The barn, the house, the grounds were all to be thoroughly searched but without unnecessary damage, he added, looking at Celimene who favored him with a dazzling smile of dimpled appreciation. She could feel Jacques-Jean between her legs. If it were not so terrifying, she considered silently, it would be quite erotic. Then, she realized she should offer the sergeant some wine.

As if reading her thoughts, Richard walked over to the sideboard and poured a generous glass of red wine.

"Sergeant, s...something to cut the dust of the road?" he asked as he walked over to Montpellier and extended the glass.

"*Merci,*" said the soldier, accepting the drink and immediately taking a large swallow. As he expected, it was of far better quality than that which they had suffered to drink at the tavern.

Celimene proceeded to engage the sergeant in casual conversation, flirting over her fan. Learning he was from Paris and was often at Versailles, gave them much to talk about. Celimene wanted every possible detail of life around the palace complete with colors, sounds, and tastes. And the sergeant was most happy to accommodate her.

At last, the three *gen d'armes* reported back. They had found nothing but poor half-witted Bertrell in the barn talking to a horse about biscuits. They had even given the hay a thorough raking, they said. Montpellier, slightly annoyed to have them back so soon, sent them to check through the cottage one more time, not because he thought they had missed anything but because he did not want to leave as yet. He was still willing her nipples to burst out and escape the confines of her bodice.

When his men returned a second time he knew he could delay no longer. Completely charmed by Celimene, he bid her a tender goodnight, again kissing her hand while fighting the strongest urge to plunge his hand into that beckoning cleavage. At last, he reluctantly took his leave and joined his men outside. Together they rode off to rendezvous with their commander at the chateau.

The sound of the horses galloping away grew fainter and fainter. When they could be heard no more, Celimene stood up, her knees just the slightest bit shaky. Jacques-Jean emerged from under her voluminous skirts. Wiping beads of perspiration from his brow, he grinned at Richard who was himself extremely pleased with the success of their little charade. Jacques-Jean poured himself a draft of wine and for a few moments they said nothing but drank deeply, each from his own glass.

"You were quite perfect," Jacques-Jean addressed Celimene, grabbing her into his arms as adrenaline continued to rush through his veins and squeezing her soft and naked derrière through the layers of fabric. "You had that poor officer utterly enthralled. You are wasted in the countryside, my darling. My father will let you stay here as long as you need but truly, you must go to court and seek your fortune," he added with a final appreciative kiss.

Celimene blushed with pleasure at his compliments. She, too, was pleased with her performance and long after her lover's departure she considered his final advice. It was true, she told herself, she was wasting herself in the countryside now that there were no other ducal heirs to impress. Paris and the Court did beckon.

When the sergeant and his men arrived at the chateau, they were dispatched to help in the search already taking place. The lieutenant soon realized it was an exercise in futility. He had hoped to catch the young gentleman at the dinner table or relaxing in front of the fire with a drink or in bed with his mistress, but obviously word had leaked out. His quarry was gone, of that he was certain, but a search must be done nonetheless to appease his superiors.

The duke played his part well the officer thought admiringly. He was controlled and gracious and cooperative yet with just the right air of surprise, upset, and even outrage. The lieutenant could almost believe that the older man was truly unaware of the intended arrest and his son's flight. Almost, but not quite. His years at his job had made him cynical and disbelieving by nature, and despite anything he saw or heard, he believed only what his instinct told him. And his instincts were telling him that Jacques-Jean Charte had taken flight to escape arrest.

One of the men came back from the servants' quarters with word about Madame Charte's cottage. The duke reacted visibly. The lieutenant noticed and decided that the cottage was worth searching.

"My son is not in the habit of visiting his mother at this time of night, but if you will I will escort you there myself," Jean-Philippe insisted. The lieutenant took five of his men along.

One of the servants had a horse waiting for his lordship. The five covered the distance to the cottage in only a few minutes. After dismounting, the duke led the way to the front door, knocking on it lightly. The lieutenant told two of his men to check around the gardens and out buildings.

Lisa opened the door and the surprise which registered on her face was evident. "*Monsieur le Duc*," she gasped, while dropping a little curtsy, "Madame is not expecting anyone and has already begun to prepare for bed."

"*Oui*, Lisa, all is quite well," Jean-Philippe reassured her while pressing into the cottage salon; the remaining four soldiers followed closely behind and filled the modest room. "Please tell Madame Charte we must speak with her for just one moment," he spoke calmly to the girl.

Under the duke's watchful eye, the lieutenant questioned Hélène who had come down dressed in a house wrap, looking very small and vulnerable. With an uncharacteristic scowl leveled at the inquisitor, Jean-Philippe protectively wrapped his arm around his love. While this was going on, two of the *gen d'armes* searched the substantial cottage while another detained Lisa at the back, ostensibly to question her.

The lieutenant knew he was getting nowhere with his questioning of Madame Charte. He sensed her anguish and fear but felt his visit was no real surprise. She had known her son was being sought but had been kept ignorant of any detail, the officer concluded. A waste of time.

A commotion came from the rear of the cottage with the sounds of pots clattering, masculine cursing and feminine screeching. Rushing to see what was going on, both the lieutenant and the duke found Lisa with a kettle in hand swinging at her interrogator.

"Stay away from me, you oaf," the girl cried out. Her cap was askew and her face was flushed with anger. "Or by the Blessed Virgin, I will clout you on the head."

"Moreau!" the lieutenant barked, "What is going on here?"

Fresh and angry scratches were evident down one cheek of Moreau 's ruddy face as he looked to his commander but avoided his eyes. "She is worse than a cat, for no reason, suddenly she clawed me," he accused, gingerly touching his cheek.

"No reason?" screeched the girl again. "No reason? You would have me bring shame to my father's house?" And suddenly she was crying into her apron. "My brother... would k..kill you if h..he knew what you t..tried to do."

"I did nothing!" Moreau insisted while his lieutenant and the duke scowled in unison.

Hélène pushed the men aside to put her arms around Lisa and draw her close. "You should be ashamed of yourself," she bit out at Moreau, giving vent to the frustrating anger she felt on her son's behalf. "Lisa is an innocent and does not run around accusing men of taking liberties for no reason. Have you no decency? No shame? Right here in my home, under our very noses, you... you... libertine!"

"My apologies, madame," the lieutenant flushed at the woman's unexpected vehemence. Turning to Moreau he hissed, "Get out of here. Wait outside. I will deal with you later." The other hastily left the room. Totally humiliated by the unforgivable breech of conduct demonstrated by someone under his command, the officer stiffened and tried to mask his emotions. "It was unforgivable. Please be assured, the man will be disciplined severely," he addressed the duke. "My sincerest apologies, mademoiselle," he bowed to Lisa. "I do regret that I must ask you a few questions, however, but perhaps you would like to sit down first?"

Hélène brought Lisa out to the salon and sat beside her on the small settee. Both women swore they had not seen Jacques-Jean since the day before and both attested to it being common to see him only twice or three times a week. From the servant, the lieutenant felt true surprise that the duke's son was being sought by the authorities. She knows nothing, he concluded with an inward sigh, only wanting very much to leave this scene of embarrassment quickly.

The only reasonable escape route was to the north and over the border into the low country and the Netherlands. How much of a head start the heretic bastard had, the lieutenant could only guess but they must press on quickly. In haste, he left the cottage along with his five men and went back to the chateau to gather the rest and head northward. Moreau's punishment could wait.

Jean-Philippe stayed at the cottage with Hélène after the *gen d'armes'* departure. Assuring her without saying anything that could be repeated or overheard, he simply held her and whispered into her ear that all would be well. He could feel her slender body trembling in his arms and knew what the pretenses had cost her. He gently commanded Lisa to retire for the night herself.

He led Hélène up the stairs to her bed. Silently, he removed her wrap. She stood passively in her silk negligeé while he turned back the covers and held the sheet and blanket so she could slip down into the softness. He sat upon the edge of the bed and drew her back up into his arms. They each knew exactly what the other was feeling. They were losing their son and there was absolutely nothing they could do about it except cling to each other.

The strain of suppressing her emotions and playacting all day finally broke her and within the safety of Jean-Philippe's arms, Hélène gave herself over to deep sobs until she was exhausted. His neck and stock were soaked with tears when she had finally calmed and he laid her down with the gentleness of a nurse with a babe.

She felt him move up off the bed and Hélène curled into herself, wishing she had the courage to ask him to stay, just for this night, just this once, and knowing she had no right to ask. But oh, how badly she needed him and his strength to ease her pain and emptiness.

The room was lit only by the bright moonlight coming in the window. Jean-Philippe had removed his waistcoat and was in the process of removing his tear stained jabot when Hélène opened her swollen eyes and realized he was still there.

She started to speak and then closed her mouth. He was trying to tug off his boots and having a bad time of it, hampered with a desire to be quiet.

"Wait," she said softly and crawled back out of bed to assist him. The task complete, she turned to him. "Does this mean you will stay the night?" she asked trying to keep her voice steady without any trace of begging.

He was undoing the laces on his breeches and paused. "I thought you might like that, I will not sleep a wink tonight anyway. I thought we could be a comfort to each other... but perhaps you would rather be alone...?"

"No, no," she cut him off as her hand darted to stay him from turning away although he had not moved a muscle. "I want you to stay more than anything but... are you certain? What about...?"

"She has retired and is sleeping by now," he reassured Hélène. "She would no more know whether I am there in my own bed or in my study or out in the stables. I will go back before she emerges from her rooms tomorrow."

Hélène reached up to him and kissed him softly on the mouth, the hairs of his moustache silky against her upper lip. Her mouth was warm and he could taste the lingering salt from her tears. "I need you, my love," she whispered with immense feeling. "I need you desperately tonight."

Responding to her with a terrible need of his own, Jean-Philippe finished disrobing quickly and climbed into the bed. They came together with an alarming intensity, each feeling the anger and frustration drive them to an almost animalistic demand to heal the awful hole torn within the heart, and each finding a few precious minutes of forgetfulness.

Chapter 9

It was an hour before dawn and Jacques-Jean, Richard, and Marie were well on their way to Paris. The trio had ridden hard by the light of the full moon on the deserted main road. As the starlit sky dissolved to slate gray, they switched to the side trails to avoid being seen and the ground was rougher, slowing them. As pre-dawn quietly dissolved into a golden pink glow they continued picking their way cross country until in full daylight they found a ravine within a small grove of trees. Resting the horses and themselves, they awaited early nightfall to be on their way again.

Marie was no horsewoman. By the time they had reached the wooded area where they had decided to rest and wait, she was in misery. Her thighs were chaffed and burned like fire. The muscles in her buttocks were screaming from abuse. And to make matters worse, she felt the spasmodic abdominal cramping that was the forerunner to her monthly cycle. She did not know if it was the tension, the excitement, or the pounding in the saddle that had caused it but she was going to be early at a most inconvenient time.

Jacques-Jean and Richard were each snoring lightly as they rested, looking very comfortable, against the tree roots. The horses were hidden in the ravine below. Marie quietly went to her knapsack, took out the rags and thin soft cord she had packed for the purpose and stole off into the densest thicket nearby.

When she re-emerged Jacques-Jean stirred. "Are you well?" he asked from his reclined position peering out at her from under his large hat.

"I am fine, m'lord," she flushed pink and tried to walk normally. "Tending to nature is all."

He grunted and closed his eyes again.

Marie settled down in an attempt to rest her weary body. Using her knapsack for a headrest, she closed her eyes thinking how much she dreaded going back up onto the horse. Sleep overcame her and she seemed to have only just dropped off when she felt something nudging her. It was Jacques-Jean's boot at her leg.

"Time to get up," he said quietly and offered her his hand.

She nodded, reached out and obediently arose denying the stiffness she felt in her muscles. It was growing dark but there was still enough light to gather their things.

They continued onward, eating food they carried with them as they rode. Making their way back out to the main road, they were able to ride briskly in the full moonlight just as they had the night before. Finally, as dawn once again lightened the sky, they came upon a marker that told them they were very near the city.

Jacques-Jean heard the sound of a small bell and turned to see a shepherd driving his flock along the crossroad, heading for the intersection where he no doubt would turn toward the markets of Paris. "Come, follow me," he said in a low voice and began trotting briskly in the opposite direction on the same road as the shepherd. They continued onward, one following the other wordlessly until they gained a small copse of trees at which point Jacques-Jean led them off the road into the brush. Once off the road they began to backtrack once again in the general direction of the city. It was getting lighter by the minute and they stopped when they found an abandoned hut. It had no roof and two of the walls were almost half gone, but it provided refuge. The men decided to take turns keeping watch since they were so close to the roads. Marie was simply thankful to have finally stopped.

She was now in constant agony but said nothing as she looked around her for some place affording privacy. Her bladder ached, she needed to pass water and she knew her rags needed to be changed.

"Ho, where are you going?" Richard called out to her in a voice meant to stop her as she hobbled away from the hut.

"I... I need to..." Marie stammered over the distance and could not be understood.

"Richard, let her go," Jacques-Jean intervened. "We have been riding all night... what do you most want to do right this minute?" he asked his tall friend.

"Before I can do anything I need to piss... oh," he replied with sudden realization. "Well, keep down and be watchful." he called out after the girl again.

Marie walked on, every step chafing and adding to her misery. On the other side of the thicket of brush, she passed her water and tried to clean herself. She needed water, but there was none. And now her hands had blood on them. She was ashamed. She made an effort to collect saliva and spit furiously on her hands, wiping them on the fallen leaves. She felt dirty and frustrated and suddenly tears were flowing unbidden down her cheeks. Why did her body betray her in this way now? It was not fair. She did not wish to disgust Monsieur Jacques. Celimene had been such an example of fastidious hygiene and now Marie felt filthy. She used her over-skirt to wipe her tears. Then, she gathered her things and what dignity she could and walked back to the roofless hut praying the men would be asleep.

Jacques-Jean had pulled the first watch and saw Marie approaching. "There is fresh water over there," he said tossing his head in the direction opposite that from which she had come. "If you are thirsty or would like to wash," he added convivially.

Marie did not pause to reply but took off in the direction he had indicated and soon came to a small brook that gurgled along flowing into a tributary that fed into the great Seine River. Marie did not know this, however, and only considered that, of course, there would have to be water for no one would build a dwelling unless there was water nearby. Gratefully, she bent to the water as it danced along over the river rocks. She washed her hands and face, then she took a long drink and finally rinsed out her soiled rags. She was not certain how the rags would dry since they had made no fire but she would have to worry about that later. Walking further, she came to the spot where the brook joined the stream. The water was deeper, quieter and tall reeds lined the banks. On impulse, she suddenly slipped off her shoes and dropped her skirt, petticoat, and the rag from between her legs onto the creek bank. She waded in and gasped at the chill of the water against her skin. It raised goose bumps over her and she shivered violently but continued to the deepest place, squatting down and washing her bruised and blood smeared flesh. She hurried but was blue with cold when she climbed back up to the bank and pulled on her skirts again.

She could have lain down right there beside the brook in the bracken and allowed the soothing gurgle of the water to put her to sleep but she knew the men would want her back at the ruins. She was tired, she ached, but at least she felt clean and Marie walked back to the hut where she found her horse's saddle set in a corner of the ruin for her to lie against. Wrapping the saddle blanket smelling strongly of horse around her, she was soon fast asleep.

From the ruin, the ride into Paris took less than an hour at a steady but inconspicuous pace. They arrived at dusk just before the city gates closed. Once through the wall and within the city itself, the smells of the raw sewage running through the streets rose up to assault them as powerfully as a physical blow. After the cool fresh air of the country, even Richard who was the least concerned with hygiene wished himself well out of the pungent stench.

"*Mon Dieu*! Has no one a nose to smell with here?" Richard exclaimed. "No wonder it is said the Parisians bathe in perfume and stick perfumed handkerchiefs up their noses. *Merde*! The whole city smells like *merde*."

"How much farther?" inquired Jacques-Jean stoically, trying not to breathe through his nostrils.

"They live near the river."

"The river runs through Paris, Richard. That does not narrow it down. Do you have an address?"

"Of course, of course. I remember it is across from the *Île de la Cité*. I think I can see the bridge ahead. *Oui!* That is it. It cannot be far to their house," replied Richard trying also to breathe through his mouth as they walked their mounts. "I cannot imagine my little cousin living like this. It is far worse than I remember when we last visited."

"When was that?" Jacques-Jean asked simply for distraction.

Richard was silent for a moment. "I cannot remember. Five years perhaps, maybe six."

"Obviously, it has grown worse... or as a boy you did not care."

"It has grown worse," Richard grumbled. "I think we should dismount and continue on foot. We will be less conspicuous." With that Richard halted his horse and slid to the ground watching his step to avoid the open gutter running through the center of the street.

Jacques-Jean saw Marie wince in pain as she tried to pull her leg up and back in an effort to dismount.

"Wait," he called out swinging lightly off his own horse. With reins in hand, he came around to the side of her animal. "Swing your leg up over in front and face me." His arms were extended as his hands gripped her waist. She put her hands on his shoulders as he eased her down.

"I am sorry," she bit her lip again to keep from crying out. "I am not used to riding a horse."

"You did extremely well," he said, giving her a wink of encouragement. "Are you hurting? Can you walk?"

"*Oui, oui*, m'lord, I am fine," she lied and attempted a smile that came out crooked.

"How far do you think we will have to go now?" he asked Richard as they crossed the bridge into the old, original part of the city.

"From here, it should be very close," Richard replied. "But I will have to ask about the street. Stay here." He handed his horse's reins to his friend who stood with Marie. Richard went off in the direction of a tavern. They heard noisy singing as he opened the door and it quieted again as the door closed.

Jacques-Jean and Marie stood quietly waiting, each holding their horse by the bridle and reins. Suddenly down a small dark alley, Marie saw the glint of something from a second story window reflecting a bit of lamplight. The sound of a grunted mutter that was supposed to serve as warning was quickly followed by the wet splat of urine and human excrement falling to the brick pavement below. The raw sewage lay in the alley awaiting the next rain to wash it down the open gutter and finally into the sewer. Marie shuddered. She had never thought of the city as being such a filthy place. Why did everyone want to come here, she asked herself?

Finally, the door to the tavern opened emitting the continuing sounds of music, singing and human babble. Richard emerged and came toward them muttering. "How was I to know, *bon Dieu?* Everything is different and it is nightfall."

"What is it?" Jacques-Jean inquired.

"It is not here, we are going in the wrong direction. Come, this way. We must cross back over but it is along the river," he pointed as he took his horse's reins back.

Marie silently groaned. She had sworn she would never give Monsieur any reason to regret his decision to bring her along but at that moment she hurt so badly, she was regretting her own decision to leave. Biting her lip against the pain, she followed along behind Richard, leading her horse behind his as Jacques-Jean followed behind her. The rags between her legs were chafing her skin raw. Each step was increasing torture and she had no thought to spare for the stench of the streets.

They walked over the roughly worn cobblestones on either side of the gutter, the horses' hoofs clopping along in the shadows. At last they came to the bridge at the other side of the island and crossed it. On the bridge, the breeze from the river cleared their nostrils somewhat. Once on the other side, the neighborhood began to improve as did the smell. Or perhaps they were simply growing used to it. Lighted windows offered cheery invitations they could not accept. Lantern posts and torches lit their way. After what Marie thought to be almost an hour, but was in reality only perhaps thirty minutes, Richard went into another tavern. He learned they were very near the Dufee's location now and had solid directions.

At last, they found the street and Richard was able to lead them to the house. At least he thought it was the right house. It looked completely dark and Marie wondered to herself if the family was even in residence. Richard knocked once by lifting the heavy door knocker and letting it fall.

Denis himself opened the door to see who was there. By the light of one candle, he half pulled them across the threshold, closing the door quickly behind them. Thick draperies covered the windows.

"Welcome, *mes amis*," he said without expressing the least bit of surprise when they were safely inside. He set about lighting more candles in the sconces on the walls quickly illuminating a pleasant interior. He wore the same dull brown conservative jerseys which Jacques-Jean remembered seeing him in the last time they had met.

"Denis, you act as though you were expecting us!" Richard said in puzzlement. "Has the news already gotten out about Jacques-Jean?"

"News? No news, but I can very well guess why you are here. And no, I have not been expecting you specifically, but since the Edict of Fountainbleau I have raps on the door in the dark of the night often... and all for the same reason. You wish passage to the Americas, *oui*? Madeleine, see who has come," he called upward as he passed the staircase. Denis ushered them into the dining room which was now well lit. "You have horses?" he asked and they nodded, slightly speechless at his quick and organized acceptance of their arrival.

"I will go tend to them, we have a stable in the rear," he said and left abruptly.

Dressed in her housecoat, Richard's cousin came quietly down the stairs. Her dark brown hair was already brushed out and hung loosely around her shoulders in preparation for bed. She looked more like a child than a bride.

"Richard," she said in a light, soft voice and embraced her cousin, her dark eyes looking up at him, large and round. "So, it is trouble for you, too?" He looked down at her and simply shrugged his shoulders. "I am so sorry," she added earnestly. She turned to the others to be introduced after which she said graciously, "You are all most welcome. I will fetch you something to eat and drink. I know you will want to retire soon after your long journey."

They settled at the large sturdy dining table made of highly polished wood. The reflections of the many candles danced upon the table's surface until Madeleine spread a gleaming white tablecloth out. Denis came back inside and the men explained the circumstances of their forced flight. Madeleine served food and drink.

Noticing how pale and worn Marie looked, Madeleine went to her and bent into her ear, asking quietly, "Can I help you with something in particular?"

Marie looked up at her with gratitude and nodded her head.

"Come with me," Madeleine gestured to her.

She noticed the difficulty with which Marie walked and guided her out to the kitchen. Off to the side of the kitchen was a small bedroom.

"This was the maid's room until Denis decided it was too risky to keep a servant in our home. Instead a girl comes each day but leaves again before sundown."

Marie only nodded.

"What can I do for you?" Madeleine asked with concerned attention.

"Could I please have a tub of warm water?"

"A tub?"

"*Oui*, a wash tub or a large bucket. I have never really ridden a horse before, at least not for any distance, and to make it worse the curse began on the way. I am so sore and chafed, if I could just sit in some warm water... please."

"Of course, I understand," Madeleine said and quickly went out to the lean-to behind the kitchen and brought in a lady's hip bath. "I am afraid there is no fireplace in this room. If you like, you can come in front of the kitchen hearth. I could close the door and..."

"No, no, I will be fine in here. Just, please, make the water very warm."

With a nod, Madeleine went to fetch the water.

Marie lit several candles and looked about the room. That it was very plain and devoid of decoration made it look especially neat and clean. It held a narrow bed, a small chest of drawers, a chair, and a small table. The single window had its shutters closed and was curtained in a bright ocher color that had faded to a rather pleasant shade of pale yellow. On the floor, a colorful peasant throw rug made of hundreds of scraps of cloth braided together added color and warmth as did the friendly glow of the candles.

In a short time, Madeleine had the small tub half filled with the water which had already been hanging by the fire. She went out to the well in the backyard for another bucket as Marie began to undo her skirts. Her petticoat was spotted over with blood. The rags tied between her legs were soaked and blood was smeared over her inner thighs which were chafed so badly they bore a strong resemblance to raw meat. Madeleine returned and saw her.

"*Mon Dieu!*" she gasped, "you poor thing, you must be in misery."

Marie sat down into the tub, leaving her legs hang out, her feet still on the floor. She gasped involuntarily feeling the initial bite of the hot water upon her abused flesh, then she relaxed to its soothing effect.

"Ahhhh," she sighed deeply. "I am so grateful. Is there more water?"

"In a bit," Madeleine brought a thin blanket to put over Marie's naked limbs. "It is starting to get cold."

"To be honest, I had not noticed."

"No wonder. Such things we women must go through, men will never know," she said with an almost comical air of sophistication, like a very young child imitating something it has heard its elders say. She went on hesitantly, "Are you Richard's ... ahh....?" she didn't quite know how to say it.

"Oh, no," Marie blushed.

"Monsieur Charte's?"

"No, no... I am only... well... I was his mistress's maid."

"Richard has a mistress?"

"No-no. Er… well, I do not really know but I meant Monsieur Charte's mistress."

"Oh." Madeleine exclaimed softly. She had been raised in the heart of the Protestant middle-class. None of the men she knew had mistresses, or at least she was not aware of any. She had always thought of mistresses as something Catholic men had, yet Monsieur Charte was a Huguenot she had been told. But she understood he was also an aristocrat, so that undoubtedly explained it. Well, she supposed, mistresses needed maids also, but it was peculiar to actually meet one in person. She looked up a little shyly at Marie and almost asked what mistresses were like, if they run a house like a wife or if they just lie in bed all day and night waiting for their lover. But that, she thought, sounded too childishly naive. Instead she asked, "Why are you fleeing, are you a Huguenot, as well?"

"No."

"Catholic?" the young wife exclaimed softly in alarm.

"No-no. I guess I am nothing... in particular," Marie shrugged slightly. "I mean, I cannot remember ever being inside a church." Seeing the other's eyes go round with surprise she hastily added, "but I know there is a God, at least I think there is. It is what everyone says, is it not?"

"But of course there is a God," Madeleine assured her guest. "And it is very important for you to know that He sent His only son to die for you. He loves you very much."

Marie shrugged a bit uncomfortably. It was a thought she did not find easy to examine. The idea of a God who loved her was difficult to accept. She only knew a God who took everything from her, sooner or later. She decided to address the other part of the girl's question instead. "I am not really fleeing, I asked to come along. I want to go to the New World and I have no idea how to get there by myself."

"You *want* to go?" the girl asked with a vague note of awe. "You are so brave!"

Marie looked up at the young woman she judged to be about her age, perhaps a year or two older but much more innocent.

"Sooner or later, we all die. I will die if I stay here, I will die if I go there but here I have nothing and there I have a chance for... for something. That is not so brave."

"*Mais oui*, it is," Madeleine nodded. "Why, I could not imagine leaving here. Leaving behind everything I know, everyone I know, my family, my friends, my comfortable life? To leave my home," she gestured to the walls around them. "To go where everything is strange and savage and so very far away? I should surely die of fear and loneliness. That is why we pretend," she added quietly.

"Pretend?"

She nodded. "We must pretend," her voice dropped to a complete whisper, "to be Catholic."

"Oh," Marie responded simply. There was no hint of judgment in her voice. She did not understand why this young matron seemed slightly ashamed. One must do what one must do to survive, was that not what Anoui had told her? "There is really nothing here that I leave behind," Marie said softly. "I suppose that makes a difference. You have a family, relatives, a husband, a home... it would be very hard to leave all this behind."

Madeleine studied Marie quietly. With sudden realization, she saw that Marie was being very honest when she said she had nothing here but was trapped in the life of a servant. Before her guest could see pity in her eyes, Madeleine turned to leave saying only, "I will bring more water."

She went back into the kitchen and returned with another steaming kettle, carefully adding the hot water to the tub without burning Marie.

"When that cools, you must get out. It is not good to soak too long; the flesh will become too tender. I have some salve; it is very good. I will get it." With that Madeleine left the room again, closing the door softly behind her.

When she returned, she left the salve and fresh linens as well as a nightgown for Marie to use. She also brought her a supply of thick spongy sheep's wool, and showed her how to wrap it in strips of cloth to make a more absorbent washable pad to staunch her monthly flow. After drying off and applying the soothing ointment to her raw skin, Marie dressed. Using the bath water she began scrubbing the blood out of her soiled clothing, hoping everything would dry before morning.

In the kitchen, Madeleine added more wood to the fire. The flames burst forth brightly and the warmth beat back the night chill. She returned to the maid's room and took the wet garments from Marie. She gave them a final rinse in fresh water and put them through a wringer she cranked by hand, squeezing out every possible drop of water. Finally, she gave each garment a good shake-out and hung it by the hearth to dry.

"They should be dry by morning," Madeleine said with satisfaction. "Do you feel better?" she called over with a gentle smile.

"Much, much better... but I prefer not to walk anymore, thank you," Marie called back through the doorway.

"Of course, let me bring you a plate of food. I saw you ate almost nothing at the table."

"You are very kind. You have been so good to me; I know not how to thank you." Marie was genuinely touched at the sweet thoughtfulness of the other girl, a complete stranger, who had helped her, waited on her, and now brought in a plate of food and gave it to her.

"There is no need to thank me. We are all children of the Lord God, and He would have us be uplifting to each other," she replied sincerely and gave Marie a sisterly hug and kiss upon her cheek.

In the dining room, the men finished eating and Denis took up the candelabra and led them into his study. It was a comfortable room full of books and maps, and again Jacques-Jean noticed heavy black curtains completely covered two areas where he imagined there were windows.

Denis set the candelabra down to light the sconces on the walls. Several maps were spread across his large desk top.

"Your timing is most fortunate; I have a ship leaving in five days for the Colonies," Denis said as he sought out one particular map. "Here, this is where it is going," he tapped the surface with his index finger, "the Dutch called it New Amsterdam, but now it is known as New York Towne."

"From there, we can make our way into New France," said Richard, tracing his finger quickly over the map.

"You had better think twice about it," Denis looked at them. "I am afraid you are going to have the same problem in the new France as you have in the old. There is not much of a population at this time, but as the Crown encourages farmers and families, civilization brings authority and the authorities have no tolerance for Huguenots in the New World, especially ones who have papers out for their arrest. Official policy now forbids Huguenots from settling in New France."

Richard scowled in surprise and looked at Jacques-Jean.

"Look here," Denis said and referred back to the map pointing out a coastal area to the south, "this they now call New Jersey and while it may be *Anglaise* they are our kindred souls who have left the Church of England behind to worship as they desire. They, too, are Calvinists. Many Huguenots have settled into this area," he pointed to the mouth of the Delaware River. "As well as Protestants from Germany, Scotland, and Sweden. Of course, there are also the original Dutch, but they are more in this area" he added, his finger sweeping the Hudson River. "You will have much company." He smiled encouragingly. "And from what I understand, they are not only tolerant but practice a form of self-government which allows everyone a voice. There undoubtedly shall be many opportunities for you... even the girl. Yes, *mes amis*, I think you are most fortunate. A week from now, that ship will be gone, the last for the season, and the next ship will go to the West Indies... a climate few white men find tolerable. And many go to an early grave because of it."

Jacques-Jean continued to inspect the map with interest. "And here...?" he asked pointing to a well marked coastal port about halfway between New York and the West Indies.

"Ahhh...Charles Towne... we put in there often. In fact, I am expecting a ship back from there in about three more weeks. It is perhaps the most tolerant of all the English settlements on the continent. They have to be," he chuckled, "because their climate is not. Oh, I must be fair. The winters are almost paradise I have been told, but in summer... as long as you are near the sea it is perhaps tolerable but inland it is fit for neither man nor beast. Few survive the fevers."

"But yet they stay... why??!!" Richard asked.

"They stay." Denis nodded with a knowing smile. "They do as little as possible in the worst of the heat but try to stay healthy and grow rich."

Richard raised his eyebrow skeptically, surely Denis was having a joke with them.

The merchant decided to explain. "All along these river ways huge rice plantations are popping up... but the watery land is also a breeding ground for fevers. Whites are safe from the first frosts until perhaps mid-spring, then, they must escape for their lives to the seaside. So they import blackamoor slaves who appear to have a natural resistance to these fevers. While the slaves are planting and harvesting, the masters stay at the ocean front and live very well. I believe it is the most prosperous spot in the colonies."

"What a life!" Richard exclaimed.

"Well, they do have to deal with the problems of absentee ownership; while the cat is away, the mouse, he will play," Denis warned.

"Forget that," Jacques-Jean grunted, "I have no desire to live in stifling heat nor to own slaves for that matter. Such a climate is good conditioning for the afterlife awaiting those who trade in human flesh."

Richard chuckled at his friend's moralistic response.

"What is here? This Boston, a very good harbor too, it appears," mused Jacques-Jean.

Denis nodded. "Excellent, but colder in climate and in temperament. The Puritans have settled in this area. They had a rough time of it, I am told, escaping their king's wrath only to become as intolerant as they said the Church of England was of them. I hear they have rules and laws for everything."

"Surely not everything..." Richard winked.

"Even that," Denis poured them each more wine. "The Puritans, they say, even have rules for what positions are acceptable when a husband and wife make love."

Jacques-Jean laughed deeply as did Richard. Now they were sure Denis was having a joke on them.

"Can you not see the sheriff sternly perched at the foot of the bed intent on ensuring obedience to these laws?" Jacques-Jean cried out in mirth. Richard convulsed beside him, doubling over with laughter.

It was late and the young men were tired. The wine was going to their heads and breaking the grip of the tension created by their forced escape. They laughed and continued to laugh so hard that tears ran down their cheeks. It was infectious and soon Denis, too, was laughing. But he was the first to finally catch his breath.

"Yes, I think you are most fortunate. You are going to the best place. You had better get some rest, now. We have a barge going down the Seine tomorrow and you three must be on it."

"I want to pay you for my passage," Jacques-Jean stood up proudly. "And I will pay for the girl, as well."

"Save your money, *mon ami*. Richard is family, and so, you are family. I want to help. Besides, if I have a trusted contact in this colony I have another business connection. You could even call it an investment. Now, let me show you both to your bed for the night."

Jacques-Jean nodded and realized he had not seen Marie for some time.

"What of the girl?"

"Do not be concerned, I am certain my wife has made her comfortable in the maid's room."

The next morning word came early to Dufee that his main shipment of merchandise had not yet arrived at the barge site.

"Do not concern yourselves," he counseled calmly. "It happens often and means nothing sinister, have no fear. The worst is that you should stay indoors. The less my neighbors are aware of your presence the better for everyone. The housemaid will be arriving soon and I have instructed Madeleine to say nothing more than her cousin from the country has come to pay a visit. One need not explain oneself to servants, *n'est-ce pas*? To do so would invite suspicion. We are in God's hands."

Marie was secretly happy for the additional time to recover. She contented herself with staying in the small room off the kitchen through the day, applying salve to her sore flesh and constructing more pads to take with her out of the rag scraps Madeleine had brought to her. Fearful she might inadvertently say or do something to give them away, Marie had a time honored excuse for her seclusion and was glad to stay away from the housemaid.

Jacques-Jean amused himself perusing through the Dufees' library of books. He spent the day reading thereby alleviating any need to speak or interact with anyone else. He melted into the background as a bookworm while Richard fell into easy conversation with his cousin, purposefully drawing most of the attention upon himself while reminiscing about playful childhood memories.

The housemaid blithely went about her routines. There was nothing untoward to arouse her suspicions and once the main meal of the day was prepared and served and the kitchen cleaned and swept for the evening, the girl was dismissed at the customary time which was just before sunset.

With the door closing behind her, everyone relaxed with a small sigh of relief.

"I think that went well," Jacques-Jean said with a quiet smile, setting his book aside and stretching. "Do you think we will be leaving tomorrow?" he asked trying not to appear impatient.

"We can hope but do not be disappointed if you are with us yet another day or two," Denis replied. "Usually when there is a delay it is at least a two day occurrence, sometimes more."

"What is it they say about house guests and fish?" Richard asked as he accepted another glass of wine from Denis. "Something about 'after three days they both begin to stink.'"

"Richard!" Madeleine exclaimed, an amused expression on her face. "How can you say such a thing? When Denis and his ma-ma came to stay with us in the summer, they would always stay for several months."

"Now that I am grown, I can understand why. We could not believe the smell when we entered the city and this is autumn. *Mon Dieu*! I can only imagine what it must be like in the heat of the summer. How can you stand it, little cousin?"

Madeleine cast her eyes downward with a small shrug.

"Most of the time it is not so bad in our neighborhood," Denis replied somewhat embarrassed. "Something about the way the winds blow in from the countryside. And in truth, I suppose we do become used to it."

"Your hospitality is more than generous," Jacques-Jean added gratefully, "if I seem a bit anxious it is only because I know by now they have gone north to the borders and have not found any trace of us. How long before they think of Paris and search every port for us?"

"Not *us*, Jacques, you," Denis replied with significance and Jacques-Jean and Richard both looked to him. "Who would or could have told them that instead of one they need to search for *two* plus a girl. That changes things a great deal, *n'est-ce pas*? A young man seeking to flee the country does not usually drag along a young girl."

Marie looked up, sensitive to her position, wondering and finally speaking aloud. "Do I make it harder for Monsieur?"

"No-no, quite the opposite, *ma petite*," Richard grinned reassurance. "Denis is saying we have changed the description of the fugitive and that is a good thing. It is as good as a disguise."

"Oh."

"Should we take a barge by ourselves to the ship?" asked Richard.

Denis shook his head. "Now that would be very unusual. Relax, my friends. God is in control."

"Come," Madeleine beckoned to her cousin, "make yourself useful with your great tall reach and help to cover all the windows for the night before all the light of day is gone."

Jacques-Jean and Denis joined Richard and together they had every window throughout the house securely covered with the thick black draperies in mere minutes. Marie and Madeleine lit tapers and they settled down in the salon.

As they sat quietly, each with his own thoughts, a cautious scratching came at the front door. Denis arose, carrying a taper and closed the salon door behind him. He proceeded to the front door much as he had the night before.

With muscles tensed, Jacques-Jean strained to hear. Marie realized she was holding her breath. Richard had come to the edge of his chair in a defensive posture. The door to the salon opened and Denis stepped through holding his taper high.

"Meet *Frère Robert*," he said and stepped aside to admit a mild looking man dressed in a somber, dark suit of clothes. "It would seem *Frère Robert* will be going with you. As a *pasteur* he has over stayed his welcome in France."

With the rescinding of the Edict, Huguenot pastors were considered unnecessary and very unwanted; officially there were no Huguenot flocks to shepherd. Even *Louvoir* realized it was not realistic to expect the Protestant pastors to convert to Catholicism but they were viewed as a cancerous entity able to spread contamination. With strength and conviction and their skills for preaching and proselytizing, they could not be allowed to remain and continue the corruption of others. They had been given two weeks to sell their homes and any other property and leave the country forever or face being sent to the galleys or hanged.

Brother Robert was a young widower who had seen his congregation disappear just as Hélène's church had dissolved after their building had been confiscated. Uncertain where to go, he had at last made the bold decision to leave for the New World where he hoped to spread the Good News of the Gospel and gather a new flock.

In the flattering glow of the candlelight, Brother Robert looked younger than he did the next day in the light of the sun. His hair was as somber as his clothing: neat and unadorned, trimmed to a convenient length all around and needing no tying. Jacques-Jean and Richard judged him to be somewhere in his early thirties, rather soft and small shouldered, but with eyes that were steady and a voice of calm strength.

"Every day hundreds of Huguenots slip over the borders," explained Brother Robert in an effort to pass along news. "I hear the English Queen Elizabeth was so appalled by the St. Bartholomew's Day massacre that she took delight in welcoming our brethren by giving them permission to hold regular services *en français* in the lower chapel of the cathedral at Canterbury. I do not know that she really wanted us in her country but it certainly was a needle prick to France's pride."

"But that was years ago," Dufee interjected.

"True. But it was something of a precedent that continues. However, I heard Charles II turned Catholic on his deathbed and without a child, his brother James who is a Catholic has the English Parliament and the Huguenots worried. But still… more show up on England's shores each day even if it only serves as a de‑parture point. Many have gone to Germany across our eastern border and to the Netherlands in the north but those who are caught trying to escape do pay very dearly."

"What happens to them?" Marie could not help but ask, surprising herself at her boldness but as yet, no one had enlightened her.

"The men are mostly sent to the galleys; life for a galley slave is not long, I am afraid. Within a year, two at the most, they are usually dead."

"Why?" Marie listened attentively.

"They are kept chained to their seat so if there is a battle and the galley is sunk, they go down with it and are drowned."

"*C'est terrible!*" she breathed softly.

"And if they avoid drowning, chances are within a year or two, depending on their condition to start with, they are driven to mortal collapse from exhaustion at the oars."

"What is a galley, monsieur?" she whispered timidly, embarrassed to be so ignorant. Brother Robert smiled at her and explained gently as if speaking to a child. "The king's galley ships patrol our shores, most heavily to the south in the Mediterranean Sea where Muslim pirates are always a threat. Pirates like to raid our coastal communities if they can, in hopes of taking captives to the North African slave markets."

Marie and Madeleine both gasped.

"Surely not women?" Madeleine half stated, half asked as if the very thought of making a white woman a slave was beyond her comprehension.

"Especially white women, pretty and young white women," Richard added. "The sultans and sheikhs are always looking for white women to stock their harems."

"Harems?" Madeleine echoed.

"To be pleasure slaves," Richard grinned.

Madeleine wrinkled her nose at her cousin assuming he was teasing. "Plea‑sure slave? But what is…"

"Madeleine, I will explain it to you later," Denis cut in with a doting nod to his wife. Marie on the other hand understood and had no trouble imagining a woman being turned into a sex slave.

"Because the galleys are smaller," Brother Robert continued, uncomfortable with allowing the topic of pleasure slaves to continue, "and more maneuverable, they are good for military patrol. This they must be to catch the pirates. They do not depend upon the winds, you see, but can be powered solely by the oars."

"Galley ships do good?" Marie offered softly.

"Necessary work... yes, but..." Brother Robert hesitated, stroking his small goatee thoughtfully. "We have long used prisoners to row the oars, men who have already been sentenced to death. It is better to use them to some purpose rather than just execute them, *n'est-ce pas?*"

Marie nodded.

"But now innocent Huguenots are being marched to the galleys and it is almost an assured death sentence – and for no other crime than practicing their Faith or trying to leave the country." Brother Robert sighed deeply. "I must confess, I feared to just openly leave even if as a *pasteur* I had permission. I do not trust the authorities anymore and now I have stayed too long."

"And the women...?" Jacques-Jean asked, thinking of his mother.

Brother Robert lowered his eyes. "They are usually sent to prison."

Denis, fearful of frightening the women, spoke up to shift the focus. "I have grave concerns for our country's future, *mes amis*. What will happen when we have lost most of our skilled artisans, our merchants and tradesmen? What happens when only angry peasants and arrogant aristocrats remain?"

"There are exceptions, but most aristocrats would never dirty their hands with trade or markets," Jacques-Jean spoke calmly knowing his own father worked very hard to administer his lands.

"There are exceptions," Brother Robert agreed, "but most aristocrats do not even know how to dirty their hands. But if I were them I would be very concerned that there are so many more peasants throughout the land than aristocrats."

"But the peasants have no education," Richard interjected, "nor weapons."

"Or craftsmanship... or common sense," Denis nodded. "They are sheep."

"Sheep are followers, all they need is a leader," Jacques-Jean said pensively beginning to realize the threat. "And *Frère Robert* is right, they have the numbers."

"As I have traveled around," Brother Robert went on, "I have witnessed such hatred for the aristocracy. Oh, make no mistake, the peasants have been raised to love their king but they have no love for the extraordinary indulgences, the inordinate privileges, the haughtiness, cruelty, and waste within the aristocracy."

Jacques-Jean thought immediately of his uncle and nodded his head.

"As a Christian preacher, I must denounce hatred but I can understand the causes."

"We are losing the very heart of our merchant class," Denis ruminated sadly. "You know the countries they seek refuge in are more than happy to receive them. They bring their skills, they bring contacts, they bring whatever personal wealth they have. They are educated and learn their new language quickly. These are good, solid people, not beggars and dolts, and they are fellow Christians of like minds."

"You are right," agreed Brother Robert, "and France is made the poorer for losing them. These men who have surrounded our king, they have no idea the ruin they bring to our country. God in His Omnipotent wisdom sees and knows all. We are not the first Christians to be martyred for our Lord. Did not all of His disciples find their lives ending in martyrdom? Did not the Roman emperors throw Christians to the lions for sport? Was there not a time when the Holy Roman armies sought to eradicate our own true believers in the foothills of France hundreds of years ago? People who sought only to follow the teachings of Christ, simply and purely, and not submit to the dominance of Rome?

"France has been persecuting Huguenots for a hundred years now. It is nothing new. The Spanish have their Inquisition for which to answer; England's Bloody Mary allowed the air to fill with the stench of burning flesh. And France, too, will have its day of reckoning for its terrible sins."

Richard stifled a disgusted grunt. "When? When do the frogs and leeches, the toadies, debauchers, and sodomites get their just rewards? When do peace-loving citizens get back their rights?"

"In God's time, *mon frère*," responded Brother Robert. "In God's time. It is not for us to tell God, it is for us to be obedient to His will."

"To turn the other cheek?" Richard grunted, twisting impatiently in his chair.

"Our great God does not ask us to be doormats, *mon ami*. In the Old Testament we read how He readied many an army to fight in His name, but for now until God gives us direction we must do what is wise."

"And what is that?" Jacques-Jean asked quietly.

"We endure. We survive," Brother Robert responded mildly, the light of Christian love emanating from his eyes without rancor and without hypocrisy. "We are called to love our Lord God and our brothers, to set the example of Christian faith in our modern world. The Church of Rome has been a political creature from the very beginning but – it did spread Christianity. And be assured there are those even within its corrupted midst that act upon their own conscience."

They were all listening attentively.

"In the south," the preacher continued, "small enclaves of the faithful have run to the protection of the mountains and hills once again; refugees within their own country, they live in caves and meet in the forests to hear good preaching and pray for their own survival. And there is one, a Catholic priest, who demonstrates the true love of Christ in how he is helping these to survive. This priest doles out the official tokens to these faithful so if it is demanded as proof, they can appear to be good Catholics.

"Others have left Rome in their hearts, but keep up pretenses. Still others pretend to have converted but continue to hear God's true Word in secret."

"Madeleine and I must play this role but we do it to be able to provide aid to those who need to escape," added Denis.

"But how long before you are discovered, Cousin?" Richard asked, his brow dark with anger.

"I am in God's hands," the merchant replied simply with a shrug.

"But you are also risking your wife."
"We are both in God's hands, Cousin," Madeleine answered proudly, looking lovingly at her husband.

Brother Robert nodded.

Jacques-Jean grew quiet again and mulled over his thoughts long into the night. In the few short days since they had received notice of his impending arrest, he had grown closer to his faith and his God than in all the years of sitting dutifully in church sharing a pew box with his mother. It was strange but seeing those who risked their lives on a daily basis for their faith was a very powerful witness. In truth, he had lived a sheltered life and had taken much for granted before this. Now, something within him stirred an awakening and a desire to be a better man, not for the approval of other men but for the approval of God.

The next morning Richard was up before dawn and assisted Madeleine in removing all the coverings from the windows before she and Marie began breakfast. With no word of the shipment, Jacques-Jean and Denis invoked the ladies' help to make Brother Robert appear less like a preacher before the housemaid returned. In a flash of brilliance, Madeleine searched through a chest to uncover a waistcoat, gifted to Denis during his student days but only worn once. It was made of calico, printed over with pineapples and quite the ugliest thing any of them had ever seen.

They insisted Brother Robert shave his goatee and amidst gentle laughter he gave over his own cassock and waistcoat and put on the pineapples and an old periwig belonging to Denis. Pleased with the transformation, they sat to eat their breakfast and when Denis excused himself to attend to his daily business transactions, the others remained around the dining table to pass the time playing card games.

As the day worn on, Richard became inventive in initiating fictitious plans for "the family" to get together over the upcoming holidays and share Christmas in the country. Jacques-Jean caught on immediately and before long he and Richard were sharing made-up stories of mischief "when they were altar boys," and the small aggravations they had given the village priest. It all played very normally as the housemaid buzzed in and out doing her chores and inevitably overhearing a word here or there. There was nothing the least bit suspicious and thus they weathered through another day.

Later that night, Denis received the news for which they had all been waiting. The cargo raft had been loaded and could leave for the ship in the morning.

By the cold foggy light of dawn, Denis outfitted Jacques-Jean and Richard with the clothing of a merchant along with phony papers introducing them as agents representing the company. Marie took on the role of Jacques-Jean's ward and the four had no trouble boarding the raft at the river's edge which made its way to the port where the modest merchant ship, *Bonne Foi,* awaited.

Chapter 10

*B*onne Foi - "Good Faith." Jacques-Jean smiled even as he pulled his cassock more closely around him. It was so like the mild mannered little merchant he had come to know and respect to throw a double meaning into his ship's name.

Jacques-Jean stood in the freezing winds where he had come to escape the smells below deck. The sun was shining brightly but gave no warmth as the winds cut to the bone. They had been at sea for four weeks and the captain assured them they were making excellent time. Jacques-Jean watched the sails billow in the wind. It had a dizzying effect and he dropped his gaze to watch the ship's prow cut through the water with speed. Froths of bubbles created by the action were mesmerizing and kept his attention as he thought of the English words for what he was seeing. He did not as yet know but the English lessons he had hired for them from one of the crew were definitely paying off. He could identify most everything important in his sight with its English name.

The captain had estimated another four weeks before they reached their destination, three if their current speed held. Three weeks. If Jacques-Jean was any judge, Brother Robert did not have three more weeks unless something changed drastically.

They had each had a bout with *mal de mer* which they now knew in English as 'seasickness.' Richard had barely noticed. Marie had been ill for three days, Jacques-Jean for only two, before each had regained appetite and good spirits. But Brother Robert seemed unable to recover. He grew weaker with each day. Marie spent much time watching over him and managed to coax just enough water, broth, and warm tea down his throat to keep him alive but try as she might, what little food she could get him to swallow he retched up again costing him more in the effort and energy than he gained. For Marie it was like watching Anoui all over again and she was growing very anxious.

Richard arrived to take a shift to relieve her and insisted she go on deck and stretch her legs. She looked at Richard helplessly but with gratitude. He was right. She needed fresh air. Taking the blanket from her bunk she made her way down the tight corridor and up the narrow steps.

On deck, she shook the blanket fiercely hoping to evict any lice or fleas which might have taken up residence. Wrapping the blanket around her against the frigid winds, she spied Jacques-Jean and walked toward him. He saw her and met her half way. They both had adapted to the rhythmic roll of the deck just as they had come to accept the cold winds of the northern Atlantic ocean.

"When was the last time you ate?" he asked.

She shook her head and shrugged. "Yesterday." Her teeth began to chatter and she sought a corner out of the wind amidst the crated cargo on deck.

"And it is now passed high noon."

"I have no appetite, m'lord. Perhaps the fresh air will help." Being cramped in tight quarters below with Brother Robert in his illness did not promote a desire to eat.

"Stay here," Jacques-Jean said sternly and strode away. When he returned he carried a hot bowl of stew and a tankard of hot tea. Marie smiled her appreciation and accepted them with thanks. The crates setting on deck were lashed together securely and served as crude seating and table tops. Marie set the bowl down and sipped at the tea. Staying out of the wind but in the sun was comfortable enough and before long she found her appetite returning.

Jacques-Jean let her eat without interruption. When she finished he asked, "So how is *Frère Robert* doing today? Any improvement at all?"

She shrugged and shook her head. "I wish there was something more I could do. It breaks my heart to see how thin he has become."

Jacques-Jean had already been to the ship's captain. They had no doctor on board and the ship's cook was only good at stitching up lacerations, setting broken bones, and making poultices for strained muscles. A merchant ship with a crew of seasoned seaman had no need for seasickness remedies. The captain could only suggest that they pray.

"We *can* pray," Jacques-Jean replied and realized he meant it. "Let us pray together, Marie, for God's intervention. Surely God does not have need of *Frère Robert* in Heaven at this time, perhaps if we tell Him how much Robert is still needed here..."

Marie said nothing.

"What is it?"

Looking sheepish and uncomfortable Marie muttered, "It is... I mean... perhaps I better not."

"Why? What is wrong?"

"I do not know how, m'lord. I am no good at praying. I begged God not to take my sister, I begged him not to take Anoui. God does not listen to me."

"Do you not remember what *Frère Robert* said when we were in Paris? God hears all prayers including yours. But sometimes He has His own reasons for not doing what we want. But now, what possible reason could the Good Lord have for taking *Frère Robert*? If we ask Him sincerely, surely He will consider our request, yes?"

"He will listen to you perhaps, m'lord, but not to me."

"Nonsense! That is a foolish thing to say and I have never taken you for a fool, Marie. I am no preacher but I know in my heart that if there is a God, and I do believe there is, then He hears all prayers. And perhaps He is even a little more attentive to the sincere, earnest prayers of the humble who do not think they can pray. What makes you think you are anything less in His eyes than… than, well, than I am for example?"

Marie's head shot up to look him in the eyes. She did not see jest or mockery. He was serious yet to her the answer was so obvious it was painful.

"Mademoiselle Celimene said she told you about how things were at the tavern."

"Yes."

"Then you know why," she said dully.

Jacques-Jean wished desperately that he knew what Brother Robert would say in response to this. The poor child saw the degradation forced upon her as evil in her own character. That was so wrong.

"Marie, I have heard it said often - no matter what you have done if you are truly repentant, God forgives you and gives you a clean slate. To pray for another is a good thing and God will love you for it. Do you think you must be perfect to follow Christ? No one is perfect. In the Bible everyone who followed Christ had his imperfections."

Marie looked up, her expression teetering between doubt and a desire to believe.

"But the real message is forgiveness. We are forgiven when we accept Christ. Now please, will you come and join me in prayer over *Frère Robert*? For are we not told *where two or three are gathered together in my name, there shall I be?*"

Marie had no idea what the Bible told them but reluctantly she followed.

Richard stood when Marie and Jacques-Jean arrived below deck and backed away to allow them closer to the ailing man. "I washed him a little," Richard volunteered, "but I doubt that he can hear us. I am afraid it is only a matter of…"

"Richard, *mon ami*, join us in prayer," Jacques-Jean invited earnestly.

The larger man shook his head and withdrew. "There is no room," he muttered and left.

It was an excuse. Richard saw no point. Brother Robert was better off going to his rewards in Heaven. He lived in a world where he was being hunted for nothing more than a refusal to pray to saints and bend to the will of Rome. What would such a mild mannered fellow do in the New World, anyway? He spoke against the sword and pistol. How would one survive in the New World without the sword and pistol? One could not even defend against the savage beasts. Richard snorted to himself. Robert was a dreamer, a good man but a dreamer; was it not better he should die here, mused Richard, and be buried neatly at sea? Better than to perhaps be torn limb from limb by the jaws of some fanged beast and have his bones scattered to the four corners?

Down in the tiny cabin, Jacques-Jean and Marie spent more than an hour praying earnestly on their knees at the bunk of Brother Robert. He made no movement and they could barely detect his breathing. Suddenly, he opened his eyes and in a voice barely audible he asked for water.

"What did he say?" Marie gasped.

"Water! He wants water," Jacques-Jean replied with excitement.

"Here, here," Marie held a cup to the lips of the ill man.

He sipped and it stayed down. He drank a bit more and cleared his throat. In a hoarse whisper he next asked for broth.

Jacques-Jean and Marie looked at each other and neither could help but smile broadly.

"I will get it," Jacques-Jean responded and was gone before Marie could reply. A repeated litany was running through her head. *Thank you God, thank you God, thank you God.* Her mind cried it out over and over again.

Jacques-Jean returned with the broth. Marie held it, making certain it would not burn the pastor. She gently fed it to him.

"I feel better, praise God," Brother Robert reassured them with a shaky smile as he croaked out the words. The perpetual nausea had indeed disappeared and he felt hunger for the first time in four weeks.

Marie began to weep tears of relief. It was a small miracle. God had heard their prayers. He really had and He had answered them. He did watch over them. He did. It was a miracle.

Two days later with Jacques-Jean's assistance, Brother Robert joined them on deck both for the exercise and for the fresh air. Wobbling and feeble but very determined, he sat down to feel the warmth of the sun seep through his all too sparse flesh and into his bones. He took in lungs full of the clean air which had warmed in a streak of fair weather while Marie and Richard worked to scrub and scour his bunk below deck.

When they brought his mattress topside to air-out in the sunlight, the Captain gave them fresh sheets from his own stores, saying it had been the worst case of *mal de mer* he had ever witnessed. "Last week I would not have bet a sou for his survival," he said and ordered the fouled linens collected and boiled by the cook before being hung up to dry.

"God heard our prayers," Marie said exuberantly, smiling broadly at the gentle preacher. He nodded in acknowledgment.

"Thank you for those prayers," he replied softly. "It appears God still has work for me to do in this world."

Jacques-Jean said nothing but he too felt the preacher was meant to fulfill some further purpose.

Only Richard felt the man would have survived anyway. It was a flip of the coin, he shrugged, one way you lived, the other you died. Brother Robert's coin simply had come up this time in favor of survival but these thoughts Richard kept to himself.

Two Sundays later, Brother Robert led a worship service on the main deck. They had been at sea for many weeks and sailors are a superstitious lot. The survival of the man they now knew to be a Huguenot preacher was for many nothing short of a miracle, a sign from God, and they listened to his words with grave attention.

"We are told the wages of sin is death," said the soft spoken man from his platform. "Let us remember it was the Father of All Lies who told Eve as he tempted her in the Garden – *thou shall not die.* But what had God said?" He paused and looked over the gathering: the sailors, the Captain, his cabin boy and the trio of traveling companions who had nursed him through his illness. "God had told Adam and Eve not to eat of the fruit for if they did they surely WOULD die. And it was the sin of this disobedience that first separated man from his Creator and they lost their perfect bodies and began dying from that very moment.

"Satan has always lied and we, it would seem, have always had a proclivity for a sinful, disobedient nature. From birth our feet are set upon a path which if left to our own devices will lead us to spiritual death and the ultimate emptiness of separation from our Heavenly Father."

Brother Robert paused while looking out at the eyes focused upon him in fearful attention. "But the Gift of God is life everlasting!" He smiled. "He loves us. We can rejoice that God so loved the world He sent his only begotten son, that whosoever should believe upon Him shall not perish but have … Life … Life everlasting. Whosoever! Who-so-ever – that is what God says right here in His book." He brandished the Bible written not in Latin but in French. "Whosoever! It matters not how many sins you are guilty of… we all are guilty, my brothers. We all stink of sin. It does not say only if you buy indulgences from Rome. It does not say only if you confess to a priest. And nowhere here does it say that a priest can forgive you of your sins. No! Only God can forgive sin. It says whosoever confesses, repents, accepts, and loves the Lord Jesus Christ, the son of the living God, the Perfect Lamb without blemish who was the sacrifice for our sin… only the penitent believer shall be forgiven. He who was without sin took all the sins for all of us - past, present and future. We need only accept Him with a repentant heart, confess our belief in Him and be baptized in His name. Do this and you become a new creature in Jesus Christ, washed clean in the blessed Blood of the Lamb, your sins forgiven by God alone and blotted out. Blotted out forever. Have you accepted God's great gift to ensure your life everlasting?"

The crowd on deck was mesmerized, held speechless in the wake of Brother Robert's powerful address. Crusty sea dogs discovered their cheeks wet with tears.

"Who wants to repent, accept God's gift of life everlasting and be baptized today? Who wants to acknowledge before this company that Jesus the Christ is his Lord?" Brother Robert cried out and nearly a dozen sailors, which was most of the crew, came forward.

Marie also moved forward. She wanted the Gift. She wanted very much to be a new creature; she wanted to be pure and washed clean of her degradations. She wanted to know she was forgiven for all her sins. She wanted to know she was saved through the Savior, the Lord Jesus. Tears of repentant joy streamed down her cheeks.

A few minutes later, they made a curious sight in an impromptu ceremony. Battered, scarred, and tattooed sailors, the cherub-faced cabin boy and one young girl, all kneeling humbly before a cross. One by one a full bucket of fresh sea water was poured slowly over each penitent head as they publicly proclaimed for the Christ.

Marie was the last and instantly she began to shiver fiercely. Jacques-Jean had a blanket at hand and wrapped it around her at once.

"I am now a new creature?" she asked with a huge happy smile.

"Yes," he nodded, smiling back. "A new creature who needs to change her clothes immediately."

"I am a new creature," she said excitedly to Richard who nodded. "I am a new creature!"

"A much more spectacular baptism than mine," Richard added.

"W...what was yours like?"

"I do not remember, I was a baby in my mother's arms. Now go, you are turning to ice. Change your clothes."

"Yes, yes. I go," Marie fairly danced away, hugging the blanket around her. "I am washed clean by the Blood of the Lamb!" she cried out happily and disappeared below.

In the years to come, Jacques-Jean would look back at his escape from France as something divinely orchestrated. They had been so extraordinarily fortunate. From the very first – receiving warning from an old family friend who never even went to court anymore, slipping between the very fingers of the soldiers-at-arms while hiding quite literally right in front of them under a woman's skirts, riding undetected through the open countryside to Paris, being sheltered by Dufee and making it safely onto his ship. It was nothing short of miraculous.

And being thrown together with Brother Robert? This too had been a gift, a blessing. Jacques-Jean the blasé young nobleman had become Jacques the man who had grown stronger in his faith.

For the rest of their voyage, Brother Robert held daily Bible studies for anyone interested but especially for the new converts while fair winds carried them onward without further incident until one day they all heard the cry: "Land ho!!"

Rushing as quickly as each was able aboard the cramped ship, Jacques-Jean, Richard, Marie, and Brother Robert stood together at the rail squinting out over the gray-blue sea until upon the horizon they saw for themselves the faint dark shadowing of land. It was their first glimpse of the New World and the new life that awaited them.

Chapter 11

I n time Marie could look back upon her arrival in the New World with the realization of how very naive she had been. But, if she had truly known what it was really going to be like, it is entirely possible that she might not have had the courage to leave France. God does us a kindness not letting us see the future.

Late in the year of 1685, however, Marie was not yet quite fifteen and she boldly faced the unknown. She did not know exactly what she had expected. A strange land, she had heard. Savages, she had heard, and wild animals and wilderness. It was all rather vague. What she first beheld, after weeks and weeks of open seas, was forest... more forest than she could ever have believed possible if she had not seen it with her own two eyes.

Her first sightings of the New World as they sailed along the coastline were of dark green, tall, giant evergreens, stretching for miles and miles, mixed with the lighter, bushy brown, leafless deciduous forests that had lost all their leaves for the winter. Trees and more trees... so dense in their growth there seemed no room to push oneself onto the shore.

As the merchant ship sailed onward into a large harbor, Marie next saw the heart of their new world. The harbor was home to several large islands just off the coast of the mainland but Marie had no idea they were islands. One, called *Man-a-hat-ta* or "Island of the Hills," by the natives had a settlement with a permanent population of scarcely more than 1000 people. This was rather small even by New World standards for a colony boasting a settlement history over half a century long. But people seemed to move on or die almost as quickly as they landed.

The town, called "New Amsterdam" by its original Dutch settlers, represented part of the only toe-hold the Netherlands had gained on the continent. To the north, the Puritans and Pilgrims had been storming the coasts of the Massachusetts and Rhode Island colonies by the shipload driven by the winds of religious zeal in flight from persecution. Although England had broken with Rome generations before, the Church of England was still essentially catholic and far too filled with idols and papist reminders to suit the Puritans.

To the south, despite marshy conditions, Jamestown, the colony of Virginia enticed a smaller but steady supply of newcomers with the promise of great wealth from tobacco trade. Just as, despite the heat, the Carolinas also grew. But the Dutch for the most part remained content to stay at home in Europe being neither persecuted nor goaded with the promise of riches from a fast cash crop. They prospered and remained a small nation of merchants, content with establishing shipping lines and trading agreements to support their lucrative dealings in commerce amongst all countries.

The colony struggled and New Amsterdam remained sparsely settled with an eclectic gathering of Europeans who seemed to feel more at home there than anywhere else. In negotiations to end a war with the Netherlands, England gained possession of the territory and it subsequently became the property of the king's brother, the Duke of York, who put it into the hands of his Lords Proprietors. The New Netherlands territory was split and renamed New York and New Jersey. The settlement of New Amsterdam became New York Towne, Breuckelen across the river to the east was now Brooklyn, Haarlem to the north was anglicized to Harlem, Hellegat became Hell Gate, and new political appointees made their presence known.

Where there are politics, there is undoubtedly corruption, and where there is corruption, there is money to be made and power to be gained and an established ladder by which one might climb upward. In New York the rungs of the ladder included being politically astute, being active in the right church, and being wise or fortunate enough to have married the right wife. Suddenly, huge land patents were being bestowed up and down the Hudson River and history would say of the royal governor, Benjamin Fletcher, that he made New York a safe haven for pirates in exchange for a percentage of their profits.

It is during these next decades that much of the "old money" of New York will be somewhat scurrilously accrued and incubated. Marie was innocent of such insights, however, as she stood gazing fixedly from the deck of the *Bonne Foi* toward land. She knew nothing of backroom political wheeling and dealing, outrageous land grants, or the developing inner power structure of corruption. She knew only what she saw.

And what she saw beyond a gathering of ships in the harbor under a myriad of different flags was the tip of a large land mass which had been stripped of all its trees and stood instead covered by the works of man. The primeval forest had been carved away, felled first to build the fort and stockade, then houses and barns. Lumber continued to be harvested as the demand progressed. It took lumber to build all the carts and wagons, docks and warehouses. And wood was the settlement's only source of fuel. But the heaviest demand put upon the forest was the demand for exporting lumber to the Old World, a world that had felled many of its forests generations earlier.

On the western side was a large river named the Hudson after one Henry Hudson, an Englishman, navigator and explorer, who was funded by the Dutch and who unsuccessfully searched for a northwest passage to Asia during the early part of the century. The river flowed from the north into the harbor and rising high above the rooftops was a large windmill, a leftover from the Dutch. The evenly laid out, straight dirt streets also reflected the meticulous Dutch whom the Puritans accused of keeping cleaner homes than bodies and cleaner bodies than souls.

Lining the streets nearest the waterfront were rows of buildings built next to each other sharing a common wall between them in European row-house style. Marie thought the architecture very odd however, unlike anything she had seen in her native land.

Neighborhoods comprised of individual houses, each sitting in the middle of their own little plot of land, had developed farther away from the waterfront. Kitchen gardens filled with vegetables and herbs each season were a very important part of these homes. On the east another river ran into the harbor. And still farther to the north running along the river fronts were neatly divided lots for cultivation, now that all the trees had been taken, and one could spot the occasional farmhouse. But the soil was relatively thin and bedrock loomed close to the surface. It was not a farmer's paradise even when the Indians ceased terrorizing the settlers on the frontier of Harlem.

The old fort, such as it was, still stood on the southern tip of the island. With only a small handful of soldiers in residence and cows grazing on the ramparts, it did not look particularly imposing. Many dwellings extended far beyond its protection and a twelve foot high wall to the north of the settlement had been constructed at least twenty-five years earlier to protect against Indian attack. The Indians had been quite peaceful for some time and for the moment at least, the French and English were not at war.

The four traveling companions had slept safely on board ship the night before, ate a hurried breakfast together at dawn, and agreed to meet back at the fort's southern most tip before sunset that evening to share information. Marie had no intention of tagging along on the men's coat tails any longer. She did not want nor did she expect them to feel responsible for her. She had begged to come along to make her own way. Only now, with the ship scheduled to remain in the harbor only a few more nights, this new world was becoming a most formidable place.

The morning mists had not yet burned away when Marie first set out to explore but the quay was already teeming with activity. She pulled her shawls more closely around her slender shoulders against the crispness in the air blowing off the water and made her way down the gangplank. As she stepped onto firm ground she was startled and surprised to feel the earth moving beneath her feet. She swayed and lurched and Richard laughed as he caught her.

"It is called *getting your land legs back*, eh? Do not worry, just take care. You have to adjust to being off the sea now. I feel the same," he laughed as he swayed.

"Oh. It is so strange, like we are on the water still." She giggled and clung for a moment to Richard's arm.

"After being on shipboard for weeks, we must again learn to walk only this time without the roll of the ocean."

"Will you be all right?" Jacques-Jean asked as he joined them and felt the strange phantom roll and tilt for himself.

"Yes-yes. I just did not expect it." She laughed as she went off trying not to stagger.

Marie progressed along the waterfront amazed at the number of different tongues she heard. Wasting no time during their voyage, she had joined the men in taking English lessons from one of the crew. Jacques-Jean was the only one of the four who had had a rudimentary knowledge of English learned from his boyhood tutor, but his tutor had not been well versed himself.

Marie occasionally heard a word that she thought she recognized but nothing really made any sense. The shouts and orders and conversations around her made everything that much more confusing, distracting, and noisy.

Everywhere she looked everyone seemed to be in a hurry. It was not a pace she had grown up with in the French countryside. Carts and wagons carrying goods, barrels, lumber, and crates filled the streets. Horses, mules, and oxen dragged sleds, drays, and litters piled high with animal skins and barrels. Brawny men carried sacks and bales on their backs while others pushed hand carts and wheelbarrows. The goods being unloaded from the harbor full of ships would undoubtedly be sold in the shops and taverns of the town. And mostly lumber, pitch, tars, resins, skins and furs were being loaded on board the vessels for the trip back home.

Marie walked slowly, still swaying a bit and dodging men, mud, wagons and animals while getting bumped or shouted at more than once. It all reminded her of the time she had watched an anthill, the workers moving, moving, moving, never stopping to rest, never straying from their path.

Finally, bewildered and confused, she turned away from the waterfront and continued to make her way along the inland streets which were a bit quieter and strangely straight, squaring up the groups of buildings and household gardens. There was little change in the traffic of those streets however. Everywhere people hurried, walking, riding, shouting, talking, yelling, arguing, whispering, laughing, but to Marie it was all just babble.

When her stomach began to growl, she realized it must be close to midday although the sun remained hidden in an overcast sky. It was time to find something to eat. She found herself once again along the riverfront but on the side of town farthest from the old fort. She approached what she judged to be a tavern by the huge wooden sign swinging from the main beam projecting several feet out into the street. On it was a large, horned bull painted upon what was at one time a background of deep sea blue but which had now faded from sun and weather. The bull stood on two feet and held a tankard of ale in one hoofed paw and a pipe in the other. She didn't especially like the looks of the place but looking around and not seeing any other signs for food or drink, she decided to go inside.

Marie felt all eyes turn upon her as she walked into the establishment. In seconds she realized to her complete dismay that she was the only woman within the dark gloomy walls. It was warm and smoky and she flushed slightly feeling a fine sweat break out over her body. It did not help, she thought, that she undoubtedly appeared to have been drinking spirits as she could not help but stagger a little.

"What kin I do fer ya?" a man with a patch over one eye asked in a rough low voice, so coarse there was a deep vibrato to every word. She approached the counter he stood behind. Marie was suddenly reminded of Bouchet and her knees went weak. For a few long moments her mind was completely blank of all English. She found her tongue and laboriously began to stumble over her words as she asked if she might have a drink of water.

"Water?" he snorted in disgust, "I ain't in business t'be givin' out water to no Frenchies; now why don't you get your little arse back up north where ya belong?"

Marie did not understand him but realized from his tone that he was not inclined to be friendly. She began stumbling between English and French.

"*Pardonnez moi*...par-don mee...excuse, pleez...*je ne comprends pas*... *le pain, pain*... ahhh...bread...*avez-vous*... have you bread, pleez, monsieur."

"Ya got money, Frenchie?" the man asked, squinting at her with his good eye and rubbing his extended fingers and thumb together.

"*Oui, oui*...." she replied, fishing her small purse from her pocket and holding it up.

"How much bread ya want?"

Marie stopped for a moment to consider the meaning of his words. She could not think of how to say "half a loaf" in English so she put up one finger and gestured to cut it in two.

"Whole thing or nothing," he said, just to be difficult.

Marie nodded and gave him a coin.

"What's this?" he snarled, looking at the French coin. "Damn French shit!"

"Iz goud," she assured him and took the bread he thrust at her. Marie expected to receive change back. "Money, pleez?"

"That's it. I don't make change on no French coin."

"Iz too much!" she exclaimed in disbelief.

"Ya want the bread or not?" he snarled.

"... water?" Marie asserted.

"There's a well at the end of the street," he shrugged and stared at her indolently. She could feel her cheeks burning in anger. She turned quickly, grabbing an empty chair back to steady herself as she went.

Marie was so relieved to be outside again, she did not notice the two men lounging just within the alley running along side the tavern. They had been inside and had left just before her. She was momentarily occupied with the act of tearing off a piece of the loaf she carried and had just put it into her mouth when she felt herself being half-dragged and half-lifted into the alley behind a cart full of barrels.

What happened in the next few seconds took place so quickly, Marie remembered it later as a blur. She felt a huge hand wrap over her mouth which was still full of bread. Instinctively, she clutched her purse tightly but it was torn from her grip. She felt hands under her skirts, grabbing her legs and groping her flesh between them. Dropping her loaf on the ground, she kicked out wildly making solid contact with one man's groin while reaching back and raking her fingernails over the other man's face. Amidst curses, she wretch her head free, spit out the bread and bit down hard when the hand came back at her. She felt the hold on her loosen for only a second but it was enough for her to break away. She began screaming and ran for the open street. A few people turned to look and the two nefarious characters took off at a run in the opposite direction, disappearing between the buildings.

Marie stopped screaming and started to cry. Hot tears of anger, shame, frustration, and indignation blurred her vision. Her bread had been smashed into the mud of the alley, her small purse was gone, she could still feel the rough hands on the flesh beneath her skirts, and her clean linen collar was soiled and torn. She had been insulted, robbed, and almost raped, and she had not been in this new world but half a day!

After a moment of uncontrolled panic, Marie wiped fiercely at her tears and pulled herself together as people passed by her giving her curious and odd glances. She was ashamed but glad for the anonymity of the crowd. Darting swiftly along the street, she realizing the people she now saw neither knew nor cared of her undignified assault. She walked numbly back to the ship. Within the safety of her tiny bunk she hid away awaiting the coming of late afternoon and tacked another collar on her frock with needle and thread.

When Marie met with her traveling companions in the late afternoon, she pretended she had had a pleasant enough day. In reality her head was throbbing from the incident which had brought her experiences with Bouchet back to her so clearly she was still trying not to tremble. And her belly was turned in upon itself from hunger. She was thankful when her companions insisted she join them for supper.

Brother Robert was eager to share his news as soon as he had said a blessing over their table. "I have found a small church," he beamed, "and they are in need of an assistant for the pastor. It is perfect for now. They cannot pay me but I will have food and shelter... and a chance to improve my *anglais.*" He chuckled, "Pardon, mee, I must speak theez now," he forced himself to begin speaking in English.

"Bon." Richard nodded and caught himself as well. "Goud. Goud for you. It takes no so long, eh? You....you....ehhh, queeek, huh? Fast to learn, eh?"

"God...He lead," Brother Robert grinned pointing upward. "And yoo?"

Richard shrugged

Jacques-Jean listened politely. He and Richard had not made any significant discoveries but he could not help but notice how unusually quiet and subdued little Marie was. She was withdrawn, preoccupied, and distracted. He attributed it to her confessed headache and exhaustion which also explained why she begged an early end to her evening so she could retire behind the curtains of her berth on board ship.

The next morning, Marie was late in rising and came into the ship's galley only after Jacques-Jean called at the curtain of her bunk before he went on deck. When she appeared her hair was neatly combed and tucked under her cap but she looked pale.

"Goud morning," he said in exaggerated English.

"Goud morning, m'lord," she echoed weakly.

"Hurry, sleepy head," he added teasingly in French and she smiled only faintly as she quickly downed a cup of strong, black tea.

"It is time we left," Richard said unceremoniously and lumbered over to the gangplank. Jacques-Jean followed and turned to offer Marie a hand as she stepped up onto the exit ramp. The breeze was brisk and the air frosty and in the early light of morning, he could see her face more clearly. She was avoiding his eyes and he thought she looked tense and uneasy. Richard was already across the gangplank and on the wharf.

"Is anything wrong?" Jacques-Jean asked quietly, his calm gray eyes studying her.

"No, m'lord," she answered a bit too quickly.

"Are you certain?"

"Of course, m'lord," she assured him. The last thing she wanted was for him to think her incapable of taking care of herself. She managed a real smile and forced herself to leave the familiarity of the ship.

"Are we to meet again at the fort corner?" she asked a little too brightly.

He nodded. At that moment the ship's captain appeared on deck and stood at the railing looking down at them.

"*Bon jour!*" the captain spoke and gave a wave at the trio. He was a God fearing man who tried to avoid the politics which kept so many people on land agitated. He received his instructions from his employer, the Dufees, which often included taking on extra passengers like this foursome. He did not ask why, nor was he told, but he suspected. And he had found the three extremely easy passengers. They had been like many before them, appreciative and undemanding. The fourth, whom they called *Frère Robert,* had been taken so ill, the captain thought for certain they would lose him but the girl had pulled the unfortunate man through. And their reasons for leaving home were none of his business. "Just wanted to remind you that we cast off day after tomorrow," he called down to them. "Space at the docks is at a premium; we must drop anchor farther out if we must wait on further business." And when they nodded that they understood he turned to go on about his duties.

Jacques-Jean watched Marie go on her way clutching her shawls against the wind and avoiding the mud of the street. He wondered if that was what was disturbing her. In two more nights she would lose her shelter and needed to find a position quickly. He knew it was none of his concern, but still he felt paternalistic toward the girl. She had been one of his servants in a manner of speaking and she was a daughter of France and only a very young girl, defenseless in a strange new environment. She had shown an amazing amount of pluck on their escape but had she really realized what she was getting herself into? Perhaps regret was setting in and the fears of being in such a foreign place were growing. Just because he could not go to New France did not mean that she could not. She might be better off there with their countrymen. Jacques-Jean made a mental note to keep an eye out for anything that might be helpful to her. He realized she had very little means to support herself although he had no idea just how little since she had been robbed. He said nothing of his thoughts as he fell in along side Richard walking in a new direction but he made another mental note to offer her the opportunity to go on to New France. He decided he would pay her passage if she decided to leave.

Steering clear of the section of town where she had been attacked, Marie continued to explore the streets but in a wary, agitated mood. The captain's warning had only served to underline her growing sense of anxiety. She had been a fool to take so much of her tiny savings out with her, she chided herself. With her purse stolen, she had only the coins which she had left knotted into a handkerchief back at the ship. She could not afford to rent a room now. And she would not beg from Monsieur. She simply had to find work.

After almost two hours of wandering Marie chanced to hear the soft, melodious sounds of her native tongue being spoken quietly... somewhere. Her eyes raked over the scene around her. It was a woman's voice. She heard it again. She saw a woman. No, that woman was calling to someone and the sounds coming from her throat meant nothing to Marie. She turned slowly where she stood, listening intently. She heard it again. There. She saw two women, standing closely together. One dressed very well in silks, the other, more coarsely attired, was, perhaps, her servant.

"*Pardonnez-moi, madame,*" Marie approached them with a warm smile while speaking softly in French. "I beg you to forgive my intrusion but I could not help but overhear that you were speaking my language. I am newly arrived..."

"Who are you?" the woman in silk interrupted and demanded brusquely.

"My name is Marie, m'lady. I have just arrived by ship and I do not know any..."

"What do you want of me?" interrupted the woman, her brow knit into a frown.

"Please, I only wish a little information..."

"I have nothing to say to you. Go away!" the woman said curtly and moved swiftly through the gate of a tall garden wall. The other woman, a bit older, much stouter and in plainer dress remained still, looking at Marie. She seemed to be hesitating, not certain what to do.

"Aggie!" came the call from behind the garden wall. "Aggie, come in at once!"

The woman hesitated a moment more and then quickly whispered to Marie. "Wait here. I will return." She disappeared through the garden gate.

Nodding a quick agreement, Marie found herself alone again. She stood in front of the garden wall. It was too tall to see over. Leaning her back against it, it did afford some shelter from the cold wind and it was warmed by the sun which was now shining brightly.

Marie continued to watch the people passing by in the street before her. Strange looking people, oddly dressed, so different in appearance from the people back home. *Home,* she mused to herself and told herself that *this* was now her home.

Oh, Marie, what have you done coming to this strange land where no one wants to speak to you and you can understand nothing? What have you done to yourself this time? You are not just a couple valleys away, now. No, this time you are a far, wide ocean away from everything you knew and you have no way to return even if Mistress Celimene would have you back.

The minutes passed slowly. With every sound she looked to see if the gate was opening. She began to wonder if the woman had been jesting with her or perhaps, once inside, had forgotten all about her. Had her mistress forbidden her to come back out? Marie could not understand why the first woman had been so unfriendly. It was true that she was only a poor stranger of no importance, but any stranger deserves the courtesy of a few simple answers.

With each passing moment, Marie questioned the wisdom of continuing to stand outside the wall like a statue waiting for a woman who may have completely forgotten her. Time was very precious. By tomorrow she must have someplace to go for the ship would be gone. How would she ever find a place if she kept waiting here doing nothing? But, she told herself, she had passed half the morning and these were the first people she had found who could even speak to her in her own tongue. She must wait, at least a while longer. The older woman had seemed kind; surely she would not tell Marie to wait just to leave her standing. And the woman had told her to wait. Marie remembered that very clearly. No one would tell someone to wait and then just forget about them, not even in this new world. Would they?

It was perhaps thirty minutes before the garden gate opened again and the woman, Aggie, stepped out. Thrusting a small napkin full of bread at Marie, she said not unkindly, "Here, take this."

"*Merci*, but you misunderstand," Marie said proudly. "I am not a beggar. I do not need food. I need only to speak with someone who can understand me."

The woman looked at her. "Oh, *je regrette...* I thought... I did not mean to insult you. Please, keep it anyway."

"*Merci*," Marie replied gratefully. "What I was trying to say before - I just arrived by ship two nights ago. I have been walking all along the waterfront... I hear people speaking every language in the world except my own. You were the first.

Whose house is this?"

"This is Monsieur Gerard's home. That was Madame Gerard. My name is Aggie," the woman replied in a perfunctory manner.

"You do not know how good it is just to hear you speak words I can understand," Marie sighed.

"You speak only French?" Aggie looked at her critically.

"I have been trying to learn *anglais* on board the ship but I have heard very little of it on the waterfront."

"*Oui*, the waterfront has many strangers, many speaking strange tongues from places all over the world. In the heart of the town, however, you will find much English, even the Dutch now speak English. Best that you learn it very quickly," Aggie warned. "To be French here is not the most popular thing. At the moment, to speak French is frowned upon."

"Why is that?"

"Do you know nothing? Do the French and English have such great love for each other? This is an English colony, *n'est-ce pas*? Do you think they have great love for us? No," she answered herself a bit imperiously. "There is always fighting between the French to the north and the English settlements. If you wish to remain here you must try to speak only *anglais*. To speak French is to invite suspicion and even hatred."

"I had no idea," Marie said softly trying to comprehend the situation. "Is that why your mistress was so...?" Marie did not wish to speak ill of the woman and did not know how to finish her question but Aggie understood. Madame Gerard had been very rude.

Aggie nodded her head not expecting the girl to finish. "Madame Gerard's husband has instructed her to speak only *anglais* outside of the house. But our *anglais* is not very good, you see. My *anglais* is terrible," she giggled slightly, causing her eyes to crease shut. "It is easier for us to speak together in French, and you caught us but... she could not continue speaking to you," the woman explained.

"I do not wish to make any trouble for you."

"No trouble... I am not Monsieur Gerard's wife," the servant woman smiled. "Are you looking for work? Perhaps I could speak to the mistress. Good servants are not easy to find."

"What kind of work?" Marie asked cautiously.

"As a house servant, of course."

"*Merci*... but," she hesitated, "if I wanted to be a house servant, I could have stayed in a very nice position in France."

"Why did you leave?"

"I wanted something more... something better." Marie didn't wish to offend her new acquaintance but how could she explain to her that the last thing she wanted was to be swallowed up into a French speaking household with little or no opportunity to learn English or to get out and meet people and learn her way around this new English land.

"And you think you will find it here?" the woman gave a short snorting grunt. "I hope you are not too greatly disappointed or you have risked coming a very long way for no reason," she added sourly. Seeing how her words stung the stranger, she continued more gently. "Ahh, well, there is always work and not many women here to do it. What skills do you have?"

"I can cipher," replied Marie. "I used to work in a tavern doing... well, almost everything that needed to be done. Are there any merchants here who speak some French? I will learn *anglais*, most certainly, but I do think I will need a little help."

Aggie thought for a moment.

"Follow this street," she gestured, "until you come to the canal. Turn northward and you will come to a bridge across the canal. Cross the bridge and continue along that side of the canal. You will come to an inn called The Pork 'n' Porridge. I have heard the master speak well of it. You could try there."

"Oh, *merci*," Marie replied, almost ecstatic at finally receiving one friendly suggestion. "*Merci beaucoup.*"

The older woman nodded her acceptance of the thanks. "If things do not work out, come back and I will see what I can do," she added. "Better a house servant than to sleep in the streets."

"You are very kind. *Merci*." And with that Marie hurried on her way and Aggie slipped back behind the garden walls.

As Marie walked in the direction to which she had been pointed, she took on the pace of the streets. She now had someplace to go, a destination, and she, too, wished to waste no time. She concentrated to remember the sounds of the English words, The Pork 'n' Porridge, and repeated them to herself under her breath as she went along.

"Zee Pooork'n'pourraghhh, zee pooork'n' pourraaghh..."

After she came to the canal she looked for the bridge. She saw one and crossed over but looking up the street along the canal she saw nothing to indicate an inn. Mustering up her courage she tapped a mild looking stranger on the arm and said in her best English, "Pardon me... zee Por kin porraaage... pleez, where?

"What's that, ye say, missy?" was the reply from a middle-aged man with a soft brogue. He wore a homespun shirt and breeches with cotton knit stockings, and a well-worn leather apron and he was in the midst of supervising the unloading of a wagon.

"Where zee Por kin porraage?... I look," repeated Marie with an ingratiating smile.

"Ye be lookin' for The Pork 'n' Porridge, ye say?" he repeated.

Marie nodded her head quickly in recognition.

"Keep on this street," he gestured, "until you hit the next, turn and follow it to the Grand Highway, then it's just around the corner... look for the sign."

Marie had no idea what he had just said.

"Sign," he repeated. "Sign? Can ye read? Do ye know what a sign be?" Marie continued to look at him blankly.

"Oh, Jumpin' Jupiter... I need a piece of foolscap," he muttered to himself. "Michael!" he yelled to a husky young lad carrying goods into the shop. "Fetch me a slip of foolscap and something to write with..." The stranger turned back to study Marie. "Where in the world did ye come from, lass? How did ye git here? A bonnie lassie like you, all alone, so far from home... and no one to be lookin' after ye? Ye be like a little lamb set out in a world of wolves," he shook his head as he muttered, "and there be wolves a plenty 'round here. Just a lamb among wolves to be sure. I wouldna be lettin' my own daughter wander aboot these God forsaken streets all alone."

Marie did not comprehend what the man was saying but he seemed kindly and so she stood silently with a smile on her lips. Soon Michael returned with a used piece of paper and a large pencil stick for his master. The man set about drawing out a replica of the sign as he remembered it, with the words "The Pork 'n' Porridge" inscribed neatly on it.

As the merchant worked, his assistant stood idly for a moment looking boldly at Marie. Fetching young women were a rare commodity in the colonies and his gaze lingered upon her too long as it traveled over every inch of her form. She chose to ignore him as she kept her gaze cast downward. He heard a distinct "herr-hummmph" and looked to see his master eyeing him sternly. With a subtle jerk of his head, the merchant ordered his assistant back to work.

"Here ye go, lass," the man said, pushing the finished drawing at Marie. "Take it. And walk this way," he drew on the paper again to indicate the path she should take. "When ye see a sign that looks like this," he gestured and spoke with exaggerated slowness, "ye be there."

Marie accepted the small drawing."Thank yoo," she said smiling up again, "thank yoo, much."

Following the crude little map, in time she saw a sign hanging off a beam that looked remarkably like the drawing she held in her hand. She walked until she stood beneath it, then she smoothed her hair, straightened her shawls and collar, threw back her shoulders and went inside.

A large, cheery fire was burning brightly at the far end of the room while the sun shone through the very large front window. The rafters hung low but the room was well lit and clean. To the side along the wall was a small narrow staircase which Marie could only guess led to sleeping rooms on the second floor.

"Good morrow, miss," a small man in a big apron called over to her.

"Good... day... sir," she replied thinking hard at each word. "I... I look for... work."

"Do you have any references?" the man replied glibly without hesitation as though he were very used to this conversation.

Marie stood silently and then spoke again.

"Sir, I... speak English leetle. But I learn fast. You speak French?" she asked in a hushed tone brought about by her recent conversation with the servant woman.

"I might," the innkeeper replied as if making a private joke, then he looked at the pretty young stranger and smile graciously. "But of course, miss," he replied in perfect French, "I speak French, English, German, Dutch and a little Swedish. I must for the sake of business. Sit down, if you please." He gestured to a chair at the table near him, waited for her to sit and sat down across from her.

"I am looking for work, monsieur," she said, relieved to be able to speak French again. "I worked several years in a tavern doing everything but cooking; I can cipher. I work hard but I expect a fair wage. I have only just begun learning English but I want to learn very much and shall learn very quickly. Someone told me you might be looking for a servant."

"When did you arrive in New York?"

"Two nights ago."

"Alone?"

Marie hesitated. She did not understand the reason behind his question.

"I am my own person, monsieur, not married, not obligated, not owned but I have friends."

The innkeeper laughed softly. "I meant did you come with family?"

Marie flushed slightly. "No, no family."

"How old are you?" he asked.

"Eighteen," Marie lied and stiffening her back, she sat very straight.

"Oh, as old as that are you, eh? Well, you have courage, I give you that, but I am sorry to say I have no need for any additional help. I have two growing boys and so, enough helpers."

Marie's face fell. "Do you know of anywhere else, monsieur? It would be of such help to work for someone who knew just a little French, while I learn *anglais*."

The innkeeper took a wrinkled but clean handkerchief from his pocket and blew his nose while he thought. The girl sitting before him was so small and looked so defenseless, he did not have the heart to simply send her on her way. There was a look of desperation around her eyes and he knew she was no more eighteen years of age than he was. A God fearing Christian man, he did not want to see her end up at the brothel down by the docks. Carefully, he wiped his nose and put the handkerchief away before he spoke again.

"Wait here a minute," he said with a gesture for her to stay where she was and he got up from the table. He walked through a door to the back of the inn. In a short time a woman came to the doorway. She wore a slightly soiled apron over her dress and her fine brown hair insisted on creeping down and out from under her white cap. She looked out at Marie as she continued stirring whatever she had in the bowl she held, and she said something to the innkeeper. He returned to the table.

"My wife tells me that one of the families in our church may be in need of a nursemaid. Can you take care of babies?"

"Oh, *oui*," Marie replied quickly, her face lighting up.

"I suppose babies care not what language you speak. You're not a papist are you?"

"A what, monsieur?" she asked in puzzlement.

"A papist... a Catholic?"

"Oh... no, monsieur."

"Good. Not that I much care but they would not want a Catholic putting the wrong ideas into their children's heads. Very well, I will have my son take you to their house. Their name is Van Hootenaug. I know Madam Van Hootenaug speaks some French."

"Oh, *merci beaucoup*, monsieur… and please, for me thank your kind wife as well."

The innkeeper called his young son in and gave him instructions to escort Marie to the Van Hootenaug house and let the mistress know his father had sent them. The father added a stern warning for the lad to hurry back before the lunch trade began at the tavern.

The boy did as he was instructed and Marie soon found herself standing in the entry of a neat wood-framed house, being scrutinized closely.

Mistress Van Hootenaug was a plump young matron with very yellow hair done up in braids that wrapped in two large coils on either side of her head. She was not unpleasant but Marie did not think her very friendly. Her hard blue eyes had a pinched, stern appearance which was accentuated by the fact that the woman was quite nearsighted and had the habit of squinting when she was not wearing her spectacles. She spoke a little French, as the innkeeper had said, and asked Marie a good deal about herself. Marie was as candid as possible without bringing up all the more sordid details of her life back in France.

The Van Hootenaugs had five children, Marie learned, the youngest being a small baby, the oldest being eight, with a five year old and a pair of twin toddlers. *Mistress* Van Hootenaug, as Marie was instructed to call her, was indeed looking for a nursemaid. Someone, she said, whose chief responsibility would be to look after the children and keep them out of mischief. Marie had the distinct impression that there had only recently been a former nursemaid but what had become of her was unknown.

"You will also be expected to set an example for the children. You will attend household vespers every evening with the family and church every Sunday, do you understand?"

"*Oui, madam.*"

"No-no, we might as well begin immediately to learn it correctly. You say: *Yes, mistress.*"

"Yes, mistress," Marie echoed.

"That is better. You shall have the room over the kitchen. It is small but it is next to the nursery and it is warm."

"Yes, mistress."

"You shall eat well and be allotted one new dress a year for church. We do not have a lot of money to give you, you understand?"

Marie hesitated for a moment. She did not want to work as a servant all of her life. If she received little to no wages she could never be independent.

"But I understood there is to be some wage," she said slowly.

"Well... yes... but as I said, we cannot afford to pay much."

"How much is not much?" Marie asked candidly.

"Perhaps Master Van Hootenaug can be persuaded to give you... say, six pence a week."

"Six pence... is that fair?" Marie asked out of ignorance, but her question was interpreted as a challenge.

"Well, perhaps one shilling but not a halfpenny more."

"I see," Marie said, now realizing that the woman was trying to obtain her services as cheaply as possible. She would ask Monsieur Jacques-Jean how fair the wage was.

"Now, I shall take you to meet the children," said the matron and led the way to the kitchen. They walked into a noisy scene. The cook was trying to keep the toddlers away from the fire while the eight year old was thumping his five year old brother and the baby was crying from its cradle.

"It is time for me to nurse the baby. Make yourself useful and amuse the girls."

"Yes, mistress."

Marie had learned that much English very well.

When lunch was over, the children were all put down for a nap and the neat little house grew quiet. Marie explained that she had a previously arranged rendezvous with her traveling companions before sunset and must leave to let them know she was well and to retrieve the rest of her belongings from the ship she had arrived on. Mistress Van Hootenaug was not pleased but she could not reasonably stop the girl from leaving this once although it meant that Marie would not be there to help feed the children their evening meal.

It was easy for Marie to find her way back using the old fort and windmill as a landmark. She made a mental note of the number of streets she crossed so she could trace her way back again. At last, she was at the correct fort corner. At least not everything about this land was confusing.

Marie did not have to wait long before she saw Jacques-Jean and Richard approaching.

"And so, little Marie, how did your day go?" Jacques-Jean asked as they came nearer. He was surprised to learn in the next few minutes that Marie was employed, had a place to stay, and had made several new acquaintances in the town.

"Amazing! You have accomplished all that?" Jacques-Jean said teasingly but was quite honestly impressed. He also noted that she was looking much like herself again and he was glad for it.

"And how much is this woman going to pay you for attending her litter of brats?" Richard asked as they sat down in a nearby tavern to eat.

"That is one thing that bothers me," Marie admitted. "How much is a *pence*, what is a *shilling*? I cannot tell if I am being paid fairly."

"You will learn soon enough," Jacques-Jean said easily. "Most likely you are being cheated because you are new and know not the labor market as yet. But consider that you are learning. You will learn the language, the money and the prevailing wages. I have no doubt you will learn very quickly," he smiled. "I am most happy for you. Richard and I have been learning too, is that not so, *mon ami*? This America is quite a place... we will make a mark here, I can feel it," he added with the easy confidence of a healthy young man who sees little impediment to mastering the world.

"One thing we have already learned," broke in Richard. "These people have little love for the monarchs across the seas, no matter which one."

"I have also learned it is not a popular thing here to be French," said Marie.

"*Oui*, we have noticed this as well," nodded Richard.

"And is it not understandable?" reasoned Jacques-Jean. "Louis can be very aggressive and there is no channel separating the French and English on this side of the ocean."

They turned their attentions to their supper. A day of walking about in the fresh air had worked up everyone's appetite.

"I did have a thought for you today, Marie," Jacques-Jean said after a few minutes when he remembered how he intended to let her know he would help her leave the English colonies if she wanted. The young girl turned her bright eyes to him immediately, very flattered to think he might have thought of her and very curious to know in what way. "It might be more comfortable for you in New France with our countrymen. Just because I cannot go does not prohibit you from settling there. You do know this, do you not?"

Marie's heart uttered a silent scream of protest as it gave a large thump-thump within her chest. "But I could not," she began to protest softly.

"I would be happy to make the arrangements for you," offered the young aristocrat, "if you should decide you would prefer to be among your own kind."

"My own kind ...?"

"Other French countrymen," he explained. "People with the same language."

She shook her head in silent protest. "I already have a position here," she said quietly. Her throat had become dry and she could feel tears threatening to present themselves. There was an unexpected sting in the knowledge that he would easily see her depart his company.

Jacques-Jean shrugged. "It is up to you. Just remember, for as long as I am here, if you change your mind, I will be happy to assist you in getting passage."

"For as long as you... are here? M'lord are you planning to leave this place?" Marie asked, feeling an unexplainable panic rise within her. The thought of being left alone without him at least nearby was both heart-wrenching and unbearable.

Jacques-Jean shrugged again, unaware of Marie's sudden pallor. "It is difficult to say what will happen. Someday I do expect to return to France," he said looking at her and suddenly seeing before him the face of a very frightened looking child. "Oh, but not for some time, I imagine. And while I wait, I suppose this place is as good as any other. Is that not so, Richard?"

Richard said nothing but grunted a nod. He was more aware than Jacques-Jean of how the girl was looking at him.

After supper that evening, Jacques-Jean helped Marie retrieve her small bundle of belongings off the ship before escorting her back to the Van Hootenaug house. With the setting of the sun, it had turned very cold but the sky was clear and the bright moon lit the way much better than the little lanterns that hung along the streets and at the street crossings.

"So, this is now your new home." Jacques-Jean stated when Marie paused before the front gate of the Van Hootenaug house.

"*Oui...* my new home," she echoed weakly.

"Do you have any regrets?" he asked nonchalantly as he stood relaxed, resting his hand on the fence post.

"Oh, no, m'lord, none," she replied quickly. "And I thank you from the bottom of my heart for allowing me to come with you."

"You were very brave to come. Things could have ended far differently, you know," he said, referring to their escape.

"I know."

"And another thing... here in America, I am no more than you. Unless you want me to start calling you *m'lady*, you must now call me simply *Jacques!*"

"I must?" she asked seriously.

"*Oui*, you must!" he laughed easily. She relaxed and smiled.

"Very well... Jacques," she replied shyly.

"And if you need anything, remember you can always call upon me."

"But where will you be once the ship is gone?" she asked, a hint of a frown playing across her forehead as she realized she would not know where to find him.

"We took a room at the same inn you went to this morning, The Pork'n'Porridge," he grinned.

"You did?" Marie uttered in disbelief.

"*Oui*. We did. It has a very good reputation it seems; it is clean and respectable."

Marie nodded and added almost shyly. "I want you to know it is far less lonely and frightening here knowing I have you for a friend."

"Now it is I who must thank you for a very pretty compliment," he replied gallantly.

"When..." she began and hesitated, "... will I see you again? I would like to know how it goes for you," she added shyly.

"Ah, *oui*, well, if I have someone to think of my welfare, I know I shall do well," he said lightly. "I do not doubt that I will see you soon, moppet."

"*Bon soir, m'lor...*" she caught herself and smiled. "*Bon soir*, Jacques."

"*Bon soir*," he smiled and bent over her hand to give it a gallant kiss.

Three days later Jacques rode out to the Van Hootenaug's on a horse he was thinking of purchasing. It was an impulsive move, outwardly simply giving him a destination but inwardly after weeks shared together on shipboard, he missed the young girl's company. Reining the steed at the hitching post, he walked in an easy relaxed manner to the front door and gave the knocker one sound clang. Mistress Van Hootenaug herself opened the door, clutching her shawl about her plump shoulders.

"*Bon jour, madam*," Jacques said easily, doffing his hat and bowing in a sweeping gesture. "Do you have a maid by the name of Marie here?" he asked in French, knowing from Marie that the woman understood it.

The matron looked him over steadily, squinting as she did. His long flowing curls, his easy grace and manner, the cut of his clothes, the rapier hung at his hip all indicated he was born of high station and it gave her much satisfaction to show no regard for it since she had no evidence that he had any station, high or otherwise, anymore.

"Yes," she replied curtly in English. "Who wants to know?"

"A friend," he replied with a smile testing his own English. "May I see her for a moment, pleez?"

"The *nurse*maid Marie is engaged in her duties. She is allowed visitors only on Sunday afternoons."

Jacques was visibly rendered speechless for an instant. The woman had to be joking. The lowest serf on his fathers' estates would never have been denied a visit from a member of the nobility. Or more aptly put, no member of the nobility would have been denied access to any servant. Ahhh... but that was it. America... he had no rank here and she knew it. It was an egalitarian chip these people seemed to wear upon their shoulders.

"Pardon me, I did not mean to inconvenience yoo," he replied with careful politeness. "Pleez tell her *Jacques* called and weel return on Sunday."

"Very well, and make it after church services," came the even reply before she stepped back and closed the door in his face.

The following Sunday was a bitterly cold, windy day and despite two shawls Marie's teeth began to chatter within moments of going outdoors. True to his word, Jacques came to call. He had purchased the black gelding and had decided to invite

Marie for a ride. But given the weather, a warm seat by the fire seemed much more appropriate.

"It is a bb..beautiful horse," Marie said admiringly, unable to keep from shivering.

"And far more able to withstand the cold than you, I think. How would you like a cup of hot tea... or coffee perhaps?" he smiled. "Come, up you go." He set her into the saddle, climbed up behind her and wrapped his heavy cape around her. From that point on, Marie found their ride about town to be quite pleasant. Jacques' body heat from within the cape was as good as a stove.

After he took her on a tour around the town limits, he brought her to The Pork 'n' Porridge where they met up with Richard.

The innkeeper recognized Marie at once.

"Good day," he greeted her in English as she walked in and immediately moved to the fire burning brightly at the hearth.

"Goud afternoon, sir," Marie smiled broadly rubbing her hands before the fire. "It iz goud to see yoo. Thank yoo much for zee direction to my work."

The innkeeper looked at her in surprise. "Excellent!" he responded. "You told the truth when you said you would learn English quickly."

"Thank yoo," she beamed, her eyes dancing in merriment. "I have zee best teachers in zee world! So I learn queekly to speak zee English, yes? I have zee childrens and they are many...? Much? No, no... *very* goud teachers, yes?"

"Indeed they must be," he agreed, smiling at her enthusiasm. He took their order and proceeded to serve them food and drink.

Marie did not deny, however, that she was working for a very strict and demanding taskmistress. "I can understand why their last nursemaid left," she confided to Jacques and Richard quickly in French. "It is not *les enfants* that are so bad, but the parents," she rolled her eyes in an exaggerated gesture and her companions laughed.

They joked the afternoon away forcing themselves to speak in English as much as they could until they were at a complete loss for a word. Marie was learning to read out of primers with the Van Hootenaug children. Peter, the eight year old, enjoyed playing schoolmaster with her. Never having had any schooling, Marie soaked up knowledge ravenously and willingly shared her newly learned language skills with her companions. They, in turn, provided a relaxing and amusing break for her from the stiff and critical environment of the Van Hootenaug household.

That same evening upon returning to her employers' home, Marie was immediately called into the family parlor where she was not offered a seat but was made to stand before the two Van Hootenaug adults. She received a stern lecture from them regarding her behavior in public. Marie felt her cheeks growing hot and flushed as she stood before the verbal chastisement. Master Van Hootenaug said nothing but sat sternly sucking on his pipe, his jaws tight in an expression of disapproval. His wife obviously had his full support as she lectured the younger female.

"It is neither customary within our society nor fittingly proper for a young un-married woman to share such a close seating arrangement with a man who is not a member of her family," she stated sharply. "And as long as you are in our employ, you will not compromise yourself in such a manner again. Do not forget that your behavior is a reflection upon our household. It is unthinkable that you should sit to-gether in such a way, your bodies hidden under wraps."

Marie clenched her mouth shut. She did not trust herself to speak and so she remained silent. She did not understand what she had done that could be viewed as so improper. Jacques had only put his arm about her waist to support her upon the horse as she had sat sidesaddle in front of him. She would have surely fallen if he had not. And his cloak had given her warmth.

"We shall forgive you this indiscretion this one time... allowing for the obvi-ously foreign background and society from whence you come... but make no mis-take, do not confuse our charity for tolerance! There must be no repeat of anything like this, is that understood, Marie?" Mistress Van Hootenaug demanded severely.

"But I was very cold," she tried to explain, lapsing into French.

"*That* is no excuse for compromising the reputation of our good family," the woman replied harshly. "I have an old cloak I will lend you if you have come so ill prepared for our weather; then you shall have no excuses for such unseemly be-havior."

"Yes, Mistress." Marie would have liked to have said much more but knew she dare not. They would *"forgive"*... forgive what? There was nothing to forgive, nothing!

"Very well, now go to bed, it is late," the woman ordered curtly.

Marie dropped a curtsy and left in silence but her mind raced in anger. What could the woman possibly think they had been doing except riding a horse? Mon-sieur Jacques was a gentleman! He was not a Bouchet to take advantage of her and it angered her immensely to have Mistress Van Hootenaug insinuate that he would. She burned with indignation that anyone could think Monsieur Jacques could be anything but honor itself. It seemed to Marie that it was her employers who were unseemly – suffering from impurity of thought.

Chapter 12

"Hmmm," the young Frenchman stared critically at his image reflected in the dim looking glass within the close and dusty tailor's shop. At least it was warm amidst the bolts of cloth, he thought as he studied the fabric he held. The worst of winter in the New World colony of New York had settled in. The days were short and often gray and the winds off the harbor cut through to the bone. A slushy frozen rain fell at times, at other times it snowed. It was their first winter in the New World and it was unlike anything the trio had ever experienced before. Neither Jacques nor Richard found the clothes they had brought with them substantial enough and Jacques had sought out a tailor. "Zee cloth..." his fingers flicked over the material draped over his shoulder and deftly felt of the weight. "No, no. This cloth iz too... how do yoo say...?" he frowned waving his hand as he tossed the cloth aside. The fabric was loosely woven and coarse. It felt unsubstantial and he knew instinctively the wind would go through it like a sieve. "Here," he grabbed up a bolt of tightly woven wool. "Theez, make it of theez."

"Yes, sir," the slightly built but dexterous tailor nodded approvingly and smiled. The cost of the material was four times that of the other. It was the finest heavy woven wool made in England, imported for the most affluent of his clients. With complete efficiency he began to measure Jacques' torso, shoulder width, arms, chest, waist.

"Mind, I need zee room, ahhh, here..." Jacques gestured to his shoulders. "I weel not be bunned, yoo understand?"

"*Bunned*, sir?" replied the tailor with a frown of concentration rippling over his sallow face.

"Yes.. I must have zee room for to move." He windmilled his arms to demonstrate.

"Oh..." replied the craftsman with sudden realization, "*bound*, sir. You mean bound. Oh, no, sir. Not at all. I'll give you ample room in the shoulders, you can be certain of that."

Jacques nodded. "Yes. Bound," he repeated with concentration. "I weel not be bound. My arms must be free for... " he suddenly did a fancy little series of movements miming fencing with a foil which almost caused the tailor to pitch backward onto the floor.

"Ah, yes, sir," the tailor nodded his understanding again, light reflecting off his bald pate. "If you could just hold still a bit longer, sir..."

"And small zee fit here," Jacques gestured to his waist. "Not... lozz... ah, *loose*, right?"

"Yes, sir." Agreed the tailor again. "And the length, sir? For winter I would recommend a little added length, perhaps to here?" He gestured to a point midway between Jacques' knee and the floor.

"Mmmm..." Jacques considered carefully. "Yes, yes, theez weel do. Very goud," he brushed his hands together in a gesture to indicate the subject was finished and stood still while the slight man with his tape measure took some final measurements. "Wheen may I return?"

"Oh, late tomorrow afternoon, sir," the tailor replied straightening up to his full height which was still not equal to Jacques. "I'll have it roughed out for your first fitting." The tailor smiled amiably as he made a few notes of the measurements he had just taken.

"Goud, yes. Goud. Tomorrow afternoon. Yes, veree goud," Jacques agreed. He turned and in the close quarters he almost bumped into Richard's large lanky frame. "Ahh, Richard. Now iz your turn, eh?" Jacques graciously gestured toward the tailor who stood tape measure in hand.

Richard shrugged. "No theez time," he said casually. "I need no thing."

"No thing?" Jacques exclaimed. "Unless yoo have a heavee coat I know not, yoo need a winter coat as well."

"No," Richard replied stubbornly. "Zee cold bothers me no. Yoo make too much of it. We seet all day by zee fire, what use have I for a heavee coat?"

Jacques almost retorted but suddenly stopped himself.

"Perhaps a fine wool scarf, sir. To wrap around the neck," the tailor offered. "It's amazing how keeping the neck warm makes a great difference."

"I am no old man," Richard jeered, pulling open the door to the shop and walking out into the street. His breath immediately came from his mouth in clouds of vapor.

"Make two scarves," Jacques said to the tailor, "from theez." He fingered a fine red cashmere. "One for heem, one for me."

"Yes, sir."

"No, no... make three," Jacques held up his thumb and two fingers suddenly inspired to get one for Marie as well. Richard could hardly refuse the present if there was one for each of them. It would be a clever little token to distinguish them as special friends. "Me," he pointed to himself, "heem" he gestured after Richard, "and *une petite jeune*... ah, a small fee-male." He again gestured indicating someone who only would come up to his chin.

"A lady, sir. Yes, of course," the tailor nodded more than pleased at the additional order. He took up the bolt of downy soft cloth. "Three scarves as well, and one a bit more lady-like."

"Can yoo have zee scarves readee tomorrow after zee noon?"

"Of course, sir," the bald head bobbed. Scarves were a simple task and he would set his wife and daughters to it that very afternoon.

Jacques nodded and putting on his hat went out into the cold to catch up with his friend. Tomorrow was Saturday and on Sunday they would see Marie.

The trio had fallen into the routine of spending Sunday afternoons together. On more pleasant days they explored. Now, with winter fully entrenched in the seaport settlement, they mostly sought out a cozy refuge before the hearth of the small coffee shoppe. There, warm and comfortable, they could sit off to themselves perfecting their English, sharing news, talking of the future and enjoying the hot beverages served to them.

Two days later when they gathered together as usual, Jacques presented both

Richard and Marie with a bright, new dark red scarf and brought out his own. Richard could do little but accept it as Marie smiled with appreciation, then laughed with delight at how they now had matching accouterments.

"Zee fabric iz so fine, Jacques, it iz so soft against my skin," she sighed audibly rubbing the scarf against her cheek. "This iz much …ah, *most* thoughtful of yoo. Here Richard, let me show yoo how to get zee most warm... ahh, warmth.

With a glint in his eye Richard stood and mimicked her, holding the scarf to his cheek and affecting a falsetto. "Zee fabric iz so fine, Jacques, so soft against my skin."

"Sit," she ordered, pretending to scowl. "Yoo are much too tall when yoo stand."

"I no think so," Richard replied blandly. "My feet reach all zee way to zee floor."

"Oh, you know what I mean. *I* cannot reach you," Marie giggled. Richard sat and she carefully set about wrapping the cashmere flat around his neck several times, causing it to layer. She tied it once over and smoothed the ends down into his cassock. "We weel look so... *fa-shen-able*, yes?" she smiled, patting her finished work.

"I have no need to look *fa-shen-able*," Richard grumbled good-naturedly. "I leave that to *mon bons amis avec....*"

"Tut, tut," Marie interrupted, "in English, if you please."

"...to my goud friends with zee eye for *fa-shen*."

"Oh, Richard, you try to act ill tempered," Marie cajoled him. "Zee scarf iz very fine, you know it iz. And yoo look very handsome. It iz a very goud color for you. And it iz very nice of Jacques to get each of us one so we can match... like," she thought for a few seconds, "like com-pan-eeons-in-arms… zat iz zee way to say, iz it not?"

Richard mutter something incomprehensible and nodded his head, distracted by her attentions. His hand drifted up to the soft cloth at which point he could not keep himself from caressing it, savoring the pleasure of the tactile sensation.

During the entire discourse, Jacques had simply sat aloof, listening without seeming to notice as if it did not matter. Inwardly, he was relieved and glad that Richard had accepted the neck scarf. It would help to warm him. Jacques was beginning to realize his friend most likely could not afford a winter coat and was too proud to say so.

After taking supper together, they conversed for some time sharing with Marie the news gathered from the docks, gleaned from any newly arrived ship seeking shelter in the harbor. They also went to less savory taverns frequented almost exclusively by the sailors, taverns into which they would never take Marie. But at this time of year, fewer ships arrived and almost always they came from the warmer waters of the south. Nothing was arriving now from Europe.

As the hour grew late, they parted company for another week, with plans to meet again the following Sunday. Richard went on his way to the inn while Jacques escorted Marie safely back to her place of employ. Marie would labor for the Van Hootenaugs for another six days, only leaving the confines of the house when sent on a specific errand. And Jacques and Richard would spend much of their time in one tavern or another, trying to stay warm while they listened and watched and learned everything they could take in. The pair had yet to decide how they were to go about the business of seeking their personal fortunes here in this vast new world.

One late afternoon Jacques and Richard found themselves sitting idling within the circle of warmth before the friendly fire on the main floor of The Pork 'n' Porridge. It was another foul, dark day and they had not left the inn to venture out save to seek the privy in the back when necessity demanded. Now, each nursed a draft of ale as they watched a dice game in progress between several burly colonials who also shared a room there. It was only mid afternoon but the weak sunshine of the morning had disappeared within an overcast and it had already grown so dark that Thompkins felt compelled to light the candles, lamps, and lanterns all around in an effort to cheer up the atmosphere. The innkeeper threw an extra log on the blazing fire and the soot blackened fireplace radiated comfort while the wind could be heard periodically rattling the casement windows as it blew a hard icy snow through the air.

"It is a good day to be inside," Richard said lazily with a catlike stretch extending his long legs out in front of him; his arms reached up high overhead. "No one should have to go out on a day like today."

Jacques did not disagree. It would take time to become acclimated to these harsh temperatures and storms and he did not know how Richard stood it without a sturdy winter coat but Jacques knew better than to say as much. As he watched the flames dance along the logs and little sap bubbles rise out of the new log, he thought longingly of home. The peaceful vineyards of the *Pouvoir* estates seemed like paradise right now. The mild climate he had grown up in lacked these cold extremes.

In his mind's eye he could see the spaciously impressive chateau of his father where one could walk from room to room all day and never feel closed in or confined. The friendly, neat cottage of his mother had seemed small in comparison but, in fact, it was larger than most of the homes here in this new land. The cozy comfortable little retreat of his mistress had seemed so rustic until he compared it to what he saw around him now. Why even his father's horse stable was a majestic structure compared to his present surroundings. And it was filled with horses just begging to be exercised in the mellow golden countryside of fields and vineyards as far as the eye could see. And in this place, they huddled along a coast whipped by winds off a frigid sea.

There was much he had taken for granted in his youth and even more so when he had become his true father's heir. For him, the chateau and the stability it represented had always been there, sedate, strong, and a symbol of the orderliness of life. In his young mind, it had neither a beginning nor an end, it simply was. Like the air simply is. He had always depended upon it. It was shelter, it was sustenance. It was more. It had been the cornucopia of all bounty, pleasure, education, and protection, the very root that gave his life substance, form and connection. He had felt *connected* through the land to the generations before him and to the generations meant to come after him. Even though the generations might be unknown to each other, they shared a common bond. He had thought it would always be this way without really ever thinking upon it. How easily he had accepted that someday the *Pouvoir* lands would become his own to run, that his children would grow up in the hills and valleys in which he had grown up. And he had assumed that some day in a far distant unforeseeable future, he would pass it all along to his own son.

It had all vanished in one night. He had returned to the chateau to be told of the *lettre de caché* and in that moment he had lost his future. Now, with each passing day he gained a clearer realization that, in all likelihood, that life was gone forever and this was now his life. He was never going to be able to go home again. He had left both a mother and a father who loved him, but that phantom stability he once thought so rock solid had dissolved faster than a sandcastle before a large wave. It had vanished like the mist over a pond vanishes in the sunshine and he had become just one of the thousands upon thousands of Huguenots who were being driven from their homes in France. His former life was as a dream now, and he had awakened to an entirely different reality.

Jacques looked around. The dice throwers were laughing very loudly, slamming their tankards down on the table top, ale spilling into puddles on the floor that glistened with firelight reflecting on the surface like dancing gold. He would admit to no one but himself that he sometimes had nightmares from which he awoke in a tense sweat feeling isolated and very alone. It was as if part of him had been torn out, wrenched from his being as he fled France. It was the part of him that was France. The family holdings, the fields, the vineyards, the juice of the grape fermented into rich wines and hardy brandies had been part of the blood running through his veins. He was reminded of the time, which now seemed so long ago, when he and Richard and their Catholic friend, du Vaille, had sat in the tavern with Dufee, discussing the New World. What if he were not his father's son, Jacques pondered? What if he had really been the old duke's son and just another noble bastard with nothing? Would he ever have voluntarily left to seek his fortune in the New World? Would he have had the courage to leave those valleys and live apart? Perhaps, he thought, and perhaps not but if he had it would have been his decision. He would have thought long and hard about it. And it would have been different if it had been his choice. If he had left under those circumstances, he would have been able to return anytime he wished. That would have made a very great difference.

But it had not been his choice. He had had to flee, run, like a coward perhaps but... no, he would not fault himself for a coward. One man cannot fight the Crown and all its minions. So, he had fled, escaped, been driven out and now he felt so alienated from everything that had been his former existence. He was in this strange land now, an ocean away from everything he had known and loved. Now he lived amidst those whom he had grown up thinking of as *the enemy*, with their hard-edged speech and strange accents. And he was expected to make something of himself here on his own. Build an existence with his own two hands. But he was not a peasant, not a common laborer. And he had no trade, no sale-able skill, no artisan talent. He was born to lead, to administer, to govern, was he not? But what was there here for him, a Frenchman, to govern in a land of Englishmen? And if he had been *born* to be his father's heir then why was he here?

Jacques considered. But he had *not* been born to be his father's heir. No, in truth, he had become his father's heir only because his father had had no other children. He had been born the grandson of a clerk, part of the Huguenot *bourgeoisie*. Why had he never learned an appropriate skill? No-no, to be fair, he had been learning to run a vast estate... that was a skill, was it not? And how was he to use that knowledge in this new place?

Jacques drained the last of his ale and signaled to the innkeeper's son for another. With a quick gesture of his hands he indicated he wanted two tankards, one for himself and one for Richard. They had had to grow accustomed to the taste of this bitter brown ale as there was no wine in this land worth drinking. The serving lad brought the fresh tankards and Jacques paid him.

And still in all... Jacques told himself as he rubbed his eyes grown scratchy in the dry air around the fire... and still in all, he was a most fortunate man. He received a generous stipend from home. His needs were modest and it was enough to keep him from feeling desperate and destitute. It gave him the opportunity to consider his next course of action. Richard, he now realized, was not so fortunate.

Jacques had come to the conclusion that whatever money Richard had escaped with, it was most likely all he could ever expect to receive. With Richard's mother dead and his father not nearly so concerned for his bastard son's welfare as he might have been, Jacques expected that Richard must have been given a lump sum as a send off of "good riddance," if he had even received that. And once out of sight, Richard was now out of mind. In that regard, Jacques was generous with his friend and had become thoughtful of his expenses. Richard, his closest and dearest friend, had sacrificed his monthly stipend to come to the New World with Jacques, but thank God Richard had come along. Jacques shuddered to imagine the loneliness of being here without him. But his companion had as strong a sense of pride as any man and Jacques was very careful in his generosity lest his friend's pride grow wounded. Richard would not take well to the thought of becoming a charity case and Jacques knew his comrade was very anxious to find a way to earn a steady income.

Richard had been watching the trio of rough men at their dice game for a long while. The game seemed simple enough and he itched to get in and try his luck. He felt very lucky at that moment and he had learned from long experience that when he felt this way he should act upon it. The men were drinking but they did not appear drunk, yet they had an easy air of disregard for the gold coins they tossed lightly back and forth amongst each other as they took turns losing or winning. In simple truth, he was down to his last silver and he could well use some of their gold. He felt lucky.

Richard suddenly straighten up and called over to the players. "Iz theez a private game or can anyone play?" he asked by way of seeking an invitation to join them. Jacques was surprised.

The three men looked up and surveyed the lanky, bushy headed young Frenchman. They all had weathered, leathery faces, still brown from long hours of exposure to the sun but their expressions were not unfriendly. One of the men, dressed in rather odd leather clothing and appearing to be the most successful of the three at the game, grinned at Richard. He was missing one tooth but on the whole his face was broad and pleasant. He gestured for Richard to come over and join them.

"I seen you around, now and again. My name is Cameron. This here is Witcomb," he said jovially, referring to the fellow seated to his right. Witcomb had a coarse angular face and when he grinned he displayed teeth darkened by stains. "And this is Red." He nodded to his left to a husky man with a tuft of red hair sprouting off the top of his head much like a coxcomb.

"I am Richard Bonchance and theez my friend, Jacques-Jean Charte."

"Too many names," Cameron grinned and waved his hand. "You got any objection to being called by just one?"

"No," Richard replied. "*Bonchance* iz goud."

"Good. Sit down. You want to join us, Charte?" he called over.

Jacques smiled in return but declined. He was still in shock that Richard had decided to gamble and was not going to play against him. Keeping a placid expression upon his face, he drew his chair a bit closer in order to see, and prayed that Richard knew what he was doing.

One of their favorite forms of amusement back in France had been gambling on cards and dice but that was when they knew that in the event they lost everything, they still had a place to sleep and would only be broke until their next allowance came due. Of course, if Richard lost everything, Jacques would keep him from beggary but still, for his friend, things would be even more desperate. Had he not heard that one should never gamble when one is desperate? Scared money drives away luck, or something like that.

Jacques sat quietly.

The game of dice was based upon the highest score accumulated in three rolls, winner take all. There were bonus points for certain combinations and it took

Richard a few rounds to completely understand. During this time he bet very small sums and lost. His new found friends smiled, laughed, and clapped him on the back as they cheerfully took his money. Jacques inwardly cringed. Richard took off his long cloth cassock as if warming to the activity and now preparing to get serious. He took another try with the dice and this time he won. With a broad grin, he just as cheerfully took his money back.

They played all evening and one look at the table and the gold sitting at Richard's elbow gave an instant indication of who was winning. "I theek," said Richard cautiously, "we queet while yoo steel have something left, eh?"

Cameron surveyed what he had lost and took up the dice. "Tell you what, one more roll... just between the two of us. If you win, I'll double what you got. If I win I take back my money."

Richard shook his head. "No, no, I no can do. I am winning but only what iz on zee table. I am satisfied. And yoo, I theek, are a leetle drunk. It was a pleasant pastime."

"You could double your winnings, Frenchie."

Richard ran his hand threw his bushy hair and Jacques sat completely still but suddenly very wary and ready to react instantly should there be trouble. "I am no greedee," Richard grinned, "it iz time to stop."

Cameron gave him a long hard look which Richard returned without malice. The colonial burst into laughter. "Well, damn if you don't beat all," Cameron said leaning back and draining the last of his ale. "You had yerself quite a streak. I guess you better buy us one last tankard for the night, Bonchance."

Richard grinned amiably and signed to the innkeeper to bring a round for the five.

"*Bonchance*. What's that mean anyway?" asked the red-haired man.

"*Goud fortune*," replied Richard with another grin, "or as yoo say maybee... *goud luck*."

"Well, hell, no wonder ya cleaned us out," Cameron continued his good-natured complaining, scratching his whiskered chin and seeking his pipe. "Ya don't make your living fleecing locals, do you?"

Richard was not familiar with the expression but he was certain he guessed the meaning. He paused suddenly and his face went dark, "Monsieur, I hope yoo do not to question my honor," he said quite seriously.

"Oh, hell, man, no. Now, don't git all riled. You won us fair 'n' square. It was a decent evening's entertainment 'n one I won't be catching the pox from neither," he winked knowingly. "I just ain't never come so close to being cleaned down to the bone before." Cameron laughed again. "So what *do* you boys do for a living, if ya don't make it gambling."

"A good question, monsieur," Jacques interjected. "It would seem we are still reviewing zee opportunities zee New World presents. And may I ask what it iz you do, as you say, *for a living*?"

"Me, Witcomb and ol' Red here is fur traders. Don't usually see us this far south. We like the St. Lawrence River area but it's gittin' a bit crowded with your countrymen. We thought we'd try going up the Hudson next season." Suddenly Cameron's eyes narrowed and he looked straight at Richard. "I'm still building a party, can always use a fella who has luck on his side so firm it's his very name. You wanna join us? We'll be leaving at th' first thaw of spring."

"Does zee invitation include both of us?" Richard asked indicating Jacques as he gathered together his winnings, carefully collecting them into his purse which was growing quite heavy.

Cameron eyed Jacques critically. The young, blond Frenchman was not very rugged looking, thought the trapper; lithe and strong he didn't doubt, but a little too pretty and civilized for the wilds. Not his idea of trapper material but he had the feeling if he wanted the one he'd have to take the other. "Of course," he replied with a nod.

Richard looked at his friend and Jacques replied for them both. "I believe we are most interested in hearing more, monsieur."

Through the following days and weeks, Jacques and Richard began spending a good deal of time with Cameron and company discussing the business of fur trapping and trading. Mildly startled at how cheaply the natives traded pelts, they finally came to the decision to officially join Cameron's party.

The next Sunday, as they sat at their usual table in the little coffee shoppe, they told Marie they planned to join an expedition into the wilderness come spring.

"We should be leaving in another month perhaps," Jacques offered amiably as they sat together nibbling on savory dainties served with the dark brew.

At the thought of their leaving, Marie went a little numb and her face grew pale.

"Iz that so?" was all she could muster in response. Richard and Jacques exchanged glances. As the news sunk in, she wondered in panic how she would survive without them. She began to miss them desperately and they had not even left.

"Whatever am I to do if I do not have yoo to talk to on Sundays?" she asked at last. "I weel go mad with no one to talk to about Mistress Van Hootenaug's latest demands," she added with a slightly hysterical giggle. She struggled to fight back tears.

"It iz time you left that *mégère*," growled Richard as though he would like to throttle the shrewish housewife himself. He slipped back into French. "You can do better than playing nursemaid to her pups, Marie. It is time you moved on."

"I agree. Your English is quite good now," encouraged Jacques, "and you read better than either of us. It *is* time you looked for something better. A better position."

"You make it sound so easy," Marie lowered her eyes remembering how desperate she had been to get a job when the Van Hootenaugs had hired her.

"You have given them good service, Marie, you do not owe them anything more," Jacques spoke softly as though reading her mind. "You are not indentured and do not underestimate your value. There is a shortage of women here in the colonies," he added.

Marie gave a small nod and decided with determination to put the matter aside for the moment and enjoy every minute they still had left together. She smiled up at both of them, "And so, you weel return with a beautiful fur for me, iz this not so?" she asked pertly, returning to English. "One that yoo have caught with your very own hands, maybe? And yoo will return in good health, eh?" She grinned as they both smiled and nodded in agreement.

Dutifully, Marie attended the popular Protestant church each Sunday as the Van Hootenaugs required. She did not mind. The people were kind and occasionally she even caught a glimpse of Brother Robert who if he saw her would always give her a broad smile of welcome. But she had to admit that for the most part she tuned out the service, simply standing, sitting, and kneeling when everyone else did but always thinking her own thoughts. To be fair, it was a rare chance for her to think of her own concerns. Each night when she crawled into her small bed after a very busy day, she would try to think about her own situation but sleep born of exhaustion came on too quickly. And during her busy days, she dare not lose focus of her tasks or Mistress Van Hootenaug was certain to scold her harshly.

One Sunday in early March of 1686, as everyone sang and she pretended, she thought again of what Jacques and Richard had said about leaving. The weather had changed and a whisper of the spring to come was blowing in from the south. They would leave soon, she knew, and with that thought she also knew she must follow their advice and find another position. Just then she caught sight of the Thompkins family and decided she must try to speak to them after the service.

Marie called to them as they were all departing the church.

"Master Thompkins," she walked quickly over the thawing ground to catch up to them, "a moment of your time, pleez."

"Good morrow to you, Miss Marie, how goes it with you?" he asked cheerfully, pausing in the road. His wife nodded in kind.

"Good morrow, and to you, Mistress Thompkins," Marie dropped a curtsy. "I wish to thank you again for zee help you gave me and to ask you once more if you might need any help at zee inn?"

"Are you not happy with the Van Hootenaugs?" asked the innkeeper's wife.

"Happy enough for a nursemaid, mistress, but a nursemaid iz not what I intend to be all my life," Marie replied with diplomacy worthy of a seasoned ambassador.

"I see," replied Thompkins comprehending more than he acknowledged. "You are learning to use English well," he said with meaning, admiring the way Marie had stepped around his wife's pointed question. Personally, he wouldn't want to be working for the Van Hootenaugs. "So, now you wish to join the world of commerce, is that it?" he added helpfully.

"Yes, yes, exactly," Marie smiled gratefully.

"What do you think, Martha, could we use another hand?" Thompkins asked his wife.

"I think not, Henry. Hank becomes more useful every day and little George does well for his age," she answered, referring to their sons. "However," she paused noticing the disappointment on Marie's face, "you might inquire of the Wingates. They own Wingate Emporium on High Street. By all accounts, business is brisk but they lost their son to the wasting disease this winter. Not only are they grieving but they are shorthanded as well. You may tell them we have sent you."

"Oh, thank you, Mistress Thompkins," Marie bobbed another curtsy. She pulled the worn borrowed cloak closer and turned to go back to the Van Hootenaug house to await Jacques' call. The challenge she now must ponder was how and when to find time away from the demanding eye of Mistress Van Hootenaug in which to visit the Wingates.

Chapter 13

Summer found Marie working at the Wingate Emporium. Thomas Wingate and his wife, Abigail, were delighted when Marie approached them after church services one Sunday seeking a position in their store. They had seen the young woman at church often although they had never actually spoken with her until she came to them saying the Thompkins had given her to understand they might need help in their store. The timing could not have been better. The sharpest, bitterest edge to their grief was slowly dulling as they labored daily to work beyond it. The promise of an eager, young, and lively presence around their home and business, both of which seemed hollow in the wake of losing their son, was as much valued as any talents Marie might possess for the work.

The Wingates lived in spacious if rambling quarters behind and over their store. They installed her in the cozy back bedroom on the second floor which had once been shared by their two daughters. It was bright and airy with sloping ceilings and a French style double window giving an unobstructed view of the back yard and garden below. It was furnished rather sumptuously to Marie's way of thinking with a large featherbed, a chest of drawers and matching dressing table, a cedar wardrobe and a washstand with a chamber pot hidden within. Marie could easily imagine herself a make-believe princess in such a bedchamber. Adding to the overall effect were the billows of diaphanous pink and white curtains, embroidered with patterns of dainty small blossoms and hummingbirds, which hung from the window and canopy bed frame. And for added comfort, there was a grate in the floor which could be opened to allow heat from the downstairs to find its way up in the winter.

The Wingates' bedroom was to the front of the second floor, at the top of the stairs and stood over the large shoppe below. Between her room and theirs was a small room which Mistress Wingate used for sewing and mending. There was also a door in the hall that remained locked. The locked room had belonged to their son.

On the first floor of the wood frame building, the large shoppe fronting the street held Master Wingate's prize possession: a large, black cast iron, woodburning stove which he had had shipped all the way from Saugus in the Massachusetts colony. It had taken four men and a team of oxen to deliver the imposing black box from the ship and assemble it in the middle of the room. The metal chimney running up through the ceiling all the way to an opening in the roof also helped warm the upstairs. During the cold months, well placed chairs around the stove were extremely popular with the customers who liked to spend a half hour or more warming themselves and chatting with fellow townsmen. Behind the store was a stock room which led into a small hall with an exterior door to the side and a door leading into the family's drawing room. From the drawing room one could pass into an equally large kitchen.

The kitchen was the only single story part of the building and for safety's sake, the wall separating it from the rest of the structure was comprised of brick and held a large hearth and chimney. The roomy interior of the kitchen held plenty of space for a large table at which the family dined informally. Stepping outside the backdoor, one discovered a lean-to sharing the wall with the kitchen. This lean-to had a separate outdoor entrance and had been the quarters of an indentured cook when the Wingate children had been growing up. The cook had served out her seven years, stayed on as a paid servant for almost seven more, then married and opened an eating establishment near the waterfront with her husband. The lean-to now stood empty and housed only odd storage.

Marie was delighted to be earning considerably more in wages than she had received from the Van Hootenaugs. The Wingates were fair people, she considered, and would never take advantage of one's lack of familiarity with the labor market. As Master Wingate liked to teach, "Never try and cheat your business associates for while you may succeed in doing so once, twice, or even thrice, eventually it will cost you both reputation and patrons." They lived by that rule.

Marie guarded her earnings closely, watching as month by month her tiny savings grew. And as an added boon, she found she enjoyed the work immensely.

She had a natural ability for putting customers at ease. She listened closely to what they said, taking an interest and making them feel special under her earnest desires to fill their orders. She was eager to make suggestions and council in selecting the wisest purchase. Above all, she enjoyed meeting the various people and getting to know them. This, she thought to herself, was what she wanted for herself someday - to have a general store of her very own. It was a worthy ambition and she dared to fall asleep at night dreaming of the day when she would have her own store, her own house, her own carriage, beautiful furniture, fine dresses, servants... it was her dream, after all, and she could dream it anyway she wanted.

The Wingates were of a seasoned age and treated Marie much more like a daughter than a servant. They, as the Van Hootenaugs before, were conservative in their ways and insisted that she go to church with them each Sunday just as any daughter would have been required but they were more gentle in their general attitudes. The elderly couple was alone now. Their two surviving daughters were both married and settled upon frontier homesteads. Their only son to survive infancy and the heir apparent to the family business had died before reaching an age for marriage and fatherhood.

Abigail Wingate, a sturdy, stable woman with a warm, generous spirit and a deep faith, found she was very pleased to have Marie's company. She had been missing close female companionship. Abigail had buried four other children through the years, an infant girl, two young sons and a daughter who had been almost fully grown. It was nothing their friends and other families all around them had not suffered as well. It was half expected. There were miscarriages, still births, fevers, infections, unexplainable diseases, and accidents. Young deaths were a part of life and surviving childhood was never to be taken for granted. But losing their last son had been especially difficult on both the Wingates.

"I know we shall all see each other again," Abigail would say whenever she felt herself becoming overly melancholy at these losses, "what a day full of joy that will be, to see them all again as we are united together in Paradise with our Lord. Fact is, we were blessed to have them even for a little while on this earth." She would sigh wistfully and add quickly, "It's only that I know it's difficult for Master Wingate. It's hard, very hard for a man to lose all his sons." She turned and saw Marie looking at her intently. "When a man works his whole life to build something, he hopes to hand it on in his old age to his sons. Now, Master Wingate has no one to whom to pass his business."

Marie was drawn back to memories of her own family. Was it not perhaps easier for a mother to lose a baby than for children to lose their mother? Then she would see Mistress Wingate sneak a handkerchief from within her sleeve and wipe quickly at her eyes. Perhaps it depended on how old the child was when the loss occurred, Marie pondered, for losing one's parent was the expectation after a long life was it not?

One evening as they were cleaning up the table from supper, Marie asked Mistress Wingate if she could borrow the family Bible to read. Just about every household within the English colonies owned a copy of the Bible commissioned by the English king, James I, in the earlier part of the century.

"Why Heavens child, have you no Bible of your own?" the older woman asked in astonishment.

"No, I could not read before," Marie said simply. "But in zee nursery with zee Van Hootenaug children I was beginning to learn."

"By all means you must continue. When we finish here, we'll sit down together and read."

"Are yoo sure yoo would not mind?"

"Of course not," the older woman smiled.

"But I want not to take up all your time."

"Mercy, I've nothing any better to do. It's the best use I could possibly make of my time these days. Once you are reading well you never need allow anyone to come between you and what God Himself says in His Holy Word," she said, looking quietly pleased.

And so Abigail Wingate encouraged Marie to read out loud while helping her pronunciation. The girl's dogged determination impressed the elder woman. Abigail was certain this was God's work they were about. Marie did not disclose that her motivation had more to do with the practical development of literacy than any desire for greater piety. But sometimes the text did promote a very stimulating conversation especially when Marie read in front of both Wingates and Master Wingate would point out a lesson.

During those long days of summer, Marie also worked hours and hours in the store doing inventories of the stock to become familiar with it. Many evenings long after supper while the light was still good, Master Wingate would find her busy with the shelves of merchandise, cleaning, stacking, and straightening. He told her she did not have to work quite so hard. But aside from her hunger to learn, the tasks helped her to forget how much she was missing Jacques. It had been months since she had heard his voice, seen his laughing eyes, and felt the warmth of his easy charm. Each Sunday in church she remembered to add him into her prayers. God had to know where he was and what he needed, she reasoned, and so she prayed fervently that God would look after her dearest friend and Richard as well and keep them both safe.

That September, as the long, warm days of summer shortened and began to cool, an event occurred which was to have a long reaching and irreversible influence on the direction of Marie's life.

Master Wingate made the decision to take in an apprentice.

Marie was shocked and upset when quite suddenly and unexpectedly a young lad almost two years her junior showed up in the store and was introduced to her as "the new apprentice, Samuel Cooper." The youth was housed in the spare room lean-to at the back of the kitchen after he and Marie helped Mistress Wingate clear the space. Most of the things were moved into the storage shed out behind the chicken coop. The women gave the quarters a thorough cleaning and fresh bedding while Samuel was set to the task of daubing a clay mixture into any cracks and chinks in the outside walls.

"Mind you do a good job filling those cracks," Mistress Wingate told him. "When the winter winds are blowing, you'll thank yourself for making the effort."

"I do not understand," Marie spoke up later that evening when she was once again alone with the Wingates. "Why did you not tell me, Master Wingate? What am I doing wrong?"

"But there's nothing that you are doing wrong, Marie," Wingate answered, very puzzled at her obvious distress.

"I work very hard... do I not?" she puzzled.

"Yes, yes, of course, you do."

"I am learning very quickly... am I not?" she added hesitantly.

"Child, I have no quarrel with your work. My decision to take in young Cooper as an apprentice has nothing at all to do with you." He removed his reading glasses and rubbed the bridge of his nose.

"But it does, it does... am *I* not your apprentice?" she looked dumbfounded.

"Good heavens, no, child, you are my helper."

"Helper? Apprentice? I am sorry, sir, but I do not understand the difference." Marie, still struggling with the subtleties of the English language, felt there must be something she was missing. "Please explain to me."

"An apprentice is someone who wants to learn a business or trade so he has the means to earn a living at it," the older man explained patiently rather like a school lesson. What he did not mention was that there was generally a contract and the master, while being obliged to teach everything including literacy, did not need to pay an apprentice for the work. It was education in exchanged for labor. And in some occupations, one's family paid the master to accept the apprentice.

"But *I* want to learn the business! *I* want to make my living at it someday!" Marie exclaimed, tears of hurt filling her eyes. "I thought you were pleased with me, sir. I thought you would keep me on and continue to teach me."

He smiled at her as though pacifying a confused child. "Oh, I understand. No, no, I have no intention of turning you out onto the street... is that what you are afraid of, my dear?" the elderly man asked kindly.

"Then why, why am I not your apprentice?" she fought to keep tears from spilling down her cheeks.

"But, that's foolishness, you should know very well," Wingate appeared genuinely befuddled. "You are a female," he said, stating the obvious and feeling very uncomfortable with her emotional upset. "Someday you will get married and settle down to raise a nice family and keep a proper home," he went on, busying himself by filling the small bowl of his long stemmed pipe with tobacco. Using a straw, he took flame from the fire in the hearth to light it.

Marie was so stunned by his answer, it shocked away her tears. "But sir, what if this never happens?" she inquired quite logically.

"Of course it will. You are a very handsome looking girl, Marie," he said, puffing on his pipe. He looked to his wife for her support. "Some day you will find a nice young man, isn't that right, mother?" Wingate looked again at Abigail who nodded her agreement. "There are plenty of single men in the colonies. Someday someone will offer to make you his wife."

"And if I am a... *wife,* as you say, does this mean I cannot run a store?"

"Why you'll be so busy keeping house and having babies you won't have time to run a store," he replied chuckling.

"But what of your wife, sir? She, too, runs the store."

"Well, our children are grown now but it is my enterprise, my responsibility. Just as having the babies has been her responsibility. That's a job no man can do," he added with sincere appreciation. "Besides, learning the gentler arts is what is important in securing a position as wife to a shopkeeper... or as most any good wife... not an apprenticeship in stock and suppliers. If you marry a shopkeeper, he will already know these things."

"So women can never serve as apprentices?" Marie asked.

Wingate puffed on his pipe. "Well, I'll not say *never.* One might apprentice to a dressmaker or a milliner, even a cook if one had not learned at home... but that is to develop a specific skill, mind you. It has always been my opinion that God simply did not give women the constitution for the rigueurs of commerce."

Marie could say nothing more but she carried her bitter disappointment to bed with her that night. For the first time in weeks she had no pleasant visions of owning her own store by which to lull herself to sleep.

Not too long after this discussion Wingate gave her a small raise in her wages. In the midst of her flush of happiness she was told by a rather jealous young Samuel that he may not be earning anything now but after his apprenticeship was served he could expect to earn four times what she was earning. And, he said rather spitefully, he would be in line to take over when "old man Wingate" retired or he could possibly buy out the business to be both owner and boss.

Marie was speechless. That night she counted out her little cache of savings. She was much better acquainted with the cost of things and the value of English money than she had been. After a few simple calculations, she concluded that it could easily take half a life time for her to save up enough to have the stake to start a store of her own. And *that* being done only by living always as a pauper. She was not going to get anywhere working for somebody else.

Marie lapsed into despair. She moved numbly through the days and retired early each night. The Wingates saw it as a mood which she would get over. Something perhaps brought on by the changing seasons, colder weather and shorter days, or perhaps one of those female upsets to which the weaker sex fell victim. Thomas Wingate silently admonished himself that it was a sign that they were teaching Marie too much. It was a well-known fact, after all, that females dare not try to learn as much as men, it taxed their spirits and caused maladies to their frailer bodies. He hoped they had not done the young girl irreparable harm and vowed to ease up on filling Marie's young head with so much information. It was a shame, however, for she was so much quicker than young Samuel and extremely helpful in reinforcing his training. Wingate knew he could leave them alone and Marie would make certain Samuel's ciphering was correct.

Keeping her thoughts to herself, Marie wondered what Jacques would say about this "apprentice" business... *if* she ever saw Jacques again. He and Richard had been gone for almost seven months now. Winter would be coming soon. Surely their trapping expedition would be returning before long, she thought. But what if he and Richard had moved on to another area permanently? Surely not, she told herself. Surely he would have told her. And why was that, she asked herself? He was not responsible for her, nor to her. They were only friends. People in this new world left friends behind all the time. Had they not all arrived here by leaving friends behind?

Through the Sunday afternoons of October, Marie took short walks alone to the outskirts of town and observed the changing beauty of the landscape streaked in colors which had no comparison to anything she had witnessed before. The climate back home had never produced such color, at least none she had seen. Here the flaming reds, startling oranges, brilliant yellows, golds, dark wines, and russets painted such a vibrant landscape it actually took her breath away and filled her with a sense of wonderment and awe that she didn't quite understand. Could the God that made such beauty really be watching over her as they said in church? And if He was, how did she measure up in His eyes? What did He expect of her? And how was she to know?

These were solemn thoughts evoking a very sober mood to match the contradictory melancholia of the season. Marie saw a large phalanx of birds flying across the pale sky, swooping, curving, moving as if of one mind. She had noticed many large flocks of birds of late all heading southward. Where did they go, she wondered? And how did they all know how to fly together like that? If God could direct the birds, why could He not give clearer direction to people? Why was life so hard to understand?

Was it true, she asked herself again? Was Master Wingate right? Were women only to concern themselves with nothing more than being wives and mothers? That certainly was the example set all around her. She realized she personally knew no woman who ran her own business. Whatever was she thinking? All around her were examples of women who only helped their husbands in business and ran a home.

Should she only concern herself with getting by until some man should ask her to be his wife? But what man? Marie sighed. Ah, there was another problem. There were men all over the colony, it was true. Indeed, there were far more men than women and she supposed if she really encouraged such attentions... But as Marie thought of all the many, many men she had so far met in the course of everyday life in the store, there was none to suit her save one. Where would she ever find a man like Jacques-Jean Charte?

Marie's heart skipped a beat just thinking of him and then it wept. She could never expect to marry a man like Monsieur Jacques even if there were any others like him. And so what was to be her fate? To accept marriage to just any man? To clean his house and wash his clothes and share his bed and do his bidding just because that was her place? To hope that he held her in some regard and did not beat her which the law said was his right, to learn to take her primary joy only in whatever children she might produce? Was that really what God expected her to do?

The autumn colors all faded and the leaves fell in thick rustling carpets under foot, but still Jacques and Richard did not returned. The sunlight now came in thin brittle shafts and it was often overcast with clouds sprung up off the sea. It rained a great deal and the winds blew in cold off the ocean. The leaves had turned to shriveled scuttling shapes being driven about by the gusting breezes. Marie needed to light the lantern in order to read to herself in her room after church.

One afternoon as she read, she sat up suddenly after reading a passage in Proverbs. She reread the words again:

"Who can find a virtuous woman? For her price is far above rubies....
"She considereth a field, and buyeth it: with the fruit of her hands
she planteth a vineyard...
"She perceiveth that her merchandise is good...
"She maketh fine linen, and selleth it; and delivereth girdles unto
the merchant..."

That sounded very much like a woman in business, thought Marie. And she read it again. This *was* a woman in business and right there in God's own book such a woman was called – *virtuous*.

In pure delight she silently hooted within herself, milling her arms and legs in the air. She was tempted to run out and find Master Wingate; to push the pages under his nose and read them aloud into his ear. Tempted – yes, but maturity took over and she knew it would be wiser not to argue this with him. This was her conversation with God. Marie felt God had answered her question. There was nothing in her dream that went against God's will. She closed the Bible and lay back on the featherbed, a smile returning to her countenance. Closing her arms about the precious book, she drifted off into a peaceful, untroubled sleep.

Marie was standing at the counter of the Wingate Emporium carefully rolling a length of calico back onto the bolt when she heard a familiar voice call out her name.

"Marie!" A figure stood silhouetted in the doorway blocking the weak, late autumn light.

"Jacques?!!" she cried out with sudden delight. She turned about quickly. She would have recognized that voice anywhere. She ran to the dark figure standing with open arms and threw her own arms around his neck.

"Jacques, is it really you? You are safe! You are here! Oh, I am so happy to see you..." and then for no reason at all she began to cry and laugh at the same time and embarrassed herself in doing so. She alternately tried to flick away her tears and stifle her giggles and generally acted just slightly addled in the head.

Master Wingate smiled indulgently and told her to get out of his store before she scared away his customers and perhaps it would be best for her to take the rest of the day off. Grabbing her heavy shawl, she pulled on Jacques' arm and hurried out into the street.

"Let me look at you," she cried gleefully as they gained the full outdoor light.

Jacques stood before her with a broad smile on his deeply tanned face. By contrast to his darkened skin, his teeth appeared all the whiter beneath his small thin golden moustache. His strong jaw was in need of a shave but his gray eyes twinkled merrily at her beneath a shock of unruly blond hair which had escaped the leather thong at the nape of his neck. He wore no lace now but a collarless shirt and leather weskit over a body that seemed to have gained a powerful density and strength. His breeches were worn and soiled at the knees, his dirty stockings were not silk but of coarser cotton peeking over the tops of his boots and his soiled coat had seen better days when the cuffs showed no fraying.

"You look well, Jacques," she said honestly, appraising him, "healthy, unhurt. A little different... a little..." she hesitantly groped for the correct words.

"A little worse for the wear I should think," he grinned.

"No. I am thinking... stronger, *tough* I think is perhaps the right word."

He laughed. "Sleeping on the damp ground and beating snakes off your path is not my idea of the most pleasant way to make a living, but it is a living none the less and it will make one tough. I need to pay the barber a visit," he added stroking his chin and raked his hair away from his eyes with his fingers.

She laughed with him. "It is so good to have you home," she beamed and squeezed his arm again, aware of rock hard muscle beneath her hands. "I was beginning to worry," she added, now feeling almost shy. "There has been ice in the mornings. I think the snow comes very soon."

"Come with me, I have something to show you," he said, brushing aside any concern and taking on the enthusiasm of a schoolboy wanting to show off a new treasure.

Taking her arm, he led her down to the waterfront where Richard, sporting a full bushy beard and long buckskin trousers topped with a tunic shirt of leather, was standing guard over several huge piles of pelts and leaning on his musket. His European hat looked oddly incongruent with the native style clothing he wore.

"They are all sold, my friend," Richard called out in a roar upon seeing Jacques and Marie approaching. "Ahhh, Marie," he grinned broadly and tipped his hat as he walked lazily toward her. "I knew Jacques could not wait to find you; you are all I have heard about for the past two hundred miles."

Marie blushed and looked guardedly at Jacques.

"It is true," he shrugged nonchalantly. "I missed your silly little face, I must confess. Having nothing but Richard and savages to look upon, can you blame me?"

Marie felt her heart jump and beat more rapidly within her breast and she willed it to slow down. They were only bantering; joking, she thought, but it pleased her, oh, how it did please her. She turned and gave Richard a quick hug.

"Welcome home, Richard," she said, hoping it did not sound like an afterthought. "Your English is much improved. Both of you!"

Marie felt her senses run willy-nilly from her, scattering to the four winds. Her dearest friends were back. Nothing bad had happened. And he had thought of her while he was gone. With her heart thumping loudly in her chest she forced herself to look at the furs and refocus her thoughts. She began to run her hands over some of the pelts. They were the most beautiful things she had ever seen.

"You came back with all of these?" she cried out softly. "*Mon Dieu,* they are *magnifique!*"

"*Il y a* enough here for every lady at Louis' Court to have a new fur cape, *n'est-ce pas?*" Jacques boasted proudly in French. "*Et...*"

"Sh-sh," Marie warned with a sudden interruption, aware and ashamed that she had said anything at all in French herself. She had led Jacques right into it. "You are back in the English settlement now, Jacques, you must be more careful of what you say and how you say it," she whispered.

"Yes, well," he glanced around self-consciously at her reminder. He turned his attention to business. "So... Richard, you say everything is sold? Did we make a good price?"

"We did far better than we hoped," Richard replied proudly and slapped Jacques on the back. "We will live well this winter, my friend, have money to supply ourselves next spring, and with a little left over besides."

Just then a stranger came up to them and began to talk to Richard about loading the skins on board the anchored ship. Marie saw him hand over two large purses in payment. She was struck dumb imagining the amount of money it represented.

With their business settled, Jacques was eager to seek out a barber, arrange for a hot bath, and find some new clothing. He asked Marie if she would like to meet them at The Pork 'n' Porridge later and join them for supper. She happily accepted the invitation and the trio parted company.

Marie was so happy her body seemed weightless and her feet hardly felt the ground. She hurried back to her room at the Wingate's to freshen up. Alone, she was now conscious of having been caught in her oldest skirt and mended apron, and with her hair tied lopsided upon her head under her coif. She went to the wardrobe, opened it and spied her new Sunday frock. Mistress Wingate had helped her make it and it was one Jacques and Richard had never seen before. She decided she would wear it to supper in honor of their homecoming.

Removing her outer garments, she stood in her shift, poured fresh water into a basin and washed. Brushing out her heavy hair, she let it fall about her shoulders. She had discovered a light scent that smelled of lemon in the store's inventory and upon admiring it, Mistress Wingate had given her a bottle. Marie splashed it on. She liked its cool, refreshing and astringent quality. Pulling on the light green frock which laced up the front for ease in dressing, she snugged up the bodice from her slender waist to her full high bosom and surveyed herself critically in the mirror.

On that fateful day when Celimene had found her, scrubbed her clean, dressed her and brought her before a mirror, Marie had been a bit startled and very surprised. Looking upon herself, she had seen a stranger. She had thought the stranger quite pleasant looking, so scrubbed fresh, pink, and in clean clothing. As time went on, however, Marie had become increasingly dissatisfied with her own appearance. She could find a dozen faults and was certain that was why she sometimes saw people staring at her. It was no wonder Jacques said she had a "funny little face," she thought.

As she stood before the mirror in her room, she noted that her hair hung thick in smooth, gentle rolling waves of light brown streaked with gold. She could hope that it would detract from her *funny little face* except the mores of the day dictated that she must hide it under a cap. With a sigh she twisted it up and pinned it atop her head. She popped the lace cap over it, grabbed her best shawl, and hurried out the door.

The walk to The Pork 'n' Porridge brought pink to her cheeks and as she stood for a moment inside looking for her friends, Marie looked fresh, bright, and very lovely but she was completely unaware of it. Neither was she aware that more than one man turned to look at her with explicit interest. If she had stood alone much longer, at least one would have approached her with suggestive familiarity. Master Thompkins saw her arrive as well and hurried to greet her before any of his more aggressive patrons could instigate an embarrassing scene. For the innkeeper, it was all in a day's work when you lived in the colonies where lovely young women were very scarce.

With friendly courtesy Thompkins escorted Marie to a table set off in a corner which he had already reserved for the two young Frenchmen. He helped Marie to her seat while making it quite clear in louder than normal tones that she would not be alone for long as her friends could be expected at any moment.

She sat there quietly and had waited only a few minutes when she saw Jacques and Richard, both in clean suits of clothing, coming down the stairway from the rooms above.

Marie's face lit up with a smile as the two young men walked toward her. Jacques looked like himself again, well groomed, shaved and bathed, with his hair trimmed and neatly clubbed with a large wine colored bow matching his suit. He looked relaxed as he took his seat. But the difference in Richard was incredible and Marie could not help but say so.

"Richard! Your face has returned," she observed teasingly. "I had forgotten how handsome you can look when you are not trying to imitate a bear."

"I feel naked," he grumbled, rubbing at his chin, but he was pleased at her compliment. Sporting a dark blue suit of clothes, it was obvious that Richard's lanky frame had filled out with hard muscles and he too, had taken the pains to bathe and groom.

"I have missed you both so much," Marie said, spontaneously reaching out with her hands and grasping each man's forearm with an affectionate squeeze. "I am so glad you are back from the wilds... and safe," she beamed as she looked from one to the other. "So tell me, did you really trap all of those beautiful animals?"

"No-no," Richard responded. "The best furs usually are found in the winter. The natives trap them and trade them to us. The only furs we might trap is during our stops at one village or another. Or since bears sleep all winter, you hunt them only summer and autumn."

"You stayed in Indian villages?" Marie's eyes went round.

Jacques nodded.

"And he caused quite a stir with his pretty curls," teased Richard.

"Only because it is different; it was the same with Red," Jacques countered.

"Red?"

"One of our traveling companions," explained Richard. "His hair is like a flame."

"What are the natives like?" Marie could not suppress her curiosity.

"The friendly ones are... friendly," replied Richard.

"I suppose she could have guessed as much," Jacques laughed. "They are different of course, but not without their own rules of behavior. Hospitality is very important and every tribe has its own peculiarities."

"Do they speak English or French?" she asked.

Jacques shook his head. "The ones we encountered... some spoke a little English and we learned a kind of gesture language to speak to those who do not," Jacques added.

"Gesture language?" puzzled Marie.

"Hand gestures which seem to be rather universally understood. They are most eager to trade," Richard said and demonstrated a few for Marie's amusement.

After a leisurely meal filled with stories, the two young men good-naturedly allowed Marie to count out their earnings and divide it into lots for them. She now understood money well. The first portion was to pay for their next expedition, they said, which they would finance themselves this time. They gave that gold to her along with a list of the supplies they would need in spring. She would arrange it through Master Wingate. The rest she divided in half, one portion for Jacques and one for Richard. Each individual portion was further divided into two. The money each man would live on this winter and the smaller portion being the money each man would save for future investment or a rainy day.

As Marie counted out the coins she was pricked again by a sense of her own frustration. In one season, they had amassed more money just for savings than she had been able to save so far in her entire life. She was not jealous of their success; to the contrary, she was very happy for them and proud of their achievement. But it made her realize sharply her handicap in being female.

As the evening drew to an end Jacques insisted on escorting Marie back to the Wingate's. "It is late and dark and I will not have you on the streets alone. Especially with our money," he added in jest.

They walked along the darkened lantern lit streets. The evening air was pleasantly mild, blowing in from the sea with the tang of salt. As they walked, Marie decided to tell Jacques of the apprentice situation and how troubled she was by it.

"It is not that I do not wish to have a family some day, Jacques, because I do, I do, more than anything," she said earnestly, "but how can I know what the future brings? I depend only upon myself. And so I want... no, I *must* build something for myself. Does that not make sense? Or am I being foolish as Master Wingate says?"

"It is never foolish to have dreams of something better," he replied thoughtfully. "Is that not what this land is all about?"

"Jacques," she stopped suddenly in the street within the circle of light from one of the hanging lanterns and spun around to look directly up at him. "I want to learn to trap! Will you teach me?"

"What?!"

"I see the money you can make. I want to learn to trap just like you."

"No-no, Marie," he objected sternly, "believe me, you do not." She looked at him plaintively. "That is not an undertaking for a girl," he added more gently but just as resolutely.

"You sound like Master Wingate!" she cried in accusation.

"Do you think it is easy to carry a load of furs on your back?"

"But ..."

"Truly, there are many men who do not survive the hardships. It has less to do with you being a female than about you not being strong enough... it is a brutal occupation. One slip in setting a trap and you can crush your own arm or lose a hand."

She turned her gaze to the ground in disappointment while Jacques, in turn, felt somehow guilty. They walked for a few paces in silence, the faint sound of their footsteps evident in the quiet.

"I know what it is to want something more," Jacques said at last. "For most of my young life I had no prospects. Then, I was an heir for a short time, but now I, too, must 'build something for myself' as you say. I do not see why you should not just because you are a woman, n'est-ce pas? But you must choose the right... mmm... *opportunity* and it will take a lot of hard work. No. More than that, it may take a willingness to risk everything, even your life."

"But have I not done that already? I can do it again."

Now he paused for a moment in the street and she paused with him. He looked at the earnest sincerity in her face, her unlined brow puckered in a frown as the wind lifted a light brown curl which had escaped from under her cap.

"You are right," he said, remembering their escape in France. "You have done that already. I have no doubt that you could do it again," he added. "All right, you must give me a little time to think on this. We will talk of it again."

Marie's spirits were suddenly lifted. Her sadness and doubts flew away and she was certain once more that she did have a future. They reached the Wingate's store and Jacques gave her hand a gentle kiss and flourished a courtly bow in parting.

Late into the night as Marie lie in her bed trying to reconstruct her happy dreams of owning her own store, Jacques' handsome face kept crowding into her mind. She was suddenly reminded of the hard warmth of his body as she had thrown herself into his embrace earlier that day, the softness of his lips brushing against the top of her hand when they had said good night, the gentleness of his hand as it had held hers, the smile in his eyes when he looked at her. She discovered her body reacting in strange ways which caused her to catch her breath. It was most peculiarly disturbing.

Marie loved Monsieur Jacques-Jean. She knew that. Could anyone help but love him, she asked herself? Who would not love the exceedingly handsome young aristocrat with his very pleasant manners and extremely considerate air? It was like loving a king or a prince, a worshipful kind of love from afar, a love that was not expected to be returned. Was Jacques not like the fairy tale prince who was so handsome, so very kind, so charming, and yet strong and clever and naturally adored by all the women and admired by all the men? That was exactly him, she thought. Only someone as odious as Bouchet could harbor ill against someone like Jacques.

Bouchet! The mere remembrance of the name sent a shudder through her body and a sickening feeling began turning in the pit of her stomach. She could still see his leering eyes. Smell his fetid breath. Feel his bulk heavy upon her, crushing her, his rough hands pawing at her, his penetrating invasion of her body. In the darkness Marie could hear the snorting sounds he had made as he progressed to his finish. The sounds were so loud, so clear in her memory that she recoiled and pushed out with her arms and hands, startled to feel nothing except the empty space around her.

Tears began streaming from her eyes as she relived her humiliation and remembered the others he had forced upon her as he took their money. She had been his tavern whore. She turned to sob into her pillow.

A common tavern whore.

A whore.

Whore.

Whore.

Whore.

The word echoed in her head with accusing degradation. She had been nothing more than an object men had used to relieve their sexual needs, an object to be used without feeling. And she reminded herself sharply that Monsieur Jacques-Jean was a true gentleman, a man of noble blood and honor, and the son of a duke. No matter how gallant and pleasant he was to her, she had better never forget her place. She shuddered deeply to think what the Wingates would think of her if they knew. Jacques knew. He knew her shame and degradation, and still he treated her with respect. He pitied her, that's all, she told herself quickly. He was so very... *kind*, she thought sadly. A true gentleman. Real gentlemen were kind and polite and showed courtesy even to those far beneath them. Is that not what made them the objects of adoration?

Marie, she scolded herself at last, *you must be grateful for his kindness and his friendship, you stupid girl. It is far more than you deserve. And do not waste your time with foolish thoughts of... of anything else. You are not the kind of person he would ever see as anything more than a... a friend, perhaps. You can consider yourself most fortunate to have that regard. He would not just relieve himself with a common whore. He has the better tastes of a true gentleman.*

The image of Celimene came to mind with memories of her exquisite beauty, her perfect, flawless ivory skin, her rounded cheeks, her lushly sculpted body with soft dainty hands and feet. And her scent. From her head to her toes she had had a scent, sweet like roses yet subtly spicy, from the herb and rosewater baths she loved to take. *She smelled so good,* thought Marie, *and if she smelled that good to me, how much more intoxicating must she be to a man. And her smile, it had been so perfect, so warm and radiant and compelling with those perfect teeth. And the easy way she captivated everyone's attention with her charm. The husky musical lilt of her voice, the flutter of her long, black lashes around luminous eyes that seemed to say exactly whatever men wanted to hear.* Marie's self-image shriveled to dust in her lengthy mental liturgy of Celimene's assets.

She recalled too well that last day at the cottage when Jacques had come to spend the entire afternoon in Celimene's bed. At the time she had marveled at the intensity and duration of their pleasuring noises. Now, for some reason the thought of them being together in lustful carnal embraces taking such pleasure in each other wounded Marie as it never had before. How many nights did Jacques lie awake thinking of Celimene and longing for her, she wondered painfully?

Marie did not want to attempt an answer and fought to drop into the oblivion of sleep.

Chapter 14

T he last lingering autumn days gave way overnight to the icy winds of winter which swept the straight little streets clean of everything that was not secured in its place. Traffic in the large harbor slowed but did not halt altogether for the weather was more temperate than in the colonies to the north. In New York Towne they had less snow and the harbor was never frozen over completely but people walked hunched over, none the less, clutching their wraps tightly about them.

Business at the store remained brisk although they had to light the lanterns long before closing time during these, the shortest daylight hours of the year. The steady stream of customers opening and shutting the door created no shortage of drafts. A large fire always burned brightly in the iron stove but beyond its immediate presence the corners of the store were chilled. Marie wore several shawls and still sought the nearness of the stove or kitchen hearth as often as she could.

She was getting to know the store's steady customers. People whose lives slowly unfolded over the weeks and months of purchases from tidbits learned here and there. She learned who had relatives in the colonies, who had a visitor bringing fresh news, where the family had sprung from, whose child had taken ill, who was planning a marriage, who had suffered a loss, how business was faring, and what news had been heard from home. People were willing to share news and information from "home." It gave everyone a sense of community. They all knew how far they were from that land which they had once called home, no matter which country it was. Europe and England were a long way back across a fickle and capricious sea.

Only the children were different. In them one recognized a sense of ownership, a complete sense of belonging right here in this place. They had little patience in hearing their elders speak longingly of some distant place although they dared not say so outright. But Marie could see they felt no sense of loss. This land was their land. This was the only home they knew and they had better things to occupy their minds and attentions than to listen to the adults waxing nostalgic about the old places and ways. And if those old places and ways had been so sublime, why had they left them? She thought it but did not say it.

Of course, there was always someone new coming into the store as well. Many were ordinary folk. They came for food stocks, supplies, things to get them through the winter before they set out for the frontier. Always they arrived so full of hope. Some would continue to return through the winter, then come in for a final spending spree in the spring when they would purchase tools, seed and those basic staples they would need before striking out into the wilderness on their own, rarely to be seen back in town again. Others would never leave the town. They would lose their money gambling through the winter, or fall victim to robbery, or succumb to sickness or some other misfortune which would steal away their nest egg. They would hire themselves out, just as she had and they would spend years talking of going out to the frontier, homesteading, or buying property, but it did not happen. Some few would live and eventually die in the town without ever achieving anything.

Many of the poor came to this land as indentured servants. Someone had paid for their passage to the colonies and now they were obligated to work off the debt. Many had arrived not knowing where they would be going or what they would be doing. The ship that had brought them sold them upon arrival at a tidy profit to pay for their one way passage. In general, they were always able-bodied, healthy, strong, and they tended to be young or possessed of a valued skill. Most were sold quickly and had no choice regarding the circumstances in which they would be living until their contract was fulfilled. If they were fortunate, they ended up with good masters. If not, they could be treated not much differently than slaves, for slaves they were until the debt was paid.

These came into the store to shop for their masters and mistresses and lived for the day when they would have their obligations worked off and be given their papers of freedom to strike out on their own. Generally that would take seven years for an unskilled laborer or house servant. It made Marie realize how very fortunate she had been that Jacques had taken her with him. Had he paid for her passage, she wondered? Whether he had or whether Monsieur Dufee had given them free passage, she was still obligated to Jacques. If it had not been for him, Dufee would have had no reason to allow Marie on one of his ships. And if she had been determined to come to America on her own, she also would have had to trade her labors for seven long years in exchange for her passage. It would have taken seven years before she could have even thought of earning her own money and saving for her future. Seven years in which she could have been worked to death. She thought with a little shudder of still working for the Van Hootenaugs and not being able to leave.

There were also people of substance who came to the colony seeking to become gentlemen farmers, seeking opportunities, or establishing businesses with investment capital. Some would stop briefly in New York harbor before finding their way down to the Virginia Colony where it was said rolling hills of fertile land just waited to be planted in tobacco. And these people would also find their way to the store to buy necessities, luxuries, medicinals, sundries, a new bonnet, a stout cane. Marie loved to meet them all. She talked with them as they made their purchases, and looked forward to seeing them again in the future.

But there was no one she looked forward to seeing more than Jacques. He and Richard dropped by frequently through the season to say hello and exchange a few pleasant words. The time they loitered making some small modification to their spring supply order or passing along a random tidbit of harbor news was a thin disguise for their attraction to Thomas Wingate's prized stove, radiating its circle of warmth on frigid winter days. And still the trio spent their Sundays together once Marie returned from church services with her employers.

"Marie, could you help me with this box, dear?" Abigail Wingate called through the door of the stockroom.

"Of course," Marie rushed to assist. She accepted a medium-sized box from the older woman who followed with another box in her arms. "They are not heavy," she observed.

"No, but be careful, the contents are breakable. Let's bring these over to the big window." It was the first working day of December and snow was falling in big, soft, coin sized flakes outside.

"What is inside?" Marie asked.

"How would you like to set up the Nativity?" Abigail smiled.

"Nativity?" Marie asked hesitantly, unsure what the older woman meant.

"Yes, the little manger scene. Oh, I know there are some who think it's idolatry but Master Wingate and I never agreed with the Puritans on that. It depicts the story of the birth of the Christ Child." Abigail looked at the girl. "No one in their right mind actually worships the statues… surely you know the story?"

Marie shook her head. "I… I do not think so, Mistress Wingate."

"Oh, my," Abigail tried not to sound shocked. "Well, let us set these boxes aside for now. I know what our reading lesson tonight will be."

After supper that evening Abigail had Marie read the story of the birth of Christ found in the gospel of Saint Matthew and again in Saint Luke. The next day the older woman led the younger again to the boxes.

"Come, let us open these boxes now but be very careful with the wrappings." She began to unroll packing cloths from one bundle and a small figurine shaped like a man in kingly robes emerged. "Ahh, here we have one of the wise men."

Marie was carefully unwrapping an object of her own. "It is another wise man, I think," she said. The figure she held in her hand fascinated her. It was richly detailed and brightly colored and unlike anything she had ever seen before.

"Yes. And here is a little sheep."

The next object Marie identified in her hands was a young boy with a staff in his hand and a lamb across his shoulders.

"A shepherd," said Abigail.

Marie nodded and thought she could almost hear the little lamb bleating, it looked so real. She unwrapped a very small baby figure.

"Ah, I see you found the Baby Jesus," Abigail smiled. "Now to find his mother."

"They are so beautiful," Marie exclaimed softly, "so beautiful."

The two women proceeded to unwrap over two dozen pieces including animals, angels, the Holy Family, and a beautiful glittering star. Each piece had been perfectly formed in porcelain, painted in great detail and then fired with a glaze that made it shine.

"Master Wingate purchased the set years ago. Came from Italy. Paid a pretty penny. Such a surprise," Abigail sighed wistfully. "We've always put it up on the mantel but I thought we could set it all up in the store window this year so everyone can enjoy it."

Sometime later Abigail called to her husband. "Master Wingate, come see what we have done." He set aside his accounting books and came out of his office. When he saw the display his expression turned very sad for a moment, then he smiled encouragingly.

"Let's see what it looks like from outside," he said, going back for his coat and assisting his wife with her cape. Marie waited for their reactions.

"It looks so lovely," Abigail Wingate said again when she came back inside shivering and red-cheeked. Marie thought she detected a tear in Mistress Wingate's eye.

Thomas Wingate came back in stamping the snow from his feet. "It is beginning to look like Christmas, Mother," he said to his wife with a distinctly sad note in his voice.

Marie heard Mistress Wingate blowing her nose. She returned having hung up her cape. "What did you do last Christmas?" she asked Marie briskly.

"We went to church Christmas Eve."

"Yes, and you did not hear the story of the Nativity?"

Marie shrugged, "I do not recall but I remember the baby was fussing and I had to take him out for a while."

Abigail said nothing but could not help wondering how this child had been raised in a Christian country and had not heard the story of the Nativity in her almost sixteen years?

Marie felt herself blush but continued. "The Van Hootenaugs did allow me to take the afternoon for myself on Christmas Day once I had cleaned up the children after their dinner. I met Jacques and Richard and we had supper at the inn."

"Supper at the inn?" Abigail replied with an indignant sniff. "Well, we shall have to do better than that this year. You are one of the family now and must have your Christmas dinner with us," she said with a positive nod. "And I want you to invite your gentlemen friends to join us as well."

"Yes?" Marie's eyes opened wide in question.

"Oh, yes, yes. I insist," the woman replied, gathering energy as she continued speaking almost without a breath. "Samuel will be going to his family and our daughter Jane won't be able to make it because of her condition. Elizabeth and Nathaniel will be here, bless them, but I do so like to have a full table. The more the merrier, I always say. This house needs to be filled with songs and laughter.

Now I insist, you and your friends must plan to be with us."

"I am certain Jacques and Richard will both be most pleased to receive such an invitation," Marie smiled.

"Then, make sure they come." Abigail stopped suddenly and looked at Marie thoughtfully. "And we must see about a holiday dress for you. Come, look at this," she said, drawing the young woman to the bolts of fabric. She selected a shimmering muted gold silk taffeta that had just come in on the last ship and pealed several yards off to drape across Marie's shoulder. "This sets off your hair and eyes very nicely, I think."

"It is much too fine," Marie protested.

"Nonsense," the older woman chided warmly, "it will be my Christmas gift to you. Time you dress up a bit; you haven't a frivolous bone in your body, child. My girls were never half so practical minded as you. Tomorrow morning we will take this over to Seamstress Perkins and she can take some measurements and get started.

When Marie extended the Wingates' invitation, Jacques and Richard accepted with sincere appreciation. They had not had the opportunity to sit down at a family dinner table for well over a year. Even Richard admitted he missed it. They had gone from eating in a ship's galley, to eating in taverns, to eating around campfires and back to eating in taverns.

It was a convenient excuse to order up a new vest and Jacques made certain that Richard went along to the tailor. The tall man greatly preferred the freedom of the Indian buckskins which continued to draw stares within the town. But Jacques teased and cajoled that within civilization, his partner might want to dress like a white man and wear shirts that were laundered upon occasion. Richard grumbled good-naturedly but consented and even planned to go to the barber for another clean shave in honor of the occasion.

Marie looked forward to Christmas Day with mounting excitement. She had never had a truly fine dress and the anticipation of wearing one was almost more than she could bear. And unspoken in her mind was the question... would Jacques think her pretty?

Several days before the holiday, the Wingates' oldest daughter, Elizabeth, arrived with her husband, Nathaniel Stone. Marie liked the rather large boned young woman immediately and greeted her with a friendly smile.

Elizabeth Wingate Stone was aware of having a choice to make when she met Marie. She could choose to dislike the petite and pretty younger woman for any number of petty jealous reasons including moving in and usurping a far too daughterly position in the Wingate home. Or, Elizabeth told herself, she could be a true Christian and adult as any married woman should be, and accept Marie's offer of friendship in its genuineness and choose to like the girl for all the many reasons she was likable. Elizabeth chose to like her and her charming accent and to be grateful her mother had some female companionship.

"I understand it was you who helped Mother with the window display," Elizabeth said to Marie. "Those figurines were my brother's favorite part of Christmas. He was always the one allowed to set them up on the mantel. He loved doing that. Did mother tell you?"

"No, she did not," Marie replied and remembered Mistress Wingate's tear filled eyes. "But it explains her sadness."

Elizabeth sighed deeply as well. "I miss him too. You would have liked him, Marie. He was very sweet natured. Too young and too good to have to die."

Marie nodded quietly. "That is what I thought when my sister, Louise, died. She was my mother after Ma-ma died." Elizabeth looked at the girl but Marie's eyes were cast downward. "Many die too young," she said at last.

"Of course, my brother's death has been the hardest on mother and father. He was their only surviving son and they had to watch..." she stopped herself and made an effort to brighten her mood and change the subject. "I am sorry we pushed you from your room. I asked mother to let us stay in my brother's room but she wouldn't hear of it. I guess she's not ready yet."

"The room is really your room," said Marie meekly.

"Mine and my sister's but those days are gone, we cannot both stay in there now with our husbands," she smiled, "unless we set up another bed. So, what difference does it make? Anyway, please feel free to go in and get anything of yours you need and have forgotten. I hope the sewing room is not too cramped."

"Not at all, I will be fine. But it is kind of you to be concerned," Marie smiled shyly.

Mistress Perkins finished Marie's Christmas gown and it was more than Marie could have imagined. Sewn into a very fetching design with a billowing skirt and modestly scooped neckline, it was trimmed sparingly with fine lace which ran around the neckline and draped elegantly from the cuffs of the elbow-length sleeves. The bodice and sleeves were trimmed with bright green satin which was also used in a panel set into the front to give the illusion of a full satin underskirt. The gold taffeta bodice fit Marie's slender body like a second skin and laced up the back. Marie thought it breathtaking and completely impractical for everyday life. That made it even more special. Since colony women rarely ever wore the fussy panniers which were the uniform of the very fashionable women of England and France, Marie felt extremely stylish with several very stiff new petticoats rustling profusely as she moved about.

Armed with curling irons, hair pins, and tiny wire basket frames used to lift and give foundation to the popular hair arrangements of the day, the Wingate women set to work on Marie's locks early Christmas morning. Parting her hair into sections, they lifted the height and created long sausage curls which cascaded in a thick mass along one side of her neck. Elizabeth skillfully defined tight, little wispy curls along Marie's forehead and set the entire arrangement off with a golden taffeta bow embellished with holly leaves and berry accents.

"My, my, now don't you look grand," Elizabeth said with a conspiratorial smile as she surveyed the other.

"Oh, but I do not mean to look… *grand*," replied Marie apologetically.

"Why not?" the young wife challenged boldly.

Marie paused for a moment. She was certain she understood the meaning of the word. "It is not right that I should seem to be... how do you say? I do not want others to think that I do not know my place," Marie said softly.

"My goodness, child," chimed in Abigail. "And what *place* is that? You have the same rights to fun and happiness as any young girl, no matter her birth place or her father's occupation."

"But I should not pretend to be what I am not," Marie replied earnestly.

"You mean you want not for others to think you are putting on airs?" Elizabeth offered.

"Yes, yes, *putting on airs*," Marie echoed.

"Don't be silly," Abigail said emphatically. "You are a pretty, young girl dressed up for the holidays. There is no pretense in that. You are one of most down to earth and selfless people I know. Especially around those two young gentlemen friends of yours."

"Oooo, you should never be too selfless in front of suitors," grinned Elizabeth, "it gives them the wrong idea."

Marie looked puzzled. She thought she understood the meaning of selfless, at least she could guess, but "suitor" made her think of clothing.

"Suit-ers?" she asked in puzzlement.

"Gentlemen callers," responded Elizabeth, "you know, *beaus*. Young unmarried ladies have suitors who court them… seeking their hand in marriage. But if they are going to value you and want you, you have to value yourself. Men have no idea what is worthwhile unless some woman tells them," she giggled again.

"Oh," Marie understood and blushed profusely. "But you do not understand," she replied hastily. "Jacques and Richard are like my... my family, my brothers. They are not suit-ers. You must not think that. I was only a lowly servant and Monsieur Jacques is the son of a duke."

Elizabeth looked at her mother and back to Marie.

"Well, you are not a *lowly* servant any longer, and your Monsieur Jacques is now a fur trader, I hear. You are every bit as good as he, I should think. Perhaps even better. I wouldn't know since I have not met him," she added, wondering what kind of exaggerated tale this Monsieur Jacques had spun for the obviously impressionable girl.

"No-no, you do not understand," Marie murmured under her breath. She could not explain. How could she possibly explain to them how low in life she had once been?

"Elizabeth," Abigail cautioned her daughter, "marriage has certainly turned on your sass. Now leave Marie alone. It is time you began dressing and then we will do your hair." Turning to Marie she added, "The main point, my dear, is that you do look very pretty and you have a right to look pretty. Every young lady should have opportunities to dress up and shine. And I do not believe for a minute that those two young men will dislike it for one second."

"Thank you," Marie said softly, so hoping Mistress Wingate was right.

When Jacques and Richard arrived at the Wingate home later that day, Marie opened the side entrance door widely to let them in. The enticing smells of roasting goose, spicy Christmas puddings, fragrant burning evergreens, and mulled cider spilled out into the cold air, surrounded the two young men and almost lifted them across the threshold.

Once inside the snug building, Richard grinned broadly in appreciation of Marie's rosy cheeked beauty and finery. He bent uncharacteristically low to kiss her hand with great formality.

"The little girl has grown into an enchantress," Richard said as his eyes lingered over her in such overt appraisal that it caused Marie to blush. "Mademoiselle, you are a vision," he added softly.

"Welcome, Monsieur Richard. You look very elegant yourself," she replied unconsciously mimicking a momentary formality.

"I agree to moments," Richard shrugged, breaking the mood with an impish grin and strut.

Jacques was standing quietly, his eyes had not left Marie from the moment she had opened the door. His mind was grappling with the image before him. She was still little Marie, the little sister, *la petite jeune*, but in such unusual finery and looking so elegant and sophisticated. Oh, nothing like the Court women, to be sure, women of the colony never dressed to the standards of the French aristocracy but still she was in a very grown up dress and sophisticated hairdo and she was positively… radiant. What had happened to her? It was a moment of confusion for the young man. The endearing little girl he had only felt paternalistic towards was suddenly something far different.

He found himself smiling in amusement. But of course, young girls all had such a fanciful way of playacting and seeming to be grown up. They were so much better at it than boys. He remembered a pair of sisters on his father's estate when he was a youth. He and the stable master's son had crept up upon them one rainy afternoon and watched for several minutes before laughing aloud and giving away their hiding place. The sisters had old ball dresses, feathers and scarves and had put on such a sophisticated act one might have thought them their own mothers.

Suddenly Jacques realized he should say something. "*Joyeux Noël!*" he said and he took her hand in a gallant bow and kissed it with exaggerated courtly politeness deciding he also could play-act.

"*Joyeux Noël*, Jacques," she replied, baffled and a little hurt at the insincerity of his greeting. He was mocking her, she thought. Making fun. She found herself desperately trying not to feel ridiculous. She should never have allowed Mistress Wingate and Elizabeth to talk her into this hairstyle, she thought. She must look very laughable, she castigated herself, a fool trying to ape her betters. She was a homespun servant girl in silk taffeta and Belgian lace and he was trying not to, but he could not help but laugh at her. Marie fought not to allow tears to rise up with the burn of color in her cheeks.

"As Richard has so aptly said, you look most charming and very grown up," Jacques continued to grin playfully.

"Thank you," she said a trifle stiffly, hurt with the idea that at almost sixteen she somehow was only pretending to be grown up. Her cheeks were scarlet in embarrassment although she bravely forced herself to smile. She avoided his eyes. "It is most kind of you to say so," she said. "Please, follow me. You must meet the Wingates' daughter, Elizabeth, and her husband, Nathaniel," she added and, despite her finery, she felt rather like the servant again at Celimene's cottage.

They walked into the cozy main section of the house where several trestles and a long plank table had been erected. Snowy white cloths covered the rustic pieces making it look every bit as elegant as a baronial banquet hall. The table was decorated with centerpieces made up of late autumn apples, nuts in their shells, pine cones, and oranges from Spain. Even with daylight spilling in the windows, the candles in two elegant candelabras at either end of the table gave everything a warm glow and reflected off the gleaming china and polished silver tableware.

Introductions were made after which Jacques and Richard each presented two bottles of French wine to their host and hostess who accepted them appreciatively.

"French wine?! Oh, my!" Master Wingate stared at the bottles in his hands and at those in his wife's hands. "Wherever did you find... ?"

"Ah, monsieur," Jacques replied with a twinkle in his eye. "That must be our little secret."

"To be sure, to be sure," Wingate accepted graciously. He didn't really care where it came from, he was just very pleased to have it.

Dinner was ready. Everyone gathered and Thomas Wingate gave the blessing. Then he opened the French wine and poured.

"Glad tidings of this season of great joy!" pronounced Wingate as he raised his glass first to the two young men who had brought the wine and then to everyone assembled around the table. They responded in kind.

Wingate stood poised for a moment over the goose which was browned to golden perfection. "Mother, you and your helpers have outdone yourselves," he smiled and commenced to carve the bird. Steam rose up from the succulent breast as he sliced thin juicy pieces and served. There was also a beautifully roasted rack of lamb. Dishes began to travel around the table, platters and bowls filled with savory dressing and thick rich gravy, smoothly mashed squashes whipped with sugar and a dash of cinnamon, several puddings and a compliment of vegetables covered in creamy melted butter.

There was also something imported from South America called *potatoes* which Master Wingate had discovered coming off a ship. And they had added another dish to their traditional meal since coming to the New World, a sweet-tart jellied sauce made from cranberries boiled with sugar.

After everyone expressed delight at the various foods and complimented the cooks, conversation grew very lively as the diverse group shared stories of their Christmas traditions and favorite foods. The Wingates spoke of Christmases years ago in England.

"Father always brought in a Yule log," the elder Wingate smiled. "We somehow endowed that log with magic. In our eyes it was the best and brightest fire to be seen." He chuckled, "A bit pagan, I suspect. Oh, well, may the Good Lord overlook our foibles. But no apology is needed for the sweet puddings Mother oversaw."

"My mother's eggnog was always my favorite," confessed Abigail. "Mother had a special way of fixing it. It was her secret recipe and I have never been able to do it just like she did... ever. Oh, I do wish Mother would have shared her secret before she passed."

"Her secret, my dear, was undoubtedly a good pint of Irish whiskey," exclaimed Wingate with a twinkle in his eye.

"Oh, hush, Master Wingate, my mother never took to serving spirits," she replied modestly.

"Only as the secret in the eggnog," he chuckled, addressing their guests.

Elizabeth smiled. "I can remember when Mother and Father used to tell us Old Father Christmas was coming and we had best be good or we'd get a lump of coal in our stocking."

"Your stocking?" asked Marie, not remembering ever having stockings as a child.

"Yes, we would hang our stocking by the hearth and hope to find a treat in the morning. It was something we learned from our Dutch neighbors. We would go to bed with such a mixture of anticipation and trepidation. If we were judged to have been more good than naughty throughout the year, we would find a treat, but if we were judged to have been more naughty, we might get a lump of coal," Elizabeth explained. "Of course, no one ever received a lump of coal, but my brother and sisters and I used to torture each other... I mean just plain torture each other over the prospect of getting that mortifying lump of coal."

"I never knew you took it so seriously," Abigail said, looking over at her daughter. "Did you really fear it so?"

"We did," confirmed Elizabeth. "Oh, don't look so guilty, Mother, we were none the worse for it. It kept us minding our manners and gave us cause to review our behavior over the year. And if God blesses us, I expect to do the same to my children."

Abigail smiled a bit hesitantly. "I do so wish your sister could have been with us this year," she said a bit sadly and it reminded Marie again that this was the family's first Christmas since their son had died. And this was the first time he had been casually mentioned. A quiet pause had fallen over the table and Marie looked over to see Master Wingate also looking very sad.

"With baby's arrival so near," Marie said cheerfully, "it was most wise of your daughter not to travel but just think what next Christmas will be like with your first grandchild... a merry little one. Christmas can be so special for the little ones. I see their faces when they come into the store. Such anticipation. Such looks of wonder."

"We were all like that once," Elizabeth laughed softly, "there is magic to Christmas when you are young... if your parents are generous. Don't you remember?" she asked Marie.

Jacques was watching Marie, admiring the way she had turned the Wingates' sad thoughts to happier ones. She was shaking her head slightly and shrugging her small shoulders. "I guess I do not," she said as everyone looked to her and Jacques thought he saw discomfort in her face. "I find it so much happier to enjoy Christmas through a child's eyes."

"Not everyone here makes so much of Christmas," Mistress Wingate added. "I understand to the north there are those who view celebrating the twelve days as very pagan. To them anything but just going to church is near blasphemy."

"In our homeland," Jacques interjected lightly, "the children find things in their shoes."

"Did you say shoes?" Nathaniel asked.

"Yes, *sabots*, wooden shoes left by the hearth. Funny is it not? Some set out stockings, some set out shoes. Of course, it is basically the same. If we were judged to have been well behaved, we found a treat from *le petit Jesus*. But I do not remember ever believing anyone but my mother left the treat there. And I remember church services at Christmas... very beautiful. The Christmas message is one of such joy and hope and there was always much singing. My mother and I enjoyed that, as well." There was now a touch of sadness in Jacques' words as he was reminded of his loved ones far away.

"Is your mother still alive?"

"Oh, yes."

"Has your father passed?" Elizabeth asked.

"No, no," Jacques responded quickly. "He, too, is alive and very well I hope, I just grew up as a small child with my mother."

"Marie says your father is a duke," Elizabeth stated bluntly and Mistress Wingate's eyebrows shot up at her overly bold daughter.

"This is true." Jacques replied.

Elizabeth continued to look at him expecting more of an explanation.

"So why are you trading in furs?" the young woman prodded and Abigail

Wingate gave her daughter a look that said such a personal question was a breach of etiquette and her daughter should know that.

"Elizabeth, mind your manners," Master Wingate said softly.

"No-no, it is a fair question. France is officially a Catholic country, you see, but my mother and I are not. We are Huguenot, what you call Protestant. All of my life we had rights in France equal to the Catholic citizens but no longer. They have been taken away and so I left."

"Oh my, that is terrible!" Elizabeth exclaimed as Abigail tsked softly and Master Wingate nodded. He had suspected as much. "So did your mother come with you?"

"No. She remains over there under the protection of my father." Not wanting to dampen the holiday spirit, Jacques smiled graciously. "We all are... how you say... mmm, always looking for the best?"

"Optimistic?" Master Wingate offered.

"Yes-yes, *optimistic.* We all are optimistic that sanity will return to France one day but until it does, I must seek what the New World has to offer, eh?"

Although she had known Marie only a few days, Elizabeth was gaining insight into the girl's alone-ness. What was it she had said, *many die too young*? It sounded as though the girl had lost everyone and Elizabeth could see clearly how Marie felt about her *Monsieur Jacques*. Despite her earlier skepticism, Elizabeth found herself completely charmed by the fair haired young Frenchman with whom she had been fully prepared to find fault for Marie's sake. Instead, she observed that his manners were impeccable and his presence undeniable. He certainly carried himself like a young lord. And beneath his charm and charisma was genuine warmth. She could well understand why Marie almost worshiped the ground he walked on. Well, Elizabeth admitted to herself, if she were not a very happily married woman, she might possibly fall just a little bit in love with him herself. No, too short. Being very tall herself she did prefer a really tall man like her Nathaniel. This one was just about her height. But Marie was small and had to look up at him. They would make a beautiful couple. Elizabeth smiled and let her eyes drift over to Richard who was watching Marie. Now that one was even taller than Nathaniel and while he was much rougher than his companion, still, he did have an appeal... in a sort of handsome animal-like way. My-my but this Marie certainly did have a very intriguing pair of gentlemen friends. Elizabeth's eyes went back to her own husband at whom she smiled.

"Well, my favorite memories of Christmas are the games we played," he was saying. "And I think later we should have some fun being children again today ourselves."

Everyone voiced their agreement and when the sumptuous meal concluded, the women cleared away the dishes after which the men saw to breaking down the table and storing it away. Soon they launched a rousing game of blind man's bluff, progressing to games of wit and words while laughter filled the warm rooms.

It was late February and the daylight hours were lengthening, bringing the smallest promise of the spring to come. One unusually mild and sunny Sunday Jacques showed up on his horse and invited Marie to go out for a ride in the countryside.

"We will meet Richard later for supper," he said as they trotted through the streets and out through the Wall gate. Housing had spread beyond the twelve foot Wall which still stood as protection against future attacks from the north. There had been little opportunity to exercise his animal through the worst of the winter. He could not take it on the trading treks which were traveled mostly by canoe and he was beginning to reassess the wisdom of even owning such a fine creature for all he was able to ride it. But now with the earth still frozen hard, it made him happy to ride.

Marie started to giggle as she sat behind him hugging his back.

"What is it?" he asked in amusement.

"I was just thinking of Mistress Van Hootenaug and what she would say if she saw me."

Jacques gave a laugh and they rode for some time in silence letting the horse set an easy trot. The farms were laid out in neat squared-off fields and fenced pastures.

"It is good to see the countryside again, Jacques," she said after a time, and she allowed herself to enjoy clinging to his back as they rode. There was something so solid and comforting in his strong straight back and she was sure she enjoyed the familiarity more than she should. "Thank you for inviting me," she said at last.

He nodded and made a small noise of acknowledgment but said nothing. It pleased him to feel her warmth at his back. He had never had any siblings and he fancied he had developed a very fraternal affection for this little girl.

He slowed the horse to a walk.

The farmland around them was still lying deep in its winter slumber and it would be weeks yet before it would begin to respond to the wake-up call of spring. A house appeared here and there with a barn, sometimes a silo and the sound of a barking dog gave them the reassurance of civilization as the horse walked along the wheel rutted road.

"Jacques?"

"Yes."

"Why did you and Richard decide to be trappers and traders? I mean... if it is so difficult. There was a gentleman that came into the store this week with his wife. They are wintering in New York with family but then they are going to the Virginia Colony to begin life on a plantation. *Plan–tay-shion*. The word is very... how to say," she gestured spreading her hands and arms wide and expansively from around him, "it sounds so much more elegant and impressive than to say *farm*, does it not? But that is after all what it is, is it not? Except as I understand, they are very, very large and produce one main crop for selling.

"Would this not be much more like having the estate of your father? To have a *plantation*? Or do you expect to return to France and that is why you do not want to do anything so permanent?"

Jacques was a bit taken back. He had no idea Marie gave so much thought to his business. And he was not expecting her to question his judgment but she spoke candidly, like a child.

"Those are a lot of questions," he replied lightly, but not completely masking a trace of irritation as he stared ahead. Irritation born more from his own lack of a personal definition to his future than anything to do with her.

The young woman suddenly realized now impudent her questions may have sounded. What right did she have to question what he was doing? It was not her place. And she should not have brought up his return to France. He had to miss his life and everything he had been forced to leave behind there. Of course he expected to return. She was rubbing salt into his wound she thought and quickly replied in an apologetic manner.

"I am sorry, Jacques... please, I did not mean...."

He waved his hand to dismiss her discomfort. "I have heard of these plantations, Marie," he said thoughtfully. "They are like large estates but instead of tenant farmers they are worked by slaves. I will not be part of such a life. I realize that at one point in our past the serfs of the land were little more than slaves, perhaps many still are but hopefully France is growing beyond that and I, for one, will not be party to seeing it established here."

"Can not a plantation have tenant farmers?" she asked as they rode.

Jacques laughed but not unkindly. "Why would you choose to be a tenant farmer upon my plantation if you could go someplace nearby and homestead a place of your very own? There is so much land here to be had, you see."

"Ohhh, that is true," she said quietly, feeling a little stupid for not having realized this herself. "But what of indenturing?"

"I have been told it has been tried but does not work well."

"Why?" she asked softly from around his back.

"Too many of our kind sicken in the climate," he explained. "No one wants to go there to work. I have heard the heat is beyond anything you could imagine and fevers have filled grave yards. But for some strange reason the black peoples can survive. The climate of their origins is not so very different and they are used to it, I suppose.

"Slaves seem to be the necessary work force for the large plantations, the work is hard, the climate is hot but they can survive it. I remember Dufee speaking of them," his voice trailed off a little. "It seems so very long ago," he said quietly, and was silent for several minutes as the horse walked along.

"Anyway," he continued with renewed focus, "it is not the life for me. As for my return to France, who knows, Marie, who knows? I am a man with a price on his head still. This has not changed. I cannot live my life as if this is only temporary for, indeed, it may be very permanent. I just do not know. The fur business is an honest way to earn one's living, *n'est-ce pas*? And earn a living I must."

In silence they continued on for a time. Jacques lapsed into thoughts of home. The door had once again been opened and a kaleidoscope of memories flooded in. His mother. His father. The estate he had been learning to run. The vineyards. The taste of the fine wines that came from the estate. His mother's cottage where he knew every nook from the perspective of a child. The sight of the chateau itself standing at the end of the drive when the sun was setting, turning the windows into mirrors of gold. The pleasant leathery smell of his father's study. The formidable, never changing Augustine. The familiar landscape. The smell of the countryside on a summer day. That fateful night when his father had told him he must flee. The sound of the footsteps of the soldiers walking about at Celimene's little cottage while he hid inches away beneath her skirts so close to discovery. And how different would his life be right now if he had been discovered? Undoubtedly he would be rotting away in the Bastille. But Celimene had been masterful and he had not been discovered. Celimene... ah, yes, Celimene. He wondered what she was doing on this fine day. He would not be the least surprised if she had gone to Paris and by now, charmed her way into Versailles. If any woman could do it, she could. He smiled to himself, she had been extraordinary and he had discovered her first, a diamond in the countryside. Why she might even be in the bed of the king himself by now. Jacques continued to smile, and if she was, he was certain she could get the king to do anything she wanted. Who knows, she might even finesse a pardon for her former lover. Jacques now broke into a broad grin, amused by the audacious scope of his imagination.

Marie was also thinking. Jacques had promised he would think about what she could do to get a start of her own. He had said he would think about it. That had been last autumn. Almost four months had passed since and he had yet to say a word. Surely he had had enough time to think. Should she remind him? She did not want him to think her a pest. *He has become so quiet,* she thought. She had the feeling that the stupid things she had said had made him angry or sad. She had made him think of home. He seemed distant now although he was right there in front of her, her arms still holding on to him. But where were his thoughts? Why had she said anything about France? She could kick herself for having mentioned France. She had left behind very little. He had left behind everything - a loving family, a fine chateau, a title... the mistress he loved. Was he now sorry he had brought her out for a ride? She must learn to think more before she spoke. But she was thinking now and deciding what to say was not easy.

Soon he and Richard would go away again and be gone for another whole season. Spring was coming and she would be left behind, struggling to keep her temper when Samuel Cooper became particularly arrogant in his attitude toward her. She knew three times more than he did about the business and yet when the Wingates were not around he often treated her like a simpleton, having her fetch and carry while he monopolized the conversations with the customers. And just last week she had caught him again making errors in tallying up a customer's bill and she had corrected it before the account was settled. And he was the apprentice, not she? How would she ever get ahead this way? She must ask Jacques about it. She might not have another opportunity to be alone with him. She did not want to push but what if he had completely forgotten and if she did not speak, he would have no time left to really think on it? Then she would regret not saying something now. It would be safest for her to remind him. But if he was still mulling it over she would seem impatient. Perhaps she should just keep her mouth shut. She should be glad he did not decide to go to the Virginia Colony and start a plantation. What had she been thinking? Why would she even suggest such a thing? If he left trapping and went to the south, where would she be then? He and Richard were her only family. They were friends, were they not? He was a friend. He had told her he was her friend. And friends can talk to each other, she reminded herself.

"Jacques?" she said softly finally breaking the silence after taking a deep breath. He grunted coming out of his reveries and was suddenly aware again of the girl's warmth at his back. "Remember last autumn, when we talked? About my being able to have a store of my own, I mean? About my being able to do more, to build something?" Once begun, the words tumbled out of her. "You said that you would think on it. Have you had a chance to think on it? I need to find a way to earn the money to start a store of my own. But I do not know how to do that, Jacques."

"Yes-yes, I remember. I remember. I have not forgotten." In his mind he gave her credit for her tenacity although he would rather she had remained quiet just at that moment.

"I am sorry, Jacques, I do not mean to pester. You have been such a good friend to me. And the last thing I want is to seem ungrateful. But since that time you have never spoken of this again and you will be leaving soon. Have you had a chance to think? What have you thought about it?"

He drew up the horse to a halt and in an agile movement he swung his right leg over the horse's neck and jumped to the ground. He turned and lifted her down. She was bewildered and unsure and for an instant she was terrified that she had made him very, very angry. Was he going to leave her out here to walk back as a lesson to not be a pest? She said nothing but went along with his actions. The horse nickered as it stood in place. Marie felt the earth beneath her feet crunch a bit with each step and the sun felt pleasantly warm.

Jacques stood looking down into her face, a frown creasing the bridge over his nose. She was so young, he thought to himself. After a moment he asked, "What would you think of going into the wilderness?"

"If that is what I must do..." she shrugged looking at him with complete trust. "But you said you would not teach me to trap."

"Could you stay alone, by yourself... with no one to talk to, no one to call upon?" he asked critically.

"If there is no one, why am I there? I do not understand."

"I *have* been thinking," he continued. He paused to observe their surroundings. They were out far enough he decided and turned the horse and began to lead it back at a walk. Marie followed at his side. "Richard and I have gone into the wilderness and there is far more profit to be made in trading for the furs trapped by others, then by trapping them oneself."

"How is that?"

"It frees you from limitations," he responded.

Marie looked at him for further explanation.

"Let us say I could trap and skin and cure five good pelts a week... which all depends on luck. Multiply that by how many weeks? Let us say twenty-six leaving some time out for travel. All right, you are good with figures, how many skins is that?" he asked, looking over at her.

"Five times twenty-six?" she thought out loud. "That is one hundred and thirty."

"Very good. Now, if I were lucky enough to actually be able to get a worthy animal a day I would have one hundred and thirty pelts and let us not forget how very hard I would have worked to walk the trap line, set the traps which is very dangerous, skin the animals and cure the pelts. Then I come home for the winter. But winter pelts are the most luxurious and I would have none. To get winter skins I have to live out in the wilderness over the winter, like the savages do. However, if we trade with the savages for the skins which they have trapped all winter, we come home with hundreds of furs, and of the very best quality."

"I think I understand what you are saying. It makes sense, but what has this to do with me?" Her brow knit in earnest concentration.

"A trading post is just another kind of store, Marie," he replied. "But it sits in the wilderness proclaiming the very edge of civilization. Your customers would be savages and rough trappers at first. They would give you furs instead of money. You would not have the companionship of your own kind, there would be no other women," he cautioned. "And make no mistake, there would be nothing soft or easy about the existence. It is a hard life. But there is profit to be made. Think about this. I want you to think about this all the while we are gone this coming season."

"But I have not enough savings to purchase goods to trade with..." she began.

"I will have the capital. We can be partners," he said gravely and stopped again to look at her. "But you must understand how it would be. I will paint no false pictures for you. I have been out there. While Richard and I are gone, you would be utterly alone; you would have to rely completely upon yourself. You would have no one to call upon. No neighbors. No friends. There will be beasts in the forest. There could be danger from strangers and the savages are unpredictable. There would be no physician if you became ill. No shop if you forgot to bring something with you.

"But it would only take a few years and if we choose the right location, civilization would spread to you. People would come and a settlement would start and your store would be the first and main supplier. And you could realize your dream." Jacques stopped and looked into her eyes. "You could also die in the trying," he added grimly.

Marie stood listening, trying to absorb the vision.

Chapter 15

Spring 1687

Jacques shifted his weight carefully keeping his balance as he stood in the flat bottomed sailboat. Richard was at the rudder and the wind in the squared off sail was strong enough that they had no need to use the oars. It was a welcome relief. The young man stretched as he stood and sucked in the fresh clean air, deeply filling his lungs and then exhaling. They had been days rowing against the current on the wide Hudson River, many days since they had gathered their supplies at the Wingates' store and bid farewell to Marie.

Jacques leaned back against a pile of goods and relaxed watching the ever changing scenery around them. The cultivated patches of farmland which had at first stretched out on both sides had grown fewer and farther apart, finally disappearing altogether as the primeval forest closed over the landscape.

It was early spring and the beauty of the new growth was just starting to make its seasonal appearance in delicate colors. The trees and brush sported varying shades of green as buds broke forth into leaves. Even the patches of evergreens were splotched with the light vibrant hue of new growth. In a short time blossoms would appear. The whites and pinks, lavenders and deep mauve of the wild crabapple, the cherries, and the red buds would be everywhere as the world pulsated with life.

Jacques had a growing admiration for the raw magnificence of this untamed New World. There was nothing back in his father's province which could compare. The countryside of his youth had been trim and tidy, sectioned and divided, fenced or walled, constructed on, or under cultivation and even the occasional stand of trees was neatly separated out. But here, the clear waters of the rivers were, for the most part, smooth and easy highways cutting deep into primitive wilderness robust in its fecund lushness, a wilderness which on foot could be quite intimidating.

Having been up the Hudson and Mohawk before, the young adventurers knew they would not have to leave the smooth liquid road to portage around rapids or small falls until after they had taken on Indian guides beyond Fort Orange and switched to light canoes.

Skimming along, they were suddenly made aware of being trespassers within the habitat of a gathering of waterfowl when quacks and flapping wings registered discontent at their invading presence. The travelers noted the movement of a large flock of birds returning from their winter homes. The shaggy hills of the landscape were growing more pronounced and closer while the river itself grew slightly more narrow.

As they glided along they could see into the forests a distance, something which after the plant life reached full maturity would be impossible. Richard pointed out a small group of whitetail deer, the speckled markings on the fawns making them blend in so perfectly with the small patches of sunlight strewn about the forest floor that Jacques almost did not see them at all. Farther on, they spotted two huge animals with large, solid racks squaring off against each other in a small, marshy meadow, their trumpeting sounding out over the landscape and echoing for miles.

With keen eyes, they watched little creatures scurrying along the river's banks. Both were able to identify river otter, muskrats, beaver, weasels, raccoons each busy with their own spring tasks. Squirrels playfully raced up and down tree trunks, chattering at the passers-by. Jacques pointed to possum sleeping up in the tree as they passed close to the river bank and later they saw two bobcats staring down at them in fixed attention which caused them to avidly steer away from the shoreline again.

At dusk each day they made camp along the river bank and always they built a large fire. It would get cooler as the sun set but more than that, fire was the best deterrent against animals and smoke helped to keep mosquitoes and other flying pests away. And so they journeyed ever deeper into the interior.

They knew they were approaching the fort when the forest gave way once more to cultivated land. Around the fort there was now a very small settlement. Large land grants had been given to political favorites as far north as this and tenant farming of this land in the relative safety of the fort was an alternative for those who had not the courage to go into the less protected, more savage frontier beyond.

At last the two young adventurers sighted Fort Orange right on the edge of the river's west bank. There was nothing impressive about it. It was small and had started off as little more than a seasonal Dutch trading post. It continued to be subject to flooding when spring thaws caused the river to rise. They glided their craft up to a weathered and rather unstable looking dock and paid an old man who sat nearby to keep an eye on their goods. They looked forward to getting supper from one of the vendors usually set up around a fort and tonight they expected to sleep within the protective stockade.

As they walked through the fort gates, however, no sooner had they opened their mouths when they found themselves quickly surrounded by several soldiers.

"Hey, look what we gots here, Sergeant," one of the men brayed in a high and grating voice, "we gots us some real life, livin' an' breathin' Frenchies!"

Jacques' pride bristled at the discourtesy but they were far outnumbered as more soldiers pressed around.

"We are only passing through," he said, trying to sound amiable.

"Yup, thems frogs by gosh," muttered another.

"Better bring 'em over to our *hospitality* room," a voice called out. It was a voice of authority and the men immediately put hands on both Frenchmen and roughly pushed them along in a specific direction.

"What are you doing?" Jacques demanded as their weapons were seized.

"We have done nothing!" exclaimed Richard struggling against his captors.

"Shut up if ya know what's good fer ya," said one man roughly jabbing a musket butt in Richard's back.

They were quickly pressed into a small enclosure defined by six inch thick timber poles stuck into the ground vertically. Pushed off balance and into each other as they passed through the threshold, they fell to the dry dirt floor. Jacques was incensed. "What is our crime?" he demanded of the guard who ignored him and shut the heavy door leaving the two to sit alone and without supper for the night.

They looked about at their surroundings. The enclosure had no roof. There was no furniture only a pile of dirty straw off in the corner and the dirt floor was so hard pressed as to seem to be rock. As it grew darker, light from the torches outside came in through the cracks and so did the chilling air.

"I have the feeling something has happened between the English and the French... again," mused Richard with an air of resignation.

"But all was quiet when we left New York Towne," Jacques replied.

Richard shrugged. "We have been on the river awhile."

"Not that long. Do you think we are at war again?"

"What else?" Richard said quietly.

"Just when we decide to venture out on our own. What do you think they will do?"

"What can they do? We are not soldiers."

Jacques did not want to think about what the English soldiers *could* do if they chose. Instead he suggested they sit back to back to conserve body heat.

It was a very long night for Jacques who could not find sleep easily. What was the worst that could happen to them? He asked himself over and over. What if they were turned over to the French authorities? No, that was ridiculous. There was no reason to turn them over to the French. But what if they were? Would a patrol out here be aware of the reward for his return to France? Was this the beginning of a long journey ending in a cell in the Bastille? But what reason would these English have to turn them over to the French? He was an expatriate seeking asylum on

British soil. This was not unusual for Huguenots.

At dawn they were roused out of their uncomfortable sleep in the straw when a pair of guards arrived. The door opened, the guards burst in and Richard was half dragged out. Jacques sat up and waited and wondered. He called out for a slop pail to relieve himself but received no reply. When he could not stand it any longer he went to a far corner and urinated through a crack between timbers and onto the ground. He thought it had been about an hour when two more guards arrived and he was taken out and roughly escorted to a small building bearing a sign stating "Post Commander" on its front beam.

The British officer behind the desk was young although not as young as he at first looked, with his apple cheeks and a very light flowing periwig upon his head. The lines on his pale brow along with the wrinkles in the corners of his eyes and the faint lines running from nostril to the corners of his mouth gave him the appearance of an aging cherub.

"State your name and spell it," he demanded with no pleasantries.

"Jacques-Jean Charte," Jacques responded and as he spelled it out a clerk at the officer's side wrote it down.

"You are French?" It was a question but came out as an accusation.

"Yes, I was born in France. What crime is it that we are thought to have committed?"

"I will ask the questions, Mister Charte. How long ago did you leave France?"

Jacques thought. "It has been a year and a half now."

"And you have been in the north all that time?"

"The north, whose north? We landed in New York Towne, we went on a trading expedition last year with a group under the leadership of a man called Cameron. We were right here at this fort a year ago," he said, his impatience beginning to show. His stomach was growling fiercely. They had not eaten since yesterday's breakfast.

Wordlessly the Post Commander signaled his clerk who left the room.

"Your friend said you came down from New France two years ago."

"No, he did not. It is a lie," Jacques said firmly with no hesitation. "From Europe, we arrived in New York Towne and have spent both winters there. We traveled up the Mohawk with Cameron, trading; that is all. Now, we go ourselves to trade. You can see our supplies in our boat."

"So you claim you are traders?"

"Yes. We are traders," Jacques replied, not realizing the double meaning of his words.

The officer jerked his head upward but saw nothing in the other man's face but anger and indignation. God, how he hated this duty. When would he ever be allowed to go home again? He was sick of dealing with the savages and the trappers and traders and the emigrant riffraff of the world. Sick of the constant outbreaks along the borders. There was never a decisive battle. There were no clear victories, something a soldier could sink his teeth into and be proud. No. Instead it just went on and on without ceasing. He longed for the peaceful tranquility of the English countryside and the diversions of London life; longed for the lush precision of his English garden, centuries old, well-tended, harmonious; the entertainments of the theater and formal balls. How he longed for the company of his own class again and his clubs. He wanted to see his family. He had a wife back in England and a son born six months after his departure whom he had never seen except via a small miniature portrait. Was it too much to want to go home?

"What are you doing in the English colonies?" he asked hoping he did not sound as weary as he felt. "If you are French, and we have already established that you are French, why are you not in New France?" So far the stories of the two men matched but there was something about this one that nagged at him. He had an air about him. He was far too polished to be ordinary riffraff. He had the bearing of an officer and the intelligence to be a spy. "Are you acquainted with the *Marquis de Denonville?*"

Jacques thought intently. There was something vaguely familiar about the name but he could not place it. "I cannot say that I am," he replied hesitantly.

"Come, come. Are you trying to tell me you do not know who the Governor General of New France is?"

Jacques continued to look steadily at his interrogator. "I regret the name is only vaguely familiar."

"And what about King Louis... of France? Have you heard of him?"

Jacques' expression changed to a scowl. "Of course."

"Well, it seems your King Louis sent orders to Governor Denonville to round up as many of our Iroquois allies as he could find and ship them over to France for galley slaves. Did you know about that?"

"No. I did not. I have nothing to do with the Court or court business."

"You speak like an aristocrat," the Post Commander pressed in accusation. "Why does a French aristocrat come to America and live only in the English colonies?"

"I have my reasons." It was the first evasive thing Jacques had said and it piqued the officer's interest as he noted his prisoner did not deny being an aristocrat.

"And what might those reasons be?"

"I am a private citizen, monsieur. I am not in the military and my reasons are my own," Jacques responded, his posture stiffening with dignity.

"Are you a criminal of France?" the officer stared at him keenly.

"I have chosen to leave France and settle in the colonies; that is not a crime."

"Why does a Frenchman of the aristocracy choose to leave France for the English colonies to become a common fur trader?" the officer persisted.

"I am... a Huguenot."

"Ah... yes, I see," the officer responded with recognition. "Well, that does make you something of a criminal, does it not?"

Jacques said nothing.

The officer rose. The scrape of the chair legs across the wood floor echoed in the quiet room. He walked around the desk toward Jacques who did not move as he approached. Reaching over to grasp Jacques' collar the Englishman suddenly pulled, not harshly but with a certain strength, to expose a broader portion of Jacques' neckline and chest. In the past, the officer had exposed more than one French Catholic trying to claim disenfranchisement through religious persecution. The crucifix they had worn so long they had forgotten its existence had given witness to their lies. This fellow had none and nothing to indicate he ever had worn one, observed the commander. His golden skin was evenly tanned where any chain would have been.

For a long moment, the officer stood very close, his eyes looking at Jacques' exposed chest line, moving up to the cut of his jaw, his full lips beneath the small neat moustache, his eyes, and the mass of natural, silky, blond hair.

Suddenly Jacques felt the hairs on the back of his neck rise with a feeling something akin to a thousand ants crawling across his skin. He was aware of the deepening rhythm of the Englishman's breathing so close to his face and it was with an instinctive repulsion that Jacques realized there was something in the other man's eyes that reminded Jacques of his uncle, the count.

The clerk came into the room. The commander drew back, let go of Jacques' collar and returned to his desk chair. The junior officer presented a huge ledger and pointed to something.

Jacques recognized the book. He and Richard had signed it along with the rest of their party the year before.

"Sign your name, Mister Charte," the commander's tone was beginning to modify. He pushed paper and quill across the desk toward Jacques.

Jacques stepped up to the desk, took the quill, dipped it into the ink well and signed his name on the paper.

The commander picked it up and compared it to the signature in the book.

"Well, we have established that you were here last year, that part of your story is true."

"I have no reason to lie, monsieur."

"At that time you were with Cameron's party?"

Jacques nodded.

"And now you are going trapping by yourself?"

"Trading. We have a boat full of goods. Has something happened that we should know about?"

"Nothing in particular," the commander said evasively, and then added, "but if I were you I would keep a sharp look-out. These borders are never very settled. If you run into a detachment of soldiers from either side, you might have difficulties."

Jacques nodded.

Just as quickly as they had been seized, Jacques and Richard found them-selves released and given a conciliatory tankard of ale, a bowl of mush, and a heel of bread.

They ate quickly.

After checking over their supplies and assuring themselves nothing had been taken, the two comrades pushed on. They could not wait to put distance between themselves and the fort. Neither man knew exactly what to make of their experi-ence. Jacques was inclined to believe that being part of a larger group had insu-lated them from the same treatment the year before.

"Did you not tell them we were with Cameron last year?" Jacques asked Richard as they rowed their craft away from the fort.

"No."

"Why not? Finding our signatures in their records seemed to be the ticket for our release."

Richard shrugged. "Everything I said they twisted around. I was upset so I said nothing more."

"Did you notice anything strange about that commander?" Jacques asked.

"Strange?" Richard asked. "In what way?"

"I..." Jacques hesitated. "Just strange."

"He is English, they are all strange," Richard shrugged while grunting at his oar. "English officers all remind me of little girls."

"And how many have you seen?" Jacques smiled broadly.

"Not many, but the ones I have seen remind me of homely little girls."

"You had better never let them hear you say that. Their musket balls undoubt-edly kill just as quickly as ours," Jacques chuckled and thought of his earlier expe-rience no more.

They took the large bend in the river which forked off to the west into what they knew to be the Mohawk River. It would not be long, they remembered, they should see the final settlement soon. It was less than a day's journey from the pro-tection of the fort.

As they came closer to their destination, they saw large bear patiently fishing for their next meal with huge clawed paws and the two men felt very glad when the breeze in the sail helped them put distance between themselves and the mas-sive brown beasts.

At last they were in sight of the settlement and while observing it from a dis-tance, they noted that little had changed from the year before. Spread out before them was a clearing of rough, hard packed ground, snarled up in places with tree roots, mud and green patches of fresh new weeds. The clearing before them was speckled with a myriad of tree stumps in various states of decay. One could see several cabins scattered about, the farthest being up on a hillside almost a mile away. The distant cabin had the look of being a miniature placed upon a space where some giant had pressed his thumb to flatten out an area of the forest just large enough to set it upon. Jacques did not recall that this cabin had existed the year before.

The split plank cabins of the settlement were all about the same size and construction. The only differences between them were the number of miscellaneous out-buildings near each. There was a scattering of sheds and privies. One had a barn, one had a crude corral. It was obvious vegetable garden plots had been planted already and the patches of ground were rather meticulously bordered in fencing intended to keep out the animals. In the distance they could see four men working at the process of clearing more land. A thin older woman struggled to hang laundry over a rope line near a wash pot to the side of one of the cabins.

Sounds of grunting drifted to them from a pig pen off to the left as a youth with a dog threw refuse into a wood trough. Chickens wandered brazenly about, clucking and pecking constantly at the ground everywhere except where the garden fencing kept them out. A rooster strutted amid the hens. Only when the birds strayed too far did the dog decide to chase them back to their roost which was to the rear of the largest and most complex building in view.

In the middle of everything sat a two story structure built of a combination of logs and planking. There was a lean-to attached to the main part of the building on either side and a floorless porch overhang ran across the front. It stood facing the river and sported a faded sign which had "Wise William's Trading Post" painted upon it. Three heavily bearded men, passing a jug between them, were sitting outside beneath the roof of the porch. They watched the newcomers approach with marked interest.

As the boat closed in upon the river bank, Jacques jumped out with a splash holding a tether rope in his hands while Richard jumped in behind to push the heavy boat from the rear. They both were trying to use the momentum of the craft to move it as far onto the bank as they could before the friction of the broad flat bottom against the ground brought it to a stop. At the same time the dog by the pig pen suddenly came running up, snarling viciously at both of them. Instantly the youth shouted a command at the beast to call it back. It continued to stand stiff and poised, its teeth bared, uttering a low guttural growl.

Jacques remained very still, wishing he had his musket in hand. To start off the season with a leg infected from a dog bite would be a disaster.

"Cannon! Git back here I say. Cannon! Back! Back!" The youth continued to shout fiercely and finally the dog ceased growling, lowered its head, and wagging its tail it trotted back to its master.

"I could have done without that welcoming committee," Richard said abruptly. Jacques nodded in agreement and relief.

They finished pushing the boat as far up on land as they could to secure it from being taken away by the river current. Richard lashed the sail tightly and

Jacques tied the tether rope to one of the tree stumps near the water's edge.

"Well, now let us see if William is around," Jacques recommended as he grabbed his three cornered hat off the boat.

The three men sitting outside the trading post were rudely dressed and had become very still and quiet as they watched Jacques and Richard approach.

"Good day to you," Jacques called out in a friendly greeting as they grew nearer. Nothing but scowls came from the seated trio who had enough similarity in appearance for him to suspect they were brothers. "Is William about?" he asked politely.

"Who wants t' know?" Came a challenge from the biggest of the three. Spittle from tobacco chew dribbled into the speaker's beard and he paused to spit.

Richard looked at Jacques. Jacques looked at Richard.

"I do not remember there being such friendliness the last time we were here," Richard said sarcastically under his breath. "It is as bad as the fort."

A big bald man stepped out through the open door of the trading post carrying a jug the color of his tanned head. He was dressed in well-worn leather breeches and a homespun shirt opened broadly at the neck. He sported a pronounced belly which hung over his pant top. Heavy stockings covered the lower part of his big legs which disappeared into heavy, thick soled shoes.

"William!" Jacques greeted the large man, grabbing his free hand and forearm in a two handed handshake.

"Charte!" William replied back with a broad smile of recognition at the handsome young man. "And Bonchance." Richard stepped up and also shook William's hand. "I didn't expect to see you fellas this far from home this spring."

"But why not?" Jacques asked pleasantly. "We told you we would return."

"It's all right, fellas," William turned to the seated scowlers, "these here is honest men from the south part of New York colony. This is Jacques Charte and Richard Bonchance. These here is the Calder brothers, that's their place up yonder." He pointed to the farthest cabin up the hillside. None of the Calder brothers moved except for a barely perceptible nod of the head. William turned back to Jacques and Richard. "It's your accents, boys. They didn't know if y'was friend or foe."

William proceeded to offer the fresh jug to Richard who uncorked it, took a long pull and passed it to Jacques who did the same before passing it back to William. They remembered the homemade brew which was harsh and had the after-burn of molten iron going down their throats. Last year they had learned that after several drinks it got easier to swallow. But too many drinks left one desiccated with a penalizing headache that lasted a full day.

The big man motioned for them to take seats on several available pieces of sawed up tree trunk standing vertically upon the ground. He sat down on one himself.

"What is happening, William?" Jacques asked. "We were stopped at the fort and thrown into what served as their jail for the night. Then, they interrogated us as if we were spies."

"Not surprised," William replied. "Rumors is flyin'. There been reports of war parties and Indian raids. The Iroquois and the Algonquin is jist spoilin' for more fightin' after the long cold winter we had. Blood thirsty bastards! I have my own sources that tell me the English are plannin' a series of raids up around Montreal Island. That's not information they'd be wantin' you to take back up to New France."

"Why would they want to go up to Quebec?" asked Jacques with a frown. "Do they think the French will not come right back down into the English land and raid as well?"

"Payback. Story I heard was the French and their Hurons raided a sanctuary mission the priests set up west of Fort Frontenac on Lake Ontario. The neighborin' Iroquois with their wives and children had been invited by the priests to visit for what was supposed to be a friendly gathering. After some torture, rape and God knows what to break their spirit, the French and Huron hauled all the bucks away and shipped them off to France as slaves. Now, you know no self-respectin' Iroquois is going to just let that pass."

Jacques and Richard nodded.

"We've had no problems here mind, but I keep all my firearms at th' ready. You two all alone this year?"

Jacques nodded again trying to remember what tribes they had traded with the year before.

"What happened to Cameron?" William asked after another generous pull on his jug before he held it out to Jacques again.

"When we parted company last fall," Jacques volunteered as he passed the jug to Richard, "he told us he wanted to go up to the river *Saint Laurent* for the winter. He kept talking about the pure white winter pelts one could find. That was the last we saw him."

"I'd hate to think he was up in the midst of French country now," said William, looking down at the ground, then he looked up with a half smile. "Well, I guess Cameron knows how to take care of hisself. He's been doin' it long enough, right? But you two had better think twice 'bout going into the wilderness this season. You'd be fair game for our side seeings how yer French. Hell, them English soldiers could jist as easy have their damn Indians slit your throats and take your hair," he added, taking the jug back again.

The men continued to talk. Jacques explained that they had had no awareness of any new hostilities before they had departed but since their path was taking them westward they saw no reason to turn back. They requested that William make contact with his Indian friends. They needed scouts, they needed canoes. They were undaunted.

"I'll send fer the scouts," agreed William, with a serious look, "but I strongly advise you boys to go back to the fort, it ain't that far, 'n' get a paper from the commander. Something to keep with you just in case."

Jacques considered and wondered what effect such a paper would have if they ran into French soldiers instead and were searched. He decided against it preferring to trust in Providence.

True to his word, William sent for the scouts. Jacques and Richard camped out by their boat while they waited and the trading post dog soon grew used to them. After several days the scouts arrived.

William introduced the pair as "David" and "Samson." They were Christians, he told Jacques, converted by missionaries and proud of their new Christian names. They wore calico shirts and matching bandannas tied around their coal black straight hair. Their leather leggings hung only to the knee and their moccasin boots came to just above the ankle. Both had rugged faces the color of soft brown leather which crinkled into a myriad of lines when they smiled and spoke in their broken English. Jacques could only guess at their ages. It was obvious they were not young but neither had a single gray hair, so how old could they be?

The Indians were strong and sturdily built. And just as importantly, they each piloted a light weight birch bark canoe which took only one man to lift and carry over portages but with goods inside it would take two.

Against William's better judgment the small party said their farewells and continued westward up the Mohawk. It wasn't long before they came to a small falls which forced them out of the water. Once up river of the falls they put the canoes back into the water and continued paddling.

After several days they came to a small village composed of a half dozen or so huts. Each hut was constructed of tree branches and grass thatching in the summer style with open walls loosely hung with grass mats and skins. It was the tribe's summer camp and in fall they would migrate to the safety of their earth lodgings for the winter. Each spring they chose to come to this spot for the hunting and fishing it offered and to meet with others for trade.

The copper-skinned villagers greeted them hospitably remembering the yellow haired man and the tall dark haired white from the year before. The headman, a large brave covered in intricate tattoos depicting his exploits, was called *Newateme*. He was pleased to receive them as his visitors, not only for the goods they brought in trade but for the prestige it gave his camp to host them. Jacques and Richard went through the formalities of greeting with the assistance of Samson and David. They noticed a small group of young females twittering and chattering, laughing and giggling amongst themselves from around Newateme's hut. Most wore only a short skirt of leather, their developing breasts left naked and exposed. Jacques guessed they were his daughters and felt himself and Richard being looked over and discussed with great curiosity. At one point Newateme turned and said something, scattering them like one might shoo and scatter a flock of chickens. The nubile young girls ran lightly away with more suppressed giggles and joined the older women in their daily tasks.

Several of the young men of the tribe assisted the visitors in constructing a shelter which would protect them and their goods from weather. The two were expected to stay for a week or more. Using forked branches as anchor posts they arranged sturdy branches around in a conical form and covered them with grass mats. When the shelter was finished it was low and cramped but provided protection from rain. In good weather, however, everyone chose to sleep out under the sky by their fire.

The first night they were invited to eat at Newateme's fire. As they ate, the drums began beating a signal call to gather for trade. The drumming continued until it was time for everyone to retire.

"It's called a *wickiup*," said Richard, crawling in from out of the drizzling rain.

"What?" Jacques was sitting up off the ground on a low pile of skins. He wore only his shirt and breeches, having pulled off his muddy boots, and he had been daydreaming.

"This shelter, it is called a *wickiup*."

"*Wickiup?*"

"Yes, *wickiup. Wickiup. Wickiup*," Richard rolled the sounds around in his mouth. "It has a nice sound to it, do you not think?" Richard grinned as he hunkered down within the low shelter.

"Wickiup," Jacques repeated again.

"Wickiup," Richard replied with obvious pleasure. "One of the natives who was adopted from a tribe to the west told me this, at least that is what his people call it."

"Adopted?"

"Well, captured… he must have been quite young or they would have slain him."

"Hmmm" was all Jacques replied.

It was a dark, wet afternoon and there was nothing to do but sit, smoke, and pass the time playing cards but their deck had disintegrated after getting wet. They had been in the camp for two weeks trading with different groups arriving every few days. Today it had been raining steadily and no one had come.

Jacques studied Richard as the taller man moved to sit down on a second pile of furs.

"What?" Richard asked feeling Jacques stare.

"Nothing."

"Do not say *nothing*. I know that look."

"What look?"

"That look."

"There is no look, I was just… looking," he shrugged.

"That is what I mean."

"Well, I have to look. I am not blind," Jacques said reasonably.

"You are not just looking," Richard muttered, "you have a look."

"What kind of look?"

"You know what kind of look."

"Obviously I do not which is why I ask."

"You know," Richard muttered.

"What would I have a look about?"

"How should I know, it is your look," Richard replied.

"Well, what kind of look does it look like?"

"A look! It looks like a look!"

"But I already admitted I was looking."

"At what?"

"At you."

"And?" asked Richard in a challenge.

"And what?"

"And what were you looking at me for?"

"Because…" Jacques grasped for a reason, "because you are there."

The individual raindrops could be heard falling softly on the shelter.

"So, what are you thinking?" Richard finally asked.

"Thinking? Ah, well, I am merely thinking that if I had not known you all of your life, I would swear you had been birthed by a squaw."

"I knew it was something," Richard grunted.

"First it was buckskins," Jacques observed.

"Yes."

"Then braids."

"They keep my hair out of my face."

"And moccasins."

"My boots were wet."

"Now feathers?"

"It is only a joke."

"Next you will get a tattoo."

"Do not be ridiculous; those things are permanent! What if one were to have a change of mind?"

"So no tattoo?"

"No, with that I draw the line," the dark haired man said stretching out against the pile of pelts. "I think they are hideous."

"I am surprised; you seem to admire everything else."

"Now, can you not see how much more comfortable these clothes are?" Richard asked rationally.

Jacques was silent.

"Admit it!" prodded Richard.

"Admit what?"

"That this is more comfortable." He gestured to his apparel.

Jacques shrugged.

"By the time you put on the shirt and the stock and the jabot and the waistcoat and the cassock, are you not feeling bound and strangled?"

"No."

"Yes, you do. Admit it."

"If you have a good tailor, there is no reason to feel 'bound' or 'strangled' as you say."

"I notice you are not wearing them now."

"Here in the forest, there is no reason and it is too hot to have so many layers."

Richard grunted. The rain continued to patter on the leaves and grass. Both men listened for a while.

"And do not tell me that the leather is not hot," Jacques said after a time.

It was Richard's turn to shrug.

"How can you stand it in the middle of a humid day?" Jacques asked.

"It protects from the mosquitoes. I would rather sweat than itch."

"Ummm."

"It also protects from the brambles."

Jacques silently fingered a small tear on his blousey soft sleeve. On one of his recent excursions out beyond the camp to urinate, a thorn had caught the fabric and ripped a hole. "But the leather does not breathe and soon you grow ripe," he added after a moment.

Richard did not respond. He put his hands behind his head and looked at the thatching above him. He wondered vaguely how long it would take before the rain would saturate through and start leaking in.

They continued to sit in silence, the gentle rain falling steadily. The camp was quiet as everyone had sought shelter in their own huts. It was a sleepy time of day.

"I wonder how much longer we should stay here," Jacques questioned at last with a yawn.

"I spoke to Samson and David. They think we should move on if no one comes tomorrow."

Jacques nodded.

"There is a fork to the north of us. Remember the village we went to last year beyond the split rock?" Richard asked.

"Yes," Jacques recalled with sudden clarity, "how could I forget? I thought you would get us separated from our hair."

"Me?" Richard looked up with an expression of surprised innocence.

"Flirting with the chief's young daughter."

"I did more than flirt," Richard grinned.

Jacques shot a look over at his partner. "When in the devil did you have the time?" he asked in stunned surprise.

Richard shrugged again.

"I seem to recall that the chief made it most clear he did not want us near his daughter," Jacques spoke with a tinge of exasperation.

"Ah, you know what they say about forbidden fruit."

Jacques frowned disapprovingly.

"She did not agree with her father... these females can be very independent."

"*Sacre bleu*! Richard, if we go back and she has your papoose in tow, what then? He could be waiting to lift our hair... or slit our throats!" Jacques was deadly serious.

"Do not worry," the reclined man became more serious as well. "I can assure you, *mon ami,* if she has a papoose, it will not be mine. I made certain of that. I am not a fool, after all. I knew we could be coming back and *Grand-père* would be very unhappy with a grandchild that looked like me."

Jacques said nothing but his face was taut and he felt a headache coming on.

"You know it might do you some good to acknowledge the attentions of one of these little fawns," Richard suggested. "You are becoming much too tense, my friend. You need a good roll in the furs."

Jacques did not reply.

"I think I could safely bet my life's savings you have not bed a woman since we left France. That is a long time for a man who is used to eating regularly to go without food."

"I did not know you were my watchdog," Jacques responded testily.

"We have to look out for each other," Richard smiled and received a glower in return. "What is the matter with you these days? There is no lack of available women here. Yet you act like a monk. And you are starting to have the face of a monk."

Jacques stared out the opening of the shelter, he was considering leaving it, rain or not. How could he explain to Richard the change he had experienced in his attitudes? He did not think his old friend would understand.

"Surely you have noticed how many unattached females are in this camp? I think we do the men a service to help keep them all happy. There are no taboos with these people... as long as the girl is not mated... or promised... and is willing. And they seem to be most willing," Richard smiled in appreciation.

Jacques sat unmoved.

"Surely you have noticed the attention you stir with your pretty blond curls. Frankly, I think you could take your pick of any of the maidens. They perhaps are looking for a baby with blond hair, *n'est-ce pas*?" he added lightly.

"I would never willingly leave a child of mine out here to be raised by savages." The reply came with such underlying passion it took Richard by surprise.

He looked at his friend and partner and decided the conversation was getting too serious so he nodded with a shrug. "You know what to do about that as well as I." Richard hummed a little. Beneath the teasing, he had a genuine concern for his friend and he could not let the subject rest. "What about the plump one who always brings us breakfast every morning? She has an untouched look about her and a very sweet smile. I have seen the way she looks at you."

Jacques tried to ignore his companion and willed the ache in his head to cease.

"I think she is wanting very much for you to take notice of her," Richard teased. "What a disappointment if we should leave here with her wanting. What a waste. It seems a crime against nature. "

Jacques was determined to ignore him.

"Or if you prefer the more slender," Richard shrugged, stretching, "what of the little one that runs to fill your pipe? She all but throws herself at your feet. My heart goes out to her. And there you are - *Monsieur Poisson Froid.*"

Richard was wearing on Jacques' last nerve.

"Why are you so aloof? Have you lost all your natural appetites?"

Jacques frowned.

"Is there no hot blood left in your veins?" Richard grumbled when he still received no reply.

"*Sacre bleu,* Richard! Will you cease your incessant chattering?! You are worse than a fishwife on the wharf of Havre! Can you not shut your mouth and give me some peace?!!" Jacques exploded at last. "My head is pounding."

"You know, you *are* becoming too tense," Richard said smoothly, not appearing the least insulted, "like a dried up old maid with a rusting chastity belt!"

Jacques glowered fiercely at him and looked away in total exasperation, mentally and physically throwing up his hands.

"It is not good to keep it all inside you. It backs up and numbs your brain!

Jacques grunted and threw himself back on the furs.

"I never thought you would develop a prudish streak," Richard said at last with a note of accusation in his voice. "What has happened? You come to this land and suddenly you become a Puritan?"

There was a long silence while the air in the tent grew increasingly heavy with more than humidity.

"Look," Jacques decided to speak knowing Richard would pout like a child if he did not. "I am not passing judgments," he began carefully. "I am sorry if that is the way I sound. I just do not understand the appeal but perhaps more importantly... I am … hmmm, how do you say, *mefiant*?"

"Distrustful of what?"

"We really do not understand these people, do we? I hope your apparent unwillingness to control your own appetites does not bring down trouble in the end. But it is your business. As for me... I simply do not share your apparent attraction to these native women."

"A woman is a woman in the dark," muttered Richard flippantly.

"Not to me!" Jacques snapped. "Now will you just drop the whole thing?"

"These natives are very free spirited," Richard continued incorrigibly. "Why do you not try to relax with one?" he coaxed. "She might surprise you, eh?"

Jacques shook his head.

"It is only sport," Richard shrugged.

"What sport? They are like sheep, like little bunny rabbits. They are too docile, too submissive. I need something more."

"Perhaps your tastes became a little too rarefied too soon in life, my friend. This is not France, you know. France has been left behind, and the life you had there as well." Richard scratched thoughtfully at his beard and spoke again. "There is a good life to be had here. A better life perhaps, if you do not overlook the very best parts, eh?"

Jacques was pensively still. After a few moments he asked earnestly, "How can you even share a thought with them when you can not speak the same language?"

"I am not looking for conversation from them, for that I have you, *n'est-ce pas?*"

At this Jacques could not help but laugh.

"*Oui.* Well, I am not attracted to them. And that is my business, *n'est-ce pas?*" He looked at his friend for agreement.

"*Oui,*" the other shrugged with a sigh. The thought came to Richard that Jacques may have begun comparing all females to the one they had left behind in New York Towne. "But still," he added philosophically, "a man needs a woman. If not a squaw than you had better find a wife." Jacques did not respond. "Remember," Richard added teasingly, "it starts to numb your brain, not to mention what it does to your disposition. I have never heard of a man dying for lack of a woman, but possibly his friends might kill him for the foul mood the condition creates." And with that the larger man laughed deeply and turned over to go to sleep.

The following day no one came to trade; they broke camp and continued up the river.

It was a short season. Jacques and Richard ran out of goods to trade and so they turned back toward home long before the first evidences of autumn. Jacques was relieved. They were picking up more and more reports of fighting and war parties and by the time they returned to Wise William's, tensions in the area were running very high. They bid farewell to Samson and David, packed their pelts into their boat, raised the sail and caught the current homeward. In passing through the fort they learned for certain of the bloody massacre which had taken place at a settlement called Lachine on Montreal Island. Two hundred had been slaughtered and over a hundred more taken prisoner which meant taken as slaves by the Iroquois.

"Well, what do we do next year?" asked Richard as they were gliding swiftly downstream toward their ultimate goal of New York Towne.

"What do you mean?" Jacques looked at him, startled out of his own thoughts. They were making excellent speed sailing with the current and would arrive back in New York Towne perhaps before nightfall. Jacques had been mulling over the mixed emotions with which he anticipated a reunion with Marie. He supposed there was a chance she might have decided against striking out for the frontier, but he strongly doubted it. And he had given her his word. Why had he even suggested such a scheme? He felt the pinch of conscience. She was over here, thanks to him. Not that he supposed she was not able to make her own way. God knew if she was stubborn enough to set her mind to it, she could have. Other women did. They sold themselves into indentured service. But if she had done that she would not have been able to just take off and go to the frontier, would she? The blame still rolled back to his doorsill. And still, he cared that she was unhappy and frustrated. If he had had a sister, he would have wanted her to get on well in life, would he not? Of course he would have. But somehow he felt that if Marie had been a real sister, daughter of his mother or daughter of his father, she would have been raised to accept a well-arranged marriage to assure her well-being and would not have insisted on tramping half way around the world to the colonies and their innate dangers.

Just like you? A voice from within sprang up out of nowhere.

But that was different, he quickly told himself. He was escaping certain imprisonment in the Bastille.

And she is escaping peasantry.

Jacques scowled to himself. It was true. And this latest complication was his own, half-witted idea. He had no one to blame but himself, not her.

"From the sound of it," Richard was saying, "the British and their Indian friends did some very bloody deeds up there. Women, children, no one was spared. You can guess as well as I what it means. Our countrymen are going to retaliate. Next summer all hell will break loose and I do not think we are going to want to be anywhere near these rivers."

"You are right," Jacques agreed pensively. "I have been thinking the same thing. We must consider. Could we not go into the interior farther to the south? Surely we could find some Indian scouts of our own."

"I am willing."

"There is something else I want to talk about," Jacques began a bit hesitantly and then decided he might as well just blurt it out. "Marie wants to start a trading post and I told her if she is willing to accept the risks she could hold down a base camp and we could use it during the winter while we trap furs ourselves."

"Marie?! What?! A trading post? But she is only a girl!" Richard was genuinely horrified. "Where did she get such an idea?" As he looked at Jacques, his expression turned into a glare of accusation. "It was from you, is that not so? How could we leave her all alone in the wilderness? It is not possible!"

"She desperately wants to have something of her own, Richard. This is a way for her to begin. Establish a trading post like Wise William's and it will grow."

"*Merde!* Jacques! This is utter madness. How could you even think to agree to such a foolish scheme?" Richard asked hotly, shifting restlessly in the boat. "A white woman alone on the frontier! It is suicide or worse!"

"Why get angry with me?" Jacques looked at his friend defensively. The conversation was doing little to mollify his feelings of guilt. "She begged me, Richard."

"And if she begged you to slit her throat?" he demanded.

"Do you know she asked me first to teach her to be a trapper? She has such spirit. You have to admire that kind of spirit. Although we know she has no idea what trapping is really like. But she is ready to march off on her own to find out."

Richard was shaking his head vehemently. "Even we did not go off initially on our own... we needed someone to show us. How could you agree to be the one to show her?"

"No, no; I did not! I told her *absolutely no*. It is not the life for a female. But Richard, she wants disparately to get away from working for others. Can you blame her? Can you really blame her? Would you be satisfied working your entire life as someone's servant?"

"Better a living servant than a dead king! You know the dangers out here as well as I do," Richard protested, "animals, snakes, illness or accident with no one to help, the savages... even our own kind. Why, if they found a girl like Marie, alone by herself, who knows what they might do to her? Can you imagine Marie alone with the Calder brothers? *Mon Dieu*, Jacques! I thought you had some regard for her. Better to let her marry some man who would take care of her."

Jacques did not bother to answer but felt his stomach tighten as he thought of Bouchet. At that moment he realized Marie must learn to use a weapon to defend herself. He would insist upon it, make it a condition of her going. "I have fully explained how dangerous it could be. And I told her to think on it while we were gone. She may have changed her mind... but if she still wants to do it, Richard, are you going to be the one to tell her she may not? I have given her my word."

"She cannot possibly understand how dangerous it is. How could you give her your word?!" Richard hit the rudder for emphasis and the boat swerved sharply.

"She only needs to be alone for the summer while we go into the interior, and we will be around in the winter tending our own traps. I plan on teaching her to defend herself. She has great courage and I cannot refuse such determination."

Richard fumed in reply. *Only alone for the summer*. If an entire village could be massacred in a day, as it had in Montreal, what could not happen to one small female in the course of an entire summer?

Chapter 16

After almost two years of working for the Wingates, Marie had learned much about running a general store and bartering merchandise. She had also learned that while she was expected to politely take instruction and orders from young Samuel Cooper, she was also expected to bear the burden of cleaning up his mistakes. The only thing that kept the young woman going was the thought of starting an outpost at the frontier as Jacques had described.

She had thought on it the entire season as he had requested. She did not fantasize that it would be easy. She knew also that it was a great risk. But, she told herself, it was a bold heart that was needed to rise above the state one was born to especially if one was born a woman. Here in the New World, it was not her peasant blood that would keep her in servitude, it was her sex. She could have been born of the very same parents on the very same humble farm but if she had been born with *un pénis* instead of under the curse of Eve, how different her life might already be. She could see that now with aching clarity and considered it quietly as she readied herself for bed in the solitude of her room. First, she would never have been left pregnant from a naive roll in the hay. And while she still might have run away from home just as Louis had, she would not have borne a child only to watch it die, and Bouchet certainly would never have raped her or whored her out to others.

Marie knew by now that there were men in the world who used other men, but she thought it doubtful that any man would have been so easily used as she had been. She would doubtless have been somewhat better equipped to fight back and defend herself. And here in the New World, if she were a male, she would be taken seriously as a shopkeeper's apprentice instead of being dismissed as needing a guardian. The Wingates were kindly people, generous and concerned, but they could not see past her gender. Well, she sighed, she could hardly blame them for being of the same mind as the rest of the world. She was without a family or independent means and, thus, it was only the normal expectation that she should marry some man, any man, who could take care of her and for whom she would provide the necessary services. There was a shortage of women here and keeping a house and having babies was what this new world saw as her duty. In that regard, it seemed no different than the Old World.

Marie was brushing her hair furiously. As far as any world was concerned, no doubt, one man was as good as another for the likes of her. No matter her more tender feelings. No matter that her heart was irretrievably lost to one particular man. What right did an orphaned peasant girl have to feelings for a nobleman?

She tossed the brush down on the vanity with a thud and dropped down on the featherbed, throwing herself back upon the pillows. She stretched and tensed, then relaxed and wiggled her bare toes. A little laugh came out without much humor. If she had been born a man would she have been one of those men who would love another man? Would she be just as hopelessly in love with Jacques? She thought for a long moment. She really could not imagine being a man. Why she might never have met Jacques at all if she had been a man. There would have been no reason to dally at that tavern. She might have joined the troop of players or found her own way to Paris. But it took her fancy to think that if they had met, she would have admired him all the same and, perhaps, he would have admired her character and they would have become great friends. Friends as they were now only as a man her heart would not have ached so at times with the thought of him. Marie closed her eyes and saw Jacques' face before her and felt her heart compress within her chest.

Well, she shook herself with purpose, pulling the mosquito netting around her bed for the night. She was not a man. She was a woman! And she would have to take greater risks and work twice as hard because of it. But there was also no one to force her to marry if she did not want to. And she would overcome the hindrance of her sex or she would die in the trying. Let it be God's judgment just as it had been His decision to make her thus. And with that, Marie turned on her side and went to sleep.

By the time the men returned to town in early autumn, Marie was more than certain of her choice. She was almost seventeen and told Jacques as soon as she saw him that she was willing to do whatever it took and she meant it. She would manage and she would survive. And no matter what, in the end, she would only thank him for giving her an opportunity no one else would have given her.

She thought he seemed proud of her decision and he told her again that if she had the courage to be by herself in the wilderness then he would be a partner in building a trading post as well as in preparing her to live there on her own. And so, Jacques began to take Marie out to the Harlem farmlands beyond the northern limits of the town where he showed her how to load and shoot a musket.

"This is the lock, this is the stock, and this is the barrel where the shot comes out." He described the parts of the musket as he held it before her. His expression was completely serious as was hers. She nodded. "Never point the weapon at anyone unless you have the stomach to kill them. This is most important, do you understand this?" She nodded again. "Anyone you feel it necessary to point a musket at will most likely be able to detect a faint heart and a weak trigger finger." His eyes held hers. "They will call your bluff and when you are at their mercy, they will not thank you for yours." Marie's brows knit as she digested this and nodded once more. "Do you fully understand what I am saying, Marie?"

"I..I think so," she replied quietly. "I...I am not sure."

"Marie, females are universally regarded as the weaker sex. If you submit,

you may be used but rarely would anyone take your life. Even amongst the savages, usually they would rather enslave you than kill you. But if you hold this," he
shook the musket in gesture, "suddenly you have equal strength, equal power, the
power to kill. It will change completely an adversary's view of you. And so you
must be willing to kill them before they kill you." As he stood looking at her he
saw resolve straighten her backbone and her shoulders squared almost imperceptibly.

"I understand," she said, never taking her eyes from him.

"Very good," he nodded quickly and continued with the lesson. "Now this,"
he pulled a thin steel rod from its holding place along the side of the barrel, "it is
called the ramrod."

"Ramrod," she echoed.

And so he began to teach.

It was only a matter of practice he kept telling her as time after time she fumbled, spilled too much powder off the pan, ruined the cartridge, or failed to remember to complete the cocking procedure and found the trigger would not move. She
learned the result of failing to ram the cartridge down completely when the flint
sparked the powder in the pan, making a small flash but not igniting the cartridge
within. Marie's hands grew dirty from the soot and her arms ached from the weight
of the long weapon but at last she loaded flawlessly and fired five times in the
space of about ten minutes and Jacques seemed very pleased indeed.

"So, are you ready to continue with the lesson?" She nodded,. "*Bon!* Now
you add the musket ball to your movements and we can practice hitting the target."

It quickly became evident that Marie had a good eye and a steady hand despite the weight of the weapon. With Jacques' continued coaching, she became an
excellent shot given the limitations of the firearm itself which was not expected to
hit its mark beyond a rather limited range.

Christmas brought another invitation to gather at the Wingate table. Jacques and
Richard arrived to the happy squeals of a small toddler and met the Wingates'
younger daughter Joan, her husband and child. Elizabeth and Nathaniel were also
there.

Richard once again allowed himself to be properly groomed and re-civilized
upon his return to New York Towne. From his cravat to his buckle adorned shoes,
he looked the part of a colonial Huguenot gentleman, ruggedly handsome and a
touch more conservative than his well-dressed aristocratic friend, Jacques, who
was trying not to look like he was searching for Marie. Richard took great interest
in watching his friend's first reaction upon seeing her enter the room dressed not as
a store clerk but in the kind of gown one would expect an adult woman to wear for
the holiday. Her dress was more conservative than the one she had worn the year
before but she looked sophisticated, very beautiful, and completely without pretense. Marie was all grown up with her thick hair pulled up into a simple top-knot

ringed with holly and wispy curls edging her soft, small neck.

All evening it was an interesting dance the two performed, observed Richard, each attempting to avoid being too close to the other without looking like they were attempting to avoid the other. He doubted that anyone else saw it. Marie joyfully interacted with the toddler until he was finally taken off to bed. Jacques spent much of his time discussing daily living at the frontier with the Wingates' sons-in-law. Did they even realize how hard they were working to pretend they were not overwhelmingly attracted to each other? Richard wondered.

By the approach of spring, everyone was aware of the mounting tensions on the frontier. There was no doubt that the French would retaliate and Jacques could not forget that if captured by them, there were still papers out calling for his imprisonment. After considerable ruminating and deliberation, the partners finally made the decision to go south along the coast striking out into unknown territory. Going southward would keep them well within English land, they believed. Between the former Dutch settlement of old New Amsterdam and the old Swedish settlements along the Delaware River there was little but unknown wilderness. Yet it all was now owned by the English Crown.

The outpost the young adventurers established would be their own stop off point for coming and going by sea, they reasoned. And the two young men, now somewhat seasoned traders, were certain they could develop their own routes inland into the territory somewhere north of the Delaware River. How difficult could it be, they asked themselves?

Marie had put off telling the Wingates she was leaving. Instinctively she expected they would try to dissuade her and she had no desire to face an unending barrage of discouragement. She felt great affection for the elderly couple although she smarted daily from Cooper's presence in the store. Deep within her being, part of her resisted abandoning everything to him and did not want him to know she was any sooner than necessary. It was silly, she realized, for Cooper was not her competition, nor was she his. There was no contest and that was what perhaps grieved her the most. There had never been a contest because she was a woman. If there had been a fair assessment between them as clerks without gender, Marie had no doubt that she would have won easily but that knowledge was of little comfort.

Marie could put off her announcement no longer. Winter was definitely over and Jacques had mentioned leaving within a fortnight.

It was Sunday evening and Marie was waiting for Samuel Cooper to take his leave and retire to the lean-to for the night, leaving her and the Wingates alone by the fireside in the comfortable kitchen. Instead, he remained, chatting idly almost as if he knew she wanted time alone with the couple. The clock struck ten and Mistress Wingate began to gather her knitting. Marie knew she was on the brink of sending them all to bed.

Marie finally spoke. "Samuel, would you be so kind as to retire for the night?

I wish a word with the Wingates alone."

Master Wingate looked up from his paper. Mistress Wingate sat heavily back down in her chair. Samuel looked thoroughly put out. Marie waited as he seemed to crawl with the speed of snail to the door.

When the outside door finally closed, Abigail asked, "Whatever is it, dear?"

As Marie had expected, they were shocked by her announcement and expressed increasing concern on her behalf.

"But whatever are you going to do out there?" asked Abigail, a vague look of confused bewilderment on her gentle motherly face. She did have two daughters who lived on the frontier so in that respect it didn't seem so terrifying or forbidding, but her daughters were both married with husbands to protect them and their reputations. "You'll be all alone by yourself with those two young men...?"

"I will grow a vegetable garden and hold the camp for Jacques and Richard," Marie answered brightly, not comprehending their true concern. "I will keep the post while they are away."

The older couple exchanged a glance.

"Marie, do you think it proper?" Abigail asked almost timidly. "After all, you are not married to either one of them. Great harm could befall you." For a young unmarried woman to set out into the wilderness with two healthy, virile men, not her kin, would mark her in their little society. Abigail feared Marie would never be accepted into any respectable circles after that. Did Marie not realize or did she just not care? The older woman puzzled.

Marie looked at her with a bright smile, thinking only that Mistress Wingate harbored fears on her behalf in regard to the dangers of the wilds.

"I am certain everything will be well, Mistress Wingate," Marie said bravely. "Jacques and Richard will look out for me. I have been practicing with a musket and I shall manage being alone for a time," she said with assurance. Then she turned and threw her arms around the gentle woman. "But I will miss you very much; you have been very kind to me."

"I would ask one thing of you," Abigail said quietly. "I know you came here on the ship with Brother Robert. Will you talk to him first, before you leave?"

"Talk about what?"

"Please?"

Marie shrugged. "Of course, if that is what you wish. I tried to find him after services today to say good-bye but…"

"Perhaps Master Wingate can arrange for Brother Robert to come here and see you." Abigail looked to her husband who nodded his agreement.

Brother Robert who was still the assistant to the pastor at their church surprised the Wingates completely. He knew the three friends very well. It was Marie who had nursed him through an almost fatal bout of sea sickness, he told them. And the French culture was not prone to Puritanical views.

"I think it is a marvelous thing you are doing," he smiled. "I myself have often thought of striking out to take the Good News of the Gospel to the natives as well as to our own. I hear there is a Huguenot settlement on the Delaware now. Where is it that you plan to go?"

"I am not certain. That is up to Monsieur Jacques," replied Marie.

"But, Brother Robert... a young girl? With no chaperon?" Thomas Wingate cut to the heart of their concern.

"Yes, yes, I see your concern. But she had no chaperon when she crossed the Atlantic for many weeks. And she came to no harm. I know these young men. They are most honorable and Jacques-Jean Charte is more like her guardian. Have no fear for her honor, my friends."

The Wingates did not feel they had the right to say more. After all was taken into account, Marie was a free agent. They could neither force her to remain in their employ nor could they stop her from leaving. The girl had evidenced exemplary moral behavior all the while she had lived with them, never flirting with the customers, never causing so much as a hint of gossip. They could not bring themselves to assume a future immorality of behavior to take issue with although the community at large might see it differently. And so they resolved to pray for her and hope for the best.

Jacques sold his horse and used the money to purchase a small craft similar to the one they had rented to use on the Hudson. The trio filled the square sailed boat with supplies packed in barrels and casks. Along with food, utensils, linens, dishes and pots, they took carefully considered tools, implements, seed, trading goods and several storage chests along with a sturdy table, three sturdy wood chairs and a large cherry framed looking glass. Mistress Wingate insisted Marie take an entire bolt of mosquito netting which she reminded the young woman would be equally useful in straining fruits for jellies and for wrapping cheeses.

"Cheese?" Marie laughed. "I will need a goat or a cow first."

"Oh, yes," Abigail flustered, "of course... but you'll need this. The mosquitoes in the wilderness can be fierce. I know. My daughters have both said so. You must be careful. Oh, my! How far are you going?"

Marie shrugged. "I do not know. Jacques did not say."

"I just worry, you know. Wild animals and savages, no other women, no white families around, it's just so frightening. My daughters have neighbors."

Marie reached out a hand to pat the other woman gently on the arm. "I promise I will be fine, really I will. And some day we will have neighbors as well."

"You have far more courage than I, Marie. Oh, do take care of yourself, child. You're so young and have so much to live for." The older woman gave Marie a motherly embrace, squeezing her tightly. When Abigail let go she turned quickly to dab at a tear.

The trio cast off and left the harbor before dawn catching the tide. At first they rowed away from the wharf, seeking the current, and then they unleashed the stiff square canvas sail. The breeze filled it immediately. It ballooned and Marie could feel the power as the boat surged smoothly through the waters and out to-ward the open sea. She was much more aware of their speed than she had been in the larger ship of their crossing. The cold wind whipped the hair from under her cap and about her face as she watched the waters flowing passed the hull. She peered at the nearness of the surface from the side of the craft. The docks and waterfront grew smaller and smaller as the unending water surrounded them. She was briefly reminded of when they had first arrived less than three years before. Now she wondered fleetingly if she would ever see this harbor again.

Jacques and Richard were very attentive in steering the craft and setting the angle of the sail. They were both uneasy about actually being out on the open sea, although neither said so. There was an undeniable vastness to the ocean which was daunting and intimidating. They did not fool themselves. They were not sailors although they knew how to handle the craft from sailing up the rivers and their fragile link with the land was based solely upon sight. A sudden fog bank or storm could break that fragile link and their craft was not meant for enduring the perils of the high seas.

Richard steered the rudder skillfully tacking to and fro, keeping the wind driving them southward but never venturing so far out as to lose sight of land. The day wore on. The sun made its steady climb up and up until it reached its zenith at which time Marie produced lunch from a hamper Abigail Wingate had packed full of food. Jacques relieved Richard at the rudder as the sun began its decent toward the forests that covered the coastline. Looking for a place to go ashore for the night, they strained against the sun's brightness in their eyes. For sometime the coast had looked rocky and uninviting, offering little foothold for a landing. then sand bars appeared that needed to be navigated around.

Squinting out over the glittering water, Marie pointed excitedly at what looked to be a small harbor half hidden from their direct view. They headed for it and were pleasantly surprised to discover that it was larger than they had at first thought, deep enough for larger sailing ships perhaps but because of the rocky outcropping it was almost camouflaged from visibility. Sailing into the small bay they spied a long strip of beach and brought the boat aground upon the shore.

The light was fading quickly as the sun sank into the trees and it was getting colder. The three gathered driftwood and dead-fall which was plentiful. In a short time they had more than enough wood to last the night. Richard set about building a fire in the center of a grass edged hollow amongst the dunes while Jacques and Marie unloaded bedrolls and food. Marie used a small cask for a table top and saw to the preparations of a modest supper out of the hamper. Jacques spread the bedrolls around the fire. The sand was dry and still pleasantly warm and would make comfortable sleeping while the steady breeze from off the water was keeping all flying insects away.

It had been a very full day beginning long before dawn and filled with nervous excitement. Now, as heavy dusk gathered around them, an exhaustive stupor visibly stole over them like a rolling fog. As they sat over their suppers, Marie was aware of wanting to stretch out in her blankets and close her eyes.

"What are you looking at?" Richard asked, noticing Jacques staring out at the darkening water's edge.

"The tide line... I think."

"Oh," Richard responded dully, then with a quick nod of recognition continued, "Oh, *oui!* Do you think we are safe?"

"Safe?" echoed Marie.

"My guess," replied Jacques, "is that it is close to high tide right now judging from the markings on the shore. I am guessing the saltwater does not come up this far or the grasses would not be growing and the sand would not be dry enough to blow into dunes."

"*Bon*," Richard grunted in satisfaction, "we will be just fine."

"The question is how far does the tide go out?"

"What difference does it make?" Marie asked quietly trying to follow the conversation. Not having much experience living by the sea, she had not thought of the tide waters coming in and posing a threat to their little camp until she heard the men speak of it but she did not understand what possible harm going out could do.

Jacques smiled slightly, brushing some sand from his mustache. "It could make a difference if our craft is beached a league from the water's edge."

"Ohhhh," Marie gasped slightly with a sudden frown. "What should we do?" She had the mental image in her mind of their boat being left high and dry, like Noah's ark after the flood.

"Surely it could not be that much," Richard objected.

"I am not a sailor, *mes amis*, I know not what to expect but we will find out, eh?" Jacques looked at the worried faces of his companions. "Do not worry. What is the worst that could happen?"

Marie thought for a moment and realized that unlike the forty days and nights of rainwater receding from the land, the water here would come back in again just as faithfully as it went out. "We would have to wait for the water to come back," she offered hesitantly.

"*Exactement.* Not a terrible tragedy, *n'est-ce pas?*"

Richard grunted slightly as if he had known this all along and with a dismissive air, stretched out on his bedroll. "Time to get some sleep," he said with a deep yawn. "I will let you worry about the tide. Wake me for the next watch, *mon ami. Bon soir.*

"*Bon soir,*" Jacques replied.

"Good night, Richard," Marie called over, keeping her English. "Sleep well."

Jacques threw more wood on the fire and the sparks leapt into the air above the ridge the dunes made and the wind quickly carried them off. The steady breeze blowing off the waters filled their ears and blew their hair but closer to the earth, within the protection of the dune mounds surrounding them, it was calmer. There was no strong surf in the protected inlet, but the water lapping gently at the shore established a calming rhythm. The fire crackled and popped, creating a ring of light and warmth within the shelter of their little hollow.

Marie arranged her blankets. She longed for sleep but did not wish to leave Jacques up all alone. She stifled a yawn.

"The sky is very clear," she said looking upward. The stars were beginning to pop out in the evening sky. She moved slightly getting more comfortable, her arms clasped around her knees. "The sand is beginning to cool. I have never slept on a beach before, have you?"

"No. Never," he replied softly, watching the fire light one side of her face, creating a play of shadows on the other.

"The sand does not stay put," she giggled, brushing her hands and her clothing. "It gets everywhere."

"I think I have some in my teeth," he grinned at her.

"But it is comfortable." She wiggled her bottom into the sand and he, finding that particular movement very unsettling, redirected his eyes if not his mind back to the fire. They both sat quietly for a while watching the dancing flames. "Does it bother you so much?" she asked at length.

"What?" Jacques looked startled, thinking for a brief moment that she had read his mind.

"The boat... is that why you are staying up, to watch the water and the boat?"

"No, not really."

"Then why?"

"Marie, are you not tired? Why do you not get some sleep as well?" he suggested rather strongly and a bit more harshly than he had intended.

"Are you not going to sleep?" she asked with concern.

"Of course, but not yet, now hush. *Bon soir.*"

She obediently made a small pillow of the sand to put her bedroll on, stretched out, and wrapped her blanket around her. The evening was becoming quite cool and the fire's warmth felt comforting. She really was exhausted, she thought, and if Jacques was not desirous of her company it was fine with her. "*Bon soir, Jacques,*" she murmured sleepily just above the sound of the wind.

Jacques sat quietly watching her, the smooth plains and hollows of her face illuminated by the flickering flames. One small graceful hand held the edge of her blanket to her bosom which was soon moving up and down in a steady, relaxed rhythm. When he was certain she was asleep, he tore his eyes from her, got up soundlessly, took his musket and moved away from the circle of light. He took up a vigil in the shadows of some brush where he could see into the moon lit darkness and watch for any signs of unwelcome visitors. After the moon had made its way halfway across the sky, he would wake Richard and get some sleep himself. And in the meanwhile, he found himself unable to think of much else but the soft, slender female slumbering on the sand.

Marie stretched in her sleep, then sat up suddenly, blinking at the sun which was already in the sky. She rubbed her eyes and had to think where she was and why. Her cap had fallen off. Raking her hands absently through her hair, she could feel the grit of sand on her scalp. She also felt it give way cold beneath her legs. Jacques and Richard were hunkered down together across the fire from her, eating dry biscuits and washing them down with hot tea. She rose wordlessly, brushing sand from her clothing and shivering. She went to the other side of the boat and into the forest to find a bit of privacy. Taking a wide legged stance she lifted her skirts just out of the way and emptied her bladder.

On returning, Marie was fully awake and noticed the boat was sitting only a small distance farther from the water's edge than it had the night before.

"It is good then," she said after a murmured greeting and the angle of her head and expression left no doubt as to what she referred. She poured herself a mug of tea and took a biscuit.

"Oh, *oui,*" Jacques smiled broadly, flashing his teeth as he took in her sleep rumpled appearance. He thought her quite adorable with her clothing slightly askew and bunched in wrinkles. She had the soft dewy look of youth in the early morning, sleepy-eyed and slightly off balance. The wind caught tendrils of disheveled hair and made it twist about her head as though alive. By contrast, Jacques was combed and tidied, his hair caught neatly back in a ribbon and his clothing arranged perfectly. Even the stubble of his beard was so blond and unobtrusive as to not detract from his overall appearance of being well groomed.

"How does he do it?" Marie asked Richard after sipping her tea. Setting the cup down, she tugged at her own clothing and pulled her skirt around into its proper orientation. "He slept on the beach the same as we did, did he not?"

Richard, looking very rumpled himself with his hair wild in the unceasing wind, only shrugged. He knew exactly what Marie was saying. "I am getting tired of this infernal wind," he said as if somehow that explained everything but of course, it explained nothing.

Marie nodded. Now that he had focused her attention on it, she was finding the incessant wind more and more provoking herself. She turned into the wind so her hair was swept back from her face and out of her eyes and she continued to drink her tea. She could feel the hot liquid coursing down her insides and warming her.

"Why did you not wake me sooner?" she asked, swallowing the last of her biscuit. "I am holding everything up."

Jacques raised his hand in protest. "Not at all. I wanted the mist to clear before we left this place."

"What mist?" she asked looking around the crystal clear bay.

"The mist that was there at dawn," he pointed southwest to a reedy shoreline. Marie followed his gesture and squinted.

"What is that?" she asked, peering at the uneven shoreline.

"That is what we are going to find out," he smiled, "if I am not mistaken, it looks very much like the mouth of a river, does it not?"

Marie nodded and drained the last of her tea.

It only took a few minutes to gather their things and douse the fire. Thanks to the flatness of the boat's bottom, it was not that difficult to push the vessel across the wet sand the short distance needed to reach the water. It needed very little to float and once buoyant, the barefooted young men each took an arm and lifted Marie in. They pushed off while scrambling in themselves.

While Richard manned the rudder, Jacques saw to the sail and set the angle to catch the wind blowing in from the sea. Before long they were sailing against the current of a fresh water river spilling into the inlet. Catching the main channel, they continued inland for a time switching to oars as the wind died away. Marie used the opportunity to brush and braid her hair in a manner she had learned from Celimene.

As they continued up the river, the sound of rushing water grew more pronounced. Jacques and Richard strained against the current until they spied a small rocky bluff jutting out at the confluence of a smaller tributary rushing into the main channel. Rowing to the far side to avoid the strong current coming from the smaller body, they made it upstream and pulled back over to land the boat on the rocky bank upriver of the rushing stream. The men were intrigued. They pulled their boots back on before securing the craft. Marie was told to stay in the boat, musket in hand while they proceeded to climb upward to survey the area.

Alone, Marie looked around her. The world was fully awake and growing pleasantly warmer. The skies were clear and birds sang and chattered in the oaks, maples, birches, and hemlocks all around her. She watched several waterfowl pursuing their breakfast making slow lazy passes over the water, diving and scooping up fish in a languid, seemingly effortless motion. Sunlight danced on the water while dragonflies droned and fish leapt up to grab the water skimming insects hovering on the surface. Breathtakingly beautiful butterflies played among the cattails and small yellow wildflowers. Tiny new leaves were visible on the trees high above while the sun streaked through the tops to illuminate dark places in the brush on the ground and spotlight patches of wild violets among the thick ferns.

So this was the frontier, Marie thought to herself in wonderment. It was beautiful. Pristine. Alive. Verdant. Rich in color and filled with the fecund scents of earthy loam, teeming river, and moistly vegetated forest.

She had become very accustomed to the straight, barren dirt streets of New York Towne, and the neat little farms beyond. But now she thought back to her first impression of the New World and how the trees seemed to crowd down to the sea allowing no room for humans to set foot. Thus the coastline had appeared as they had traveled yesterday but the small beach upon which they had landed had turned out to be deceptively broad. And here she was, a short distance inland, with the trees looming over her and crowding to the water's very edge. There was barely enough room to pull up the boat which was lashed to a scrubby tree hanging over the waters. Rocks lined the river bank here as though pushed by the force of all that was living while the smaller, faster stream just below her was unrelenting in its efforts to join to the sea.

This was the wilderness up close and it beckoned to her. Marie stepped carefully from the boat onto a large rock, taking care that her wooden sabots did not slip and send her sprawling. She was drawn onward by curiosity. For a moment her heart quickened as she thought of the daunting task of trying to clear all of this wood and make something out of such a wilderness. Then calm settled over her. It was the opportunity to build a dream with her own two hands. To have something the Bouchets of the world could not take from her. A chance to prove she was equal to any Samuel Cooper. Here, somewhere in this place, she would reap the rewards of her labor and would not be used to unfair advantage by anyone. She would be her own mistress with no one to say she could not... or she would die trying.

Such were the thoughts of Marie's heart when out of the corner of her eye she caught sight of a large, copper colored snake slithering along the bank. With a squeak and a shudder she made a hasty retreat back into the boat and sat nervously watching all about her.

A short time later the men returned, both grinning broadly as they traversed back down through the brush.

"This is perfect!" Jacques called out in delight. Marie gave him a quizzical look. His fair hair was snarled with brambles now and there was a light scratch across his left cheek. "High ground is always best," he explained with enthusiasm, "it is safer from flooding and it is healthier. Here we have high ground. From up there you can see up and down the river all the way back out to the bay. The land continues at that level and looks to be very fertile. It should grow just about anything."

"It will be easy to defend," added Richard. "Here are three sides which are difficult to approach leaving only one side to guard and watch. No one can come upon you without your knowledge," he concluded.

"And there is a waterfall back up that small stream," Jacques said with excitement. "It is not very big but do you know what that means?" he asked.

"No," she shook her head hesitantly.

"That is energy!" he cried with a laugh. "It is a mill waiting to exist! A means to grind meal and to cut lumber."

She smiled catching his enthusiasm. If he said it was good, it must be so. And so it was decided that there was no reason for them to travel on any farther.

Leaving the boat moored at the river's edge, Jacques and Richard took up their tools and began to cut a switched back path as they climbed back into the forest and up to the top of the ridge where they commenced to begin a clearing. Disturbing the cool damp of the underbrush sent the mosquitoes, midges, and gnats up in gray-brown clouds. Marie helped with the small bushes and dead-fall, brushing gnats from her eyes and slapping mosquitoes from her cheeks and neck all the while. It took no time for a large pile of rubbish to accumulate and they began a controlled fire. As Marie tended the blaze she realized thankfully that the smoke deterred the flying pests. If they could stand to work in the smoke they could escape being molested but she did not know which was worse, choking on the smoke which burned her eyes or having gnats up her nose and midges in her eyes while mosquitoes bit every exposed inch of her flesh. Finally, she realized Jacques and Richard had put handkerchiefs over their noses and mouths and she pulled the kerchief from around her neck and did the same.

Once the underbrush from a sizable area had been completely cleared, the men began chopping down the saplings. As quickly as they trimmed off the smallest limbs, Marie carried them to the fire. The larger limbs were trimmed and neatly stacked by size. When the trunk itself was stripped and bare, it too was stacked aside to be used for building.

They worked with the exuberance of youth, stopping only briefly for a midday lunch. It was a pleasant day with light spring breezes stirring the air overhead but the arduous work had them sweating in abundance and the heat of the fire only made it worse. The men thought of removing their shirts but decided against it. Aside from the smoke, the cloth was their only protection from the fiendish pests that plagued them in the shadows.

All too quickly, deeply slanting rays announced the coming of the day's end and Richard and Jacques called a halt to the activities. Assisting Marie in raking up the charred ground around the fire, they assured themselves that it could burn harmlessly through the night until it completely consumed itself. The men gathered their tools and weapons while Marie shoveled up a bucket of burning embers to carry back down to the river's edge.

Wiping a sleeve across his sweaty brow, Jacques caught a whiff of himself and twisted his face in disgust. "I smell like a goat!" he observed contemptuously as they neared the boat.

"A smoked goat," Richard joked.

"I need a swim."

"Last one in takes first watch," Richard challenged and after dropping his load of tools, he pulled off his boots and was in the water before he had bothered to remove his clothing. It was just as well. His clothing needed the wash as much as his body did.

Jacques stopped to find a tin of soap, not really caring that he should take the first watch again that night. He followed Richard around the small bend of the river and removed his own boots and breeches before plunging into the cold stream of water rushing in from the tributary.

Marie, itching, scratching, and reeking more strongly of wood smoke than either of her companions, looked after them with vague envy as they disappeared from sight. She dumped out the hot coals she had carried onto a broad flat rock formation near the water's edge and added kindling for a cook fire. Over the fire she set down a deep iron pan having three feet on its bottom which allowed the air to circulate to the fire beneath. She added water to the pan to warm before looking for the salt pork. It would have been nice to have some fresh fish for supper, she thought, but it was too late to try and catch any. Surely the fish had all been frightened away by now, she thought wryly as the sounds of playful cavorting and laughter wafted back to her. She scratched at her sweaty scalp and mopped at the sweat running down the back of her neck. She made the sudden decision that there was no reason in the world why she could not have a wash as well. Quickly unlacing her small corselet, she dropped it on the neighboring rock at the edge of the riverbank along with her skirt and blouse. Kicking off her sabots, she walked gingerly into the water on the upstream side of the boat, the opposite direction from the men. For modesty's sake she had left her thin shift on and it ballooned about her as she carefully went out into the reedy water.

The water was cool but not nearly as cold as she had expected. It was traveling at a slower, lazier pace than the rushing tributary just a few yards downstream. She could hear her companions whooping, yelping, and splashing like young boys and she smiled to herself. She had no doubt that their water was much colder. *Hers,* as she thought of it, was sun warmed and gentle but still most certainly revitalizing. And considerably cooler, she observed, when she proceeded in deeper.

Careful not to lose her soap bar or her footing, she scrubbed herself thoroughly and sighed as she bent her knees and submersed completely. The cool water tickled as it crept up over her hot, itchy scalp. She began to scrub her thick hair which was full of bits of foliage, burrs, tiny twigs, sand and God only knew what else. Washing her face, she sensed the bumps rising up where she had been stung. Ah, very good, she thought mockingly to herself, she would look like she had the pox. She determined she must not and would not scratch at them.

The young girl could not swim and was careful not to stray far from the river's bank. Afraid that the riverbed might suddenly drop into a deeper channel, she stayed cautiously in her place just off from the reeds where the water came up only to her waist unless she bent her knees. She continued to submerge herself, holding her breath for as long as possible each time. She had never bathed in deep waters before and she found the experience extraordinarily sensual. The water engulfing her body was silken and soothing and she could feel the current ripple over her skin.

She dipped under the water again and again, losing all track of time, mesmerized by the feeling of the water flowing freely through her hair and over her scalp, caressing every part of her. She did not notice when Jacques walked back up to their landing place and began calling out for her until she came up out of the water at last with a gasp and a splash, wiping her nose and shaking her head. Then, she heard his voice.

Jacques had lathered himself liberally and rinsed with a swim. After indulging in boyish silliness with Richard, he more seriously washed out his shirt before leaving the water. Slipping on his breeches and boots, and with a promise to fetch back dry clothes for Richard, he carried his wet shirt back to the small camp intending to hang it up to dry. He had also intended on getting a fresh shirt of his own but all thoughts of that had left him when he discovered the campfire deserted. Throwing his wet shirt up in a bush, he turned round quickly, surveying every direction and seeing only the cook pan on the fire with the water in it bubbling.

"Marie?! Marie?!" Jacques voice became sharp as he called out in alarm; all thoughts of bringing clothes to Richard disappeared. He scanned the boat, the embankment, the brush. Her musket sat beside a tree. To where had she disappeared and why was she not answering him? "Marie!"

She heard him and answered back. "I am here," she called out.

Jacques spun around. He had learned on their crossing that she could not swim and never expected to find her in the river. In the dimming light he saw her beginning to rise from the water through the reeds, her wet shift as transparent as glass clinging to her slender young body as she languidly wrung water from her hair. For a long moment he could not breathe. With her arms lifted, elbows akimbo, hands busied with her soaking tresses, her breasts were lifted forward, each dark, hard nipple straining against the water soaked fibers of her shift. He heard his own breath catch in his throat as he stared. Then he heard Richard calling out to him from the other direction.

"Jacques! Hurry up with my clothes! Or do you intend for me to go naked?" Richard was yelling. "It is all the same to me, I do not mind," he grumbled loudly. "At least I would not if it was not for these little pests." Richard slapped at himself in several places where he felt the mosquitoes biting him as he left the water so he submerged himself again.

Jacques jerked around thinking only that he did not want Richard to catch even the smallest glimpse of Marie like this. He grabbed for Richard's clothing satchel and hurried back to his friend. As soon as he saw Richard, Jacques threw the breeches to him.

"Here, cover your hairy arse," he cajoled. "Marie has no wish to see it."

Richard grabbed the garment as it sailed through the air. "That is what I am trying to do. These damned little beggars are draining my blood." He hopped on one foot, shoving the other into one leg of his breeches and frantically brushing at his genitals as he did. "*Merde!* That is the last place I need to itch," he grunted and uttered several more oaths. "Do you have my buckskin shirt?" he asked.

"No. Here." Jacques tossed the satchel. "Get your own shirt," he retorted. "As I must get mine," he muttered now realizing he had forgotten his shirt as he brushed and slapped at his own attackers. "Where are your wet clothes?" he asked, stalling to block Richard's path, wanting to ensure Marie enough time to cover herself.

"Damn! I am being eaten alive! I can worry about the wet garments after I get my buckskin on," Richard replied digging in his satchel until he produced his leather shirt.

"Ah... you might lose them in the dark," Jacques suggested as Richard tried to push passed him.

"Lose what?" Richard muttered from within the leather and he stopped to pull it over his head.

"Your wet clothes. An animal might carry them away. You do not have so many that you can afford to lose them. You better get them now."

Richard looked at him fiercely as his head emerged from the neck hole of the buckskin. "Oh, fine, fine!" He hurried back to the bank of the stream and retrieved his soggy clothing which he held out from him, dripping all the way.

"Where do you think we should bed down tonight?" Jacques asked, halting in the path in front of him again, putting his arm around Richard to turn him. "Do you think there... or perhaps we should go back to the beach."

"The beach?!" The idea surprised the taller man who looked at his companion in the gloom as though Jacques had lost his mind. "It is too late to go back to the beach. We still have to eat. I have worked like a mule today. I need food. Where is Marie?" he asked, suddenly realizing her absence as he thought of food and surveyed the empty pan.

"I am right here," Marie answered, coming up behind them with her blanket wrapped about her. Once out of the water, she had quickly realized for herself that her wet shift was no covering. Thanking Providence that Jacques had gone back to Richard, she had made a quick dash for her bedroll, stripped the cold, wet shift from her and wrapped up in her blanket. There had been no time to put on fresh clothing. "I … ah … could not help myself. I simply had to wash before I did anything else."

"Of course," Jacques said with feigned nonchalance.

"It felt good, *n'est-ce pas*? But now I am hungry enough to eat the boat," Richard complained, rubbing his growling belly as he began digging into the provisions on board the craft.

"Ahhh... I would really like to put on a change of clothes. These reek from the smoke," Marie wrinkled her nose at her cast off garments. "Could I ask... that is, would you mind... ?"

"What?" Richard looked up only after he had found a hard biscuit. He held it like a prize and munched on it eagerly.

"I think she would like us to turn our backs... like gentlemen," Jacques said pointedly.

"Yes," Marie nodded. "That is exactly what I meant. If you do not mind... just for a moment, please."

"Of course," Jacques smiled agreeably and gestured for Richard to get out of the boat and allow Marie to get in. The taller man climbed out concentrating on his biscuit while Jacques offered Marie a helping hand to steady her as she stepped into the sturdy craft. Once she was safely within the confines of the boat, Jacques turned his back and turned Richard so they both stood looking up to the ridge where they had spent the day clearing.

It was gratifying to survey the work they had accomplished in that first day. One could see a definite difference although the large trees still remaining were daunting. They would have to be tackled next and neither young man looked forward to the task. As they stood looking upward Richard spoke quietly.

"I suppose getting a look at that fine limb was worth the cost of a late supper," he said, just the vaguest hint of a smile in his voice as he referred to the glimpse of leg Marie had revealed stepping into the boat. He felt Jacques stiffen beside him. Well, that was interesting. The Jacques he knew in France would have laughingly agreed. Had he not said himself once that the fine sculpting of a pretty limb showed the genius of the Master Artist?

Jacques refused to acknowledge Richard's remark. He was determined to completely ignore it. It had never happened. Marie was not to be casually jested about. And if his friend was going to be so crude, he would have to be taught a lesson... sooner or later. "I have been thinking," Jacques said with deceptive calm. "You see that smallest tree up there," he pointed up at the ridge.

"Yes," Richard responded, deciding not to push Jacques any further.

"And see the crooked one just to the left, and the one to the left of that?"

"Yes, yes ?"

If we cut down those three, it looks to me as though we could build a cabin snugly right in the middle of the rest."

Richard stood staring up.

"Well, do you not see? Taking out those three trees gives us enough room. We will not have to cut them all down. It would save a lot of labor."

Richard nodded his head in growing recognition. "Do you really think so?"

"We will pace it out tomorrow."

"But if we do not take down more trees, will there be enough lumber to build with?"

Jacques turned to look straight at Richard. "You forget, Richard. You are not thinking." Jacques continued to hold Richard's gaze as though his words meant something else. He turned again and looked up at the ridge. "The trees will shelter the cabin but we must clear a garden plot; that means several more must be taken down over that way. I should think we must cut the tops off of many others to allow the sun to get through, that shall make sufficient kindling for Marie for the season. The garden will need sunshine, *n'est-ce pas?*"

Richard nodded his agreement.

As Jacques and Richard talked, Marie hastily dropped the blanket and with a shiver, donned a fresh change of clothing. It took her little time and just as soon as she had dropped her skirt in place, she told them they could relax and go about their business. She continued tucking and smoothing her shift as she laced up her corselet and went to the fire to dry her hair.

"Are you not hungry?" Richard asked incredulously as he turned to survey her, an obvious complaint in his voice.

"Richard, there is salt pork and leftover bread. Help yourself," Marie responded amiably. "I must comb out my hair now or it will dry in such a snarl I will have to cut it all off. Would you wish me bald?" she joked.

Jacques chuckled. "Come on, Richard, we fed ourselves well enough on the trail and shall have to do so again. Let Marie attend to herself."

"But the food is better when she fixes it," Richard grumbled pettishly.

"Richard," Marie exclaimed in good humor, "it is only salt pork and two day old bread. There is nothing I would do to it except perhaps warm it. You can warm it. This is why I set up the pan." Marie cajoled with a smile and continued to work the comb through her thick tangles.

Jacques did not comment that he, too, thought food better coming from her hands. He skewered the bread onto a sharp stick and propped it over the steaming pan. When it had softened he served up the food and Richard's spirits began to improve as all his attention dwelt upon his plate. Jacques sat back with his own plate and was absorbed in watching Marie laboriously comb through her heavy tresses. Her back was to the fire and as her hair began to dry it grew lighter and floated about her head. The firelight sparked off the lighter golden streaks and created a red nimbus that encircled the pale orb that was her face. Her comb went easily through her locks now. She was finished and drew back from the intense heat of the blaze, leaving her hair to fall freely about her shoulders.

He brought a plate to her. She began to thank him, only gasping as she caught sight of his hands. "Jacques!" She reached out with her free hand and grabbed his strong wrist, moving it to get a better view in the growing gloom. "*Mon Dieu!*" she exhaled and gingerly touched his palm. He did not pull away but only shrugged. "You cannot continue like this," she exclaimed. "Tomorrow these blisters will grow worse. They will begin to break open and bleed. You could get a very bad infection. You could lose a hand!"

"They will toughen up," he replied trying to brush her concern aside but enjoying the attention all the same.

"You must wrap your hands in rags. I never thought to tell you. It is what the peasants do to protect their hands because they cannot afford gloves. Where are your gloves?"

"The gloves of a gentleman are not made to work in. The only gloves I brought with me are for the cold weather. I cannot work in them," he said half scoffing.

"Richard, let me see your hands," she demanded of the other. Without missing a mouthful as he shoveled food to his face, Richard reached out to her with his free hand and she saw that it, too, was covered in blisters. "This will not do, gentlemen," she said censoriously, a small frown knitting her smooth brow. "Your hands will be reduced to raw meat within the week unless we take care. Tomorrow, we must wrap your hands in rags before you begin your labors."

"If you say so, *ma petite*," Jacques said in a low quiet voice and gave her a smile that lit up his eyes. She felt that smile in the pit of her stomach and felt the blood rise to her cheeks. She was content to say no more but lowered her gaze and was thankful the twilight hid her blush.

Finally able to settle down to her food, Marie discovered the fresh air and exercise of the day had given her an appetite as well. She pulled small bits off the hunk of bread in her lap, and as she brought them to her mouth she realized that when these loaves were finished there would be no more such bread for them until she could devise a way to bake it. Pan bread was the best she could hope to produce until that time.

A prolonged hush fell over the trio as they sat quietly around the small fire. The birds had grown completely still overhead. For a time the only sounds were of running water and the popping sap in the burning sticks but soon other sounds filled the evening air; the throb of crickets, the ponderous croaking of frogs, the mysterious pulsing of insect song, all creating a rhythm like the heartbeat of the sleeping earth in the night.

"And what is Marie thinking, so quiet and serious?" Richard asked at last, pouring himself a cup of rum to cap his supper. His mouth was still full with the last of the food he had unceremoniously stuffed into it to free his hands. Casually, he tapped the cork back into the small cask and stretched out his long legs as he leaned back against an available rock. He looked musingly at the pensive girl.

Marie looked up and smiled. "I was just thinking about the last time we were together like this… well, something like this. Remember our journey to Paris? It seems a lifetime ago." Just then an owl hooted in the dark and Marie turned quickly to peer into the darkness in the direction of the sound.

"This is not the French countryside," Richard observed, casually picking his teeth with a wood splinter.

"No, of course not," she responded, turning back.

"And to think we could ride at night by the light of the moon," Richard continued. "Could you imagine trying to ride a horse through this?" he gestured vaguely. "Not even in the daylight. The poor animal would break its leg within a quarter of the first hour."

Marie nodded. "Remember there we were trying to hide ourselves? We felt so... exposed... did we not? Here, the wilderness can just swallow you up; it is a hiding place in itself. A protection."

"But here we do not need to hide," Jacques observed.

"But if we did, it would be much easier, would it not?" She asked quietly not really expecting an answer.

Jacques looked at her steadily, wondering what was going through her mind. Far in the distance came the faint echo of a feline scream.

"What was that?" Marie asked in a startled reaction.

"A mountain lion," Jacques said calmly.

"In France we slept during the day when the creatures of the night are asleep," Richard spoke with a teasing touch of foreboding.

"Oh, stop it, Richard. I am not a small child to be frightened of the shadows. It is a different place but I do not find it a frightening place. But one must have care. I can tell you right now, I saw a snake here this morning..."

At this both men reacted, sitting up straighter and vigilantly surveying the ground around them.

"Did it have a round head or triangular like this?" Jacques shaped his fingers in a gesture.

"I did not see, why?"

"Because the ones with the round heads may scare you but they are not venomous," responded Richard.

"Oh. Well, I do not find these rocks a very appealing bed. I have decided to sleep in the boat tonight. Frankly, I think we all would be wise to sleep in the boat."

Jacques had finished his food and took up the rum cask. He poured a small amount in a cup and held it out to Marie. "Here, have a little of this. It will warm you and help you to sleep."

"Thank you," she said accepting it and took a sip. The dark sweet liquid burned as it went down her throat.

"The mountain lion looks much like a house cat," Jacques continued evenly, "only it is perhaps four to six times larger. They are a formidable foe with their agile power, sharp fangs, and lethal claws, make no mistake, but fortunately they do not much care for the company of humans. We are not their natural prey and given the opportunity they will generally flee from any contact with us. If you should ever come upon a cub, however, for mercy sake, do not be beguiled by it. Put distance between you and it as quickly and as unobtrusively as you can."

"Surely a little cub cannot be harmful," Marie replied naively and Jacques realized with sudden horror that in all their talks, they had completely overlooked some of the basics in Marie's wilderness education.

"Marie," he cautioned intensely, "please remember for your own well-being, if you come across a cub, any cub, the mother is surely not too far away. Even the most timid animal will fight viciously and boldly to protect its young... you must know this."

"Ohh, of course, of course," she replied quickly, and stifled a yawn. Chagrined at her own stupidity, she looked apologetically at Jacques. "I am just very tired."

"Of course, and I quite agree with your choice of a bed," he said amiably.

"And I plan to join you in the boat, whether Richard is as wise remains to be seen." He finished off his drink and looked at his friend who was hanging his wet clothing to dry in the trees.

"I have no love for snakes," Richard said finally as he looked around to see both of them looking at him. "And I do not care much for beds of rock either."

Marie and Jacques both nodded.

The boat was still full of their goods and finding room for three adults to stretch out was not easy. They draped the mosquito netting over the casks and burrowed themselves into their piles of goods beneath. The fire was built up to ward off the insects and animals but in the boat the fire did little for them but give off a glow of flickering light by which they could arrange themselves. Toward the bow, Richard stretched his long frame out along the small aisle they had left for walking among their goods. Closer to the rudder Marie found a niche between some medium casks and the wheelbarrow.

Jacques again took the first watch but from within the netted protection of the boat. He sat near Marie with his back against a large barrel. He was aware of her soft breathing and the nearness of her warmth and Richard's snoring coming from the bow. Jacques pulled his blanket up closer and leaned back to watch the reflections of the fire on the mast. He fought to stay awake but after the heavy labors of the day, Jacques lost his battle and nodded off without ever waking Richard.

Deep into the night, fog undulated along the water's surface and caught among the reeds and thickets along the river banks like wool caught in a spinner's comb. As it rose, it spilled into the boat with a cool, clammy presence. Marie unconsciously sought out the warmth of Jacques' slumped body and cuddled up against him. Never waking, he finally stretched out in his dreams and put a protective arm around her, instinctively gathering her soft warmth to him.

Dawn was readying itself to leap forth on another day and drive the fog back into the magical invisibility from which it had come. In response to this quiet, casual drama, the birds in their tree top abodes awoke, one by one, to chirp, cheep, trill, whistle, and call to one another with total disregard for the slumbering humans lying beneath them in the small craft moored to the bank. In short time a most lively din filled the upper air. Richard stirred first, feeling a pressing need to relieve his bladder. He became aware of the exuberant bird song and the growing light in the sky. He sat up quickly wondering why Jacques had not called him for his turn at the watch. The sense of alarm which accompanied that question dissipated instantly when he stretched to peer over the casks in the mist and saw Jacques and Marie sleeping peacefully... together.

Rubbing the spot on his back where something uncomfortably pointed had been jabbing him, Richard rose and took a closer look. Careful scrutiny revealed Jacques curled around Marie as blatantly as you please. Pushing passed a very ugly twinge of jealousy, a broad smile broke over Richard's face. He thought he knew exactly why he had not been roused for his watch. And he expected that his friend would now be in a much more agreeable temper. Quietly, Richard left the boat and walked a few feet away to urinate against a tree.

The vibration of Richard's tread in the boat woke Marie and as she became aware of Jacques' warmth and presence next to her, his arm about her, and his breath in her hair, her heart began to beat wildly. It was almost more than she could bear. Then, for some inexplicable reason she grew fearful of his waking to find himself unwittingly embracing her. A tiny wave of panic rolled over her. It was her fault, she immediately told herself, she was way over on his side and should not be there. He might be angry at her audacity. Certainly he would be chagrined at the ridiculous position she had put him in and insulted by her invasion of his space. He might be laboring like a peasant but he was, in fact, a young lord. It was she who was the peasant. Marie took great pains to move carefully and not disturb the sleeping figure beside her. Slipping away, she left the boat to start breakfast.

She found Richard stirring the embers and adding more wood to the fire. "Good morning," she said shivering and drawing closer to the small blaze while reaching out her hands to the warmth.

"Good morning," Richard grinned at her. Suddenly she realized that Richard might very well have seen how they had been sleeping. "Did you sleep well?" he asked with the silliest inflection in his voice.

He had seen, she thought. "The sleep of the dead," she replied quietly.

Richard nodded and continued to grin. "Not completely dead, I think?" and he winked.

"Richard!" she gasped at his implication. "It is not what you think... I...I must have moved over in my sleep," she stammered a little, then looked at him imploringly. "Please do not say anything to Jacques about this, Richard, please? It was an accident and completely my doing. He did not know. Do not tease. I do not want him to be... upset."

"Upset? Why should it upset him? I envy him. To sleep with one's arms around a beautiful woman is an upset most men do not mind, eh? And I do not think you minded either."

Marie blushed profusely. He was partly right, she had not minded at all. But she also thought he was mocking her. Maybe what he said was true but she could hardly think of herself as a beautiful woman even without a face covered in mosquito bites. And with them she was certain she was quite repulsive. "Please do not say... You know nothing happened. I... I just rolled over in my sleep," she pleaded, "and I am embarrassed by it."

He shrugged not understanding at all but nodded a silent agreement anyway. He had never fooled himself into believing that he understood women, but this one? This one was a unique puzzlement.

Several yards away, Jacques awoke with a vague sense of loss. His arms felt strangely empty as he looked around in the fog and realized both Richard and

Marie were already awake and gone and that he was alone in the boat. He stretched, shivered, and rose to his feet to head for the murmuring voices of his companions and the friendly crackle of the beckoning fire.

Chapter 17

After a week of backaches, scrapped hands, bleeding knuckles, and bruised shoulders, a small, one room dirt floored cabin of rough hewed logs had been erected amongst the biggest trees still standing on the small bluff. It wasn't a perfectly squared cabin. One wall, in consideration of a very large tree, angled slightly and so the back wall holding the fireplace was slightly longer than the front wall. At the front were the main door and a small shuttered window. Another window opened out in the angled wall facing the river and in the opposite wall which did run a true perpendicular to the front and back, a second door had been placed as they planned to add a second room in the autumn.

Employing the wheelbarrow, Marie had gathered river rocks with which to construct the hearth and chimney and did so by herself as Jacques and Richard raised the walls. They learned as they went but they were also cognizant of the passing of time. Since Marie had become quite expert at mixing river clay with marsh grass, they left her to fill in the cracks between the logs as they put together a quick roof of lashed tree limbs and branches covered over with a crude thatching made of ferns.

"You will have to keep your food stored well," Jacques cautioned. "The squirrels will most likely find a way in but we will have to wait until we return to put on a shingled roof."

With the roof in place, it was time for the men to leave. Marie had her own supplies, bags of seed and a musket with plenty of cartridges. They had lashed together a crude bed strung with rope so she could sleep up off the ground and the small supply of milled boards which they had brought with them were stored directly over the bed protecting her as she slept from dropping pests or debris. The modest table, three chairs, and storage chests, represented the only true furniture they had. One chest held food supplies and the other held everything else not to be left out. It wasn't luxury but it was basic shelter from the elements and the animals for the summer. Jacques knew they could not put off their departure any longer. They must press on up the river and make contact with friendly Indians with whom they could trade. That was, after all, why they were here.

The night before their departure, Jacques could not settle down and sleep was long in coming. He and Richard had spread their bedrolls on the floor of the cabin, the ground was hard packed but he had grown used to that. It was not the ground that was keeping him awake. It was thoughts of Marie. Now that they were on the brink of leaving he knew he could not leave her here alone. Whatever had he been thinking?

Richard was snoring lightly when Jacques sat bolt upright. With cat like grace he moved to Marie's bed and called to her quietly in the light of the hearth.

"Yes?" she whispered back. "What is wrong?"

"It is no good, Marie. I cannot do this."

"Jacques, what are you talking about?" She, too, sat upright.

"I cannot leave you here. We know nothing of this place. Nothing at all. It is insanity to leave you here alone."

She reached out and found his hand in the darkness. At her touch, his palm, calloused by his manual labors, closed around hers, his fingers holding her tightly. "Jacques, you must. It is the plan, remember? I will be well, really, I will."

"I know not what I was thinking," he said in a low voice, a tinge of disgust mixed with disbelief coming through. "It is a stupid plan. One woman all alone by herself. What if...."

"We cannot live by *what ifs*."

"I know, but..."

"No-no, Jacques. Please, I want something of my own, remember? And I am willing to take the risk to achieve it. It will not be that long. I have plenty of supplies. I will work very hard and put in a garden. I will be careful, really I will. And in these passed days, we have seen no one else. Just make certain you come back to me."

He started to protest again, thought better of it and leaving the side of her bed he stretched out again on the ground with the words *just make certain you come back to me* echoing in his mind. What if something happened to them and they could not come back? He had never even thought of that. *Mon Dieu!* She could be abandoned here forever. No-no, he could not even consider that. Between himself and Richard, there was no reason why one of them would not return and he knew Richard would not forget her. Marie was bright. She was capable. And he had taught her to defend herself. And from what they did know of the area, the Indians were said to be very friendly to the white traders. The Swedes had been settled along the Delaware to the south for sometime. The port of New York was only a day away to the north, at least it was only a day by sea. It would only be for a few months, just the summer, he assured himself as sleep finally overcame him.

In the morning, Richard approached Marie outside the cabin. It was barely dawn and the light from the east was streaking the horizon with rosy mauves swirling around a dark red orange glow that pointed to the rising sun. The air was chilled and the ground cover was wet with heavy dew.

"Marie, are you very certain of this?" the big man asked, setting his gear down at his feet. She knew what he meant and only nodded as she drew her shawls closer with a shiver. "I am not comfortable about this scheme you and Jacques have concocted. I never have been. There is still time to change your mind," he said gravely. "No one would think any the less of you if you decided right now that this was not what you wanted to do."

"But this is what I want to do."

"Yes, yes, the trading post, I know, but staying here alone. That is what I mean."

"It is not what I want but it is something I must do."

He shook his head. "We could take you back to New York Towne and find someone to stay here with you next year..."

"Richard," she touched his arm affectionately. "I will be well. I promise. Look at the strong fine house you have built for me," she said earnestly, gesturing at the humble little crooked cabin. "No one can come in unless I allow them to. And I have my musket right here," she gestured.

Richard frowned. "The thatching is very thin. If it starts to leak you must add more ferns and river reeds. We will put a good roof on it for you in the fall, I promise."

She nodded. "Just come back safely, both of you." She gave him a farewell embrace and he hugged her back so fiercely that for a moment she could not draw breath.

"There could be bears," he said earnestly. "I am not trying to frighten you. It is true. And there are the wildcats. And perhaps wolves. Always keep your musket with you and be very careful."

"I will, Richard," she assured him. "And thank you for caring."

He gave her a strong look, intense but one she could not interpret. He bent to pick up his gear once again. They walked down to the rocky river bank which was considerably less rocky now that the hearth and chimney were completed. Jacques was busy at the boat repacking and rearranging their trade goods and supplies. He finished just as Richard approached and climbed into the boat. Jacques stepped back out and went to Marie.

"It is time," he said looking down at her. She was smiling up at him bravely. "Are you very sure about this?"

She nodded.

"Remember to keep your musket with you," he said, "all the time. And keep the powder dry or you will have trouble firing it."

She nodded again.

"With any luck we should see you when the leaves begin to turn. Marie... I... take care of yourself," he added almost fiercely after a brief hesitation.

She threw her arms around him and hugged him tightly to keep from crying. "Just come back safely, Jacques. And I will be fine." He held her close, suddenly aware of a hot sting in his own eyes. "I will keep you in my prayers," she whispered.

"As I will keep you," he replied, then on impulse he held her shoulders and kissed her forehead tenderly. At last he drew back and gave her a broad brave smile. He could not allow himself to think of all the things that might happen before they returned or he would never leave.

He turned and bent to push the boat from the bank, jumping in just as the wind caught the raised sail. The craft began to move very quickly. He balanced and waved at her. Marie watched and waved until the boat was no longer in sight.

It was their first foray deep into the unknown, alone, without guides, and without a map. There were no maps to be had of this area. It was unexplored. Jacques felt a quickening rush of adrenaline as they turned a bend and lost sight of Marie and the small clearing they had made.

"Well, we can certainly say that everyday shall be an adventure," he said with an intended bravado as he held the rudder. "Now we have become explorers!" It took effort to sound enthusiastic. He had hardly slept all night. Tossing and turning in his bedroll, he had been haunted while debating the wisdom of leaving Marie all alone. He knew if anything happened to her, he would blame himself for the rest of his life. In the beginning, it had been his idea and once he had expressed it, there had been no way to take it back.

Richard looked out over the river. His gut was knotted and he held a picture of Marie in his own mind. They were fools to leave her alone, he told himself. If anything happened to that girl, he and Jacques would have to live with the knowledge that they had left her all alone and unprotected in the wild. If anything happened to her, he did not think he would ever be able to forgive his best friend. They should have never brought her here. But once she had the idea in her head what could they really do? She was so blasted pig-headed in her determination. Yes, she was determined but they could have refused, that is what they could have done. Even if she hated them, at least she would have been safe.

Wordlessly, they put in the oars and each taking one, they found solace in the monotonous activity of rowing. The wind was blowing in the wrong direction and they had taken the sail down. They progressed in silence with only the sound of the oars pivoting in the hardware and splashing in the water. At nightfall they made camp on the bank.

They repeated the same activity the next day, rowing against the current with no help from the sail. It was slow progress. After several days they noticed how easily they could see the river's bottom.

"Have you noticed?" Richard pointed and Jacques simply nodded.

The next day they continued knowing they were nearing the end. The wind changed in their direction and assisted them through the following day until early in the afternoon when they found themselves caught on some rocks. Working themselves free, they went on until the rocky formations jutting up out of the river were no longer far enough apart to maneuver the wide craft through. They had gone as far as they could in this boat. Sorely disappointed, they pulled the craft off onto the bank, wishing now that they had pack animals.

It took some ingenuity to split up their cargo and bundle it in such a way as to be able to carry it themselves. Some they were able to load onto their backs and the rest they hung from a pole which they carried between them.

Struggling under the load, they tramped slowly along the river's edge blazing a trail through the thick brush. Last year's dried up brambles and thorny branches grabbed at their bodies while the tangling vines tried to trip their feet. At dusk they made camp for the night. They were sapped and they ached.

Jacques suspected Richard felt just as unsure as he about what they were doing but neither of them was going to admit to misgivings. They had no idea where they were going or that there was anything to go to. Jacques suddenly realized that they might have been entirely too hasty in building the cabin. Perhaps the wiser course would have been to travel up the river first. They would have discovered no Indian encampments and the quick end to navigation. Why had they assumed that any river they found would be an opening into the interior? *Mon Dieu,* they had been stupid! Perhaps there was a better river just a league or two to the south along the coast. Perhaps there was no river before the Delaware that reached into the wilderness. A part of him wanted to go back to Marie and a part of him indignantly refused to admit defeat.

In the morning the two awoke with sore muscles and stiff limbs. To take up their burdens and continue on was a struggle through which each man silently grit his teeth. They took turns leading, hacking at the underbrush and pushing on through. The stiffness in their bodies worked itself out by midday and the aches became dull and deep.

The pair continued for several more days, each silently questioning the wisdom of their course of action, each unwilling to vocalize his doubts. To make matters even more difficult they were in a constant uphill climb but it did give them the excuse for their mutual silence as they needed to spare their breath. As they climbed they broke into a pine forest where the ground cover was sparse, and traversing was easier. Even so, the heavy loads on their backs made it easy to lose balance and they often fell to the soft needled floor. All the while they saw and heard no evidence of any other peoples and finally the river which had narrowed to a small brook simply ran out. They had reached its head, a spring gushing from a rocky crevice.

Richard and Jacques set their loads down and sank to the ground looking at each other. Where would they go now they each wondered? And how would they remember their way? They had not run out of river on the Mohawk. How different that had been. How easily they had traversed miles. It was impossible to get lost on a river. But on land, the trees all looked alike in every direction. The forest blended together as if to purposefully confuse the traveler. And there certainly were no road markers.

"Any suggestions?" Richard grunted as he took a bite of hardtack.

"I would suggest we follow this ridge," Jacques replied thoughtfully. "Perhaps we can find headwaters flowing westward and can follow that."

"Hm-mm."

"Can you make a better suggestion?" Jacques asked a bit piqued.

"Only that we start to make a map. We need to notice the landmarks, things that will not change as the seasons change so we can find our way back to our river and our boat."

"Agreed."

And so they began to make a crude map and take great notice of natural formations that marked their way and would remain immutable with the changing seasons.

§

Marie went to work with a practical common sense that did not allow her to feel the loneliness. First things first. She considered her food supply and rigged netting to catch fish off the bank of the river. Then, she turned to the creation of a vegetable garden. She spaded the ground around the tree stumps and planted her seeds in neat rows. Toiling each day from sunrise to dusk, she finally had every available sunny patch of earth planted. Next, she worked doggedly to weave a roof of tender saplings and branches to shelter the wood pile from rain and future snow. As the weather grew warmer, she established a simple fire ring upon which to cook outside the cabin to keep the heat from indoors. But when a rainy day came along, she was glad for a small fire upon her cabin hearth to keep the damp at bay and deter the small scavengers.

One day as she was drawing a bucket of water from her favorite spot along the rushing stream, she noticed an oddly flat piece of rock just below the surface of the water. On impulse, she reached in soaking her sleeves as she tilted up the rock. From the texture and look of it, she concluded that it had split off from a larger piece.

Employing the wheel barrel, she brought it back to the cabin. There were perhaps a dozen uses she could put it to but for now she was content to lean it against the fireplace. Later the thought came to her to use the same river clay mixture with stones to construct an outdoor oven. And just as quickly as that idea came to her, she saw the oddly thin piece of stone being employed as the oven door.

From that point on, Marie's thoughts were fully occupied with the idea of creating an oven and with it, gaining the ability to make fine crusty French bread. What a surprise it would be! To be able to serve fresh, hard crusted loaves with tender white insides. She smiled to herself. She could do it, she determined. She would do it. All she had to do was use her brain, she told herself.

Thoughts of an oven followed her through the days. As she watered and weeded her sprouting garden or cleaned and gutted fish, she thought on how she might construct such an oven. As she rigged snares to catch the rabbits worrying her tender plants, as she butchered and made stew of them, she conjured images of ovens. At the end of each long day, as she dropped her clothes on the river bank and stole naked into the waters for a refreshing dip, she thought on how she might create such an oven. She also knew she needed to start growing her own bread yeast.

Marie tried to remember every oven she had ever seen. The baker in the village where she had been born had a huge oven. But being a small child, undoubtedly it had seemed much bigger to her than it really was. She vaguely remembered going there once or twice, but it had been so many years ago. She remembered only that the man could stand at the oven's door and withdrawn golden crusted bread with the assistance of a huge flat wooden paddle. But the details of construction escaped her. There had to have been a fire somewhere, she was certain of that, but she could not remember seeing it. Where had the smoke gone, she questioned?

Rising naked from the water to dry in the warm air, she picked up a few choice stones and carried them up to the cabin in her basket to join the stack that was accumulating there. Surely the fire's smoke had not escaped through the door of the chamber or the bread would have smelled and tasted of smoke. No, there had to have been a hole at the top but she had been too small to see it.

Bouchet. Involuntarily she shuddered even now at the thought of him. She tugged on a clean shift. Bouchet had baked his own bread behind the tavern and she tried to remember that oven. Images of Bouchet himself blurred her mind and she realized that she had never paid any great attention to his areas of work. She had always wanted to stay as far from him as she could.

Slowly some details did come back to her, and they, along with logical reasoning finally set her to work. With diligence and care, she selected the site for the oven and decided upon the area out at the point of the small bluff. It was far enough away from the cabin, but not too far. It was a spot where any smoke and heat could benignly dissipate without offense or danger. And the soil there was almost nonexistent being mostly solid rock and unfit for planting.

When she had finally accumulated a massive pile of stones, she began. Dressed lightly in only a very old shift and skirt without a corselet and with a cup of hot tea in her hand, Marie squatted down by her clay works and put all her concentration into the business at hand.

First, she wanted to construct a platform foundation to lift the level of the oven floor off the ground by two feet, making it easier to work with in the future. She began assembling the rocks and soon realized she needed something to keep them from rolling out and collapsing at the edges.

Jacques and Richard had left planed boards in the rafters over her bed and she borrowed these to create a framing which she staked into place. Using clay rich mud to hold all the rocks together and to fill in the empty spaces, the first step was finished.

By the next morning it had dried. Marie returned the boards to their place in the rafters and made up a mixture of river clay, sandy dirt, cut up bits of dry grass and water to smooth a final finish over the platform top and sides. She protected it from the threat of rain and left it. This took several days to completely dry and some cracks appeared but she filled them with more clay. Finally she piled dried brush and tree debris over the entire form and lit the fire to harden the clay.

When the ashes cooled and she could sweep them aside, she repeated the whole process creating a second higher level built upon the first. Once this was fired she was satisfied with the platform and began to lay out the oven itself. It would be round and large enough to hold long loaves of bread, but there was no reason she could not roast a turkey or a haunch of venison just as well.

The thick wall began to go up slowly using smaller stones and her clay mixture. It took time but she was patient. After all, she told herself with a small laugh, she had no place to go and no one to whom she must answer. She made certain she left an opening large enough to fit a large turkey and yet still matching the size of the large flat stone piece she had put aside for a door.

As her wall grew higher she needed to make it thinner and less weighty so she could begin to curve it inward toward itself and into a dome.

She needed something thin and straight. Something lightweight, yet sturdy enough not to fall apart as the clay dried. Marie looked off over the edge of the small bluff and down to the river below and was pondering various materials in her mind when her eyes lit upon the clump of pussy willows. Could anything be better? In a sudden epiphany with one thought growing out of another at lightning speed she realized the unique plant would be ideal to serve as the support for the upper walls and ceiling of the oven, they had sturdiness and yet flexibility. Marie gathered the pussy willows and anchored them into the top of the wall before it dried completely; then she left it all to dry overnight.

The next day she carefully pulled the pussy willow top ends together with thread causing a natural arch. Using only clay she continued to build the walls around the willow branches and the dome took shape. She left a chimney hole in the top slightly larger than her fist but the willow branches made a kind of screen to keep debris out.

That night the mists were heavy which kept the clay from drying too quickly and when Marie inspected her work the next morning she was pleased that it showed no cracking but she was worried by the prospect of rain in the clouds overhead. Taking precautions, she rigged a covering over her work to protect it from any rain and inadvertently protected it from too much sun as well. When it began to sprinkle lightly late in the afternoon, Marie watched with concern having no idea that the heavy humidity in the air was actually helping her clay cure at a safer pace. All Marie knew was that day passed day and no distortions or cracks appeared in her work.

When at last the oven was completely dry, Marie gathered a great amount of kindling. She built a fire within and without, burying the oven in a bonfire to bake it stone hard over the course of several days. When the fire finally had burnt itself out and she cleaned the ashes away, Marie was overjoyed to find her creation sturdy and whole. The clay had baked stone hard and no amount of rain or snow would ever dissolve it back into mud again. She now had an oven in which she could make real crusty bread, just like the bread of home. Marie spontaneously did a joyful dance about the clearing, feeling immeasurably pleased with her accomplishment. She sang and laughed and kicked up her heels having no idea that she was being observed from a distance.

Finally she stood still, hands on hips and proudly looked at the oven for a long time. Would not Jacques be very surprised? Perhaps he would even be proud of her. She could not wait to try it out and to learn to use it with proficiency.

The summer waxed hotter. There was now an abundance of work as weeds threatened to take over the garden and long periods of no rain had her fetching bucket after bucket of water from the creek for her thirsty growing plants.

Exploratory walks upon occasion always brought some new discovery. Along the river she found varieties of berries to harvest, some of which she made into preserves and some she dried. When she found a grove of long needled pines and felt the spring of them beneath her feet she knew she had found the material with which she could make a mattress for her rope strung bed if she only had some ticking.

Her days were long, very exhausting, and lonely but she was never afraid, not even the day the red men came. So silently did they approach, she had no warning that they were there.

Humming to herself and with flour smudged on her face, she was kneading bread on a makeshift table outside the cabin where she had better light. Out of nowhere they appeared, four of them. Completely naked except for their tall footwear and small suede loincloths, their nakedness looked so completely natural.

Their hairless skin glistened with the vermilion tinted clay mixed with bear grease they used to paint themselves up and fend off pesky insects. They had large quivers stuffed with arrows slung upon their backs and each carried a bow, either in hand or slipped over a shoulder. Their heads, smoothly hairless from their necks halfway up their skulls, were crowned with a shock of thick coarse hair which stood straight up, like a coxcomb. Two had very black hair while the other two looked as if their hair was dressed with colored clay that stiffened the hair as well as tinted it. Marie noted that whether by shaving or plucking, none had eyebrows but their faces were blocked out in patches of red, yellow, and white. Looking beyond the colorful markings, she found them quite striking in their own way, with high cheekbones, prominently arched noses, and black eyes. All except for one. Marie noticed when that one looked at her, he had startlingly green eyes!

They made no hostile gestures to her but wandered through and around and into her cabin as though they felt perfectly at home. She was a lone female, no threat to them and they were very curious as to her purpose in being there. A series of guttural syllables came from one or the other, by which she guessed they were talking to each other. One brave, bigger and taller than the others with very black eyes and hair, poked his dirty finger at her yeasty bread dough and without thinking she slapped his hand away. He jumped back from her and then laughed displaying strong white teeth in a broad grin. He said something to the others and they all laughed. Another helped himself to a drink from her water bucket without the use of the dipper; he simply scooped the water up with his hand and slurped. After satisfying their curiosity, they disappeared into the forest just as quickly as they had appeared.

From that time on, Marie never felt completely alone. She sensed that they were out there in the forest, close by and perhaps watching her. If they had wanted to harm her, she reasoned, they easily could have done so. They had been four, she was only one and without even her musket close at hand. They had not harmed her however; they had not even taken her musket off the wall of the cabin. They had taken nothing. They had only poked at her things rather like curious children, and then gone off again.

The next visitor was quite another story. Hearing a rustle in the brush and expecting to see more natives, Marie looked up and found herself standing almost face to face across her small outdoor fire ring with a large black bear. It halted while its huge head bobbed uncertainly from side to side. It looked at her and smelled the fire. The creature appeared as startled to smell fire as the girl was to see the beast. It stood halted, uncertain which direction to take. Its large, moist black nose wiggled while its small brown eyes stared at her nearsightedly. The wind was blowing gently toward Marie and she could smell the strong acrid odor of bear mingled with the scent of the wood fire. She picked up a small burning log and slowly backed her way to the cabin. It was only a few feet but it seemed to Marie more like yards. The creature stood rooted, picking up unfamiliar scents of human and unable to decide which way to move. Gaining the door, Marie tore the musket from the wall and fired from the doorway to frighten the beast away. There was only a small pop and a fizzle. She cocked the musket and fired again. There was only another fizzle but just then the breeze took a swirl of the scent of gunpowder and brought it to the sensitive nose of the confused beast. It turned immediately and disappeared in seconds. Marie stood looking after it with a thudding heart, astounded by its speed.

From that time on, Marie rarely forgot to take the musket with her any time she went out of doors. And she adopted the additional habit of refreshing daily the gunpowder held in the pan.

The red men came back with beaver skins and tried to trade for her mirror. It was a funny scene of bartering in pantomime but somehow they had communicated. They wanted her mirror. No-no, Marie shook her head, she would not part with her mirror but she did not wish to discourage them and thus offered them knives, pots and spoons instead. The tallest brave continued to insist on having the mirror. Finally, Marie tried to convey that it would take a much bigger skin, a large bear, and she lumbered across the yard trying to do her best imitation of the bear she had seen. In the end it was the growl she imitated that brought understanding nods and smiles to the previously puzzled faces. The braves settled amiably on other trinkets and left.

Weeks later, they came back again. Marie was hoeing in her garden. The tallest one, who she recognized and had dubbed "Looking Glass" in her mind, approached the edge of her plot and laid a huge cured black bear skin at her feet and pointed to her cabin. Well, a bargain was a bargain, she told herself, and she went inside to fetch her cherry framed wall mirror. She took one last look at herself knowing that until she could get to New York Towne and purchase another she would have nothing by which to comb her hair. The image staring back at her was lightly tanned and vibrant. She absently smoothed a wayward lock and then handed the mirror slowly to the brave. His face exploded in a look of pure pleasure and glee. His black eyes glittered with excitement while he flashed a grin of delight. He took the mirror and disappeared into the forest with the other three following closely behind. Marie was left in the clearing with a heavy, cured bear skin on the ground before her. She looked down at it and bent to scoop it up.

"I wonder if you were my visitor," she mused aloud. "If so, then you have learned a lesson, Monsieur Bear. This is the only way you and your kind are welcome into my home."

Chapter 18

Jacques and Richard were walking a ridge when Richard suddenly stopped and pressed his finger to his lips. Jacques at the other end of the pole they carried between them immediately halted and remained silent. He strained to hear whatever it was that his friend was listening for but he could hear nothing but the birds, the drone of insects, and water.

"Water!" he exclaimed in recognition.

"Yes," grinned his companion. "This way, eh?"

They pushed on through a thicket and had to catch themselves on a downward slope that ended abruptly in a drop. The ceaseless sound of water falling many feet and the mist it created in its drop filled the air. Directly below them was a churning pool. Silently, they worked their way down the side until they stood on the rock formation holding the pool. The temperature was at least ten degrees cooler than it had been just a few yards back in the forest.

"The beginning of another river," the taller man said as he laid down his end of the pole and shucked off his burden. He bent to one knee, scooped up water to wash his face and saw a small green lizard dart away. "It must be good water," he observed with a grin, "or the little lizard would not like it." He bent over and drank. "Come," he gestured above the sound of the falls, "take a rest. We have been walking for hours, we deserve our lunch."

Jacques considered. Now that they had found head waters he was eager to follow the stream to see where it led but at the mention of lunch his stomach growled its own reply. He, too, slung down his load. He flexed his shoulders and stretched his aching muscles before he dropped to the dry rock with a sigh. "This has the promise of growing larger than our river. Perhaps we may find a village of natives living beside it," he said, taking out his rations.

"Yes, perhaps," Richard said optimistically. It was something to hope for. They were due for a bit of luck.

The sun had disappeared into the trees, a reminder that it would soon grow dark. Re-energized by their quick meal and respite, they were now proceeding mostly in a downhill pattern. They had traversed several miles when the stream had widened sufficiently to force them to make a choice. They had chosen to follow the northwest side. Now the stream was the width of two men lying head to head and appeared to be about two to three feet deep. But there was still no sign of any other humans.

"We had better stop and make camp soon," Jacques said wearily. "The water is deep enough to support a canoe. I had hoped that by now..."

"Look!" Richard whispered sharply, pointing as he did. Jacques saw smoke drifting above the trees down stream.

"Well, we have our wish, my friend. We have finally found some natives."

"Let us pray they are friendly."

It took another ten minutes for the pair to come upon the village. They made their way past a very rocky narrowing of the river which created impassable rapids and explained why they had not discovered a village before. Beyond the rapids the river smoothed out to a wider, slower pace. As luck would have it, they found themselves on the opposite side.

"What do you think?" Jacques asked cautiously.

"I do not see them roasting any white men over the spit," grunted Richard.

"Yes, well maybe they just finished picking the bones," Jacques replied dryly.

The encampment, in fact, looked peaceful and ordinary with a half dozen children playing a game with a skin ball and several others running with a small skinny dog. Squaws were engaged in a variety of domestic tasks, cooking, grinding meal, treating skins which were hung up and stretched between trees. There were a few braves visible, mostly occupied in making or maintaining their weapons and tools. One older brave sat knapping stone spearheads while a youth looked on attentively and struggled with his own stone trying to imitate his elder.

For a few moments Jacques and Richard stood on the opposite shore completely unnoticed. Then someone saw them and pointed, alerting the others. Soon many had gathered and were staring back. "Remember what we learned, approach with hands out and open," Jacques said softly and they waved slowly with open hands. Two craft were launched by stocky looking braves who paddled over without any obvious weapons although Jacques noted each carried a knife of some sort in his waist band.

They had stumbled into a small Mohegan village. It was difficult trying to communicate but even so, they did not do badly. It was obvious that they were being offered a ride across the water and they each boarded a dugout, their trade goods making a separate passenger. The people were curious and friendly and once they had been transported across the river the elders gathered to greet them. Using gestures they had picked up in their previous Indian dealings, Jacques and Richard communicated their desire to trade. That was good, the chief man seemed to say but gave no attention toward conducting any business. Instead, with gestures, they were invited to join the men around the campfire. The women, bare chested and wearing over-sized loin cloths, began bringing dishes of food, most of which Jacques found only slightly more palatable than their travel rations but he managed to eat something lest he should insult his hosts. After they had eaten, they were offered pipes and sat around the fire smoking.

"Do you feel like we are over dressed?" Richard said as he eyed the more attractive of the women serving them.

"I am sure you do, but I am not going to strip off my clothing and don bear grease," Jacques said with a chuckle, then added calmly, "I'm more concerned that they do not appear interested in trading."

"Perhaps their business day is over," Richard replied with a smile.

Jacques considered. It was possible. After all, it was now growing dark. Better to relax, get a good night's sleep and wake to trade in the daylight when both parties could see what they were trading. He relaxed and drew on the sweet tobacco.

Sitting as they were, cross-legged on the ground, amiably smoking with the other men, Jacques' blond hair was attracting the curiosity of the children as well as many of the women. He was aware of a small cluster staying well back from the men's circle but watching him intently none the less. Suddenly, one small boy of perhaps five or six years came darting out and touched Jacques' hair before running as fast as he could back to his group. Jacques had seen him coming out of the corner of his eye but was surprised at the behavior all the same. Still he showed no sign of having taken any notice.

After a few minutes a second child, perhaps the same age, perhaps even younger, darted forward. This time Jacques was prepared and before the child could run back Jacques held him prisoner in his arms.

Richard was immediately aware of the sudden tension amongst the adults who watched closely, wondering what would happen next and looking fully ready to pounce upon Jacques should he hurt the child in any way. Jacques growled at the small boy whose eyes rounded like saucers. Then he proceeded to begin tickling the youngster who collapsed into peals and squeals of laughter. One squaw had come running forward but stopped when she heard the child laughing. The braves around the fire also relaxed and laughed as well.

Having given the little marauder a good tickle, Jacques finally released him to run into his mother's waiting arms. Jacques smiled respectfully at the woman and made a sign praising the little boy's bravery. She nodded and quickly pulled her son off into the shadows.

This now became a game in which all the children took a turn while Jacques and Richard doled out a tickle punishment to each child who wasn't quick enough to get away. The initial curiosity over the white man's hair turned into the thrill of the dare. At last, when each child had taken a turn at touching one of the white men and some were beginning to indulge in a second round, one of the elder braves at the fire spoke out sharply. The children ran back to their mothers and the little pack melted away leaving Jacques and Richard in peace.

That night they slept around the large campfire with their goods and several of the younger braves, the smoke keeping the insects at bay. Shortly after dawn, the camp began to stir. They were each offered a hot drink which they accepted gratefully. It was a berry flavored tea sweetened with honey and it chased away their morning chill but soon sent them into the underbrush to empty their bowels before they could address their purpose. Trading began shortly thereafter.

When all the fresh pelts the tribe possessed had been bartered, Jacques and Richard were forced to consider their next move. The concept of looking for another village to trade with was not one they knew how to convey in signs and most likely neither could they have understood an answer if they had been given one. While they were still lingering at the village trying to decide what to do next, more visitors arrived. Within their midst were two brothers who Jacques and Richard soon learned could speak a halting English. This was the stroke of luck for which the two young adventurers had been hoping.

The visitors were called *Lenape* which in their language simply meant *"the people"* but the English and Swedes referred to them as *Delaware*. Lenape were spread throughout the region and they lived peacefully interacting with several other tribes. Their language, *Unami,* was a universally known tongue amidst the eastern tribes and used in communicating with each other. The young Frenchmen understood that the various Indian tribes each had their own language or dialect, much like the different countries of Europe. Jacques and Richard equated *Unami* with the French language which was universally known throughout European courts.

In English, the brothers were called *Bear Claw* and *Two Feathers*. They arrived wearing only a leather loin cloth and tall moccasins but their bodies were covered in a red tinted layer of bear grease for which some Europeans referred to them as "red skins." Each wore a small leather pouch about his neck on a rawhide thong. At their waist, a larger pouch hung from a belt as did a leather holder securing a white man's steel knife.

Bear Claw was the elder of the two. His head was plucked to a high line above his ears and the exposed flesh was decorated by an encircling tattoo of geometric figures which continued across his high forehead. He wore a splay of large bear claws on a thin thong high at his throat while on his back the old scars of a mauling were highlighted in blue clay. The implication was that he had fought the bear and won and he proudly carried a musket and horn of powder. The second brother, Two Feathers, was obviously younger but it was difficult for Jacques to judge how much younger when he first met the young brave. It surprised the Frenchman greatly to later discover that Two Feathers was only in his fourteenth summer.

Two Feathers got his name from the feathers he wore. His straight, coarse black hair hung loose with a braid at each temple. The braids were drawn back serving to hold the rest of his hair in place. At the back of his head the two small braids met and were joined, and two small feathers were caught into the arrangement. Two Feathers, who did not own a musket, carried a quiver full of arrows and a bow across his back. Both men had the suppleness and feline grace found in well-flexed, sinewy muscles devoid of excess fat. Their lean bodies exuded a powerful strength as well as an unerring sense of balance.

"We need guides," Jacques said slowly in a soft voice. "Will you take us to the other villages to trade? Speak for us with your people?"

The young brave bristled with obvious interest while the older brother showed more control and restraint.

"If we take... what you pay?" he asked, his face betraying no emotion of any kind.

"What is fair price?" Jacques asked wisely, looking steadily into the brave's face. He and Richard had learned it was always advantageous to allow the other party to begin the negotiation first.

The elder brother sat in a contemplative silence, his younger sibling betraying his eagerness with a nervous plucking at the grass blades on the ground before him. Richard was the picture of amused serenity as he watched the scene.

"Horse," stated the elder at last. He knew the white men had no horse but he had started and now would see what would be the counter offer.

"No," Jacques replied almost instantly, "too much, we have no horse. Musket?" he offered.

The Indian sat quietly for another moment. "Five musket," he retorted holding up his hand with fingers spread.

Jacques shook his head. "Two musket, he countered, one for you, one for your brother."

"Four musket," the wily Indian replied raising the first two fingers of each hand, holding one hand to himself and pointing the other toward his brother. "Two muskets," Jacques repeated, "and an iron pot for your women." He saw the Indian hesitating so he rose quietly and went to his large pack and withdrew a bolt of material. It was a bright shade of sky blue muslin. "And ... enough material for each of your family to have a new shirt or shift or whatever you wish," he offered holding the bolt out. The Indian sat immobile for a long moment, staring at the material while trying not to stare at it. Then, he nodded his agreement.

An instant later he broke into a grin. "Would have done for two musket," he said and took the material. Jacques sighed and turned to see Richard doubled over in laughter.

The trading expedition that season did not last long despite the late start. Jacques and Richard ran out of goods and yet they knew they could not have carried another iota of anything on their backs going in. It was a problem that occupied Jacques' mind for many hours on the return trek. Horses were scarce among the Indians, so they could not just hire a pack animal. He thought of the horse he had purchased upon his arrival in the colonies. It was a fine animal but not suited to pulling a plow or using as a beast of burden. What was one to do? How did one transport goods in the wilderness when the river ran out unless one found Indian carriers?

The two scouts accompanied them all the way back to where their boat had been abandoned taking them part of the way on an Indian trail which the young white men had no idea existed. By the time they reached the boat, they had worked out a plan for the next season. Jacques and Richard were going to leave the heavy sail boat with Marie and wait for Bear Claw and Two Feathers to come to them with canoes. The scouts would also arrange for more carriers who could help to transport their goods on land.

§

Marie harvested from her small garden, wasting nothing and preparing the food for safe keeping through the winter. Onions hung from the rafters of the cabin and so did bags of dried beans. She had pumpkins and squash which she tried to keep cool. Most of her garden was in roots: onions, turnips, parsnips, carrots, rutabagas and beets. She wished she had a root cellar. She worked to preserve and pickle what she could but left most of the roots in the ground as the best form of storage until it should freeze.

In autumn, Looking Glass and his band returned and left half of a freshly gutted and skinned deer on her doorsill. She was delighted with the present. She had grown tired of fish and rabbit and had been wishing for something different. The next frosty morning she awoke to find the Indians in her cabin, sleeping around her fire on her bear skin rug. She wouldn't have minded if they had not brought the rank smell of aging bear fat with them. She got all of them back outdoors by bringing the cook pots outside. Like most men, she mused, they thought a woman's natural purpose was to feed them. Well, it was only fair, she supposed, they had brought her half a deer after all.

With the sudden turn to cooler weather, Marie began to watch the river more closely. It was still early autumn but her hope of seeing Jacques and Richard grew every day. She found herself taking extra care with her appearance and regretting she no longer had her large mirror. Each morning she awoke wondering if this would be the day. And each night, she went to bed joyful in the knowledge that it had to be one day closer to their return.

On a still and mild day meant to be relished with utter abandon before the inevitable cold comes to stay, Marie awoke flush from a dream that her friends had returned. After a hurried breakfast, she stepped from the cabin and felt the joy of being alive with a throbbing pulse in every cell of her body as the sense of happy expectation filled her heart. The skies were a pure azure without the hint of a cloud from one horizon to as far as she could see toward the other, and the breeze smelled lightly of the salty sea. The forest shimmered with light as sunshine vibrated off the colored leaves in radiant bands. She could not be still and decided to go exploring into the woods. Much of the ground brush was withered and already falling leaves had covered the forest floor. She took a sickle to whack a path before her when necessary and carried the musket across her back.

Keeping the river in sight she knew she would not get lost and so she continued to explore until she found herself amidst a small grove of walnut trees. Delighted with her discovery, she set about gathering nuts into her apron. Stomping the ground and beating fresh areas with the sickle as a precaution against snakes, she soon had gathered her apron full. Then, as if in response to her expectations she caught a glimpse of something on the river and turned to look.

She was overjoyed but more pleased than surprised to see the familiar boat moving swiftly along with Jacques and Richard aboard. She shouted down to them and waved gaily. They returned her greeting in surprise as they sailed passed. She grasped the apron full of walnuts tightly in one hand, the sickle in the other and took off running back the way she had come as quickly as the rugged landscape would allow.

"Jacques! Richard!" she cried out in delight as the boat came nearer the shore by their landing spot. She had left the walnuts, her musket, sickle and apron at the cabin before hurrying down to the river below to meet them.

"Marie!" they both shouted in greeting. She was almost jumping up and down for joy, so great was her pleasure at seeing them home. When the pair finally landed the boat, they bounded out to greet her. Jacques swung her around and had no sooner set her down when Richard picked her up like a child and lifted her into the air.

"Put me down," she laughed breathlessly. And Richard complied with a grin.

"So how is our little Marie?" Jacques asked unnecessarily, so happy to see her alive and well, he ached.

"Happy! Very happy. So happy. I knew you would come soon. I had a dream just before waking this morning. I dreamt you returned. I had the feeling in my bones it would be today. And I was right! I was right! The Indians were here a few days ago because it was so cold that night and..."

"Indians?!" interrupted Jacques.

"Yes," she nodded brightly. "I have made friends with them, they come to trade with me. We cannot talk but I have a small pile of skins. Of course some of them are rabbits. Those I caught myself. Wait 'til you see! Anyway, with the cold coming, I just knew you could not be much longer. The garden came in well. We will have many vegetables for the winter. And today I found a walnut grove; this is where I was when I saw you. The Indians have brought me meat as well... and I built an oven to make real crusty bread and roasts. Oh, I was not going to tell you. It was to be a surprise. But you will see it anyway. Oh, Jacques, Richard," she embraced each of them again. "It is just so good to see you, to have you home. I am so very glad... but I said that already. I repeat myself. I am sorry." She giggled a little and blushed happily. "After saying almost nothing all summer with no one to understand me or speak to, my words just tumble out; I cannot stop them."

The men were laughing with her. They felt the burden of unspoken anxiety drop from their shoulders, replaced with an almost giddy sense of relief to see the young woman healthy, well, and in such good spirits.

There was a party mood that evening at the small frontier encampment. Marie worked to prepare an especially delicious meal of home baked bread, vegetables, and venison steaks in honor of the homecoming while Jacques and Richard sorted through their gear and scrubbed up in the river. Freshly bathed and shaved, the men inspected Marie's progress around the site and were extremely impressed with her outdoor oven. Sitting down at last to a meal that was as good as a feast after months of their own camp cooking and they savored sitting in real chairs. They knew they had all winter to entertain Marie and felt no sense of urgency to share stories of their adventures, letting her talk on, enjoying the sound of her voice and the lively animation of her face. Marie told them the story of the bearskin rug, how it had been bartered and then put to use.

"You can imagine how surprised I was to awake and find Looking Glass and his little band sleeping on my floor," she smiled as she accepted a small glass of rum from Richard.

"Sleeping on the floor?" Jacques exclaimed with mild shock.

"Yes, yes," she nodded.

"How did they get in?" Jacques questioned.

"I do not know. I have not really thought about it." she replied lightly.

"So much for safety and security," Richard observed with a frown creasing his heavy brow.

"This disturbs me, Marie," Jacques said solemnly.

"But they are so quiet. I never even heard them."

"They just came in here? In the middle of the night?" Richard asked sounding uncharacteristically offended.

"But they would not hurt me."

"Did you pull the latch string inside for the night?" asked Jacques.

"Yes, of course."

"Are you certain?" he pressed.

"Jacques, I did... I think... I am certain I did," she started to hesitate. "I guess... I am not certain."

The room went suddenly quiet as both men looked at each other and then at her.

"I really feel very safe here," she tried to shrug off a sudden sense of guilt. "These natives are very pleasant... really."

"Not all people are pleasant. Not all Indians are friendly," Jacques warned. "You must be more careful! We expected you to be more prudent in watching out for yourself. I cannot believe you slept here, alone, with the latch string out for anyone to open... allowing a group of savages to just walk in. I cannot believe it!" he repeated rather harshly.

Marie looked at him. She was stinging with hurt and feeling her cheeks growing hot. This was her home and her life. Why should she feel guilty? She spoke quietly, a tight control to her voice. "Jacques, I cannot live my life in constant fear. I am sorry but I just cannot. I have come here to build a life but it is no life to be always afraid. I carry my musket because of the animals. I am not foolhardy. I latch my door. I can do no more. I have come to know Looking Glass and trust him as a friend. I refuse to dwell on it. I thought it was an amusing story. I am sorry now that I said anything."

The party atmosphere had suddenly vanished and it had become very quiet. The only sound was the crackle of the fire and it was Richard who finally spoke.

"Marie, you must forgive us if we feel too responsible for you. But we are the ones who brought you out here away from civilization. If anything were to ever happen to you..."

"Richard, I appreciate that," she replied softly, interrupting him. "I understand your feelings, really I do. But what you must understand is - I am not a child anymore. I am here because I have chosen to be here. And I accept responsibility for myself. If anything were to happen to me, you are not to blame yourselves."

There was a silence as both men looked at the young woman sitting with a straight back and dignified air.

"That is easier to say than to do, Marie. We cannot help but feel very responsible. But you are right. You are not a child anymore," Richard agreed as he looked steadily at her.

She looked at both earnest young men sitting across the table from her and her expression softened. "I think perhaps we have very different views on the relative safety of civilization," she went on in a reasonable tone. "You," she looked at Jacques, "had to run for your life from our very civilized France, *n'est-ce pas?* And civilization has never been a haven of safety for the likes of me." Jacques started to say something and she stopped him with a gesture. "You know what my life was like in the midst of our very civilized village," she said to Jacques pointedly. "But what you do not know because I chose not to tell you is that on my very first day in New York Towne I was attacked, robbed, and almost raped. That is again a very civilized place compared to this, is it not?"

"What?!" Jacques exclaimed.

"Why did you not tell us?" Richard demanded, overriding Jacques' sudden outburst.

"What could you have done, Richard?" she asked softly. "There was nothing to be done. It happened in broad daylight. I fought. They stole my purse. I lost my money and the lunch I had just purchased but I kept my honor. I survived."

Jacques thought back and remembered very clearly the stressed little fourteen year-old who seemed reluctant to leave the ship on the second day. No wonder and she had never said a word about it. She had kept it all to herself. How frightening it must have been for her, walking the streets looking for employment after that experience. "Marie," he said demanding her attention.

"Yes, Jacques," she looked at him.

"I ask you to accept my sincerest apology," he spoke now in a subdued and gentle tone. "I had no right to take you to task like a schoolmaster scolds an errant pupil. It is only that I have great concern for your welfare and well being."

"I understand. And of course I accept," she smiled and her face regained its look of joy. "I told you a long time ago that the world is much less frightening in having you for a friend. And I am most appreciative that you care… both of you."

"Can we all kiss now that we have made up?" Richard teased and laughingly they stood and hugged and kissed each other's cheeks.

Later that evening Jacques and Richard accepted Marie's almost formal invitation to spend the night on her bearskin rug by the hearth. She climbed fully clothed into her bed and the men spread out their bed rolls. Richard turned over and was soon fast asleep. But once again sleep did not come easily to Jacques in Marie's presence. He was much too aware of her. Marie had changed. He had left a young girl and had come back to find a woman, a strong, independent, and unsettlingly attractive woman. Her scent seemed to permeate the cabin, amidst the smells of herbs, onions, fresh bread, and roasted meat. He could smell her now, musky, feminine or was it only his imagination? Imagination or not, it stirred his blood.

Watching the fire throw shadows and reflections upon the cabin walls, Jacques thought long on what Marie had said. There was much truth in her words. Where was there any safety? One never knew where danger would come from. One could die just as easily from disease in town as from an animal in the wilderness, yet one did not worry all the while one lived in town. And it was in the peaceful countryside of France, free from any wild animals or native savages that Marie had been the most brutalized.

Jacques' imagination provided a rapid series of mental images of Bouchet and what he had done to the defenseless child. Jacques found himself clenching his fists. He was filled with anger and hatred for the tavernkeeper who was now an entire ocean away, and Jacques startled himself. Why? When Celimene had rescued Marie and he had gone to the tavern, he had not felt this kind of hatred, this kind of anger, this kind of rage. If he had, he would have killed the fat gutted swine right then! Why now, after all this time, did such intense feelings, such desires for vengeance fill him?

She had been only a child. *She had been at his mercy and he had taken the worst kind of advantage of her.* Who had said that? Celimene had said that and he had not really been listening. What had changed? Jacques asked himself as he tried not to think of putting his fist through Bouchet's face or burying his foil hilt deep into the man's bowels. Then, he realized he had an overwhelming desire to protect her. He never wanted her to suffer hurt or pain or fear again. He wanted to keep her from all harm. It grieved him to now find out that on her very first day in the New World she had been attacked while under his patronage, practically under his nose. Why had she never told him? Pride, perhaps. Or was it her damnable need to feel independent? Whatever it was, he wanted only that she should never have to endure the like again. He wanted to enfold her into his arms and protect her from everything... for the rest of her life!

Chapter 19

Marie walked out from the forest with a huge sack of pine needles balanced rather precariously on her small back. The hems at the front of her skirt were tucked carelessly into her apron strings to keep them from tripping her. This made the skirt festoon out about her in front, rather coquettishly exposing side glimpses of shapely calves, knees and lower thighs and it was totally incongruent with her posture. She was deeply stooped, bent over low and moving slowly as much in consideration of keeping the awkwardly cumbersome sack in its place on her back as of the weight she bore. But the sight she presented was at once both flirtatious and pitiful.

Standing atop the ladder nailing shingles to their newly constructed privy, Jacques caught a glimpse of her from the corner of his eye and stopped mid-swing. He gave a double take, stared, and then yelled out, "What are you doing?" Kicking out his foot to nudge Richard who was standing below holding the ladder, he growled, "Never mind this, go and help her before she breaks her back."

Obligingly Richard let go of the ladder and was at Marie's side in several swift long strides. "Here, let me take... *mon Dieu*, what is in this?" he asked feeling the shifting weight of it.

"It is only pine needles," Marie grunted as she gladly relinquished her hold on the sack, then she indulged in the simple blessing of being able to stand upright again as she pulled her skirts modestly back into place.

"Pine needles?"

"Yes, if you would, please bring them to the front of the cabin." She led the tall man to where she had rigged a makeshift frame upon which mattress ticking was stretched.

"What is all this, eh?" he asked as he looked over the scene.

"I am making us each a mattress, now that I have the material for the ticking. First, I spread the needles out to make certain they are dry. We do not want them moldering in the mattress if we can help it." She grabbed a load of needles from the sack Richard had just dropped to the ground. Shaking and spreading the freshly gathered needles out over the material, she inspected them. "And," she added, her hand swiftly plucking an insect out of the needle pile and throwing it to the ground, "we do not want any uninvited company either." Richard watched with rapt attention as she continued to spread each new handful of the long, yellowed needles, raking them back and forth until she had satisfied herself they were clean and then leaving them to thoroughly dry in the sunshine. "Once this is done, I will add yarrow and lavender..."

"Mattresses, you say?"

"Yes, of course. We will need them for our beds. Surely you do not want to sleep on the ground all winter. It will get very cold, you know. And the ropes will be no insulation. I fear until I have some chickens and geese I cannot hope to make a feather bed but someday..." her voice trailed off optimistically as she wiped a few stray curls from her face and gave him a smile.

Richard continued to look at her, his face strangely expressionless. He looked as if he was going to say something but stopped himself. At last he spoke again. "That is very clever. You are quite a woman, Marie."

She shrugged looking back to her work. "We all work very hard but," she sighed pleasantly, "it will be worth it, eh? And if we can lay a fur or two on top, it should be quite excellent and we should be pleasantly snug this winter. I just hope I will have enough yarrow to harvest for all three of us. Mistress Wingate said it helps to keep the pests away." She glanced back in his direction. "Thank you for carrying these. I will have to gather several more bags before I am finished. Fortunately, the pine forest floor is covered with them."

"So many?" he questioned with raised brows.

"The plumper the mattress, the warmer we will rest."

"There are other ways to stay warm," he responded teasingly but she didn't seem to hear him.

"Besides, it will take many bags just to fill a mattress large enough for you to lay that long body upon, *n'est-ce pas?* But go back to Jacques now, he may need you."

Richard turned to go and then came back. "We will go with you to bring in more bags."

"Oh... no-no, that is not necessary, you are very busy," she shook her head and giggled. "I will take care of the pine needles and you and Jacques must supply the furs."

"Ah-ha, so, I see now how that works," he laughed.

"Well, I am afraid it will take many too many rabbit skins to do the job and that is the largest game I have caught."

That tickled Richard immensely. "I understand... but we are not so busy we cannot make the time to fetch the needles; it is for our own mattresses after all."

"All right," she smiled and pushed him slightly before going back to her business, "now go and help Jacques."

Jacques and Richard had made a trip back to New York Towne shortly after their return to the cabin. They had sold their haul of skins as well as those Marie had bartered and bought such staples as they needed to get through the winter. They could hunt fresh meat, and they had Marie's store of vegetables but such goods as coffee, black tea, flour, sugar, and salt had to be purchased. Afraid to leave the cabin and her garden stock to the mercy of the scavengers for even a short time until a secure roof was in place, Marie had, instead, supplied them with a list of trade goods she wanted as well as replacements for the things she had already bartered away. At the very top of that list had been a large looking glass. Mattress ticking had been on the list as well.

When the men returned, they quickly set to the task of building the second room of the cabin. At first the room was to be a bedroom for Marie. Then, a cold rainy spell caused Jacques much concern; he was more set on installing a properly shingled roof and weatherizing the entire structure than in taking the time to put in a second fireplace. Marie thought it was a mistake and tried to reason with him.

"It will be too cold," she exclaimed. "Without a fire when the snow comes and the winds are blowing, it will be freezing in here, Jacques."

"It could snow any day," Jacques had answered rather shortly, "Richard and I will sleep in here. You will stay by the fire."

"Jacques! You must put a hearth in. I will build it; it will not take so long. I have become quite good at mixing up the clay."

"Richard and I will be fine," he insisted with a stubborn disdain for their comfort. "It is better we have a roof over our heads, after all. We can always add a fireplace next year."

Marie looked to Richard who shrugged, unwilling to say anything one way or the other. And so Marie had shrugged, too. It was unlike Jacques to be so obstinate. She did not understand why a few drops of rain drove him to skip over the building of a hearth. And how were they to add one once the wall was there? By tearing down the wall? From experience, she felt it would be some time before the snows came to settle in. They had not yet had what the Wingates called *Indian Summer*. They could certainly continue to sleep all together in the main room for as long as it took to finish the chimney. She had verbalized that very fact. The main room was not large but the floor space had accommodated four braves after all. There was ample room. The icy storms of winter were many weeks away but when they came, Jacques was going to regret not having another hearth in the cabin. She was certain of that.

No sooner had the room and roof been completed when a very mild, dry stretch of weather began and Marie had to bite her tongue to resist saying *I told you so*. Richard, on the other hand, felt he knew exactly what had driven his friend to rush to complete the second room and she was about five foot one or two, and weighed no more than a baby fawn.

Rather than waste the sunny days building beds, the young men had moved their bedrolls onto the dirt floor in the second room and set upon the task of constructing a smokehouse. They had been exposed to the idea in the Indian villages where smoking and drying meat was used along with salting for long term storage and preservation.

"I hope this works," Jacques grunted as he wiped the sweat from his forehead despite the coolness of the day. "I can imagine the trick is going to be to dry the meat without burning it to a cinder."

"That is why we make the pit," Richard grunted over his shovel. "The fire should be far from the meat, it is the smoke and steady warmth, not the flame, that does the job. Hickory wood is especially good, I have been told."

"We should have done this first so we could already be preserving. The forests are plentiful now but soon game will be harder to find. I cannot believe we forgot our bellies."

"You seemed to have other things on your mind beside your belly," Richard said casually, without looking in Jacques' direction. "And when Marie fills our... stomachs each night," he grinned to himself, "our bellies are easy to forget." He received no response from his friend. "She has turned into a fine cook, do you not think?"

Looking hard at Richard who kept his face expressionless, Jacques was trying to guess his friend's motive for asking such a question. "Well, I will not say she would rival a master chef in *le palais royale* but the fare she serves up is far better than the swill of the natives. God knows it is better than you or I can manage but that is no real compliment. My cooking is terrible and yours is a disaster."

Richard laughed in an agreeable snort and added teasingly, "Such a delicate pallet as yours must have a hard time accepting the idea of plain wholesome if somewhat common food. Marie is not pretentious enough to serve the showy little dishes served at Versailles."

"And how would you know what they serve at Versailles?"

"I have heard what they do to food, same as you."

"And just what have you heard?" *Does Richard really think my tastes are pretentious? Just because I have some taste, does not mean I am pretentious.*

"You remember your uncle talking about the little birds roasted whole with their bellies stuffed with their own eggs. Their feathers reattached to their little roasted bodies." He shook his head with obvious disgust. "Is it not like a cannibal slitting the womb of a woman to take out her unborn, roasting them both, putting the babe back into its mother's belly and dressing her for the dinner table?"

"Mon Dieu! How can you even think of such a thing?! That is truly disgusting. And who mentioned cannibals?"

Richard shrugged. "We were speaking of pretensions. A cannibal who would have to have his meal presented in such a fashion, I would consider a pretentious cannibal."

Jacques did not laugh as Richard was expecting. Instead he was reminded of the story his grandfather used to tell of his own mother's horrifying end. "I do not think anyone has ever thought of a savage as being pretentious," he finally said sternly.

"But if a savage did such a thing, would you not think him pretentious?"

"I would think him horrifying."

"Yes, but pretentiously horrifying."

"I suppose so," Jacques agreed. "And I also must say savage behavior is often found among the *civilized.*"

Richard nodded in satisfaction. *"Exactement!* Just give me good wine. A good cut of meat and some hard crusted bread covered in sweet butter. Now, that is a meal fit for any king!"

"One might say your tastes are just a trifle... provincial."

"One might. I do not consider that an insult." Richard raised his stubbled chin, a jocular gleam in his eye. "There are many fine things that have come out of the provinces."

Jacques finally chuckled as he came down from the ladder. "Yes, my friend. I quite agree." He slapped Richard on the back. "And quails tongues are very pretentious. Most certainly one will not find any hanging in this smokehouse, eh? Unless, of course, they hang in the beak of the birds themselves. Speaking of which... we need to gear up and do some hunting. We must try to fill our larder for the weeks ahead."

"If we are lucky we might find a bear before it goes into hibernation for the winter."

Jacques looked at Richard. "Are you so fond of bear meat?"

"Marie is looking for furs to put on the beds."

"Oh."

They hunted for several days and accrued a variety of wild birds: turkey, quail, pheasant, even duck but they came upon no sign of bear. On the river, the beaver were plentiful and busy laying up stores of vegetation for the winter. The young men had learned beaver made excellent eating as well as sought after pelts, so when they came upon a beaver lodge they knew they needed to lay traps.

Jacques and Richard gave the game to Marie to gut and pluck and dress before hanging it high in the smokehouse while a hardwood fire of hickory and maple burned slowly beneath.

Still winter held off and so Jacques and Richard decided to dig a pit in the downward slope of the knoll top behind the cabin, far from the spring stream that supplied their drinking water. Marie had come from her own chores to see what they were up to and found them stripped to the waist and sweating from their labors despite the coolness of the day.

"What are you doing?" she asked in puzzlement kicking absently at a clod of dirt dislodged by their spades.

"Perhaps you will recognize it more easily when we put up a little house with a bench inside," Richard grinned up at her. His face was shadowed with several days whiskers made darker with the smudges of dirt through which sweat had run streaks.

"Oh..." Marie suddenly understood. "All the comforts of civilization," she murmured, "I have become so used to going off into the bushes I had almost forgotten about this luxury." *And so much more important than another hearth in our cabin*, she thought but she did not say it.

Jacques paused and was standing nonchalantly while leaning on his shovel, resting and watching her. His lean muscular torso was sun baked a deep bronze now, his skin glistened with exertion and Marie found herself staring at him. Then her eyes rose to his and she realized he was looking at her and saw her staring at him. Her face went pink.

"We would not want any important parts to freeze," Richard quipped easily.

"I...I suppose it will be good to have some shelter in the winter," she added absently.

"Just be sure you do not get a splinter in that little bottom of yours," Richard said with a wink and her face grew even redder

"Well, just be certain you sand the seat very smooth ," she quipped back, "or we all might get splinters, eh?"

"We could help each other take them out," Richard teased, "it might make for a very entertaining evening on a chilly winter night, *n'est-ce pas?*"

At this she blushed even brighter. "I do not think so," she replied tonelessly, and straightening her back, she turned and made a hasty retreat leaving them to continue their project. Richard grinned and rubbed his behind in appreciation of the thought.

"Why did you say that?" Jacques asked with a frown.

"What?" Richard grunted without looking at his friend.

"You embarrassed her," he accused. "It was very crude."

"Ahhhh, but if I had to get a splinter," Richard grinned without hesitation, "I cannot think of anyone I would rather have remove it, can you?" he saw the frown on Jacques' face. Chuckling to himself, he picked up his shovel and returned to his digging without another word.

That had been two days ago and now the privy roof was all but finished. Watching Marie spread the pine needles over the ticking, Richard nodded with an appreciative smile as he stood near her.

"Marie," he said almost as an after thought.

"Yes?"

"You know I only tease. The other day, if I embarrassed you, I apologize."

"Whatever are you talking about?"

"When I was joking about the splinters... you know I was just teasing, do you not? Sometimes I just want to get a reaction out of Jacques. But I do not want to make you uncomfortable around me. I am harmless."

"I know you are only teasing," she nodded and then looked up into his eyes. "But why do you wish to bait Jacques?"

"He is my best friend and I love him better than a brother... but sometimes... oh, never mind. It is not important. I just do not want you to be upset with me."

A puzzled frown still creased Marie's brow as she watched Richard walk back to Jacques at the new privy. Sometimes she thought they were the most unlikely pair to be such fast friends. They were so completely different. And yet both men had very good hearts.

"What is she doing?" Jacques asked as soon as Richard approached.

"Pine needles. She says she is making us each a mattress."

Jacques grunted quietly as he nailed the last of the homemade shingles. "That reminds me, we must select the saplings to frame out our beds. If we cut them now, we can always lash them together later. I think it is better we get the pieces selected, stripped down, and into the shelter and warmth of the cabin before we have to deal with ice, do you agree?"

Richard shrugged. "I do not know if I can survive all this domesticity, it is too much work," he complained good-naturedly.

"It has always been a lot of work. You just never had to be bothered before."

Richard looked up at his friend with a wry expression. "And I suppose you have?"

"Yes, as a matter of fact. An estate does not run itself. I thank God for the time I had learning before we left."

"And you were doing manual labor?" Richard's tone had turned sarcastic.

"No, of course not but I observed closely. I took my responsibilities seriously. I learned a great deal more than if I had continued to spend my days in bed with my mistress." Jacques' tone had become sharper than he had meant and he realized this last had sounded more than a little reproachful. For some inexplicable reason he had felt a sudden flush of competitiveness and had been compelled to point out anything that might smack of achievement to his friend. Just as quickly, he felt both shame and regret.

Jacques gave a small laugh as he jumped down from the ladder. Hammer in one hand, he barely backhanded Richard in the stomach with the other. "Besides," he tried to sound lighthearted, "an honest day's labor will keep the fat off you."

"Fat! What fat?" Richard accepted the lighter change in mood and reflected it. "You have worked every ounce of spare flesh off me. I am nothing but bones going into the winter when I should have some fat. And is that all you can say?"

"About what?" Jacques asked, a small stab of guilt going through him, he had hoped Richard had forgiven his former words. He peered unnecessarily inside the privy at the well-sanded wooden bench with a large hole in it and pretended to study it intently.

"About the fact that Marie is making us mattresses."

"What am I supposed to say?" Jacques asked, a hint of relief tingeing his honest surprise at the shift in subject.

"I find it rather touching, do you not? She does not have to do this for us. It is a lot of work."

"Of course; she does not have to but it does not surprise me that she does it. She works very hard, she always has, and she pulls her share."

"*Pulls her share*," he gave Jacques a withering look, "she is a delicate little flower and you speak as though she were a draft mule." Jacques returned the look. "Does it not make you feel... oh, I do not know... ummm, a certain shall we say *intimacy* to know she has made you a mattress with her own two little hands, put so much of herself into every stitch... something for you to lie naked upon? Or is she no more than one of the peasants who worked for your estate?"

Jacques scowled at Richard in earnest. "I never think of her as a... a... peasant. That is unfair!"

Richard looked unruffled. "So, does it not create a certain sense of intimacy?" he persisted.

Jacques avoided looking at Richard as he climbed back up several rungs of the ladder and busied himself picking together the scraps from the finished roof. "Our whole living arrangement is rather full of... intimacy."

"Yes, but there is intimacy... and then there is *intimacy*, eh?"

Jacques looked around sharply at his friend. "I have no intention of lying naked upon my bed and she is not one of your squaws, Richard. I do not like the idea of you thinking of her in that way." He stood on the ladder, slightly above his tall friend, motionless and tense.

"What way?" Richard feigned ignorance.

"You know exactly what way," Jacques' voice had grown quietly intense.

"I have a great deal of respect for Marie. She is very special. But I also think she is a very beautiful woman and that it would be a pure waste and a sin for her to sleep alone in the cold of winter with a healthy man under the same roof."

"So you intend to warm her?" It was barely a question and Jacques' voice had gone hard.

Richard looked directly at him for several moments before speaking. "As you say, I have my squaws... but I do not understand what concern it is to you one way or the other unless you perhaps have some intentions of your own."

Jacques jumped the remaining distance to the ground, anger evident in the stiffness of his posture and precision of his movements as he packed the tools up and gathered his clothing together. He stalked off to the river seeking to cool down.

He said little to Richard the rest of the evening. He attempted to be pleasant at the supper table for Marie's sake while she in her guileless manner chatted about this and that. Richard was his best friend but at that moment Jacques was unsure how he felt toward him. Richard had never shown any real interest in Marie before. Acquaintance? Yes. Friend? Yes. Traveling companion, dinner companion, yes, yes, but never... Damn him! Richard had had a string of squaws ever since they had arrived on this continent and Jacques was not going to let him treat Marie like just another convenient bed warmer.

And yet... Marie could do as she wished and he could not stop her. He had no right to presume to decide what kind of relationship she could or could not have with anyone. She was free to do whatever she pleased with whomever she pleased and there was nothing to stop her. No, he could not stop her but he could damn well stop Richard if he must. If he had to, he would call him out on the field of honor.

That night the wind shifted and the air outside grew considerably colder. The thought of a mattress of pine needles buffering him from the cold ground was very appealing as Jacques turned restlessly and tried to find a comfortable position on his pallet on the hard earth floor. The cabin was quiet except for the sound of the fire in the other room and the closer sounds of Richard's heavy, regular breathing. Marie had insisted they leave their room door open in order to share the heat from the hearth.

Jacques opened his eyes and barely kept himself from snorting outloud. He could see Richard's outline, a long, dark silhouette against the darker shadows of the wall. Pine needle mattresses! Who was he trying to fool? He asked himself. No mattress would cure what was fast becoming a painful ache between his thighs which was the real discomfort of his night. Devoid of the distractions of the day he could not keep his mind's eye from conjuring up images of Marie coming up out of the river, dripping wet and all feminine curves. *Mon Dieu,* she was... No, he could control his mind no better than his dreams. Did Richard realize? Was that it? Was he purposely goading him?

Jacques looked down at himself and in the dim glow of the light coming in from the other room, he could clearly see the blanket tented above his hips as he felt the flesh which propped up the blanket throb with each beat of his heart. *Dieu!* He wanted her and would have given anything at that moment to simply climb into her bed and bury his flesh deeply within her. How dare Richard accuse him of thinking of her as a meaningless peasant? If that was all he thought of her, he would have eased his misery long ago.

Turning uncomfortably onto his side with his back to Richard, Jacques took matters into his own hands. There was no help for it or he would never get any sleep.

The next morning after the sun was well above the horizon, the trio went out together and gathered more pine needles. After carrying them back to the cabin, the men left Marie to her tasks while they went into the forest to select saplings for their bed frames.

"We can be glad the weather has held off as long as it has," Richard observed casually breaking the silence between them. "No more, I think. Look to the north. Those are storm clouds and I smell snow coming."

"What do you mean you *smell* snow?" Jacques snorted in disbelief. "You cannot smell snow."

"But of course I can... do you not?"

"No." Jacques looked up at his friend to see if he was serious. "How can you smell snow?" he asked after a moment.

Richard shrugged. "I just can. You can smell rain, can you not?"

Jacques nodded. "What does snow smell like?" he asked in a challenge.

Richard pondered the question. "Like snow. I do not know how to describe it. It smells like... like... a kind of flat, but sharp, almost like metal, like cold, like ice and..." he gave up in frustration with a shrug. "I cannot describe it; I just know how it smells."

"Mmmmm," Jacques responded, unconvinced. "And the Indians can smell snow as well, I suppose?"

"Of course."

Jacques looked at Richard and raised an eyebrow. "Well, smell or no smell, the sky does look bad and before nightfall we had best collect together everything we do not want to lose for the season."

Richard grunted in agreement but looked mildly hurt that Jacques did not believe him. He knew he could smell snow in the air. He also knew Jacques was peeved with him but he had taken a calculated risk. He loved his friend more dearly than a brother but there were moments when Jacques could test the patience of a saint. It was obvious to Richard that Marie was hopelessly besotted with the fair haired young lord, yet Jacques seemed oblivious to her more tender feelings. If yesterday had proved nothing else, it had shown Richard very clearly that Jacques did care whether he realized it or not. A man who became jealous was not without feelings. Maybe a little dose of jealousy was exactly what his friend needed to progress to the next step.

That night Jacques had just as much trouble sleeping as before. Outside the cabin, he could hear the wind gusting as snow in fine grainy bits fell for hours. He stretched upon the cushion of pine needles and he did think of her small hands stitching so diligently. Twice he rose to add wood to the fire and stood a long while warming himself and silently watching Marie sleep. If she awoke he could easily excuse his presence, he told himself, in his attendance to the hearth.

Finally, back on his pine needle pallet, sleep did overwhelm him and it seemed he had no sooner dozed off when they all awoke to the novelty of a white landscape with Richard mumbling in self-satisfaction, "I told you I could smell snow coming."

Chapter 20

"Jacques! Jacques!" Richard called to his friend as he ran out of the forest. The snow under foot was light but he was knocking it off the bushes as he ran. Jacques was at the woodpile chopping more kindling and looked up in alarm.

"What has happened?" he asked immediately alert to danger.

"Nothing… yet. Bring your hunting gear, quickly, quickly… hurry."

Jacques swung the axe and left it embedded in the stump they used for a chopping platform. He grabbed his musket and bag of ammunition which was always close at hand and as he ran he donned the coat and hat he had removed as he warmed to his task as wood-chopper. At the yells, Marie came out of the cabin and watched them leave as Jacques followed Richard back into the forest.

"What did you see, a bear?" Jacques asked.

"No-no, the bears are all asleep now but I went to our beaver pond to check the traps and just before I stepped out of the trees I saw it, grazing along the water's edge on the pond grasses."

"Saw what?"

"A *moos*, the Indians call it." Richard was speaking in hushed tones.

"I know not what that is," Jacques replied. "*Moos*. Is it the big deer I have heard called *elk*?"

"No-no, twice as big with antlers that are flattened out like the sails of a ship. And a huge head with a wide bulbous nose… you will see it if we are lucky. It is so huge, it will feed us for weeks. This is the time to get them but I am told never hunt them during the spring mating season. At that time the meat becomes very gamey and you can do nothing to make it palatable. Shhh..."

They continued on the mile long path to the beaver pond up their little stream, Richard slowed and became more stealthy as they approached.

"There," he whispered at last, pointing to a huge bull moose easily ten times the weight of the average man. The massive creature stood steadfastly munching the grasses it was finding just below the snow.

"It is giant!" Jacques whispered, "How are we to get it home?"

"First we must kill it. You go that way," Richard pointed carefully. "If it comes your way, I am told it does not see well. Just aim for its eye."

Jacques did as Richard requested, creeping low and careful to stay downwind as he neared the pond's edge. *How did one survive being charged by such a beast?* He asked himself. He looked and spied the closest tree he thought would give him the best chance at survival. Now that he knew in what direction he would run if need be, he approached cautiously and took aim.

Jacques and Richard both shot at the same time. The moose stood on its feet for almost a full minute although it probably died instantly, then it fell over with a thud that shook the earth. Both men felt it in their feet.

Richard ran up laughing at their triumph and immediately cut off the head to let the blood drain out. "We save the head," he said with a smile. "Tonight we feast on boiled tongue!"

"What about the brains?"

"No, those I need to cure the hide. I must soak the hide in its brains and boiling water. It loosens the hair so I can scrape it clean. It will make the strongest leather we could hope to find, much tougher than deer or elk."

"Oh, yes, did you learn this from one of your Indian women?" Jacques teased.

"As a matter of fact, I did," he smiled and began the process of butchering.

The lungs were tossed aside along with the bladder and anything else they could not identify as useful but the heart, liver and kidneys were put into a sack for safe keeping. They debated on whether the intestines would make good sausage casing and decided there was enough to deal with and tossed them and the stomach aside as well.

Richard took great care in removing the hide; when he finished the weight of that alone was all that one man could safely carry. He took it back to the cabin while Jacques continued to cut up the animal into manageable pieces. Richard returned with more traps so Jacques left with the bag containing the heart and liver and one containing the four forelegs and hooves. The hooves would be boiled down into a gelatinous material which would be the basis for a meat aspic or perhaps a fruit jelly. Each of the haunches was a load to carry in itself. They took turns, one always remaining to butcher and keep away the scavengers and one carrying pieces of the kill back to Marie and the smokehouse.

The cold weather would preserve some without smoking so Marie salted down pieces she thought they might prefer not to have smoke flavored and asked Richard to hang these outside high out of the reach of any animals. She put one good sized roast into her outdoor oven where it slowly roasted in its own fat for hours. But the tongue she immediately put into a pot to boil per Richard's earnest request. Along with onions, parsnips, and fresh baked bread, this was a treat they could all look forward to having when the butchering was completed.

When the men were down to the last pieces of meat to carry back, Richard used the leavings to bait the traps in the hopes they might draw fur bearing predators.

"What about the beaver traps?" Jacques asked

"Naww, you know the beavers only eat their sticks."

"I meant did you ever get a chance to check the beaver traps?"

Richard laughed at this misunderstanding. "No, I guess not. Well, while I set these, you could make yourself useful. Do you remember where they are?"

Jacques rolled his eyes. "Just be careful with those bigger traps. Do you want me to help?"

"No, just check for the beaver, eh?"

When Jacques returned he held two beaver to add to their haul. Richard had set a series of traps in and around the bloody waste and marked them each with a thin branch stuck in the ground and rising up like a tiny flagpole. Each man gutted a beaver and used the blood and entrails to cover their scent on the traps. To a wolf each trap would smell like beaver and moose.

Finally, they gathered the last of the meat along with the beaver still needing to be stripped of its pelt and they left the beaver pond.

"This was most fortunate," Richard remarked on the last trek back to the cabin, "to get such an animal so close to home has saved us a great deal of time and struggle."

"I was just thinking the same," Jacques replied and grunted under his load. "Without a mule, dragging this kill back in one trip would have been impossible. What do you think we will catch in the large traps? A wolf perhaps? Fox? Wolverine?"

"Mmmm, I do not know. I heard a wolf two nights ago but who knows where they are now. What would you like to catch?"

"Oh, well, if I am to put in a wish request I would like to see a fine pair of lynx in the trap with beautiful soft fur."

"Just right for a bed?" Richard teased and Jacques said nothing.

It took Richard several days to transform the raw moose hide into usable leather and he started by commandeering the bedroom and dropping a veil of secrecy. He borrowed Marie's bath tub which was the only container large enough to hold the hide and she kept him supplied with boiling water. Jacques accepted moving his mattress onto the bearskin rug before the fire. It was warm and quite com-

fortable and entirely too close to Marie but the smell of Richard's project perme-
ated the cabin and covered up her alluring scent.

While Richard was busy with his hide, Jacques skinned the beaver and
stretched the pelts by nailing them to the outside of the cabin until they were completely dry.

He and Marie put up storage shelves for the foodstuffs creating a small pantry
in the odd shaped corner of the crooked wall.

Periodically, Marie or Jacques would peer into the bedroom or stand at the
door a few sociable minutes and watch Richard scrape and work the hide. They
could both see that it was odious labor and because of it neither begrudged the big
man the small inconveniences they endured.

"How are your hands holding up?" Marie asked Richard the first evening.

"Surprisingly well."

"Let me see," she stood before him like a mother bent on inspection.

Richard held out his hands to her.

"So much work in water, I would have expected them to be dried out," she
murmured, checking between his large fingers for any cracks. "I have a small mixture of rendered fat and beeswax I can give you which helps to protect the hands."

"No-no, not necessary," he smiled in appreciation of her attentions. "I think
that is it… all the fat coming off the hide keeps my hands protected."

"Very well," she agreed and gave his hand a motherly little pat, "but if you
start to dry out, let me know."

Richard nodded with a grin and looked at Jacques who was pretending not to
notice. Marie next turned to Jacques who was making up more hunting cartridges.

"And you? How are your hands holding up with the cold weather?" she
asked.

"I am fine, *merci.*"

"Oh no, Jacques, look at your cuticles," she tsked, grabbing hold of his hand.
"Here try some of this." She produced a dollop of fat & wax ointment and began
rubbing it into his fingers.

He jerked away as if he had touched a hot iron. "Thank you. I will rub it in,"
he said rather gruffly. Richard stifled a laugh by clearing his throat.

Finally, Richard took his hide outside and stretched it out to dry between two
distant trees. He invited Jacques to join him on the trek back to the traps to see
what they had caught.

"So does this mean I can finally build my bed frame and return to our room?"

"Yes, my friend and I appreciate the inconvenience I have caused you this
past week but I would caution against stringing your bed with ropes just yet."

"Why?"

"How would you like to have a nice thick, strong sheet of *moos* leather to
stretch on the frame rather than those ropes that always move and stretch and let
your mattress and your knees fall through?" he asked brightly.

"It sounds quite decadent," grinned Jacques, "and most generous. Richard, you did not have to do all the work yourself."

"I know, I know, but I have never done it before and chose to try it alone. I think it worked out well. We have been tanning leather with piss for centuries, the natives do it with the animal's brains and amazingly, I have been told no matter the animal, it has just the right amount of brains to cure its hide."

"Really?"

"A sign that God approves of leather, n'est-ce pas?"

Jacques laughed. "Perhaps you are right. Did He not make the first garments of animal skins?"

"I thought it was fig leaves."

"No-no, that was Adam and Eve who did that, God used animal skins."

"Ah well, you know your Bible better than I."

They continued to walk in silence for a time and then Jacques added, "That is a very large piece of leather. I take it there is enough for three beds?"

"It is not a bearskin but I think it will please Marie nonetheless, do you agree?"

"I am certain it will," Jacques replied and he was uncertain what he thought of that.

When they arrived at the beaver pond, they discovered no more beaver. Undoubtedly the animals had gone deep into their lodge for the duration of the winter so they collected the smaller traps to take them back home. The larger traps did yield a fox and a wolf. They gutted the animals and used the entrails to re-bait the traps.

That night Marie slept on her new bed foundation and greeted Richard the next morning with an enthusiastic but sisterly hug and kiss in gratitude. He smiled like the cat who has stolen the cream and Jacques was gentleman and friend enough to voice his own appreciation. It was, in fact, the first night since they had left the inn in New York Towne that the men had slept up off the ground.

Jacques and Richard created several collapsible chairs made with small fur skins stretched over a pivoting frame and it was a decided improvement to their comfort in sitting before the fire.

Richard fashioned cone shaped containers of birch bark to fill with tallow skimmed off the fatty roasts which they could use for fat lamps wicked with river reeds. And melting bees' wax along the stitching on the outside of their boots as protection against water seepage was a regular task.

As the long cold evenings progressed, the trio sat together around the fire puttering, each absorbed in his own project. It had become the favorite part of the day for Marie, several hours of quiet companionship, relaxed, warm, and peaceful with nothing to disturb them as they shared this little world together. She was justifiably pleased with herself at how well she had managed alone all summer but she never pretended for a minute that she was not much happier now with them here, beside her, around her, giving her a sense of homey security - sometimes speaking, sometimes not speaking only sharing a nod, a smile. Marie was very content.

After all their stories had been told, she would often read aloud to them from books she had brought with her from Wingate's store. Her clear voice with its softly accented pronunciations, rose up soothingly to relax and entertain as the men sat back with a pipe of tobacco, sometimes closing their eyes to let her words paint pictures in their minds and sometimes with eyes riveted to the gentle slopes and planes of her smooth expressive face.

As the gloomy weeks of winter wore on with day after day of little sunlight and heavy overcast, Marie noticed a tense and irritable mood come over Jacques that she had never before witnessed. One day he stormed out of the cabin after Richard had said something to him which she did not fully hear.

"What is troubling Jacques?" she asked with concern.

"Nothing that is not his own fault," Richard replied easily.

"What do you mean?" It came out more sharply than she had intended.

"Jacques is used to having a woman," he shrugged in a typical Gallic manner.

"Oh." Marie felt the color rush to her cheeks. "I see," she said calmly hoping her voice did not betray her emotions, "and he has none here."

"He has had none since we left France," Richard said bluntly.

She was silent for a moment realizing that this information pleased her a great deal. "And it troubles him?"

"It troubles any man, if he has blood in his veins and is used to such things."

"But it does not seem to trouble you," she observed naively.

Richard smiled. "Of course it does, Marie, but I do something about it."

"I do not understand." She looked at him blankly.

"I told Jacques he should take a squaw," Richard said honestly, "an Indian woman. I have."

"You have?" Marie hoped she did not sound too surprised.

"What else is there?"

Marie visibly swallowed.

"A man has needs," Richard continued.

"But he would not?" Marie asked softly, not looking up.

"No," Richard grunted. "He will have nothing to do with them. He says they are no better than sheep. They are not so bad, I told him. Besides, I asked him if he was an Englishman to know what it is like to sport with sheep," he laughed until he saw Marie's expression. "Oh... ahh, I should not have said that," he said contritely. "It was only a joke. I am sorry."

"Forget it, Richard. I have heard far worse. At least you are honest," Marie sighed. After a moment she added, "It will be hard for Jacques to find a mistress such as he had in France."

"The only mistresses to be had here are the squaws. A white woman would be stoned to death by all the fine hypocrites in this new world. I told Jacques if he does not want a squaw he should take a wife."

"And what does Jacques think of that?" Marie asked, barely breathing.

"He does not say," Richard shrugged again and grinned, "He only growls like the bear. But every life should have a little death, *n'est-ce pas?*"

"What?" she looked at him in question.

"*Petit mort,* little death," he was still grinning.

"Oh," Marie looked away. She had no idea what Richard meant.

That night it was Marie who could not sleep. She kept going over Richard's words and thinking of Jacques. She was almost eighteen and the physical abuses of her past were fading from her mind. Other feelings stirred strongly within her. The desire for a good man's affection, children of her own, a family. She remembered the day in Celimene's cottage when she had offered herself to Jacques as a bribe to take her with him. She had learned that sex was a commodity and she had numbed herself to the act. But he had given her a sense of pride when he told her she did not have to whore to make her way. He had implied that she was better than that. What did he think of her now, she wondered? If he was needing a woman, did he not see that she was a woman? Perhaps not so fine as the mistress he once had, perhaps without any skills in lovemaking, but was she not better than a savage?

In the days that followed, Marie's behavior and attitude toward Jacques changed ever so subtly but Richard noticed it and smiled to himself. Long ago he had concluded that these two were a pair well matched. Beneath the surface, Marie was a lusty French girl who was not afraid to get her hands a little dirty and Jacques needed a wife and was nothing short of blind not to take notice of her and her nicely rounded bottom. Richard had. But he had also decided that she had grown into the kind of woman who wanted a home with curtains on real window panes and children and a faithful husband who would be a father. Richard was not cut out for that kind of life he told himself and he was honest enough to admit it. He would only disappoint her in the end and break her heart. Besides, it was very obvious to him for whom she had the eyes.

One night after noting quietly to Jacques how especially fine Marie had grown, Richard excused himself to retire early leaving the two alone together in the main room of the cabin. Very pleased with himself, Richard smiled as he stretch out under the thick furs on his bed. He had planted the seed, now to see what would grow in the quiet of the winter.

Jacques nodded good night as Richard left the room. He sat thinking and continued to pull at his pipe. He did not need Richard to tell him Marie looked fine. He was very capable of noticing for himself how exceptionally fine she looked.

Living and working together, side by side and day by day, in the close confines of the small cabin, Jacques had noticed much about Marie. She had completely changed from the dirty, stringy-haired little serving child who had been so abused by that cockroach Bouchet. She had blossomed into true beauty and grown into a literate woman of intelligence and reason who was able to discuss things rationally and logically. She was now a woman who always managed to smell fresh and sweet, who was thoughtful and generous, and who could look so vulnerable while doing the most ordinary of tasks. And still, she was a woman who could load and shoot a musket like a man and was brave enough to live alone in the wild but who, all the same, made it clear that she was thrilled to have your company, a woman of humor and insight and a very special quality. Yes, there was something more, something beyond the obvious, beyond the inviting curves of her body, the delicate loveliness of her face; something even beyond her intellect. It was a quality of feminine capability, sturdiness and raw courage that was very compelling. A man needed a bold mate such as she in this bold new world. She was really quite remarkable, absolutely unique; he was beginning to see that more and more clearly. He doubted that in all the world there was another quite like her and the man who won her heart would have a prize beyond value.

Jacques felt an all too familiar surge in his loins and was uncomfortably aware that he was not at all oblivious to her innocent sexuality no matter what Richard seemed to think. His gray eyes darkened as they wandered easily and slowly over Marie's form and came to rest upon her face. Her brow was smooth as she sat looking down at the mending in her lap. The lashes of her wide, large eyes were long, almost brushing her well-colored cheeks which still held traces of a summer glow. Here at the frontier she never wore bonnets and seldom a cap he had noticed, even in the winter if the weather was fair, and her light brown hair was streaked vibrantly with those golden highlights, bleached by the sun. Now silky tendrils curled down over her small shoulders, clung to her smooth, graceful little neck, and fell upon her bosom.

She looked up and saw him looking at her, a look so compellingly intense that she felt an unexpected physical response within her own body. She returned his gaze for several moments and felt the heat of her own blood rushing to her face. She looked back to her handwork without speaking. Her heartbeat had increased and her fingers had turned inexplicably clumsy. With every ounce of her being she wanted to fling herself into his arms and tell him how very much she loved him. She did not care if he could not love her back in the same way. As long as he needed her, that was all she asked. She would share his bed and never ask for more than his affection and tender regard. But she was not a *putain* to be making the first move.

Jacques had not meant to stare. He saw her flush and pretended to look back at the fire but he continued to sneak glances at her. He saw the line of her breast rise and fall with her breathing. He was aware of the swelling within his breeches. He shifted position and crossed his legs at the knees. Richard was right about one thing, he told himself, he had been much too long without a woman; he had no control anymore. He now wished he had accepted the last native girl offered to him if only to clear his head and allow for more control over his own flesh.

Even as he yearned for the young woman sitting only a few feet from him, Jacques was cognizant of a fear dogging him, a fear of upsetting the delicate balance in which they now lived. He, Richard, and Marie were mutually dependent upon each other, bound together for the season, sheltered here at the frontier in a single two room cabin in the very midst of winter.

He was certain she held a basic affection for him, that was obvious, but how deep did that affection go? She was no longer a desperate child in need of his rescue. He could no longer play at being her knight in shining armor. She had grown up, grown strong, grown independent. She treated both Richard and himself generously as family, as brothers. And while he had started out thinking of her as a waifish little sister, obviously his feelings were quite different now.

Think of her as a mere peasant?!! He remembered Richard's words and mentally scoffed at them in irritation. Far from it. Without knowing exactly when, he had fallen completely in love with this enchanting young woman sitting before him in the firelight. He wanted her as his very own, not as a mere mistress but for always, his and his forever - the mistress of his heart, his lifelong companion, and the mother of his children. She was everything he desired in a woman, both wife and mistress. She was warmth and humor, intelligence, candor, and resourcefulness, sturdy courage and delicate beauty. Indeed, she was everything. So very desirable was she, and perhaps doubly so because she seemed totally unaware of her own amazing qualities.

Jacques had taken a long private look within himself and realized that after three years of being a man without a home, a family, a country, a man whose very roots had been savagely torn away from him, he was driven with a need to reestablish all that he had lost. He craved a home of his own. Something he had never had to think about in France until it was gone. It was a necessity to him to establish a real home in order to derive a sense of himself, give him solidarity, structure, and security. And he wanted this woman sitting before him to be at the very center of that home. For the first time in his life, Jacques was passionately in love, and he knew he would always love her. He wanted her to make and share that home with him. He wanted family and children but even more he wanted her love, admiration, and respect.

Yes, this was what *he* wanted but what if she did not feel the same? What did he really have to offer her or any woman for that matter? He was no longer an heir; he could not even provide his wife with the protection and largess of his family's estates. And worse, he was a man with a price on his head. He could offer no security. He had no network of influence. He had nothing but the allowance from his father and he lived day to day by his wits. He had not made his own fortune, at least not yet. What had he accomplished to earn her respect? Why would she want to take a chance on the uncertainty of his future?

How stupid, Jacques, look at the chances she has been willing to take already, one voice within him said.

Yes, but, answered another voice, *what if she really has no deep feelings for you beyond homely, sisterly affection? Why would she want to commit to a life with you when you can offer her only uncertainty? There are other men who could offer her a great deal more. And once you have declared your feelings for her, can your pride stand having to face her every day if she rejects you? It is bad enough that Richard seems to sense your feelings. Can you live with her pity? It will be months before the winter is over. You cannot possibly avoid each other within the confines of this cabin and its two rooms. How impossibly awkward it will be once you profess your love if she cannot return it.*

Yes, but how impossibly awkward is it now? He answered himself. *I cannot stop thinking of her, wanting her, or being aroused by her.*

No, Jacques, you are a man, not a schoolboy besotted and lovesick. A civilized man, not a rutting animal in heat. And a civilized man learns to control his baser desires. The debate in his head was over. Fear for his pride had won out. And he would have to deal with the rebelliousness of his less than cooperative appendage as he must.

"I think I had better retire as well," he said suddenly and left the room quickly calling a muffled "Good night" over his shoulder.

"Good night," she replied softly, offering a quick smile as she looked up. But he was already gone and her smile disappeared.

Left alone, Marie's heart returned to its normal rhythm. She forced herself to take a deep breath which came out in a sigh. She tried to refocus upon her mending. She was being so foolish, she scolded herself. She thought of the beautiful Celimene and cringed at any comparison. How could she imagine for a moment that she could take Celimene's place in Jacques' bed? After having Celimene, Jacques could not possibly find Marie attractive. Unconsciously, she moved her tongue over the tiny chip on her tooth. Suddenly she felt homely and unfeminine and very certain Jacques could never want her any more than he wanted the Indian women.

Richard was pretending to snore as he heard Jacques move quietly into the room. *What in the name of all that is holy was he doing in here?* Richard thought in disappointment. Had he not been given the perfect opportunity? The old Jacques he had once known would have been spending tonight in Marie's warm bed. What did Richard have to do, draw him a map? How blind could one man be? Was it stubbornness, or... stupidity? No, Jacques could be a bit arrogant and he might be stubborn, and he did have his prejudices but it could never be said that he was stupid. But, by God, he was blind. *If she would only look at me just once like she looks at you, my friend, I would not hesitate. I would take her in a heartbeat before she could change her mind, and I would enjoy every minute with her. There would be plenty of time later to hate myself.*

Richard heard the creak of the lacings attaching the leather to the bed frame as he knew his friend had stretched out upon his bed. Another night alone like a monk, Richard thought, sadness tingeing his incomprehension. Mentally, he shook his head.

Morning dawned bright and glistening. Marie was up at first light. She stirred the fire and added more wood. Then, pulling three shawls about her, she went to the privy first and then to the stream to fetch a fresh bucket of water. The stream was still running swiftly but the edges were iced and she had to use a stick to break through. By the time she got back to the cabin she was chilled to the bone and hung over the fire trying to warm herself.

When the men emerged from their room, she had tea ready. They also went first to the privy and when they returned, Marie had hot water for them to wash with and Jacques took the time to shave. She made biscuits at the hearth and had homemade jam from summer to serve with a grainy porridge sprinkled with walnut bits. They sat together and ate. But all three were unusually quiet. As they finished the last of the tea, Richard announced that it was time to check the traps. He and Jacques pulled on their heavy clothing, took their muskets and packets of smoked fish and bread for lunch, filled their canteens with boiling water and disappeared into the forest.

Marie spent the rest of the day alone. She had taken a turkey from the smokehouse the day before and brought it to the cabin to thaw and warm. Now she cleaned it, dressed it up and placed it into a large iron Dutch oven which she set upon her hearth. She began a barley based soup to which she added onions, turnips and carrots. She cut an acorn squash in two, scraped out the seeds to dry, filled it with dried cranberries and honey and wrapped it tightly with string. Placing it in the ashes, she left it to roast very slowly through the day. Next, she set about making bread for which she began a roaring fire in her outdoor oven.

As evening fell, the smell of fresh baked bread led the men home. They had nothing from the traps but they had caught a rabbit in a snare. It would make a stew for tomorrow. The small turkey was ready and the squash was roasted to perfection. After the all day trek outdoors, the men's sharpened appetites were robust and they dug into the meal with zest, beginning with the savory vegetable soup. Marie, however, found she had little desire to eat. She had been smelling food all day and it had no allure for her.

She was feeling restless and dissatisfied but she did not know what she wanted. She had worked all day but it had not been hard labor and she felt as though she had more energy than she knew what to do with. She dallied over a small bowl of soup, looking often at Jacques through lash veiled eyes, not really wanting to appear to look at him. He was being unusually quiet and seemed to be concentrating only on the dinner plate before him. She shoved her food about her plate, back and forth, back and forth, and was conscious of willing herself not to fidget. She caught herself shifting absentmindedly in her chair again and looked up to see Richard looking at her with a small smile but when she looked directly at him, he turned his attention to his plate.

"Is there a moon tonight?" she asked suddenly, her voice sounding unusually loud as she broke the quiet.

"If it is not clouded over, there will be a moon," replied Richard.

Marie nodded.

"You did not eat much," Richard observed. Jacques looked up.

"I am not very hungry," she replied with a shrug.

"The supper is excellent," Jacques said quickly. "The squash... very tasty."

"Thank you," Marie responded absently.

"Are you feeling unwell?" Jacques asked after a moment with a frown of concern.

"No... I just... have no appetite."

He continued to look at her with an expression of puzzlement.

"I am used to doing things," she said defensively, uncomfortable under his scrutiny. "All winter there were still tasks to be done at the Emporium. I have not really done anything all day," she went on, avoiding eye contact. "I am sorry. I think I just need to get out of this cabin for a while."

"But it is night," he responded in surprise.

"Yes, I know," she nodded, "but I want some fresh air. I am going to take a short walk."

"A walk?! It is freezing out there," he exclaimed.

"It is not so bad. The wind has been blowing from the south; it has actually warmed a bit."

"But you could get sick," he argued, and looked at Richard with an expression that seemed to say *help me stop her.*

"Take my coat, Marie," Richard offered. "You will need more than just your shawls if you mean to walk any distance beyond what it takes to get to the privy."

"Thank you. Are you certain you will not need it?"

"I plan on staying right here. I have done all my walking for the day," he grinned.

"There might be wolves," Jacques interjected.

"I will not go far and I have never seen any sign of wolves around the cabin," Marie replied, undeterred as she went over to the peg and removed Richard's large fur lined coat. She slid her petite figure into it. She looked like a child playing in her father's clothing. The coat hung all the way to the ground, the sleeves extended far beyond her finger tips. She had no need for gloves.

"I will not be gone long," she said softly. "Could you close the door behind me, please?" she asked lifting her sleeved hands as an explanation. Jacques stood immediately, fighting the urge to grab her and tie her up so she could not leave. "Do not be concerned about clearing the table," she added stepping out into the evening. "I will do it when I return. It will be something to do."

Jacques moved to close the door but watched her through the narrowing crack. "What in God's name is this all about?!" he asked Richard with a frown.

"It sounds to me like a touch of... what do they say... cabin fever? She has been cooped up day after day. We go out hunting, Marie goes nowhere. We check the traps, Marie goes only to the stream and the privy. She needs to get out," Richard reasoned.

"At night?"

Richard shrugged.

"Not one bit do I like the idea of her being out there alone in the dark, I tell you! I like it not at all! She could fall or... something could attack her."

"You could always go with her," Richard suggested nonchalantly.

The ground was hard but clear of snow. It had been a while since they had had any snow, Marie thought as she walked along by the light of the rising moon. She sucked in the cold air. It felt stimulating after the warmth of the cabin and it was not uncomfortably cold. The air was still. The night was quiet. She could walk like this for hours, she thought, if only there was someplace to walk. But there was only the little switchback pathway down to the river. She craved a long walk. Like the walks she and Jacques had taken along the streets of New York Towne. Soon it would be Christmas, she thought and was reminded of the last Christmas. A sad smile tugged at her lips. It was a happy yet melancholy memory. It had been another opportunity to wear a pretty dress. She had asked Mistress Wingate to keep her two fine dresses until... until when? When would she ever have cause to wear such dresses again?

Marie's mood darkened as she recalled Elizabeth's foolish chatter of suitors. If she only knew how wrong she had been. Jacques a suitor? "Hah!" she snorted aloud. He did not even consider her good enough to be his mistress at the frontier.

Marie had never anticipated that living with Jacques while he took no notice of her would be so difficult. It had been different before she knew he was actually craving a woman. It hurt to think that she was not good enough to be his mistress even out here in the wilds. It hurt more than she thought possible. Her heart ached with a fullness of affection that longed to be let out. Suddenly, Marie's eyes burned hot and stung with tears and she thought her heart would burst. Her vision blurred and she could not get a hand out to wipe her eyes. She stumbled, regained her balance and stopped before she could stumble again. She stood in the moonlight struggling with the overlong sleeves, finally bunching the length until she could free her fingers and wipe her eyes as her tears flowed freely.

Standing in the quiet of the winter night, Marie looked up at the canopy of stars. These were the same stars that hung over France, she thought, but how different her life was now, here in the New World. She must stop dwelling on her feelings, she told herself. *Stop it! Stop it! Stop it!* Had she not always known he was too far above her to give her notice? *He is like the stars, so beautiful but impossibly out of reach. Very well, Marie, you know that!* She had always known that. How could she have forgotten? It was this new land. There was something about this land that made you forget your place, forget the past, and believe in all your dreams.

Marie turned from the river's edge and marched doggedly back up the hill. She walked briskly about the small clearing which included her garden plot, and marched back down to the river again. But there were all kinds of dreams, she told herself. Some of them were possible. Her store, that was possible. That was a dream that could come true. She must concentrate on what she could accomplish. Learn to tell the difference between dreams that were possible and the dreams that were only fantasy.

The exercise was having a positive effect and when she reached the top of the hill the third time she was feeling slightly better, more relaxed within her skin, rather like a kettle that had just released its steam. She would take one more turn, she thought, or maybe two, then she would go in before Jacques came out scolding her like she was a child. That was all she was to him, a child. He did care about her in his own way... as a child. She sighed. Perhaps, when she went back in, she would read.

Marie never saw Jacques' figure in the shadows watching over her all the while. But when she finally went back indoors, he returned as if just coming back from the privy.

Chapter 21

"It is time to check the far traps again," announced Richard early one morning as he packed together some gear. "I will be perhaps two weeks," he shrugged, "maybe more. So do not worry."

Jacques nodded as he drank a second cup of strong hot tea.

"Two weeks?!" Marie exclaimed and caught herself, remembering what Richard had said about having a squaw. "Ohhh... well, ahhh... be sure you … ahhh, find good shelter and do not get too cold. And... Godspeed," she added a little awkwardly.

Richard smiled at her. "You might check the near traps," he suggested to Jacques with a wink and trudged out the door in the direction of the Indian trail.

The sun was bright and water dripped slowly from the edges of the roof making various plopping sounds as Marie stood in the doorway and waved. The sun was warm and it felt pleasant on her face but the air was frigid. At last she shut the door and for a few moments the cabin seemed to be swallowed in darkness.

Jacques watched her, at first silhouetted in the bright doorway and then standing still, blinking and waiting for her eyes to adjust to the darkness of the cabin again. These were stolen moments when he could look at her without her knowing, without Richard seeing, without giving himself away. He saw her look at him and smile. He smiled quickly and grabbed up his cup, draining the last of his tea in one gulp.

"Would you like more?" Marie asked hospitably.

"No... no, *merci*." Jacques shifted on his chair. "I suppose I had better check the nearer traps as Richard suggested. And I think we could use some fresh meat, *n'est-ce pas*? Perhaps I will have good fortune." Jacques stood and began putting on his outer wraps. "I will see what I can find, but know that I will return before nightfall. Will you be all right?" He filled his canteen with hot water, took down his musket and slung both over his shoulder.

"Of course. I will pack you some lunch," Marie volunteered and hastily put together a pouch of seasoned dried meat and bread which she handed to the young man.

"*Merci*," he replied again quickly and took the packet from her, gingerly avoiding any direct contact.

"Be careful, Jacques," she said softly. She moved her hand in a gesture as though she meant to press his arm but she stopped herself short. "It is going to be a pretty day," she added cheerfully, pulling her hand back. "Take care."

"*Oui*." He looked at her full lips and did not want to leave.

"Keep safe."

"I will see you before nightfall," he repeated with a nod before putting on his broad hat and exiting the little cabin.

Marie watched him trudge off in a different direction from that which Richard had taken, the sound of wet snow compressing beneath his booted feet. When he was no longer in sight, she turned and closed the cabin door again. She was alone and suddenly she felt like taking a long, quiet, hot bath.

Marie decided to take advantage of the opportunity for privacy and took out her large tub. After heating plenty of water, she stripped off her clothing and used the scented, soft soap she had brought from the Wingate's store to wash her hair over the tub. She rinsed it thoroughly until she heard it squeak, then pinned it up off her neck and shoulders and finally got into the tub herself.

It was Celimene who had taught her to appreciate regular bathing and, although it was an unusual custom for the times, Marie had found a way to bathe regularly ever since. This past summer, just walking into the river had been very convenient, but since the colder weather, the men had been very considerate in giving her privacy whenever she wished. They had been most obliging although she did not like to impose on their cooperative spirit too often. Usually, they left the cabin and stayed outdoors until she signaled she was finished. Once when they were having heavy rains, she could not bring herself to ask that they go outdoors. Still she had just ended her monthly flow and was desperate to bathe. So, she had waited until they were ready to retire and simply requested that they stay in their room.

Marie sighed deeply as she relaxed into the warm enveloping water. Celimene had been very right; having a warm bath by a warm fire was extremely soothing. Very soothing. And abruptly she realized that she did, indeed, feel a need to be soothed.

These were the shortest days of the year and night came very quickly once the sun fell behind the trees. Marie tried not to worry as lavender shadows stretched out longer and longer upon the frozen ground. The windows had been covered over with oiled skins for the season and so she found herself stepping outdoors frequently to peer out into the mounting gloom. The shadows of the landscape had turned deep purple, the sun had set, and the wind had turned frigid. She shut the door again and hurried to shutter the windows against the cold and light the lamps. When she finished she went to the door again and hung one lamp on a tree limb. It was almost completely dark as she peered beyond the light spilling from the cabin door and the lantern.

She saw him emerging from out of the forest beyond her garden space like a dark shadow that quickly took on substance. She felt the knot of tension in her stomach relax. He was struggling under an awkward load which she could not detail but as she stepped farther out toward him she realized he was carrying what appeared to be a deer or perhaps a small elk over his back.

"Jacques!" she called and waved. He looked up only briefly, staggering but waving back.

Jacques had spotted the animal sometime after lunch and had taken aim and killed it before it had occurred to him to question how he was going to transport it home alone. It was a young doe, but fully grown. He had beheaded and gutted the animal before attempting to lift it. He had even removed the forelegs. Even thus reduced in weight it had been a very arduous task to carry it homeward. He was used to doing these things with Richard. Jacques had needed to sling it over his shoulders. The weight was easily the equivalent of carrying a person and the walk home had taken much longer than he had anticipated. He had left the pelts the traps had yielded half way back hanging from a tree. He could retrieve them at another time.

Jacques had been tempted after several miles to simply cut the doe in half and leave half for the animals but having carried it that far he had stubbornly refused to give it up. It wasn't as if it was life or death, it was just a straining challenge.

He was stiff, aching, and exhausted but it was a rewarding exhaustion. He was also foul from hours of contact with the raw carcass. He dropped his load to the ground beneath a high limbed tree which they used for the purpose.

"I will skin it tomorrow," he called to Marie standing in the warm light spilling from the open cabin doorway. "For tonight, it will be enough to hang it. It should be safe."

She nodded her head in agreement. "Supper is ready for you, Jacques, but you will want to clean up first," she suggested. "I have hot water ready."

"Good, I will be in directly," he nodded and went about his task.

It took another ten minutes or so before he had secured the carcass up off the ground and out of the reach of most scavengers. He made his way into the cabin feeling a tremendous sense of relief at being home at last. His legs grumbled from the extra weight they had carried over the miles and he yearned to just sit down.

It was very pleasant in the cabin, like walking into a warm pocket filled with delicious smells. The main room was brightly lit with a multitude of fat lamps, several lanterns, and two hand dipped tapers on the table which was all added to by the brightly crackling fire. Jacques removed his coat and scarf, noticing the stains of blood and raw animal fat on them with distaste.

"I will wash them for you," Marie offered softly and he looked over at her in the light for the first time. She had on a clean apron and there was a fresh glow to her skin. Her masses of hair hung in shiny, thick, loose curls about her shoulders and down her back. She had bathed, he thought, and suddenly he felt extremely dirty, trying to remember the last time he had plunged into the icy river below. Not since fall and he had only bowl bathed since. Taking the kettle from the fire he poured out some hot water into the large bowl and quickly washed his face and hands.

"If you do not mind," he said as he finished his ablutions, "I would very much like to borrow your tub tonight. The river is a little too cold, I fear and," he joked, "the deer was a little too big and bloody to avoid."

"Of course," she nodded agreeably and put more wood on the fire before filling the large water pot to heat.

They sat down to eat. Jacques tried to appear relaxed as he gave her gallant compliments on the food but he was awkwardly embarrassed by his soiled appearance. He felt filthy beyond words. Marie thought she understood his discomfort and tried to help assuage it. She could not help but smile, however. It was the first time she could remember ever seeing the sophisticated young nobleman so ill at ease. He usually conveyed a powerful sense of confidence and self-assured control, but now he appeared almost awkwardly shy. When she heard the water begin to boil, she got up and dumped it into the tub in order to begin the next pot heating.

"Wait...!" Jacques cried out as the water hit the tub bottom. He halted. It was already too late to stop her.

"What is it?" she looked over at him in mild surprise.

"Well, I did not think you were going to put the water in so quickly. I must move the tub into the other room before..."

"Oh, no, Jacques," she frown in disagreement. "You need to stay by the fire tonight. Now that the sun is down, it is freezing outside. Your room is much too cold without a hearth."

She was right of course, he silently cursed. He should have listened and taken the time to let her put in the blasted hearth.

"Besides" she went on with only the vaguest touch of mischief in her voice, "you will need someone to scrub your back, monsieur." Marie could not believe her eyes when she saw the worldly young aristocrat turn red in the face and stiffen. "Of course, if you would prefer me not to scrub your back," she added quickly and more formally, wondering if somehow she had offended him, "I will be happy to do you the same favor you have done me and stay in your bedroom until you are through." Now, he seemed to almost strangle on his food and had only just started to reply when she added thoughtfully, "Of course, you are going to need some help rinsing the soap from your hair if you want to get the filth out. And there is no one else to help, I am afraid."

His hand flew involuntarily to his head and he grimaced at the greasy, crusted and caked residue of animal blood and fat he felt there. "I... ahh..." he seemed to be undecided and she concluded that he did not find her offer of assistance completely intolerable. And why should he, she thought somewhat piqued? He had no manservant here and this was just a little more difficult than jumping into the river. And had not Richard said that the Indian women had bathed them once. If an Indian woman had bathed him, he certainly could tolerate her doing the same. She set about gathering together soap and towels with an attitude that said the matter was quite settled.

Jacques got up swiftly, poured himself a cup of rum and downed it in one breath. The warmth of it curled through his belly but it did not make him any more comfortable. He was about to begin unlacing his shirt with great reluctance when Marie spoke again. "I think perhaps you should put your coat back on and bring another two buckets from the creek before we start."

"Oh," he jerked his hands from his shirt. "Yes, of course."

"But hurry," she advised almost primly, "before this water begins to get cold."

Jacques threw on his coat, grabbed both large water buckets and marched out into the night air to the stream running near the cabin. The full moon was up and it was as easy to see his way to the creek as it might have been on an overcast day. After filling both buckets, he took a deep breath of the frigid night air as though steeling himself before beginning his return into the snug warmth of the cabin and the presence of Marie. The air was so cold and dry it made his nostrils pinch together and chilled the rest of him as well. Suddenly, he undid the flap of his breeches, exposing himself to the biting cold, and emptied his bladder, making a stream beside a tree. A faint vapor cloud rose from his urine. He refastened his breeches. He was thoroughly chilled now and quite shrunken he thought with some satisfaction.

He could not imagine what she must be thinking of him. Women, old and young, had seen him naked in the course of service at the chateau and it had caused him no more thought than breathing. He had never felt the need to dive for cover like a maiden just because a scullery maid came in to scrub out the hearth. And here at twenty-three, he was blushing like a virgin at the thought of her seeing him. But Marie was not the scullery maid, he told himself. She was someone very special for whom he had feelings and he feared his body would betray those feelings. No, to be more precise, he feared his body would betray only the lustful portion of those feelings. His breath caught in his chest and a small lightning bolt of panic raced through his insides. The true depth of his feelings scared him. This woman and what she thought of him had become the most important thing in his life.

Marie added cold water to the boiling hot water already in the tub, then, she poured a second pot of steaming water. She refilled the pots over the fire with the water Jacques had brought in while he removed his boots, stockings and was very slowly removing his shirt. The cold from moments ago had not helped at all he thought miserably holding his shirt in his hands in front of him. Marie laid out her soaps, several towels and turning back to him was arrested by the sight of him standing stock still, bare-chested, shirt bunched in his hands, and staring at her. She felt the blood creep up her cheeks and she turned suddenly, keeping her back to him, her eyes averted, busying herself with nothing.

"Go ahead and get in," she said quickly. She could hear the scuffling as she imagined Jacques removing his breeches. His clothes were very dirty, she thought to herself, forcing her mind to concentrate on something practical. She must do a wash tomorrow even if she had to hang the clothing inside to dry. She heard the distinct *plunk* that occurs when something enters water. He was getting into the tub and she waited patiently for him to say something... anything. At last she heard him clear his throat.

"If you would be so kind as to assist me, now," he finally said with the slightest hint of imperialism in his oddly gruff voice. "I would be grateful."

"Of course," she replied graciously turning quickly toward him. "Is the water a good temperature?" He was squeezed into the tub, his knees thrust up at an awkward angle and a large towel was draped over his lap and the tub. "Is it too hot? Too cold?"

"No-no, it is just right," he replied rather briskly.

"Good." It was not as if she had never seen Jacques without his shirt before, but she did so like looking at him. The skin of his back and arms was a smooth, golden hue, still tanned and stretched tautly over his muscles and bones. The play of sinews just beneath the surface when he made a movement was mesmerizing. She already knew his hard body tapered to a narrow waist and hip without an ounce of excess fat but the sight of the ivory coloring beneath the water's surface made her heart thud in her own ear. Just looking at him made her slightly light headed but now to touch him?

She picked up her low stool and brought it up behind him. Taking a seat she willed her trembling hands to act naturally and commenced to give his hair a thorough cleansing. When she was quite sure she had scrubbed out all the caked blood and animal grease she went on with the slipperiness of the soap to his neck and across his shoulders. She shrank from her own boldness and picked up the washing cloth to continue scrubbing down his back. Plunging the cloth down beside him into the water and beneath the covering towel, she deftly grabbed it back trying not to think, not to feel.

Caressing him without seeming to do so, she was aware of his varied textures as her slender fingers spread out around the rag. The soft bristle of his whiskers, the hard skull bone behind his ears. The skin of his shoulders was smooth and firm while the golden mass of small tight curls adorning his chest was crisp, glistening in a V of tiny bubbles as her sudsy hands and cloth ran over them in a slow thorough manner. The small of his back was softer, while his backbone was sharply depressed, making a valley through the defined muscles of his back.

She should not feel this way, she told herself. She should not touch him with such enjoyment. She had no right. She remembered the sight of him carrying the heavy carcass and on impulse she put aside the washcloth and began to massage his shoulders.

"This... is very tight," she said quietly, working at the tense muscles beneath his warm skin. "Does this feel good?" she asked hesitantly.

Was she joking? It felt like heaven. "Very good," he said and then gave a sudden involuntary gasp. She had found a particularly sore spot where the muscle was knotted and hard.

"I am sorry. Did I hurt you?" she stopped quickly, withdrawing her hands.

"No, no, please do not stop!" he responded just as quickly and she continued massaging. "It is only that I did not realize how sore I am... that feels... quite... wonderful..."

"How about here?"

"Ohhhhh, yes."

"And here?"

"Yes, there as well," he sighed deeply letting out a long groan of contentment. She continued for several minutes feeling his flesh become more and more pliant, the muscles softening, easing, and relaxing.

"And where did you learn this?" he asked at last in curiosity.

"I was reading in a book... there are some cultures which believe such massage is the secret to good health."

"Really?"

She nodded but he could not see her. When she realized this she added, "Yes." He said nothing after that and she continued to knead the muscles of his neck and between his shoulder blades, his shoulders, working her way gradually down his spine past the waterline. He leaned in giving her unspoken permission and she observed the whiteness of his compact buttocks glowing up from beneath the water. "The muscles feel much better now," she said after a time. "They are looser, not so like a board. There," she announced as she finished. "I will rinse you now. The water should be warm enough." She got up and went to the fire. Testing the water in the first pot with her elbow, she brought it up before him and paused.

"What is it?" he asked seeing her hesitate.

"Nothing... only... well, your towel. It is going to get very wet when I pour this over your head."

"Do you have another?"

"Of course."

"Then it does not matter," he stated rather curtly. Marie carefully turned the bucket over his head while he held his breath and closed his eyes, finally sputtering like a child with his darken hair sleekly clinging over his face. She laughed then and dropping to her knees in front of him with a fresh towel, she began to towel his hair off his face and lightly pat his countenance dry. When he opened his eyes, her breasts were only inches from his face as she reached out in her task, trying to dry his hair. He grabbed her hands to still them and pushed her away. She was startled, almost lost her balance and did lose her smile. His expression was tight-lipped.

"I am capable of drying myself, thank you," he said sternly.

"Of course. I am sorry," she said drawing back. She did not understand what she had done to make him angry but he was frowning fiercely as she went for the next bucket. Setting the full bucket of warm water down within his reach, she wiped her hands quickly on her apron. "Y..you may want to use that to rinse yourself after you finish washing," she said quickly, her eyes downcast in humiliation. She could not look at him. She turned and went back to her place by the table, gathering the dishes and keeping herself turned away.

Jacques picked up the soap and brush and began to scrub himself furiously. He was fully aroused and he was hating himself. He had had to push her away or in one more second he would have been on top of her, wash tub and all. Did she not know that? How could she possibly not realize?"

Marie could hear the beating of her own heart over the splashing of water and the sounds of a soapy brush being scrubbed over flesh. He could not have made her feel more ugly and undesirable if he had purposefully meant to. She had only been trying to help him, to be of honest service. Were they not friends? Yet, he was repulsed by her nearness. It hurt her to the core. Richard had said Jacques needed a woman. *A man has needs.* Was she so very unattractive that even with no other woman around, he could not bring himself to accept her? In an effort to distract herself from the conclusions she was all too quick to make, she paid minutely detailed attention to the supper dishes, wiping them very slowly and putting them carefully up on the shelf. At last the scrubbing stopped and she hastily flicked a tear from her cheek. She could not let him see her crying. She would not let him see her cry. He would ask why she was crying and what could she say in reply? *Because you do not want me?*

She heard him stand, water falling into the tub as he rinsed himself. There were more splashes. Then, the sound of his foot coming out of the water. The second foot. Silence. Finally, she heard his voice.

"Merci."

She turned after a moment and the room was empty. He had gone into his room to dress. She flicked at another tear while condemning herself. What had she done? What? She had done something stupid again, she told herself, but she did not understand what. She took a deep breath and sought activity as a means of controlling her emotions. She began to tidy up. In a flurry of movements, she gathered up his dirty clothes, all but his coat, and impulsively threw them into the warm bath water and began to scrub. It would do for an initial cleansing. She put the clothing in one large bucket filled with soapy water to soak overnight and began emptying the rest of the bath water outdoors, taking a blast of cold air each time she stepped outside the snug cabin, the wind ripping through her shawls. When Jacques reappeared in fresh clothing, she was shivering violently and it took little for him to snatch the bucket from her hand.

"Go sit by the fire!" he commanded. *"Mon Dieu!* Warm yourself. You do not have to clean up after me."

"I know," she shrank away slightly. *But it gave me something useful to do,* she wanted to say but did not. Jacques slipped on his coat and, oblivious to the freezing cold against his damp hair and skin, continued to empty the tub. Finally, he carried the tub outside and finished draining it.

"You are not my servant," he said as he came back inside grumbling. "I can dispose of my own dirty water." He punctuated his words by shoving the door shut tightly with a bang.

"But you are still wet. You might catch cold," she offered defensively.

"So? You would rather catch cold?" he almost growled in accusation as he removed his stained coat. "That is all I need... to have you take sick. I am no good at tending a sick-ling."

She jerked up at that and turned to glare at him. "Well, then I will make certain that if I ever do get ill, I will quickly kill myself so as not to put you to any inconvenience, your Majesty!" The sharpness and sarcasm in her tone made him turn around full to look at her in startled surprise and it was her undoing. She felt the tears spring to her eyes, too hot and too fast to be held back. She felt her face crumple as she spun away. "Nothing I do is right. Nothing. Why? What have I done? The bath should have relaxed you. You should be pleased." She grabbed at her apron and brought it to her face to hide behind as she broke down into full sobs.

Jacques had tried his best to control the effect her presence had upon him but he could not. Richard was gone and she was here and the reality was he could not continue to exist an arm's length away from her for another day without telling her how he really felt. It was just not possible. And now he had made her cry.

Suddenly Jacques' arms were around her, holding her to him as he was kissing her, murmuring and brushing the salty tears from her face, asking her to forgive him and begging her to stop crying. Marie was stunned into silence and stopped crying instantly. She did not resist as she became aware of his body touching hers. Her heart was beating a hard tattoo against her ribs and before she knew it his mouth had covered hers. She could hear her blood pounding in her ears. His lips were caressing hers, tender yet firm, gentle and yet with increasing demand. This was not a brother's kiss he gave her. Was this not exactly what she had been wanting? Reacting to the feel of his tongue as it demanded entry to her mouth, she opened for him until he was taking her breath away quite literally. Her nose was stopped up from crying and she had to pull away to gasp for air.

"Wait!" she cried, pushing him away with a sharp inhalation through her mouth. "Please. A moment. I cannot breathe." She plucked off her apron and using it as a handkerchief, she blew her nose fiercely, wiped it thoroughly and let the soiled garment fall to the chair.

"Jacques," she said softly, looking at him. It was a mixture of surprised question, statement, and summons. Their eyes met in that moment and she saw something in his look that caused an involuntary response deep within her, her eyes opened wider, her breath caught in her throat, her pulse had increased, and she felt a pleasant sensation stirring in her very depths. It frightened her and she broke the gaze. "I...I do not understand..." she uttered in genuine confusion.

In restraint he reached out and brushed a lock of shiny hair from her eye. "Oh, ma chérie, is it so hard to understand? This is not the way I wanted to... I could curse myself for making you cry... forgive me, please, forgive me." His voice was husky as he moved into her again, enfolding her in his arms, drawing her tightly to him. "I do not wish to make you cry... ever again. Never. I am a fool. You are perfect, ma belle. Perfect... do you hear? You did nothing, nothing wrong. But you are irresistible." And he was kissing her again.

This time Marie could breathe through her nose but his kiss was still taking her breath away. His words did not make sense to her confused mind but her body found no difficulty in understanding. Molding into his embrace, melting against him and feeling his hard male flesh between them; now she understood and began to kiss him back. It was a long kiss that started a liquid fire creeping through her body. She opened her mouth to him and instinctively met his tongue with hers, timidly at first and then emboldened. The fire coursed through her veins bringing on an aching need of her own like nothing she had ever felt before. Anything, she would do anything to satisfy this need, this hunger, this longing to be his. It was all she wanted, all she desired, to be his woman, to feel his touch, to satisfy his need. To hold him, that was her need, and to be held and caressed. To be made love to if not to be loved.

When their lips finally parted, Jacques continued holding Marie closely, his breathing soft in her ear causing the goose-flesh to rise on her. "I have been such a coward," he was murmuring and that made no sense to her at all. She thought Jacques one of the bravest men she knew. She was also vaguely aware that her breathing was ragged. Her hands were under his shirt caressing the heat of his chest. She could feel his heart beating beneath her finger tips. His breath in her ear and his lips on her earlobe were making her dizzy. He moved to her neck just below her ear and she went weak.

"It was the only thing you could have done… " she sighed dimly.

"No, I should have spoken long before…"

"She should have gone with you… you must forgive me if I am glad she did not… but you will have to teach me how to please you…" Marie's sexual experiences had taught her nothing about making love her muddled brain concluded as she thought of the skilled Celimene. "I have developed no skills in lovemaking…"

Jacques had moved down her throat, his tongue circling the small dip there, then went to the valley between her breasts; the scent of her skin was intoxicating. He felt her shaking in his arms, quivering like a new born colt trying to stand for the first time. His mind was befuddled at the sensations of her surrender but suddenly her words registered.

"What are you talking about?" he looked at her in puzzlement.

"Fleeing France," she gasped, "wh..what are you talking about?"

"You… me… us… I should have spoken to you long ago…"

"Oh… of course, I understand," she looked up into his face, the fine structure of his bones enhanced in the firelight. Tracing the outline of his mouth under her fingertips and stroking his soft golden mustache, she added humbly, "I am yours for however long you want, Jacques. I will be yours," she whispered, "I will gladly be your woman… Richard explained."

"Richard?! What does Richard have to do with this?" he asked gripping her arms suddenly with a pressure that held her fast.

"Nothing… only that I understand… you have needs… all men have needs he says."

"Is that all you think this is?" he asked stepping back just a little as though a trifle offended. *But of course she does, you imbecile, what else is she suppose to think with your enormous lack of clarity?*

"Marie," his voice went husky, "please stay right here. I will return in a moment." As he retreated into the room he shared with Richard, she sank into her chair by the fire, quietly panting while her head swam with confusion.

By the light of the candle he had left burning on a side shelf, he sought the package under his bed. Bringing it out, he took it with him. Walking over to where Marie sat, Jacques suddenly went down on one knee and presented the bundle to her. "I meant this to be your Christmas present," he said quietly, his voice soft and silken, a model of constraint. "It is close enough to Christmas and I want you to have it now."

Marie looked at him. He did not look angry or puzzled but eager. She was so drawn to him. She wanted to reach out and touch him again, draw him to her for another long and passionate kiss. Instead, she accepted the packet with genuine surprise. Undoing the lashing and pulling apart the thick paper wrapping, she rolled out a large, soft thick fur cloak.

"Ohhh..." a gasp of complete astonishment escaped her.

"I had it made in Boston," he explained, the firelight dancing in his eyes, "these are the very finest of the winter pelts we took in trade from the last year up the Hudson. I shipped them to a well known furrier. They are perfectly matched, you see? You will never need to shiver in the winter cold again," he added, hoping she was pleased.

"Oh, Jacques," she sighed, running her fingers over the silky fineness of the thick, light gray fur, "It is... too beautiful... I do not know what to say..." she brought the fur to her cheek, the fine loft was high and felt airy, and yet, there was an abundance of warmth to it. She stood up and away from the fire, carefully letting the garment fall to its full length. He stood as well, watching her slip it on and rush to her new wall mirror. It draped about her regally.

"It is magnificent! No queen has had a cloak more lovely," she said softly, her voice was genuine but he could hear the confusion in it. "I do not know what to... *Thank you* is not enough for such a handsome gift, Jacques. But you did not have to give me anything..." She walked back toward him ready to explain that he did not have to give her gifts to win her. He stopped her with a gesture, then took her hand and led her to sit down again. He dropped again to one knee before her, still holding her hand.

Her eyes were riveted to his, and she trembled in response to an overwhelming sense of his masculinity.

"Marie... I want you to hear me out," he began softly. "My beliefs of faith have brought me to this new world of new beginnings. And I have no desire to re-engage in the cavalier habits of my old life. I do not want a mistress. I can hardly deny that my body burns for you, but I also desire foundation and connection. I am tired of being a mere feather in the wind, a loose pebble pushed and shoved and pulled on the shores of time. I need the roots that a family can give; I need the stability of a home that a wife can make."

A small gasp escaped her. He was saying he didn't want her, he wanted a wife but what was the meaning of their kisses only minutes ago? Marie went still. Did he feel sorry for her? Was she so pathetic in her need for affection that he thought to appease her with a gift? She did not know what to say. She could not think. He leaned over and she found herself being kissed again, very gently, and she could not control the trembling within her.

Beneath the warmth of the fur, Jacques knew it could not be the temperature that made Marie tremble so and he realized he was trembling just as profusely. The silken waves of his unrestrained hair floating about him as they dried and he looked at once both masterful and totally vulnerable, his eyes, glittering with emotion, searched hers with such feeling it took her breath away.

"This is all I have to offer to you, Marie." His voice had grown very husky with emotion. "It is a harsh life, I know, and fraught with perils and uncertainty.

But I do hope to give you better some day. For now, I am only what you see, just a man. No longer an heir. No longer an aristocrat. I have no estate; there is no grand house to bring you to, no fine furniture, no fancy parties nor servants bowing to our whims..."

"Why do you talk of these things? I care nothing for such things," she replied vehemently, her hands reaching up to stroke the sides of his face, her fingers memorizing the sculpted bone beneath the warm clean skin of his cheeks. "None of that matters to me, Jacques, nothing but you!"

"Oh, Marie, my Marie," his face flushed in happiness at her words as he gathered her up to him again. "You are, indeed, the very woman for me. We will build a life here... together. And we have something the richest noble at Louis' Court, nay, something even Louis himself does not have..." Her eyes went wide trying to concentrate and understand his meaning but the fullness within her heart was distracting her. "We have the freedom to dream of a future with endless possibilities." She stayed in his embrace, hanging on every word that came from his lips. She had become so weak she would have fallen if he had not been holding her securely locked in his arms. "Will you share this life with me," he continued softly, earnestly, his eyes holding her as surely as his arms, "as my wife? Will you have my children, my sons and heirs... and share the possibilities of this future with me? Will you promise to stay by my side, for better or for worse? Join with me as one flesh? Husband and wife together forever? And together, we can pass on to our progeny what we create in this new world."

"Your *wife*...?" she gasped, staggered at the thought, feeling her heart would burst from her chest. She had not dared to think of such a thing. Marriage? He was offering her marriage. It was stunning. She had only dared to think she could be his mistress. Surely he did not mean a real wife but he was saying... *forever.*

In a sudden flash of realization an unknown vista opened to Marie. Marriage! A legitimate family of her very own. The solemn promise of a lifetime together with Jacques, forever, until death parted them. "Your wife," she repeated as though finally comprehending.

Jacques saw the shadows of disbelief and shock play upon her face. "I want you by my side, Marie... always. I can give you only my heart and my name, but I would offer you no less and our children will be legitimate," he said, looking at her with feverish intensity. He was more serious than she had ever seen him before, even during their escape from France, and it fed the passionate response within her.

"Oh, Jacques... Jacques, my wonderful, gallant sir," she cried out softly, clinging to him. "I have loved you with all of my heart for as long as I can remember. Please tell me I am not dreaming. If I awake to discover this to be but a dream, I will surely die. Tell me this is real," she murmured.

He pulled back to look into her face, his expression was without the hint of a jest. "It is not a dream, *ma amoure.* This is forever." He let go of her and went to retrieve the small Bible he had brought with him from France. He held it out and she put her hand upon it while he placed his other hand over hers.

"I take thee, Marie, in the sight of Almighty God, to be my wife, to protect you with my body and life, to provide and care for you, to cherish you always, to be faithful to you and forsake all others, for better or worse, in sickness and in health, 'til death parts us from this world." His words hung soberly in the air of the small cabin. "And now, Marie, do you accept me as your husband with God as our witness?"

"Oh, yes, yes, Jacques," she said simply and without hesitation. "I take thee to be my husband with all my heart and soul, forever, forsaking all others, with God Almighty as my witness."

At that moment, he took the signet ring his father had given him and slipped it onto Marie's finger. "Marie," he whispered hoarsely, "my dearest, my darling wife." He cupped her face in his hands and kissed her sweetly, chastely, and with tenderness itself he tugged at her full, flushed lips. He released her and set down the little Bible. Stepping back he gently removed the fur from her shoulders. "I do not think you will need this for a while," he murmured softly. "*I* wish to warm you now." With care he laid the cloak across the chair, then doffed his own fresh shirt to lay with it.

Coming up from behind, he began to plant kisses along her slender young neck, his hands working deftly at removing her garments piece by piece, leaving them puddled on the bearskin beneath their feet. Kissing and caressing as he progressed, watching her smooth, flawless skin pucker into goose-flesh, she soon stood before him wearing only her thin shift.

"I want to look upon you," he breathed and pulled the muslin shift off over her head. Her arms lifted of their own accord, not resisting him but feeling strangely paralyzed like the rest of her. "*Mon Dieu...* you are so... very... lovely," he said softly.

With appreciation he took in everything. From the curving line of her delicate shoulders all the way down to her tiny ankles and the bony definition of her small feet. His attention was brought back up to the juncture at the top of her legs, a patch of shiny brown curls with its promise of ecstasy buried within.

"And I want to look upon you," she said at length, reaching out to untie the lacing of his breeches which held in the proud flesh straining to be free. She tugged the fabric down his legs along with the stockings he wore; her gaze was riveted upon him. In her eyes, everything about him was glorious. She was on the brink of touching him when he suddenly dropped to his knees and began planting kisses on the curls between her legs. She might have lost her balance but that his hands held her buttocks, trapping her there and keeping her upright.

She felt his lips and tongue on the insides of her thighs, up her belly, slowly trailing, his breath warm and moist upon her skin. Somehow they floated onto the bed and she gave herself over to the waves of mindless pleasure being wrung from her by his mouth and hands.

She was vaguely aware of the noises she was making, gasping, panting, moaning slightly until he released her breasts and came back up to look at her, his gray eyes now dark and heavy lidded. Instinctively, she felt a need growing within but for *what* she still did not understand. "Tell me what to do," she whispered. His hand swept down between her legs as he reclaimed her mouth. She opened for him and felt his fingers explore her gently. He groaned.

"*Dieu,* you are so wet!" he exclaimed hoarsely. "Forgive me, this first time may be quick... I fear I will not be able to hold back for long."

Marie's mind flashed back to Bouchet's tavern and she thought how often she had prayed it would be quick, a quick end to the hurt and humiliation. But this was different, she was telling herself, she loved Jacques. She loved him with all her heart and soul. She wanted him to take her; she would not mind the hurt. For him she would do anything and he made her feel so special. She tensed slightly as she felt him enter her in a swift smooth movement that was both surprising and pleasant. He paused, his flesh filling her so completely but without any pain. It was a sensation of utter rightness. Then, he began moving slowly and every nerve in her body was tingling. She thought she would explode with the pleasure of it. But he had been correct, it was over too quickly. She felt him thrust hard as a primal groan tore from his throat. She did not want him to stop but she felt his muscles tense and bunch and it was over. She recognized well when it was over. At the tavern she used to pray it would be over. She now knew she must compose herself for she did not want to show her sudden disappointment.

Jacques collapsed beside Marie alternately cursing and blessing the moment, vowing to give her double the pleasure next time, berating his own lack of self-control, and assuaging his guilt with logic. After three years of abstinence and several months of foreplay, a man would have to chop off his vitals to keep from instantly succumbing the first time he encountered what he so desired. He accepted this as his mind cleared and his breathing grew more steady.

Jacques drew up on one elbow to look at Marie. She lay quiet, small beneath him, barely breathing, her eyes closed. His finger traced the curve of her soft cheek. "I am sorry," he said quietly. Her eyes popped open, the question clear in them. *For what*, they said, *you did nothing to me that has not been done to me many times before.* "I used you and I could not help it. But sweet heaven, it is only that it has been such a long time."

"No-no," she shook her head in denial. "It does not matter. I love you and it is fine. I wanted you to...to.."

"Next time it will be different, I promise you."

"I love you with all my heart, Jacques, and my body is yours. You may do with it whatever you please. I only want to make you happy."

"Oh, Marie," he sighed sweetly, "do you not see, that is also what I want... to make *you* happy. Next time it will be different, you will see."

She looked at him, a shadow of confusion passing over her eyes.

"You are so very beautiful," he sighed and stretched out beside her, nuzzling her nose with his own as his gentle fingers stroked the small column of her neck and traced her delicate collar bone. She timidly reached out herself, mimicking his caresses with caresses of her own.

"No," she whispered, "you are beautiful." He bent toward her, kissing her seductively and Marie tried to match him kiss for kiss, nuzzle for nuzzle, caress for caress. She wanted so much to be everything he wanted her to be. But the more she thought the more awkward and nervous she became. Why did her mind keep taking her back to that horrible tavern, why did she remember so clearly the disgust she had felt?

Jacques felt her quivering beneath him as he continued to kiss her neck, her throat, her breasts. He moved down over her small feminine belly, his tongue pausing to play in the hollow. He kissed the tender skin of her inner thigh and felt the goose-flesh rise on her again.

She could feel his warm breath as he progressed downward until he was kissing her thighs. Then, for a split second she felt the warm wetness of his tongue in her and her entire body tensed and stiffened as she rose off the bed, her arms extended to push him from her.

"No!" she cried out softly, "No, you must not! Not there. You do not want to kiss me there."

"But I do," Jacques looked at her boldly with quiet assurance.

"No," she shook her head emphatically, "not after the others..." She closed her eyes and could see Bouchet and the others pressing themselves into her. She could not let Jacques put his mouth where they had been. "I am not... I..." she felt so unclean.

He drew himself over her, dominant and undeniable. "You are not what?" he asked firmly. She looked up at him, meeting his eyes and then looking away. She was burning with shame, her face felt scorched, her eyes hot, why was he making her say it? Why now, now of all times, did he want her to speak of the past? "You are not a virgin?" he suggested evenly, the hint of a smile beginning to tug at the corners of his mouth.

"Of course not... you know that," she twisted in a desire to escape his penetrating scrutiny of her thoughts.

"Of course I know that," he continued mildly, "I have always known that. Do you think that makes a difference to me?"

She was still not raising her gaze to look at him but at last he saw her small delicate shoulders shrug and her head moved slightly from side to side.

"So what is it that you are not?" he pressed.

"You know what I was," her voice became so small he barely heard her.

"Marie," his voice was very soft. "When you catch a splinter in your finger, what do you do?"

Her eyes moved back to him. "Pull it out."

"Why?"

"Why? Because it will grow sore, perhaps fester and..."

"Exactly," he nodded.

She looked at him, at first not understanding then trying to pretend she did not understand, and then knowing the pretense was ridiculous. "So?"

"This is our wedding night and I have taken you for my wife. But now I seek to extract any thorn left in my dear wife's side."

"Jacques..." she whispered suddenly giving in helplessly, "you know how they used me, many, nameless, faceless, shoving themselves into me, spraying me with themselves... how can you want to touch me there with your mouth?"

Jacques' eyes had gone very tender as he became increasingly aware of the hurt that welled up within her. He had never realized how much degradation she had been hiding within her. For all this time, after all these years she still felt so strongly the cruel shame of being violated as she had. "Oh, Marie... the first time you bathed, the soil was gone." She shook her head, tears spilling from her eyes. "Yes. Yes, it was. As if it had never happened, except that you hold it in your mind."

"You do not understand..." she whimpered.

"No," he considered thoughtfully, "I do not suppose I really do. You are right, *ma Marie*. I do not understand, but I want to. Tell me; please... was it so painful?"

"It... it was not the physical pain," she said softly, the tears running unimpeded down the sides of her face. "It was harsh at first but after a time I learned to relax and shut them out. It was... it was how they made me feel."

"How did they make you feel?"

"They made me feel like... a... *pot de chambre.*"

Jacques thought the image a little funny but any thought of laughter disappeared when he saw the anguish in her face and knew she was not trying to be the least bit amusing. She radiated shame.

A chamber pot. What would it be like to be made to feel like a chamber pot? A thing. An object without heart or soul or feeling to be used carelessly. A thing to be used without feeling and abandoned without thought. What they had done had made her feel like this? Like a slop pot? His heart was suddenly overwhelmed with an anguish of his own as he came to an understanding at last.

"Oh, my darling, my sweet Marie, I am so sorry," he said gathering her to him, holding her, stroking her. In the tender moments that followed with Jacques gently rocking and caressing her, a healing began to take place. She felt a catharsis at having finally shared her sense of deep abasement. The thorn had been removed, the poison drawn. Jacques shared the burden and seemed to lift it off her. He reaffirmed her sensibilities, her humanity, and her dignity. He did not mock, nor laugh or scoff. And he had not refused to hear or try to brush it aside dismissively. She felt something deep within her begin to knit back together.

After a time, Jacques pulled back and looked at her. She saw moistness in his eyes. "A chamber pot, you say? That is completely wrong, you know. Do you want to know what you really are?" he asked insistently. She barely nodded her head. "A beautiful rose, with gentle pink petals. Your flesh is as fresh and smooth as a baby's. And you taste of salt," he whispered as his lips grazed over the tear streaks on her face. "And your scent makes me go hard with desire," he added passionately. "And I *do* want to kiss you there, just like this." He thrust his tongue deeply into her mouth and she, too, tasted salt. When he finally withdrew, she was panting.

"I...I..I am sorry," she offered apologetically.

"Sh..sh, no-no, you have nothing to be sorry for. Nothing. But, Marie, you must now leave it behind you, it is passed, leave it in the past. We left it all behind us in the Old World. We belong to each other now. That is all that is important."

"Tell me what to do," she replied urgently and a little desperately, "whatever you want, tell me and I will do it."

He took a deep breath. "I want you to relax, *ma petite*. Because I want you to have the same pleasure you give me. Your body is ready for me, *ma chérie*, but I want you to want me within you. What part?... it should make no difference."

"Oh, Jacques, I do, I do," Marie reached out and grasped him to her, her fingers twisting in his hair. "I do want you," she echoed and pulled him to her as she thrust into his mouth with her tongue, teasing him back into hers.

While her eager little tongue was a delight, he knew exactly what she was trying to do and he was not going to be distracted. He pulled back, smiling at her warmly. "You must trust me. Think only of this moment. You and me. Breathe deeply and let your mind float. Free your body to enjoy the sensations."

Marie exhaled with a sigh and began to breathe regularly again as he worked his way down her body with his kisses. He felt her relax and saw a little smile pulling gently at the corners of her mouth as his fingers traced over her sensitive skin almost tickling as he went.

He felt himself trembling as he stroked over her belly, then scooped under to hold her perfectly rounded derrière in his hands. He moaned very softly wanting to pull her onto his re-aroused flesh but not this time. This time he could suspend his own need for just as long as it took. He was going to finish what he had started.

It was not long before Marie was overwhelmed. So immersed was she in the sensations and the desires he was evoking within her that she could not help but give herself over completely to his touches. She heard herself crying out to him in a voice that sounded like someone else. Her hands dug into the mattress as she arched up begging for release. She felt the moistness of her body's responses and she now needed more, she needed him. She knew she wanted to feel him within her, filling her in the way they had been designed to fit together, filling her as he had before. She was arching to him, calling his name, begging him not to hold back from her any longer. It was exactly what he wanted to hear.

He felt the energy surge through her body as she accepted him then bucked and arched against him, taking him in completely. He shuddered and fought to hold back as he moved slowly within her tight wet heat. She began to match his slow undulating rhythm causing every muscle in his body to strain. Jacques gritted his teeth and forced himself to focus on her pleasure, denying his own until the searing molten heat of her sudden volcanic eruption pushed him over the edge. It was like a sun bursting within. He wanted to melt into her; he wanted her to melt into him. And they were melting together as one flesh.

She was limp and languid, covered in a thin sheen of perspiration, with a smile of supreme contentment upon her face as she lay beside him. "Is that what you feel?" she asked in hazy satisfaction.

"Uh-hm, I believe it is," he nodded, holding her close to him and breathing softly into her hair. "C'est petit mort."

"Petit mort? Petit mort, little death. So that is un petit mort," she said with sudden understanding. She turned and rolled over so their faces were only inches apart. "It was more than wonderful, Jacques. I had no idea."

He looked exceedingly pleased with himself, accepting the accolades as his due. "Give me a little time, ma chérie," he grinned, "and we will do it again."

"With you it does not hurt," she said almost to herself. "It always hurt before."

Jacques looked at her tenderly, his hand stroking her. Despite it all she was such an innocent. "Marie, when a woman does not want it, her body does not make itself ready. A man who cares for her will not take her without preparation. Unfortunately, there are those of my sex who seem to receive enjoyment by inflicting such hurt."

After digesting this, she let her own hand roam down to the soft flaccid flesh that had only recently been so vitally rigid. "And what about you?" she asked, with a mixture of curiosity and mischief. Her fingers seeking within the wiry golden hair for the appendage that nestled there quite peacefully, she tickled lightly at first and then grew increasingly bold.

"Ahh, gently, my love, we are most sensitive there."

"So it would seem," she teased, feeling a slight response to her persistence as his flesh grew firmer. Then she wriggled down and out of sight.

Suddenly Jacques gasped in a moan of pleasure. He could have sworn she had actually uttered some nonsense about having no skills.

Chapter 22

When Richard finally returned he had only to look at the two to know. He grinned at them broadly but said nothing until he was alone with Jacques. "It is about time," he said when they were outdoors working over the pelts Richard had brought from the traps. "In fact it was more than time. You look relaxed again, my friend," he said in a congratulatory manner. "You were becoming more unpleasant to be around than a beaver with a toothache."

Jacques laughed deeply. "I admit I have been in much better spirits of late."

"You are admitting I was right?" the larger man said and looking up to the heavens he cried out in mock protestation, "I do not believe it! That I should live to see the day."

Jacques began to form a bantering retort and then just shrugged and grinned. "What is the use? In fact, I am much too happy to debate with you. Whatever you say. I do not care."

"Well, she is not a squaw," Richard observed pointedly while glowing from his minor victory.

"No, and as you said this is not a land in which to have a mistress," Jacques added smugly.

"Then, she must be a wife."

"Absolutely. We will get the final blessing from the church in spring and I will buy a ring to replace the signet ring I gave her. But we have taken our vows before God and any issue will be legitimate."

So, I must mark the day for all of history. The day Jacques admitted Richard was right!"

"What do you mean? Right about what?" Jacques feigned incomprehension.

"I told you what you needed was a wife and I was right," he was emphatic.

Jacques burst out laughing. "Go on, you fool, enjoy the moment. Right now I am happy enough to agree with whatever you wish to ramble about. But do not think to take advantage of it."

"Of course I must take advantage of it. How often can I expect to have such an opportunity?" Richard's face was split from ear to ear with a self-satisfied grin.

The two men continued their work in high spirits. Richard kept glancing at Jacques and grinning. He was sure he had not seen his best friend in such a good mood since before they had left France. Jacques needed Marie more than he realized, Richard thought, and Marie had been in love with the fair haired young god since the tavern days, of that Richard had no doubt. What was the point of such unnecessary frustration? It was a perfect match, they were good for each other and, unlike him, they were meant for marriage.

"And so," Richard couldn't help but tease, "I guess this means I shall have a room to myself and will not be assaulted all night by your snoring."

"*My* snoring...*MY* snoring? You old sawmill, you are a fine one to talk. You shake the shingles when you get going."

Never had Marie known such complete contentment. Each day flew by as her light heart sought numerous ways to express her affection for Jacques. And each night she curled up next to his hard, lean body to share the warmth, the pleasure, and the joy. He wanted her to be naked in their bed with him and that experience alone was liberating, opening a world of sensuality she had never known. She marveled at the feel of the soft furs caressing her sensitive skin, brushing her breasts, nipples, hips, and thighs as she stretched voluptuously against them. She would move provocatively against Jacques and enjoy his reactions. And if Richard could hear the sounds of her ecstasy, she did not think about it nor did she care.

Afterward, they would always sleep like spoons. He would pull her in close to him and curl around her soft, warm, round curves burying his nose in the sweet fragrance of her hair, smelling her spice-like muskiness laced with the scent of burnt candles and fat lamps. And when they turned she would curl against him, holding him in her arms, their legs entwined, her fingertips buried in the tiny curls on his chest, her nose drinking in the ambrosia of his healthy male scent.

She tried never to think of Celimene or remember the noises she had over-heard in the cottage. That was the Old World, she reminded herself, and as Jacques had said, it was left behind. It was not Celimene who gave Jacques pleasure now; she was not the one by his side sharing his days and nights. It was Marie.

Thus, the dreary dark days of winter passed more pleasantly than ever before but in time Marie became concerned for Richard. She and Jacques found such pleasure in sharing their bed together, it made her feel a trifle guilty that Richard was all by himself each night. then, one day, he again told them he was going to check the far traps and not to be concerned if he was away for a while. She and Jacques knew Richard had gone to see his squaw but neither of them spoke of it.

For several weeks at a time through the winter, Marie and Jacques had the cabin completely to themselves. Those were weeks of sensual abandonment as they remained naked within the cozy confines of the crooked cabin and cavorted about, and experimented. Under Jacques' tutelage she was learning to give herself over into complete inhibition and under his touch her body throbbed with desire. She felt beautiful, prized, and adored and he taught her all the ways she could please him until she grew inventive enough to surprise him on her own. The memories of Bouchet and the others and their crude usage were washed away until she could look back on that time with no more significance than the times she had burnt her fingers or skinned her knees, momentary pain in the distant past and something to be forgotten.

It turned very cold that winter but deep snows insulated the cabin from the frigid winds. The traps began to yield excellent furs of great thickness. Spring was late in coming and when the thaw finally began, the trio was eager to return to New York Towne for two reasons. They had beautiful pelts to sell but even more important to Jacques and Marie, they wanted to have their marriage recorded with a formal service and a blessing by a pastor.

Upon reaching the harbor in late evening, they first sought rooms at The Pork 'n' Porridge, and the Thompkins family was pleased to greet them. They shared their good news, which did not seem to surprise Master Thompkins, and the entire family was invited to the wedding service. After all, they had known the Thompkins since their second day in the colony.

The next morning, Jacques went off in search of Brother Robert. The young couple agreed they would most like to have him officiate. Richard took the responsibility of selling their furs and Marie went to the Wingates with both Jacques' list of supplies and her own and to invite the couple to join them at the church for the wedding.

The Wingates were delighted to see Marie. It had been a full year since she had left and they had become quite concerned when her friends had returned in fall without her. Many a prayer had been said in consideration of her rash decision to go off into the wilderness as she had. Now, the elderly couple breathed a sigh of relief on hearing the word *wedding*. As Master Shakespeare had written, *all's well that end's well*. They were not going to judge and it was better to forget the unorthodox beginnings.

Master Wingate took the supply lists from Marie and excused himself, being too busy in the store to visit, but Abigail took Marie into the back and made a hospitable pot of tea.

"It is so very good to see you again, child," she said graciously, her motherly face was more round and her figure plumper than Marie remembered. "I suppose there is no real reason to ask if things have been well with you," the older woman smiled kindly, "you are absolutely glowing."

Marie blushed. "We took solemn vows before God at Christmas," she hastened to explain. "I have been a wife for many months now."

Unconsciously Abigail's gaze went straight to Marie's waistline which was as slender and trim as ever. "I see. Well, it's done often on the frontier I understand, for lack of a preacher, I believe they call it *hand-fasting*."

"But we do want the church's blessing, and to share the occasion with our friends," Marie added hastily.

Abigail smiled again and nodded.

"And how have things been with you? How is your grandson?"

"Doing well and growing like the proverbial weed," Abigail exclaimed with a flush of pride. "They were all back to see us this past Christmas. The whole family was together. Elizabeth asked about you. It was you we were missing last Christmas, child. Your ears should have been burning you were spoken of so often. And you were right."

"About what?" Marie asked.

"Why the baby, of course. You said our Christmases would be brightened by our grandchildren and you were right, bless you. Mercy, he really understood more this Christmas and we spoiled him something fierce, I'm afraid," she laughed but her eyes were moist. "It was wonderful. I do miss them. Oh, and the best news is that Elizabeth is now expecting. She has waited to be blessed, poor lamb. She was the first to marry and yet saw her younger sister beat her to the cradle. Well, that's all over now."

"When is she expecting?" Marie asked in interest.

"Oh, not long now. She was three months gone at Christmas... soon I'll have two grandchildren. Can you imagine?"

"Of course, and you will have many more as well, I am certain," Marie said pleasantly.

Abigail sighed. "Still, I can't help but wish they lived closer. How 'bout you, child? Do you have any neighbors yet?"

"No. Well... I have made friends with some of the Indians."

"Really?"

Marie nodded.

"But no white folks yet?"

"No."

"Well, you can come back here anytime and visit us, you hear? There is always a spare bedroom for you... and your young husband, of course. Speaking of which, when is this wedding of yours going to take place?"

"Jacques is making the arrangements now. Unless the preacher is unable, it should be later this afternoon."

"This afternoon?" Abigail's eyes opened in surprise. "Why, we've no time to plan anything. What are you going to wear?" she asked with directness.

Marie looked taken back and a bit bewildered. "Wear? Why... I had not thought..."

"Mercy, child, you are just as thoughtless for yourself as you always have been. I hope that young man of yours appreciates you. Many a wife has cost her husband many a pretty penny just putting clothes on her back," Abigail laughed. "Of course, if they didn't, Master Wingate and I wouldn't have had quite so good a living."

Marie smiled and sipped her tea. As she put the cup down, she spoke thoughtfully. "Mistress Wingate, do you still have my fine dress, the golden one?"

"Why yes, of course."

"Do you think we could bring it out? You are right, of course, I should take some pains for my own wedding. I want Jacques to be proud of me. Do you think the fabric will be wrong for a wedding?"

"No, no, not at all. It's a lovely dress. It's up in the storage chest in the girls' bedroom, your old room. Why don't you run up there and take a look. It may smell a little of cedar but we can air it."

Later when Jacques came to the Wingate's in search of Marie, Abigail Wingate clucked and chattered with a happy sparkle in her eye. "Now, you just go on down to the church there, young man, and we will bring the bride to you. A bride only anticipates having one wedding in her lifetime and they all want to look especially nice. You can't blame us, you know. You wouldn't have it any other way," she chuckled and shooed Jacques back out the door.

Two hours later, Jacques and Richard stood waiting with Brother Robert in the dimly cool little frame church. Jacques considered himself fortunate to have found a plain gold band of first quality at the goldsmith shop and he hoped it was going to fit Marie's slender finger. He had stopped to get a bath and a shave at the barber's and purchased a fresh shirt, cuffs and cravat from the tailor. There hadn't been time to get a complete new suit of clothes but when he heard that Marie was "dressing" he realized he needed to give some thought to his own appearance. Life on the frontier was changing him, he considered. A short time ago, he would have never thought of attending a public affair such as a wedding, much less his own wedding, without a proper compliment of clothing. Yet, now, what good was fancy clothing when he was chopping wood or skinning animals?

The small church door opened lighting up the aisle and Jacques spun around in anticipation. It was the Thompkins family and they filed in with happy murmurs and took seats near the front. Mistress Thompkins had picked a bouquet of spring flowers from her own garden and sent her youngest son out to watch for the bridal party with instructions to give the flowers to the bride if she had none and if she had, to bring them in for the altar.

Jacques paced back and forth on the smooth wooden floor. He was actually beginning to perspire. It was a little ridiculous. By common law, he and Marie had been married for a quarter year. This was hardly the time to become the nervous bridegroom. Yet here in God's House, with an ordained minister and witnesses, he felt the solemnity of the event even more acutely. Before he could pursue this line of thought, the church door opened again. This time Mistress Wingate entered, followed closely by Marie holding the large bouquet of spring flowers young Thompkins had given her. Master Wingate's portly girth followed the women into the church and he shut the door. Flanked on either side by the Wingates, Marie walked down the aisle toward Jacques.

She was radiant, elegantly coiffed and dressed in a fetching dress that made her glow. There was something familiar about the dress, he thought absently as he puffed up fairly bursting with pride. It didn't register that he had, in fact, seen it two years ago. It wasn't important. He only knew that this bride was his and anyone who cared to look could see she was the most beautiful bride in this new world.

After the short service, Richard, as best man, was the first to wish the happy couple well. He gave Jacques a kiss on each cheek and then with a wink he took the liberty of kissing the bride straight on the mouth and as hard as he had once kissed Celimene. Silently he compared. Celimene had returned his kiss with the practiced expertise of a courtesan. Marie blushed scarlet with the modest confusion of a wife. He grinned and did not miss the momentary frown that creased the new husband's brow, a frown he had never had for his kissed mistress. Well, it was the only real kiss Richard was ever likely to be able to give her and whether Jacques liked it or not, Richard wasn't one to pass up such a singular opportunity.

The Thompkins lined up to shake hands and kiss the bride's cheek. Mistress Thompkins, usually a portrait of composure, was crying.

"I always cry at weddings; I don't know why," she excused herself, wiping her eyes with a lacy handkerchief and smiling balefully as Marie consoled her.

Thomas Wingate gave Marie a fatherly kiss on the forehead. "You see, my dear," he said, "I told you some day a fine young man would want to make you his wife."

"You were right," Marie smiled, looking lovingly at Jacques and then she looked back to Wingate, "and I was right as well. I have started my own store on the frontier."

"You have?" he said, his eyes opening wider while Abigail tried to stifle a broad grin.

"Right now my only customers are the red men, but time will change that, too, I think," Marie added good-naturedly.

"You're setting up a trading post on the frontier?" Wingate asked Jacques.

"Oh, no, monsieur, not me. I was not cut out to be a shopkeeper. It is all in Marie's hands. She is most capable, do you not think?" Jacques asked proudly.

"Very capable," Abigail Wingate agreed, adding her congratulatory kiss. Then she added, "Young Cooper has a lot to learn before he catches up to Marie, don't you agree, Master Wingate? You know it is amazing how young Samuel's work has suffered such lapses since you left," she said to Marie with a wink, "and after *we* thought he was coming along so nicely."

Marie said nothing but smiled.

"Yes, yes...well, I do wish you good fortune in your venture and in your life together. Many, many years of happiness to you both," Wingate added graciously. "And many healthy children."

"Thank you, sir," Jacques replied with a small bow of respect.

That night they celebrated together with their friends at the inn where the Thompkins threw a small party. In short time the tables and chairs were shoved against the walls to make room for dancing. Musicians appeared and lively music began. There was food and drink aplenty and the other guests at the inn were pleased to join in. The savory smells of the kitchen mixed with the sweet fragrance of garden flowers, the heavy alcoholic vapors of ales and wines being liberally passed round, and the warm delicate aroma of beeswax candles. It didn't take long for the temperature indoors to rise and the pungent acrid scent of sweat to mingle with the other odors. Windows and doors were thrown open and with lanterns defining the outdoors, the dancing pushed outside in the cool of the evening with others from the community joining in.

Marie was the star attraction. The lovely bride was expected to dance with all who asked her while Jacques found himself dutifully dancing with what seemed to be every matron in the entire colony. There were many toasts to the handsome couple, and Marie felt the flush of the wine set her senses spinning and make her world tip slightly askew. The spring night grew chilled but no one thought so as they continued to drink and dance and sing.

While enjoying the party, Richard was also interested in picking up any news regarding French and English hostilities. What he learned he would save until he could share it with Jacques privately. No need to worry Marie. Last season while they were finding new trading contacts in the New Jersey territory, a settlement he was certain they had passed by the year before at a village called Schenectady right on the Mohawk River had been savagely attacked by the French and their Indian allies in retaliation for the massacre at Lachine. He had been right and they had been wise to keep their distance he thought as he unconsciously caressed his own scalp.

It grew late and the Wingates were the first to leave, pleading fatigue. A short time later Jacques and Marie bid everyone good night and retired under the usual barrage of ribald jokes and suggestive remarks from the rest who were content to continue making merry.

Jacques, carrying a taper in one hand, helped his young wife navigate the steep stairs up to their rented room. She weaved and giggled and catching herself, she giggled again. In her hand she still carried a tankard into which someone had poured wine. At last, inside their own room, Jacques pushed the door closed and instantly the noisy laughter and music was put off at a distance.

"Oh, it is so dark. I cannot see," Marie giggled slightly. "Light another candle... better to light one candle than to curse the dark, is it not so?" She took another sip from the tankard and found the small dressing table with a clunk. "Ouch! I really did not need to stub that toe. Oooo- Oooo. Poor little toe, it has already been stepped on all night."

Jacques had a second candle lit and was shrugging out of his coat after which he swept her into his arms. "Have I told you how proud I am of you?" Jacques said softly. "And how glad I am to finally get you to myself again?"

"No," she smiled; her cheeks flushed rosy from wine and exercise in the fresh air. "But I am very pleased to have you rescue me, good sir. I think I may have lost several toes tonight." With that she threw herself back on the bed and stretched her feet out to him. "These little slippers are no protection from Thompkins boys with two left feet and now they pinch my toes as well."

Jacques gently removed her shoes and then her stockings. Massaging her tiny toes, he began to kiss each one in a rendition of *Piggy Went To Market.*

"Hmmmm.... you still have five on each foot," he observed.

"Five what?"

"Toes, of course."

"Oh, toes... of course," she giggled again and convulsed into shrieks as what he was doing lightly tickled her foot. "Oh, stop... stop, please...."

"Shhhhhh... do you want the other guests to think you do not want me," Jacques feigned concern.

"I cannot help it, if you tickle; besides they are still all at the party."

"I think you have become just a little bit tipsy, *ma chérie,*" Jacques smiled at her indulgently. She was breathless and her eyes sparkled brightly.

"Perhaps... but not so very that I do not know what I am doing," she grinned boldly and ran her hand slowly up his leg to his crotch. "Oh, husband," she whispered. "I think you are thinking what I am thinking."

"And what is that?"he asked seductively.

"That it will be wonderful to sleep in a featherbed tonight."

Jacques laughed out loud at that. "Come, up on your feet and turn around, and I will help you with your laces."

She obediently accepted his helping hand, stood and presented her back to him so he could commence upon the task of unlacing her gown.

"The dress is very pretty, is it not?" she slurred slightly.

"Very."

"But not practical."

"No, but all things do not need to be practical."

"That is what Mistress Wingate says. But...." He had opened the laces and she turned around letting him remove the dress from her. "It is not even something I can put on or take off by myself."

"I know," he smiled rakishly. "Is that not what husbands are for?" He set the gown aside.

"I think husbands are a very nice thing to have," she observed. "Can you find the tapes?" she asked as she turned back around so he could untie her petticoats. "I have two you know."

"I know. I have to get the first undone before I can deal with the other."

She giggled again uproariously. "No... I mean two husss..bands."

"Oh, I thought you meant petticoats," he chuckled.

"Well, I have two of those as well, as you can see. And two husbands... one I married in the wilderness, and one I married here in church."

"Ahhh, I see... ah, turn just a little *ma petite* so I can get some light, oh, there it is..." he fumbled with the petticoat tie and finally pulled the second from her. "And what about me?" He bent to kiss the tender side of her neck and continued the lighthearted nonsense, "With two husbands what chance do I have?"

Standing in only her thin linen shift, she shivered dreamily at his caress. "Ohhhh, when you kiss me there I really cannot think."

"Then, perhaps you will keep me around for a while?" he teased.

Suddenly, a sobering sense of panic washed over her as she realized that he was going to leave her again and very soon. "Oh, Jacques!" On tiptoes she threw her arms about his neck and clung to him fiercely, burying her face in the hollow of his shoulder.

Jacques folded his arms around her. "What is it, *ma petite?*" he asked softly.

"Nothing... I just love you so very much." She kissed him almost fiercely. "I do not want this evening to ever end," she whispered against his lips as she moved her body slowly against him and felt him respond to her.

The next day the trio saw to the loading of their supplies and took their leave after Jacques had arranged for one more wedding gift for his bride. On board the small craft heading back to the frontier post was a new plump feather bed.

No sooner had the trio returned to the cabin, when the Indians, as if by some mysterious signal, began arriving to trade. Marie concentrated on her business and her tasks, trying not to think that all too soon Jacques would be gone. His leaving was much harder to face this year. She was going to miss him intensely.

The young Frenchmen checked over their own trade goods and readied their maps for a deeper trek into the wilderness. Richard was eagerly looking forward to the arrival of Bear Claw and Two Feathers. He was ready to be off and on the move. Jacques, on the other hand, steeled himself for this inevitability. It was the only way he had to build his fortune, but it grieved him to think of leaving Marie.

She had managed through the first summer very well, in fact, exceptionally well. She was getting to know some of the local natives and those natives were proving to be friendly. With this knowledge both men found it easier to accept and nurture a belief in the young woman's security. Still it was dangerous and Jacques could not allow himself to think of all the things that might happen. It was easier to think only of how much he would miss her.

Bear Claw and Two Feathers arrived as agreed upon, each in a canoe of his own with a third in tow. They loaded the supplies and trading goods, along with their personal packs and weapons. All was in readiness.

Jacques drew Marie aside and after an impassioned embrace during which he silently invoked the Almighty to keep her safe, he tore himself away with manly dignity and took his seat in one of the canoes. The party pushed off and began their trip up river against the current.

Marie stood at the shore smiling, waving, and blowing kisses until they could no longer be seen. Then she turned in the quiet and felt the loneliness fall upon her like a mantel. She shook her head and scolded herself. There was much to do and gloominess was not productive. Anoui had taught her that. The summer would be over before she knew it, she told herself, and then Jacques, her Jacques, her love and life, would come back to her again.

In a matter of minutes, Marie and the cabin were left far behind and the four men had fallen into a steady rhythm of paddling, one canoe following the other and slipping quietly through the clear, clean waters. The forests of hickory and chestnut, elm and ash slipped by them as the shaggy hills grew higher around them.

By canoe they were able to travel farther up the river but the chief advantage came when they had to leave the water. The canoes were portable, lighter and less bulky, capable of being carried over land at a portage point.

When the party could travel by water no farther, they made camp and waited. Three days later, two strong-backed braves walked into their camp. They called a greeting to Bear Claw and approached, arms wide, hands spread. They spoke no English nor any French, and did not communicate with the white men except to nod and look agreeably non-threatening.

Redistributing the weight of goods evenly, they began their trek. The trading party made its way by Indian trail through a pine forest up a small mountain making camp on the western slope. By mid-afternoon of the next day they had made their way to another river, flowing northwestward. A short time on this river brought them to their first friendly village.

Chapter 23

It was July and they were long used to all the normal sounds of the forest as their canoes glided noiselessly over the water. So adept had Jacques and Richard become at paddling, they, too, could cut through the water without a sound and keep from scaring the wildlife. Jacques could feel the sweat trickling down his scalp. He also sensed something troubling in the air. No one spoke a word. The farther they pressed on, the more they perceived something different in the feel of the forest around them. But it was difficult to pinpoint exactly what the difference was. There was nothing tangible to point to but Jacques and Richard were both aware, as were the scouts, of a deepening feeling of uneasiness. The canoes continued onward, the men saw nothing, they heard nothing. After a time, Jacques realized it was what they did not see and hear that was so disturbing. It was too quiet.

The wildlife had become conspicuous by its absence. There was no bird song in the trees above. The gentle rustling of leaves and bushes betraying the movements of small animals was not there. Their guides sensed it too, and as they continued on, each man grew more tensely aware of even the smallest sound. After a time, Bear Claw spoke to Richard and Richard called back to Jacques in a re-strained voice.

"The village we want to trade in should be around the next bend," he said in guarded tones.

Jacques nodded but he had a strange sense of foreboding. If they were that close to an Indian encampment, should there not be telltale smells of cook fires? He sniffed the air and smelled nothing of food but something faintly rotten.

The bend in the river came and as they glided around it they paddled toward a small sandy shore. There was no sound, not even the careless noises of children playing. The wind shifted and they caught the scent of something so foul it took their breath away. Stepping onto the bank, a noisy buzzing caught their attention. They pulled their crafts up onto the sand and the sound grew louder. Flies were now buzzing about their heads. They also became aware of a powerful stench, acrid, putrid, unlike anything they had encountered before in their young lives.

"What th..." exclaimed Jacques, totally at a loss for words.

Richard was swatting at the flies but uttered no sound.

They walked up from the river and suddenly a large group of scavenger birds took flight before them as simultaneously each man spied the carnage.

Bodies or what was left of bodies lay strewn about in various grotesque positions testifying to a violent end. A few had arrows protruding out of them, some had been shot with musket balls, but most had been hit with something far blunter, a tomahawk most likely, which had dealt a crushing fatal blow. And on every body the hair from the head had been cut and ripped away along with the flesh from the forehead to mid-skull. Hundreds of flies busied themselves over the remains, feasting and laying eggs, emitting a drone of maddening intensity as their movements gave a pulsating, oozing quality to the corpses.

The putrid stench was the smell of rotting flesh.

Some of the bodies were partially cooked, some burnt to a crisp. Small carnivorous animals had already been there while the raw meat was fresh. Now, as it decomposed, the scavenger birds plucked and shredded the remains.

The village was no more. The small dwellings had all been burned to the ground. The charred remnants of leather wall flaps and thick main posts were all that remained. The nearby vegetation showed the effects of the intense heat created by the flames which had devoured the structures. Some trees had been severely singed; leaves and branches had withered and turned brown in the lushness of summer. Other trees stood as lifeless posts, mute black witnesses to the obscene and senseless loss of life.

Jacques stubbed his toe and looked down. He was standing in the midst of a fire ring where the cold ashes of a small wicker carrier mingled with the small charred bones of an infant whose skull appeared to have been cleaved in two before it was heaved into the flames. He jerked his foot away and felt the bile rise up from his stomach.

"Let us leave," he said sharply in a raspy voice.

Without objection, Richard and the natives turned away and quickly retraced their steps to the waiting canoes.

The tribe who had lived there had been peaceful and friendly, and would have willingly hosted the trading party and exchanged skins for the goods that Jacques and Richard had brought with them. It had been a village of perhaps thirty adults and half as many youngsters. They had been in the wrong place in the midst of a blood lust and now they were no more.

"Do we go forward or go back?" Jacques asked of Richard in a hushed tone. He shrugged. "Ask Bear Claw," he suggested.

Bear Claw grunted and pointed in the direction they were to go next.

The small party did their trading quietly, warily, and ever mindful of the dangers but always managing to stay out of harm's way through the intelligence gleaned from the natives they visited. The massacred village was the only carnage they witnessed first hand. But they heard of other raids and counter raids, attacks and ambushes. It was a very tense season. As the daylight hours grew shorter they ran out of trading goods. Jacques considered that they had been extremely fortunate. By the grace of God, they had escaped the war parties and the troop movements and it was now time to go home. It was time to return to the coast and to Marie.

A new challenge arose. They would not be able to return the way they had come unless they were able to hire more carriers to help carry all the heavy furs over the mountains. Jacques was beginning to realize just how very inhibiting the absence of an easily navigated river was to their movements. This was why the St. Lawrence, Hudson, Mohawk and Delaware rivers were such favored pathways.

Bear Claw knew a different route he told them, a route which was all water and would bring them back to the white man's fort on the Delaware River. Jacques and Richard knew that from the settlements around the bay of the Delaware, they could connect with a packet boat to take them out to sea and northward to home. It was mutually agreed that this was an acceptable plan.

They fashioned a small raft which was piled high with all the furs they could not put into the three canoes. The canoes themselves were so full they rode dangerously close to the water line until they parted company with their two extra hired carriers.

They were making excellent progress traveling downstream with the currents when Bear Claw led them into a detour up a tributary where they soon pulled over and left the water. Set back from the river branch was a large rocky escarpment forming a shallow cave beneath; it was perhaps fifteen feet above the river's level. It was only midday but a long prelude of distant rumblings and light flashes told them a serious storm was on its way. Bear Claw knew the area well and after they secured the canoes and raft, he urged them to quickly gather up as much dry firewood as they could find and drag it within the protection of the overhang before the skies opened up.

Once the rain began, it came down needle sharp and cold and soon created water flows and channels all about them in the forest. They remained on the higher level of rock, safe, dry, and protected within the shelter of the shallow cave. Through the next two days, the storms continued. Jacques and Richard had never seen the like of such natural violence in their entire lives. At times the world grew deafeningly loud with a cacophony of thunder claps like cannon fire booming non-stop, one upon the other. Almost constant flashes of lightening strobed and flickered, illuminating the night as though it were day. It was as if they were caught on a battlefield between the heavens and the earth. At times a fierce wind drove the men to the very back of the rock wall in order to stay dry. At other times the wind was calmer but the cold rain continued dumping from the sky in steady ongoing sheets as though poured from massive cauldrons by some unseen hand on high.

Suddenly the rain stopped and ice began to hail down in pellets the size of musket balls, bouncing inches up off everything which was not under water: the rocks, the vegetation, the unflooded ground. It accumulated rapidly in white patches all around them. France did not have such storms as this and the young men from the Old World became apprehensively unnerved. What cataclysmic event were they witnessing, they wondered, in the roar around them? Had the end of the world truly come just as the preachers so often warned from their pulpits?

A sudden flash of lightning ripped through the sky hitting a tree only some ten yards away. The thunderous boom hurt their ears as white energy spiraled down the tree trunk with a sizzle, splitting it open to its core, leaving a black singed rip and felling the tree's top in its wake. It had all happened in less time than it took to take a breath and simultaneously every hair on Jacques' body stood up and away from its root as an energy wave hit them.

Jacques and Richard looked at each other in the deafening roar and then, they looked to the natives. The two scouts showed no fear but exuded an air of calm acceptance as they squatted near the fire and attended to the routine maintenance of their weapons. If the weather was not common, it appeared that it was at least not that uncommon to them. Had Bear Claw not read the signs and foreseen it coming? It would seem it must have happened before. The native had anticipated its severity and brought them to reasonable, protective shelter making provision for their prolonged stay. And now that they were protected by the rock and kept warmed by the fire, they simply waited in acquiescent patience for Nature to run her unpredictable course.

During the third night, the rain ceased altogether and the quiet was a welcome relief that woke Jacques momentarily. He heard his companions stir as well. With the realization of what had changed, he returned to his slumbers anticipating moving on in the morning. Daybreak was a long time in coming. The dripping forests were shrouded in misty fogs. The clouds, still ominously gray, overcast the skies so thoroughly the sun was impossible to detect. But, after three days of being mute, the birds trilled and sang with a voluptuousness of birdsong giving assurance that life, indeed, was returning to normal. In time, the overcast thinned and the mist began to lift. They ate and while Jacques and Richard were eager to continue on their way, Bear Claw insisted they must wait.

"What is it?" Jacques asked in frustration. "The sky is clearing."

Richard just as eager to get their furs back to the coast, shrugged in acceptance of the brave's greater knowledge. "He says we need to stay put until we see the ground dry up."

"But that could take forever! We have lost three days already."

"I know but what is our rush, eh? It is not as if we have a ship to catch," Richard replied pragmatically.

Jacques muttered something unintelligible and sat down by the fire with a sigh. He was impatient to return to Marie but what could another day or two hurt?

They used their time to uncover the canoes and raft, and repack their pelts and skins, ensuring they were dry and secure. Finally, on the morning of the seventh day they broke camp. Standing water had been absorbed and the small tributary was flowing more gently. Each man pushed off in his own canoe with Two Feathers pole-steering the raft securely piled high with furs.

Coming out of the tributary, the flotilla of canoes and raft were swept swiftly into the main channel of the river. Jacques was shocked when he realized just how rain swollen the main river had become. Waters the color of brown clay carried them along at a growing speed. They moved rapidly in the swift current keeping a sharp lookout for debris. Broken branches and rotting logs were also being carried along by the rapid waters.

The current reached a dizzying speed. Before they knew what was happening, they were being swept over rapids for which they were not prepared. The landmarks which should have warned the scouts were buried out of sight in the rising waters and the speed of their travel had brought them much farther much more quickly than Bear Claw realized. Now the sluicing waters moved them with a strength they could not fight.

The lead canoe began to take in water and grew more difficult for Bear Claw to steer. Jacques heard a crack from out of the sound of the rushing river. Two Feathers had lost all control of the raft and it had collided with Jacques' canoe, forcing him against a jagged rock. His canoe was breaking apart. Without warning Jacques found himself in the cold murky liquid being sucked under as it carried him along at a startling speed. He made out a dark shape looming toward him and realized he was being hurled toward a boulder. Just before hitting it he managed to kick off it with his boot and passed by without harm, only grazing a knee. He gained the surface to gasp a lung full of air before being pulled under again in a whirling tumult. The river continued to buffet him onward, propelling him over more rocks, sucking him under again until he thought his lungs would burst. Then it spewed him up to the surface like a Jonah being vomited by a watery whale only to be swallowed again and made prisoner without air. Finally, by a stroke of fortune, when near to blackout from lack of oxygen, the raging waters cast Jacques away, tumbling him into a shallow side wash.

Coughing profusely and gasping violently, Jacques took advantage of the reduced momentum to cling to a rock at the water's edge. Dazed and still breathing hard he mustered the strength to grab a root and climb up and onto the bank. Almost immediately he looked around for Richard. Where was he? Where were the other canoes? The scouts? Everything had happened so quickly. Had he been carried so very far away from the rest of them? He saw a canoe come careening off a rock in the river above him. It sailed through the air like a suicidal bird heading directly for a large rocky formation in the middle of the river below him. The craft splintered violently upon impact. The furs were swept onward and lost in the surging foam. Jacques stood helplessly as he next saw Bear Claw being carried by the current and dashed against the same rocks with bone cracking force, his body instantly went lifeless and was quickly pulled beneath the surface.

Soaked to the skin, Jacques' teeth were chattering as he instinctively searched for his partner and friend. Climbing up along the steep side of the river bank to gain a visage of where he had come from, he scanned the river with eyes stinging from the grit of the water he had been in. Then, he saw something. It was a hand, an elbow. Jacques dropped onto a narrow overhang and holding fast to a small stunted tree there, with his free hand he grabbed Richard by the neck of the tough buckskin shirt he wore. In a fight with the river for his friend, Jacques pulled with all his strength to drag Richard toward shore.

At first Jacques thought his wrist would snap from the water soaked weight of the larger man but he was able to adjust the awkward angle as he held tight and gradually pull his partner to safety.

For a long time the two lay entangled, clinging to the rock, the only warmth within their grasp being that which their bodies created being pressed together and against the hard rock surface. They were dazed, breathless, and in shock. For several minutes it was enough just to breathe and let the sun shine down on them.

As they lay panting and stunned, gradually coming to their sensibilities, neither man wanted to say what was going through his mind. Winter was coming. They had just lost everything: their guides, weapons, gunpowder, the skins that represented the entire season's work and investment, and their means of transportation home. They were now on foot in a hostile wilderness and they were defenseless. They had no food. No tools. No compass. No weapons. They did not know where they were and had no means to communicate to anyone they should meet save by rudimentary sign language. They had nothing but the clothes upon their backs and their lives.

"At least we are still alive!" Jacques said at last and disentangled himself from Richard's heavier body. He pulled himself to his feet, the water running from his clothing in rivulets to the ground. "Are you hurt, Richard, can you stand? Can you walk?" He had to raise his voice to a shout to hear himself above the sound of the rushing waters.

Richard responded by forcing himself to stand and take assessment.

"Nothing broken," he replied, then he checked his arm beneath a dripping, shredded buckskin sleeve.

"What is that?" Jacques asked, grabbing Richard's arm and checking for himself. He looked at the scrape; there were only thin lines of blood. He satisfied himself that it was superficial. "I would say, in all, we are most certainly fortunate."

Richard did not argue as he discovered his hunting knife in its sheath, entangled in his buckskins. "My knife!" he cried out, holding it up like the treasure it was.

Jacques clutched at his own side where an empty leather sheath hung. His knife was gone. "We need a fire," he observed clinically as he twisted and squeezed the lengths of his coat to wring out the heavy water, "a way to dry out. Since we have nothing to start one, I suggest we keep walking and see if we can recover anything from the wreckage. Perhaps we may find Two Feathers."

"Bear Claw?" Richard asked bleakly.

"Dead, may his soul rest in peace. I saw him die. What did you see?" Jacques asked as he led the way downstream.

"After the raft rammed you, I tried to paddle to the shore," Richard answered in loud gasping bursts as he maintained the rapid pace Jacques set in an effort to warm them. "I almost made it... but I was hit broadside by a tree... that came out of nowhere. It pushed me back into the rushing water... by then the canoe was filling... sinking beneath me. I managed to jump free."

"What of Two Feathers?"

"I do not know."

"Then there is a chance he is alive. We are!" Jacques exclaimed stopping abruptly. He cupped his hands to his mouth and gave a mighty shout. "Two Feathers! Can you hear me? Two Feathers! Are you there?" The sound of the torrential water was a formidable barrier to hearing anything else. Jacques felt his words go nowhere. Again he cupped his hands around his mouth when he felt Richard's hand upon his shoulder.

"Save your voice. No one could hear you unless they were standing as close as I."

Jacques nodded. "We must continue downstream," he said hoarsely and led the way while Richard followed.

They had walked for twenty minutes, struggling over the slippery rocks, searching the shoreline for any sign of either the Indian or any part of their belongings when at last, they saw him.

Two Feathers lay like a heap of rags upon the rocky river bank. His young brown face looked ashen with pain. He saw them and a spark of life came into his black eyes. His leg was twisted in an unnatural position and one arm hung lifelessly at his side.

"Two Feathers!" Jacques cried out and ran along the river's edge. He halted, not quite knowing what to do for the angry river rushed on between them.

It was a frustrating moment. Jacques forced himself to stop and consider. The water currents were very powerful even at this point. He and Richard had ended up on the north bank, Two Feathers was on the south bank. The river would only continue to get wider as they went on and, in a quick calculation, he realized that they just might need to be on the other side of it to get home. He had not even thought of this.

"Any suggestions?" Jacques looked at Richard. "We have nothing to make a boat with. We have no rope. Dare we try to swim across?"

Richard collapsed down in a patch of sunlight without answering as if to think. Jacques joined him. When Richard stood up again he moved into the forest. Jacques would have asked where he was going but it required more energy than he seemed to have at that moment. He felt totally drained. He heard his partner thrashing around but sought to conserve his own strength and did not speak. He looked across the brown rushing water to the crumpled body of the scout. If they could have asked the native what he would do, what would he have told them, Jacques asked himself? Jacques tried to calculate the width of the river, the power of the water. How much strength would it take to swim across the current? He did not think he could do it. He had never been a strong swimmer. And he was more exhausted from his ordeal than he had at first realized. No, he could not swim the river here; they were now passed the rapids but the current was much too strong. But then where? Must they go farther down river? Should they wait for the river to calm? But how long would that take? What if it rained again? No, it might take many days for the river to calm. Two Feathers did not have that time and neither did they.

Jacques' head was throbbing painfully. He was aware of a swollen knot upon his skull. He touched it gingerly and his fingers came away pink with blood. He must have hit his head and not even realized it. He could not think. In dismay he reached out mentally to his Creator, a prayer, a plea... before blackness enveloped his conscientiousness.

Richard came out of the forest and saw Jacques slumped against a tree. How can he sleep at a time like this, the big man asked himself with an angry snort. And in wet clothes no less, is he crazy?

"Hey, Sleeping Beauty, awake," he said briskly, kicking Jacques' boot. Richard was absorbed in cleaning the dirt from edible roots he had found and did not really look at Jacques for a moment. Then he realized his friend was not moving. "Jacques? Jacques! *Mon Dieu*, what is it? What is wrong?" Richard's heart began beating rapidly as he observed the blood streaking through Jacques' yellow hair and the pallor beneath his sun tanned flesh. Had he been bleeding all this while, he asked himself, cursing that he had not noticed it as they had hiked.

"Jacques! Jacques, speak to me! Do you hear me, damn you? Say something. Jacques?" Richard's sense of panic was multiplied with the thought of having to face Marie if... Well, by heaven and hell, nothing was going to happen to Jacques now. He grabbed his friend's soaking lapels and sat him up straighter, gently slapping his pale, cold cheeks until he saw his eyes begin to flutter. "Thank heaven! Say something! Anything!"

"You are kneeling on my chest," Jacques whispered with a grimace.

"Oh..." Richard backed off a bit. "Your head... it is bleeding... did you know?"

"It is nothing."

"Nothing? You just passed out."

"No, I am only tired, that is all. I must have fallen asleep."

"*Asleep* my hairy arse, you were out cold. And your skin feels like a corpse. We need a fire."

"I will be fine," Jacques insisted, his voice getting stronger.

"At least sit in the sun," Richard said dragging Jacques into the growing patch of sunshine where it was now pleasantly warm. "Let me look at your head," Richard added gruffly, masking his sense of relief. He gingerly fingered the matted hair and peered over Jacques' scalp. "You have opened your scalp the width of my thumb. You must have hit something sharp in the water. But I do not think it is deep. Damn it, Jacques, did you not feel it?"

"No... not until I sat down," Jacques uttered meekly.

"You need a bandage. The bleeding does not stop. And you made such a fuss over my scraped arm, *sacré bleu!*" Without further discussion, Richard helped Jacques remove his coat and shirt. He tore strips from the soggy hem of the soiled cotton garment and bandaged Jacques' head as best he could to stem the bleeding. "I hope that helps," he said when he finished.

Picking up Jacques' soggy garments, Richard wrung every drop he could from them before spreading them on a nearby rock to dry. The roots he had carelessly dropped in momentary panic, he brushed off and tossed one to Jacques. "Here."

"What is this?"

"It is food, just eat it."

"I do not think I can."

"You have to, damn it, you need something for strength." The concern was evident in Richard's voice despite his attempt to mask it.

"I will be fine, *mon ami*. You think I would leave you in this mess alone, by yourself?"

"You damn well better not," Richard half-laughed. "I have not the courage to face Marie alone. Now eat, I say."

"*Dieu*, when did you become such a bully?"

Richard ignored the remark but inwardly grinned. Invoking the name of

Marie had the desired effect and he saw his friend bite into the wild tuber.

Jacques bit into the root and found it palatable, slightly bitter perhaps, and smelling pungently of dark, rich soil but not unpleasant. As he chewed, he thought his head was actually feeling a bit better, his body was drying his breeches and he turned his thoughts once again to the river. Looking over he saw the Indian laying exactly as he had been, unmoved.

"Richard?"

"*Oui*?"

"While you were prowling about back there did you see many fallen limbs?"

"Some, why?"

"Because fallen limbs need not be chopped down."

"Chopped down for what?"

"A raft.."

"Ohh, yes, yes, a raft... that is good. And where is the rope for the lashing?"

"How many times have I heard you curse because you have gotten your foot tangled in the vines?"

Richard did not respond at first and then a slow grin broadened on his face. "It just might work, *mon ami*."

Together they gathered every downed limb they could find and brought them all to the river's edge. They broke off what minor branches they could with their hands in order to make the limbs easier to deal with. What they could not break off, they worked around. It took hours but by using massive amounts of green vines they lashed the limbs together. It was very crude and the end result hardly resembled a raft as much as an enormous clot of fallen debris. Jacques had no way of knowing how long the construction would hold together. But even if it all broke apart halfway across, he told himself, they would be that much closer to the other side. Saving the tallest limbs for rafting poles, they were finally ready to attempt their crossing.

Richard paused and turned to Jacques. "You realize it will be dark soon and my clothes are only just beginning to dry out?"

"Mine as well."

"And if we get wet again, we will sleep in wet clothing." It was an ominous prospect almost guaranteeing that they would catch a chill and take a fever.

"What do you suggest?"

"We could wait until daybreak tomorrow to try this."

"And leave Two Feathers to the creatures of the night? We cannot do that, he is helpless."

"Right," Richard nodded grudgingly.

"So we take off our clothes and bundle them tightly. If the raft does break apart we will hang on to this one log here. It has these high spreading branches. We tie the clothes in this fork," he gestured to a pair of limbs sticking far out into the air from the log. "It should keep them dry."

Richard agreed. They stripped quickly and using more vines bundled all their clothing into a packet and wedged it securely into the elevated fork.

Completely naked and barefoot, the pair pushed the misshaped raft off into the cold water and tried to pole and steer for the other side. It was awkward and difficult to maneuver the crude raft. The river current swept along so quickly that by the time they did make it to the other shore, they were almost half a league farther downstream.

"Well, after all that, we could have kept our clothing on," Jacques said lightly, as they rescued their clothes from the perch in the high branch. "I am amazed at how well the vines worked, they were as good as any rope," he said, pulling on his ragged garments. He began to laugh.

"And what is so amusing?" Richard grumbled.

"Can you imagine the sight we made? If any savage had seen us, he might have died of pure fright. You look like a hairy beast and.."

"And your arse is as white as a ghost!" Richard snorted in amusement.

"Something like that," Jacques nodded with a grin. "It matches my lovely chapeau you see," he added, referring to his bandage. "And there stood the two of us, Hairy and the Ghost, clinging atop a wild pile of timber, pushing and shoving like madmen. Now you have to admit it is an amusing tableau."

Richard grunted. They were both dressed again and grew serious thinking of the injured guide.

"Come, we had best hurry back upstream before Two Feathers thinks we have left him to the mercy of the wild," urged Jacques.

"Just mind how fast you go with that head of yours," cautioned Richard but Jacques had no patience to be concerned for himself.

"The leg is broken," Richard observed as they approached the scout. He had guessed as much from the other side of the river. Two Feathers grunted in reply but they could tell he was very pleased to see them. "We are going to have to set it and brace it," Richard added.

With his good arm the Indian pulled his knife from his belt and handed it to Richard. "Cut saplings and birch bark," he grunted through gritted teeth. Richard took the knife with a nod of understanding and handed his own knife to Jacques before going off into the forest.

In a preliminary examination, Jacques discovered the scout still had the bag about his waist which contained a flint and a striking stone. He made a mental note to equip himself in like fashion next time, *if there ever is a next time*, he thought grimly.

He set about gathering the driest wood he could find to start a fire. It was a slow and difficult process to get a flame going in the soggy surroundings but the smaller wood pieces had dried out in the days since the rain had stopped. With the first blaze, he carefully set up larger dead-fall to dry in its heat.

In the meantime, Richard returned with several sections of green sapling and a sizable piece of birch bark, as well as strips of soft mosses.

"You see willow?" the scout asked weakly.

"What?" asked Richard.

"I think he said 'willow'... a willow tree perhaps?" Jacques asked and the scout nodded. Jacques looked around, thinking. "Did we not pass one coming up this side of the bank?"

"Get bark. I chew."

"If you want a piece of bark to bite on, must it be willow?" Jacques asked practically.

"Get willow," the scout groaned.

"It has medicinal properties," Richard said and took off, going back downstream looking for the willow tree.

"Soak in water," Two Feathers grunted to Jacques, pointing with his good hand to the birch bark. "When leg straight, wrap."

"Yes," Jacques nodded. "I understand."

When Richard came back with the willow bark, Two Feathers took some and bit into it savagely, chewing and sucking despite the bitter taste.

Together in the twilight, they commenced the painful task of straightening the broken leg. Jacques took the pliant birch bark and molded it to the scout's skin, bracing it with splints cushioned by moss, and then tied the whole thing together using more of the creepers and vines which grew abundantly all around them.

Through the entire process, Two Feathers only winced and cried out once.

"I do not know what to do about the arm... do you?" Jacques asked Richard.

Richard shook his head.

"I do not think the bones are broken but it just hangs there," Jacques touched the Indian's shoulder lightly and saw him grimace in pain. "I think it has come out of the socket but do you know how to put it back?"

"I have seen them put back but I cannot say how," Richard replied. "I would not want to try."

"Where is the closest village?" Jacques asked the scout who was feeling somewhat more comfortable now that his leg was set.

"Down river... maybe half day more, small river. Lead upstream to fork, go up morning branch, take you my village."

"Then, that is where we need to bring you," Jacques said resolutely.

With careful tending, the Frenchmen kept the fire going all through the night. At times it was more smoke than flames and barely kept them warm but they looked at the broken body of Two Feathers and thanked God for their relative comfort. They both dozed off close to dawn when the air becomes even colder and just as the sun rose Jacques was startled awake by Richard's cursing.

"What is it?" he jerked up and cried out in alarm.

"A snake! A damned slithering son of the devil!" shouted Richard, grabbing at his chest and pulling a long tan snake, with brown markings edged in black, out from under his shirt where it had crawled in for warmth. With a snap of his arm he bashed the creature's head against the closest tree trunk and it immediately went limp in his hands.

"It bit me! The damnable thing bit me!" Richard pulled up his shirt and looked down at the fang marks on his chest very near his heart.

"*Mon Dieu!*" Jacques exclaimed in an agonizing cry, rushing to his friend's side. In an instant he imagined Richard falling dead at his feet. But as his companion continued to curse and mutter, it occurred to Jacques that if the snake had been poisonous, surely a bite so close to the heart would have killed almost instantly. He took a closer look at the wound. "Do you think it is a poisonous snake?" he asked cautiously.

"Naww, it has a round head. But it hurts all the same," Richard replied petulantly, rubbing his chest. "Well, at least we have breakfast," he added with a grim finality and used the knife to slit the snake's skin and gut it.

They attempted to cook the pieces and tried to feed some to Two Feathers but the scout was now delirious and in a fever. They wasted nothing but carefully plucked the flesh from the bones and ate the meat themselves with grim determination. It was warm but more raw than roasted. They knew they would need the strength and fought their gag reflex in order to swallow. When they finished, the pair set about fashioning a crude litter to assist in carrying the injured Indian.

By the time they started on their way the sun was high in the sky. It was a difficult job to carry the dead weight over the uneven terrain. The ground was often very muddy and slippery. The underbrush was dense and heavy from a long season of growth. The vines which had helped them build their raft now tried to entangle their feet and trip them. Thorns tore at their clothing and skin, producing scratches and lines of blood to mark them. Onward they pushed in grim determination, ignoring the ever present mosquitoes.

Two Feathers' leg was swelling and they had to stop and readjust the birch bark wrapping. Jacques noted the young scout's fever was growing steadily worse. He moaned almost constantly, a clear indication that he had lost touch with reality. Indians were taught to face pain stoically and did so unless they were unaware.

The sun was on its downward path in the autumn sky when they came upon the tributary stream and followed it. The day had turned very hot and humidity radiated from the wet landscape. Sweat rolled down their brows and their bodies as they continued to pick their way along the river bank trying not to jar the injured youth. Jacques led, Richard followed. In the cooler underbrush the mosquitoes attacked them viciously and with their hands full they had no means to defend themselves.

"I understand why the Indians grease themselves up with bear fat," Richard said dully, a dozen mosquitoes sucking at his face. Jacques tried not to think about it.

They asked Two Feathers again about the village but he was no longer coherent and had begun rambling in his native tongue. It was all they could do to get water into him without choking him to death.

"Did he not say we would come to a fork?" asked Jacques.

"Yes," Richard barely grunted.

"He said we have to go to the *morning branch*... that must be the east fork. That means we have to cross water again."

Richard grunted.

They walked on for another hour before stopping for a rest. Carefully setting the scout down, they dropped to the ground themselves.

"I am so hungry, I could eat another snake," Richard groaned.

Jacques nodded in agreement and went to the river again to drink. When he came back he said, "I think we are going to have to make camp here tonight and try to forage some food." He took a long look at Richard and was struck by the comic ridiculousness of their situation. They were carrying a half-dead Indian up a river into the midst of God-only-knew-where, trying to find his people who well might blame them for his misfortune. They had no idea where they were going or whether he had directed them correctly. And even if he had been correct, they had no way of knowing for certain that the village would not also be wiped out as a result of the infernal warring. Which Indians were these? He had forgotten the tribal name. And what if they got there and Two Feathers was already dead? How would they make themselves understood and get assistance back to civilization? Civilization! It seemed a lifetime away. Civilization and Marie. Marie, dear, warm, sweet Marie. And what would she think of her gallant hero now, he thought, with not only feet of clay but a head full of holes?

Jacques burst out in laughter, humor was an antidote to misfortune.

Richard frowned. He didn't know what was so funny. His back and arms ached. His skin itched. His chest felt bruised and swollen where the snake had bitten him. His shoulders were numb from the pressure of the weight of the load they carried. He didn't think there was anything amusing about the peril they were in. Everything had gone wrong and they could hardly ask for worse trouble.

"Just what is so funny?" he snapped.

"You! You look like hell!" Jacques choked out between guffaws.

The answer surprised Richard and made him think of the pitiful sight they made and as he thought, he too, was struck by the humor of it and began to laugh as well. He looked at Jacques' fair hair hanging in dirty, mud and blood encrusted strings from beneath his filthy bandage and down his face, a face swollen with mosquito bites and sporting an ugly purple bruise along the forehead. It really was quite funny. Jacques' coat was tied about his waist, hanging torn, shapeless, saggy and muddy over his rear-end. His shirt, equally filthy, torn short at the bottom, ripped and stained with bloody scratches showing through. His breeches, mud splashed with a hole in one knee, and shredded from thorns, showed glimpses of his bruised and blood streaked legs. His friend looked nothing like the impeccably dressed young gentleman who was to have inherited a dukedom.

"So do you!" Richard bellowed back with a roar of laughter. "The peasants of France slopping their pigs look better than we, *mon ami*!"

Hearing Richard laugh made Jacques laugh even more, and hearing Jacques laugh harder made Richard double up until they both were laughing so hard the tears were running down their cheeks. At last they stopped.

"Enough, enough," Jacques gasped and wheezed, sucking air and trying to regain his composure. His head was hurting again. "As horrible as things have gone, let us be honest. It could be worse."

"Uhmm," grunted Richard soberly. "Things can always be worse until the moment one is dead ... and then? Who knows."

Jacques nodded and sought to be positive. "Surely there are fish in that river. Why do you not try to catch some, eh? I will gather wood and look for nuts, berries, perhaps a fat squirrel will beg to be skinned and roasted. We will get a fire going. We cannot go any farther today."

Richard nodded in agreement, wiping the tears from his face while leaving dirt streaks behind. He moved to the river and stripped off his clothes as a precaution before wading in. The water was cold but felt good and in time, with patience, he managed to catch a large trout with his bare hands.

Jacques made his way into the forest seeking nut bearing trees. He saw nothing. He gathered his arms full of wood, brought it back to the camp and started a fire. Then he set off in another direction. The squirrels were scampering about in fright as he walked and he didn't know how he would actually catch one. He was no good at this sort of thing, he thought. Foraging like a native, eating off the land, this was not his strength. He had been brought up to eat off fine linen tablecloths and forage only at markets. He needed a musket to hunt with or at least a snare. Jacques stepped down on something that rolled and he almost lost his balance. He looked down and saw dozens of small greenish spheres. Walnuts! He began to gather them up, twisting his jacket around and using it like an apron in which to hold the nuts. They would have to be cracked open but they would give nourishment.

With his jacket full, Jacques turned to go back and felt the painful goring of yet another very sharp, thorny branch as it caught on his back. He uttered a low curse and tried to gingerly disengage himself without further pain and without dropping his harvest of nuts. It was then that he noticed the blackberries. He tied his load of nuts into his jacket and took off his shirt, using it to collect the berries. This was excellent, he thought proudly gathering all he could see.

Walking back to camp, he spied yet another treasure. Bright red stalks with berries of deep wine purple. He had never seen these before and picked several stalks with his free hand before continuing on. He walked into camp just as Richard caught a second fish. Thank goodness for Richard, Jacques thought. They would eat well, considering.

Jacques looked to Two Feathers who was in an uneasy sleep. He managed to get the young scout to take more water. Richard came back from the river's edge with his two hands full of cattail plants.

"If we can figure out a way to cook these, they are almost entirely edible."

"How do we do that?" Jacques said a bit impatiently. "I seem to have misplaced my cook pot."

Richard said nothing but looked over what Jacques had foraged. "Throw those out," he commanded, pointing at the smooth purple berries on the red stalks. "Those the Indians use for dye but they are not edible."

Jacques looked up half in disgust that Richard should know this while he did not and half in humble thanksgiving that he had not been able to pop them into his mouth coming back from his gathering expedition. He tossed the attractive berries into the brush.

Still naked and not wanting to take the time to dress, Richard strode back to the river's edge and picked up a series of small round stones. He brought them back to the fire and placed them on the hot coals. The daylight would not last forever. He hurried off to a distant birch tree barely visible through the darkening forest.

Meanwhile Jacques found a large flat rock and a smaller one to use in cracking the nuts and brought them back to the light of the fire. He was curious as to what his partner was up to but had been unwilling to ask. He began scaling and gutting the fish, after which he skewered them on a sturdy stick and set them to roast over the flames.

When Richard returned, he had a large piece of birch bark, fresh, green, and supple but it was made even more so by soaking in water. He had seen that from Two Feathers' leg cast and left the bark set in an eddy off the river while he dressed. With the bark softened, it was easy to draw up at the edges, punch out a hole with the knife tip, and thread a vine through to tie it in place. He did this at about four equal distances around the edge of the piece and the effect was to draw it into a shallow vessel. Next he cut the cattail roots up very finely, placed them in the bark and added water.

Jacques watched as he tended the trout but said nothing. He knew Richard could not put the bark on the fire to warm. Even soaked, eventually it would burn up. Just how did he expect to cook the roots?

Richard took two small sticks and using them like tongs he plucked one of the stones, now exceedingly hot, from the fire and dropped it with a sizzling sputter into the bark vessel. He added another and then a third and a fourth. The liquid began to simmer as the stones radiated their heat into the water. After a few minutes, Richard took the stones out, putting them back onto the coals, while plucking out the remaining stones he had put there. One by one he placed the fresh stones into the vessel. The water was now visibly boiling.

Jacques sat observing.

Richard knew he was being watched. He looked up at last with a big grin. And as if to answer an unspoken question he replied, "I saw a squaw I know do this. And the little ash that gets into the cooking is not bad, it gives a salty flavoring. The brown top of the cattail we can try roasting and the green stalk can be eaten raw."

While the roots continued to simmer, Richard found a smaller stone, went to a flat rock by the riverbank and began cracking nut shells.

The sun had not yet set and Jacques decided to bathe in the river himself. He checked the fish which were securely spitted; there was time. Shucking his breeches he took his shirt with him as he walked into the river. He did his best to wash the tattered garment. Later he could put on his breeches and his coat while his shirt hung over a shrub to dry.

He worked as quickly as he was able. The water felt soothing on his mosquito bitten body and swollen face and eased the itch of his scalp. He removed his bandage but took care not to soak his wound. Best hurry, he told himself. When the sun went down the pests grew even more bothersome unless the temperature dropped as well.

As the sun disappeared the temperature did begin to drop and their bellies growled in response to the smells of the cooking food. Their fish was done and they built up the fire, bringing Two Feathers into the ring of warmth. Settling down to eat, they gingerly picked at the hot fish with their fingers and had to patiently avoid the fine bones while their mouths watered. Trout never tasted so good. The cattail roots had softened and they used clean twigs to scoop them out by the mouthful, adding starch to their meal. The berries added sweetness. The raw stalks were almost like a salad. They did not waste a morsel.

When they finished Jacques had a thought. "If willow has medicinal qualities perhaps we could do the stone and water trick to brew tea for Two Feathers to drink," he suggested cautiously. He had learned from Augustine years ago that just because a little of something is helpful does not mean a lot will be more helpful. He looked questioningly at Richard.

"A little could not hurt," the other man said and went to the river to clean out the birch container and bring back fresh water.

By the light of the fire, they continued to crack shells and eat nut meats although it was often hard to distinguish the meat from the shell. They had to chew slowly and when a too rigid crunch hit their teeth they spit out the offending mix.

When the water was hot, they added some of the willow bark still in Two Feathers' litter and allowed it to steep for a time. They let the liquid cool and managed to get the resulting bitter brew down the young Indian's throat. It seemed to calm him after a while. Richard wrapped the cattail heads in another scrap of birch and buried it all at the edge of the fire to roast until morning.

At last, totally exhausted, they sat on the ground against a tree and went to sleep.

Jacques and Richard slept fitfully, waking several times during the night to add wood to the fire and checking each time on Two Feathers. Jacques was certain the lad's fever had eased, Richard was not so sure. At first light, they were ready to continue their march but before breaking camp they made more tea for the Indian to drink. Jacques silently considered the dull ache of his head and decided to drink some as well. He was pleased when before too long his headache disappeared.

Richard pulled the cattail heads out of the coals. Some were burnt, some still raw and without seasoning they were barely palatable but he urged Jacques to eat what he could. It was sustenance.

Chapter 24

T he sun was well up in the sky when they came to the smaller fork they had been looking for. The stream did not look very deep and they crossed the western fork without any difficulty, getting soaked only to their knees. Continuing on up the eastern fork, it was not long before they were confronted by a young Indian boy who took off running before Jacques had the breath to call out. They followed in the boy's wake and soon found themselves in a woodland village of multiple long houses. Two Feathers was recognized and taken by his family who conveyed him to the hearth of the shaman where he could be cared for and his dislocated shoulder reset. Jacques and Richard were offered food and they dropped in hungry exhaustion to eat. After a few minutes of no real communications, a young brave in clothing unlike the others approached and spoke to them in broken English.

"You English?" he asked.

Richard started to shake his head and Jacques gripped his arm to stop him. Some instinct came surging forward at the question. Not - *do you speak English*, but an implied question of their nationality and perhaps their allegiance? In times of peace, a white was just a white to the Indians. Why did this one wish to know their nationality?

"We come from southeast," Jacques gestured. "We come in peace. We trade for furs," Jacques responded in the simplest possible terms.

The Indian instantly recognized the accent to his speech and replied in almost perfect French.

"*Vous es français,*" he stated. It was not a question.

"*Parlez-vous français?!!*" Jacques exclaimed in surprise.

"*Oui.*"

They continued to speak in French.

"We are from the country of France, across the water. But we are not soldiers."

"You do not fight the *anglais*?"

"No. We do not wish to fight anyone. We live in peace."

"But you must know of the fighting between the *anglais et français*," said the Indian, his face revealing nothing of what he really thought of the matter.

"*Oui*," replied Jacques honestly, "but we have kept to ourselves. We have been on a trading expedition all summer. We only desired to trade and go home."

"But you have no goods," the Indian observed.

"No, we lost everything in the river," Jacques said without hesitation and commenced to relay the entire story of the tragic events after the storms.

They spoke for some time. The Indian listened patiently and never took his eyes off of Jacques and Richard. He was judging them, they knew, and in the end he judged them to be truthful men. It was not so difficult. They had returned the scout to his people. And the white men knew Two Feathers could verify the truth or falsehood of what they said.

The native told them that as a child he was adopted and raised by a Frenchman who had called him "*Giles*" and that they might call him this. His adopted father was now dead and he had returned to his own people.

"Are these your people?" Jacques asked.

"No," Giles replied, "I, too, came to trade. But now I must tell these people of Bear Claw's fate. I will return."

Giles got up and walked away. He was gone for some time and when he returned a female was with him. She carried goods over her arm and a vessel.

"This is Corn Field Woman, mother of the brave called Two Feathers," Giles said formally, as the two visitors stood to greet her. "She wishes to thank you for returning her son."

"Tell her we deeply regret the loss of her other son," Jacques said sincerely.

Giles translated. The woman spoke quietly never raising her eyes.

"She says the two brothers were sons of the same father, but Bear Claw had a different mother."

The woman spoke again softly and offered forth the vessel she held.

"This is salve, to ease the pain of your flesh. It will help heal the cuts, scratches and insect bites," Giles explained. "And she has brought you a change of clothing to replace your rags."

"Please tell Corn Field Woman that her kindness will be long remembered," Jacques said suddenly taking on the presence and self-assurance of the station to which he was born. The lordly tone of his voice, along with his words and gestures, was gracious and gallant. "Tell her we are most grateful and appreciative, and that we are in her debt," he ended with an elegant bow that mocked his beggarly appearance.

Corn Field Woman knew the intent of the white man's words before they were translated and she stole a look up into his face. Jacques was startled to see that her eyes were a vivid dark blue. She was a very striking woman, he thought with practiced appraisal. An oval face, high cheekbones, thin well-formed nose, delicately sculpted lips, coal black hair and brilliant blue eyes under well shaped brows. He marveled that she could be the mother of a son as old as Two Feathers. Her skin was smooth and firm, and her breasts stood high upon her chest. His guess was that she was very close to his age and he was only twenty-four. She must have given birth when she was no more than eleven or twelve, he thought. And how did she come to have blue eyes? Unless her father had been white... or her mother? Jacques would never know. A sharp command came from a few yards away and the woman bent her head again and turned the clothing over to Giles before making a hasty retreat back to the lodge.

Giles brought them to a small sweat lodge where two stout squaws helped them wash the mud from their hair and bodies with a lathery herb. Jacques managed to convey the desire for a sharp blade with which to shave. Next, they were taken to the river to rinse after which their skin was sponged with the soothing astringent they had been gifted. Special care was given to Jacques' angry looking head wound. The young men finally emerged feeling refreshed and were assisted in being dressed into the soft, clean buckskins smelling sharply of fresh leather.

"What news, if any, have you heard of the fighting?" Richard asked of Giles as they approached and hunkered down beside him.

"The French have gone deep to the south and attacked Fort New York." He saw the briefest reaction from Jacques. "You do not live amongst the French?"

Jacques paused for an instant and decided to be completely candid. "No, we live in the English colony. I have had a... disagreement with the French Chief," he tried to simplify his situation. "I worship my God in a different way than the French Chief. For this they have made me an outlaw."

Giles considered Jacques' words. He remembered the Black Robes amongst his adopted father's people. They taught of shame and an angry God who punished severely those who did not worship Him as the Black Robes taught. The whites reverenced this and yet they sinned against the laws they professed to believe in. How was this better? "What kind of man makes another an outlaw for the way he worships the Great Spirit?" he asked bluntly.

"A man who has other motives to do you harm," responded Richard.

Giles nodded and was quiet.

"We have lost everything but we need to get back home, back to the great sea in the east," Jacques began and then asked, "Is there anyone who can take us?"

"French soldiers are there," Giles said gravely.

"What?" Jacques and Richard exclaimed almost simultaneously.

"The French have claimed all the land for the Big French Chief."

"Surely not passed the mountains and all the way to the coast?" Jacques questioned in disbelief.

"I do not know how far," the Indian said calmly. "What is today is not neces-sarily what is tomorrow. But for this winter, you are not safe here," he added. "The French soldiers were here a short time ago and they will return again."

Jacques' face was tight and sober. "What can you suggest?" he asked.

"You cannot go back to the English land now without going through French held land. You cannot go to the French land you say because you are an outlaw. I will take you to my people. They live near the shores of the big water, to the north-west."

"Lake Ontario?" asked Richard. "But there are French forts all over that area."

"No, we will go to the land of the Erie, farther west. My people. They will shelter you through the winter because I will speak for you. They will not betray you to the soldiers if they come around," he added in reassurance. "But we must hurry. The signs say winter is coming soon."

§

Marie placed the small hickory logs neatly together on the leather piece which wrapped around the bundle like a sling when its two handles were brought to-gether. It was a clean and comfortable way in which to carry firewood and saved her skin from scrapes and her sleeves from snags.

Although it was late autumn and the trees stood bare of their foliage she worked without outer wraps. The sun was warm as her little corner of the world was enjoying Indian Summer, the return of mild and pleasant temperatures after the first cold frosts and before the onset of the long, tedious winter. She brought the hickory to the smokehouse and threw some of the logs onto the fire within. The smokehouse was full. Pheasants, turkeys, venison, rabbit, duck even a beaver hung from the rafters soaking up the hickory smoke which both preserved and flavored the meats. Fish, scaled and gutted, hung on poles strung across the width of the structure.

Marie stood back, wiped her brow and brushed her hair back off her face. She felt grimy. She had been chopping wood all day in preparation for winter. It was a task Jacques and Richard would have done if they had been there. But they were not there. Marie told herself she would take out her wash tub later and treat herself to a hot bath before sundown. It would, perhaps, be her last opportunity to bathe outdoors this season. The river had grown very cold but using the tub outdoors af-forded her the ease of simply dumping the water where it stood as opposed to hav-ing to carry it by buckets back outdoors.

She looked around the clearing. With the exception of the squirrels chasing each other and rustling through the layers of fallen leaves, it was very quiet. The song birds had all flown off for the winter.

Outside of the small area of cleared land immediately around the tiny cabin, smokehouse, privy, and garden patch, the forest loomed close but naked. There were trails used by the savages to move about and hunt but they were narrow, often difficult even for a single person to traverse and easily lost to the lushness of new undergrowth. Now that it was autumn, one could see farther into the forest. The sunshine broke through lighting up the thick carpet of leaves which made everything look the same. It was deceptive and easy to lose one's way if one wandered too far.

From where she stood, she had no idea how many days it would take to walk to New York Towne. Her eyes fell upon the boat moored on the beach and covered over with tarp. Jacques and Richard had thought to cover it before they had left. That had been in spring when the Indian guides had come to get them. Summer was long gone and autumn would soon be ending. She had expected them back before this.

Marie had not been totally without company through the course of the summer. Toward the end of May she had had her first white visitors. A family, passing by in search of a spot to homestead, had stopped to rest and spend a few minutes in neighborly conversation before deciding to continue on up the river, seeking to homestead on the southern banks. They were the first to bring news of serious fighting to the north.

In June, there seemed a small migration. Marie counted a total of five families who had sailed into the harbor and after saying a friendly "hello" had pushed farther into the forest via the river to find a place of their own on which to build. She invited them to come back down river to see her when they needed supplies.

It was one of these families that told her the fort at New York had been attacked by the French in retaliation for raids that had been made on their settlements near Montreal. The attack had come by sea and it made Marie wonder if she would see any French Navel ships. The fighting seemed to be going on more heavily in the New England colonies, however, and this perhaps explained why more settlers were beginning to show up in her harbor. Some were new to the continent and had been told not to go north because of the trouble, others had moved south from farms not worth fighting over in the rocky terrain farther north.

The most lurid part of the ongoing hostilities was that both sides had allied with Indians, the French with the Algonquin and the English with the Iroquois. And both groups of Indians were known to be brutal, fierce warriors and unrelenting enemies. Horror stories traveled quickly, even on the frontier. To Marie's shame, it was said the French had taught the Indians to take scalps as proof of the numbers they had killed. One family coming into the harbor brought with them a catatonic sister who had miraculously survived the rape of a war party but had seen her husband and two small sons murdered and scalped right before her eyes. The woman had been a ghostly figure, Marie recalled, unlike anyone she had ever seen before. A breathing body that walked when led, sat when gently prodded but had no will and held no expression of face. Eyes totally vacant clearly stated no one lived there anymore but somehow her heart had forgotten to stop beating.

For a long while through the summer Marie saw nothing of Looking Glass and his people. She did not know what Indian tribe they were from, nor did she know who were their allies. For all she knew, Looking Glass and his band might be involved in the fighting as well. She hoped if they were, it was for their side, which was to say, the English side. And she hoped he would be safe. Then, in autumn, the Indians came to trade. Their animal kills had been bountiful and they were generous to her, seeing her all alone again without her men. Most of the things in the smokehouse had been gifts or near gifts easily bartered from Looking Glass.

The young woman relaxed quietly in the still autumn afternoon enjoying her warm bath in the fresh air. She thought about all she had managed to accomplish since spring and she was justifiably proud. She had planted another garden, somewhat larger as she had tilled up more garden space. And the bounty the dark, rich soil put forth was amazing. As the garden had grown, she had hit upon the idea of digging a small root cellar. Not knowing exactly how she would build a cover or closing, and not knowing how to protect it from the animals without a cover, she decided to dig it in the corner of the second room of the cabin. She reasoned that when the men returned, they could build a trap door to cover the hole before anyone fell in. They might also decide to enlarge it, but she was certain that in order to make it any larger it would have to be braced and supported with planks to keep the ceiling from collapsing. As it now stood, it wasn't very big, but it had been tedious and backbreaking work to do as much as she had.

Hour upon hour, she had labored to dig up the earth, filling the wheel barrow, making the trip to dump it only to return to fill it again. She had given some thought to her dumping. The first layer of top soil she had spread out into the garden area. Then as she dug into sandy clay and stones, she had begun dumping each load at a low spot near the privy. The spot was no longer low but level with the rest of the yard. And her onions, carrots, squash, turnips, rutabagas, and beets were safe in the cool recesses of the cellar for winter.

Sacks of husked dried beans were hanging from the rafters of the small cabin where they were certain to stay dry along with her harvest of garlic. The dozens of glass jars the Wingates had given to her as a wedding present were filled as well. She had raised peas and spinach and had gathered enough berries during the season to make jams. When she found a wild crab apple tree by following a trail of blossoms on the water in spring she kept an eye on it and in late summer, she gathered the fruit by shaking the limbs over a sheet of muslin spread upon the ground. She rendered out apple butter from the tiny little apples once they were cooked to a mush and strained through her cooking sieve. Full jars now lined the pantry shelves they had constructed.

She had gone back to the small walnut grove along the river and was delighted to discover the trees heavy with their fruit which now sat in a sack by the hearth. Shelling was a task that could wait; she thought to occupy herself with it during the long, cold winter days. Perhaps she could coax Jacques and Richard to help.

Marie sighed. She did not know what else she could do to prepare for the season ahead but it bothered her greatly that the men had not yet returned. She had done as she knew Jacques would have done and made certain everything was properly stowed away in case of snow. Experience had taught them that Indian Summer was short-lived and ended with a swift change to hostile weather. The woodpile was overflowing and the axe and hatchets were safely indoors. There was a large supply of wood beside the hearth, as well as two large baskets of kindling. The privy and smokehouse were secured from animals. The oil lamps were all filled. Finally, she had toted the water from the creek, warmed it at the outdoor fire ring and settled down for the luxury of a hot bath.

Early that evening, after emptying out her bathwater and bringing the tub inside, Marie threw more logs on the fire in the cabin. She prayed earnestly for Jacques and Richard's safe return and went to bed in her shift. She had not slept naked since Jacques left. In his absence she chose to cocoon her sensitive skin from sensual stimulation. She longed to hold him in her arms again and ached with the need for him to caress her.

As she burrowed beneath the blankets and furs into the snug warmth of the featherbed, she could tell the weather was indeed turning colder. She had banked the fire and watched the flames from a single fat lamp cast shadows and reflections upon the bearskin rug. Vaguely she wondered if she would wake to find Looking Glass and his comrades asleep by her hearth in the morning.

Marie awoke. The fire needed to be tended. Stirring up the embers, her first concern was to get the hearth blazing again. The light coming in through the cracks in the shutters was oddly bright and she suspected they had just had their first snow fall of the season. Once the fire was crackling and strong, she put on her boots, pulled the fur cape Jacques had given her around her shoulders, and opened the door. She squinted at first until her eyes had time to become accustomed to the bright scene of fairyland enchantment. Everything was covered with a thin pristine blanket of pure white snow.

Coming back from the privy, she detoured to the stream, and dipped out a bucket of water to bring inside to boil for tea. If it had snowed here, she thought, it had undoubtedly snowed harder in the mountains to the west. She looked around her. The distant hills were all awash in white. Where were Jacques and Richard? Never would they be gone this long by choice, she told herself. Something had happened.

There was no longer any doubt in her mind. Something was most definitely wrong or by now they would have been home. But what? That she could not answer. It could be as simple as a detour that had cost them time. They could be arriving at any moment, she still told herself with hope. Or had they become in-volved in the fighting? Perhaps they had been hurt. They could have been cap-tured. They could be half frozen in the snow. *They could even be dead* a voice whispered in her head, and she refused to listen but the hobgoblins of the unknown had descended upon the cabin to take up residence with the young woman. Day by day they invisibly tormented her, chipping away at her peace of mind and invading her dreams. Marie grew quietly terrified.

Winter had rolled in to stay and the little cabin was soon half buried in the drifting snows. Only the steady rising wisp of smoke from the chimney gave evi-dence of life while Marie stayed within, besieged by her private demons. She went out only once each day to empty her slop pail, bring in fresh water and another load of firewood. Long hours of lonely monotony and gloom wore down her spir-its and natural buoyancy. She lost her appetite and forgot to eat. She tried to read, but could not keep a train of thought that did not dissolve into worry. She paced like a prisoner in a small cage. All alone with no other living creature to relate to, depression grew like an insidious cancer.

In all her life, she reflected, she had known only flashes of happiness. Why had she thought it would be different just because she had fled to the other side of an ocean? She had been learning to get along alone well enough when last winter had truly changed everything forever. The admiration, affection, and love she had long felt for Jacques had suddenly become so much more. Perhaps it had not been so sudden. When had she first known, she asked herself? When had she first been aware that she loved him so completely the passion scared her? It had scared her so badly she had tried to deny it. Pretending she could accept being just a mistress to be discarded in the future. It had been self-preservation, a defense mechanism. On some instinctive level her heart told her that feeling too much had the potential of being much too painful, perhaps even fatal.

But he had taken her by breathtaking surprise and had turned all her carefully controlled feelings upside down by confronting her with a passion of his own and by asking her to be his wife! He had asked her to share a lifetime together. Had it all been too perfect to last?

If she had never known the sweet security of Jacques' strong and gentle arms, the idea of life forever without him would not now seem so absolutely terrifying. If she had never felt the heat of his embraces, she would not now know how cold and empty her existence without him would be. If she had never experienced the potent fervor of their coupling, she would not now know all that she might lose.

With his fine talk of a future with endless possibilities, she had allowed her-self to visualize bigger dreams than she was meant for, she told herself. Visions of complete happiness with him, making a real home, having a real family for a life time. Now, the piper stood in the dark corner and awaited his pay. Had she not rec-ognized long ago that she lost everyone who meant anything to her? Her mother. Her sister Louise. Her infant. Bo-bo. Anoui. Better for Jacques if he had been meaningless to her. She was cursed!

Why, oh, why had he ever shown her how it could really be between a man and woman? She cried silently in despair. She had not known. She had been blissfully ignorant. Now, had she lost him and he had not even left her with a child to fill the empty void in her heart? It was just as well, she told herself, staring into the flames of the fire as they danced hypnotically before her eyes. For doubtless, the Fates would have snatched that from her as well. Like the first one. Like everyone she had ever loved. She remained alive while Fate took everyone she loved away from her.

Marie's mind drifted dangerously in her solitude. Perhaps she was not meant to have children, she considered. Perhaps she would never have a child. Perhaps that was God's punishment, His judgment upon her for her sins. All last winter, her monthly flow had continued to make its appearance. As many times as she and Jacques had made love, she had not conceived. All the times Bouchet had forced her, she had not conceived then either. And while it was true that Anoui had conceived no children by Bouchet, Jacques was a virile young man, healthy and strong. His seed had filled her to overflowing and yet, there was no baby. Was she now barren? Perhaps her foolishness at twelve with a traveling player had left its mark on her forever. Was it such a big sin, God? She cried out to Heaven. Was it so unforgivable that she was to remain barren for the rest of her life? What had Jacques said? *Will you have my children, my sons...?* She had given him a promise and that promise had included children. What if she could not fulfill her end of the bargain?

Will you have my children, my sons?

And she had said yes.

Will you have my children, my sons? Do you promise before God?

And she had promised.

Will you have my children, my sons?

Will you have my children, my sons?

The words echoed over and over in her head. Perhaps she had no right to make such a promise.

Her depression grew deeper as night followed day and day followed night in the endless soul searing solitude. She slept for hours and hours at a time, waking only to tend the fire then falling exhausted into her bed again. Dreams conjured up images of Jacques. She saw him standing by the fire in his dark breeches and soft, white shirt open at the throat. One fist resting on his hip, the hip where he used to carry a rapier. His thick, blond hair pulled back neatly at his neck. He looked at her with kindness, with smiling clear gray eyes. She wanted to go to him but could not move. He held up a glass in a toast. Suddenly, she saw his eyes grow cold, like sleeting rain. He turned from her in hurt, in disappointment, in disgust. He no longer held a glass, he held - Celimene! She could see him turning into a passionate embrace with Celimene. Celimene with her loose negligee hanging off her plump ivory shoulders was offering up her perfect breasts to him, pulling him to her. Celimene, opening his clothing with easy familiarity, her hands seductively assaulting his flesh. Celimene, with her wide, ripe full mouth, was reveling with Jacques as she had so often in the past. Marie could envision his impassioned responses to Celimene's adept caresses. She could see his explosive reaction, his sated look and then, spent, he looked back to Marie. A look that said she had cheated him and he loathed her. He had married her only because she had promised to give him sons. A promise she had no right to make. She was a cheat, a deceiver.

Marie awoke sobbing and she thought her heart was breaking in her chest. If he did come back, he would grow cold to her, she could see that now. He would grow to hate her she thought as tears streamed down her face. He would grow to regret their marriage and see it as his biggest mistake. He would be miserable and take mistresses and ignore her, ignore her to shrivel like a plant deprived of the sun. She could not stand it, she sobbed hysterically, she could not live. It would be better to die. It would be better to end it now, have it all over. Finished!

She was far down in the bottomless pit of her despair, and sinking farther and farther every day into the depths of her aching loneliness and agonizing depression. Torpidity encased her as life ceased to be worth living, air ceased to be worth the effort to breathe. She cried herself into a stupor of exhaustion and then she did a very foolish thing.

Totally drained, she fell into a sleep unmindful of the dwindling fire upon her hearth. She had failed to bank it and as she slept in tortured fatigue, the fire burned smaller and smaller until only embers remained. The embers consumed themselves until snow began falling down the chimney, dampening the remaining bits. The hearth grew cold. Marie slept on, warm within her bed of furs and feathers. More snow fell, covering the hearth, and the cabin grew cold. And still Marie slept, enervated and unaware.

Cold comes as a silent enemy, stealthy, mute and numbing, tumbling in as warmth rises and leaves. Noiselessly, cold spreads its fingers out over the ground, stealing under furniture, fondling shoes and rising to creep like fog between blankets, sheets and fabrics. Cold steals through shutters and fills the corners and sucks the warmth from within pillows, cupboards, baskets, pails, books, containers, chests, and beds. Piling onto itself, climbing over itself, like a serpent sliding, gliding, stealing the warmth from all it touches, rising higher until all remaining warmth is surrounded, smothered into chill and soundlessly turns frigid.

§

Jacques felt Marie's warm lips on his. Her firm taut breasts filled his hands, silken beneath his fingers. She was under him with her legs wrapped tightly about his hips, then she was over him, weightless, her slender legs bent at the knees and tucked along side his thighs. Her hot moist flesh enveloped his. His body reacted and he groaned a little, savoring the sensations she evoked. He tried to draw her even closer, tried to bury himself more deeply within her, seeking the rhythmic stroking that would bring release but the more he sought her the less he could feel her, the more ephemeral she became, the less he could feel anything. Suddenly, she disappeared completely like a mist, a vapor, and he was left with an ache that went far beyond his physical need. It was an ache that went to the very center of his being.

With a sudden intake of breath, Jacques started up in a reflex reaction. He was now aware of his surroundings and knew he had been dreaming. He turned gruffly onto his side. His ache was all too real. In the gray darkness of the early morning, he lay within a bed of furs and listened to the ferocious fury of the wind as it howled, whistled, and thrashed through the tall pines outside and shook at the small hut like a giant beast trying to gain entrance. Less than three feet away from his head, Richard lay snoring, totally unaware of the maelstrom, a young Indian girl asleep beside him. The small peat fire in the center of the hut was glowing, radiating warmth, but the angry wind drove the drafts that tried to steal the heat away.

Jacques sighed, burrowed deeper into the furs and sought to shut the noisome wind out of his mind by thinking of other things. Last winter he had been with Marie in their cabin. They had felt so safe and secure. One never feared the wind was going to tear apart a sturdy little cabin of logs. They had been sublimely happy sharing an intimacy they had only just discovered with each other. And this winter? He shivered a little despite the fur layers about him. This winter he was not even completely certain where he was and he could only hope that his dearest darling was safe.

Did she have supplies? Somehow he knew she did. She was not a woman of weak vanities, he thought proudly. She was resourceful and intelligent. In fact, he had no doubt that she was doing much better than he.

Dear God, how I miss her, he cried out silently.

Alone with his thoughts, Jacques had time to consider how his feelings for Marie ran far deeper than anything he had ever felt for anyone before her, far deeper than he had thought possible. The way he felt about his wife, he analyzed, must be the way his father cares about his mother. *My wife.* Never had he thought he would so like the sound of those two words. He was so proud of her, admired her grit and determination and he wanted to give her everything. But he had nothing to give her and now they were miles apart. How he longed for her presence, just to know she was there, to hear her breathing even if they did not speak or touch. He wanted to share himself with her, his thoughts, his dreams. He wanted to grow old with her. She had become his other half, a half without which he no longer could feel complete. The Biblical mystery of cleaving together and becoming one - it was very real.

He had no fancy for other woman. This was how he thought it should be. *Forsaking all others*, those were the words they had pledged. And Jacques had been very serious about his marriage vows. Unlike his father, he had been allowed the precious gift of being able to wed the woman he loved and for that he was truly thankful. In this new world, he had been allowed a love match.

In the gloom of the hut, Jacques sighed again, and raked his hand through his tangled blond hair which he knew was in great need of cutting and washing. It felt greasy and itched. He felt like an animal. He would plait it, he decided, like the Indians, like Richard. At least it would keep it out of his way.

A thick beard covered his face and as he scratched he was certain it was inhabited. He wrinkled his aristocratic nose at the smells around him. This was not how he expected to spend his first wedding anniversary - holed up for the duration of the winter in a rank hut infested with lice, with an Indian girl who reeked of rancid bear grease and putrid musk, and Richard smelling like the devil himself! Jacques smiled as he reminded himself that he undoubtedly reeked like a goat as well but had progressed beyond the point of being able to smell his own stench. They had been wearing the same clothing day in and day out for what seemed like forever. And the last hard rain of autumn in which they had been caught was the closest thing to a bath they had had since they had almost died in the river and then been tended in the village of Two Feathers.

With a smile Jacques thought of Marie's little tub and how she had washed him that first time. He sighed. And there had been other times after, much more relaxed and unquestionably delightful. Then he recalled his first experience in this village's sweat lodge. It too was supposed to be cleansing and relaxing but sitting in close quarters with a half dozen sweating, naked savages just was not the same.

Life was full of ironies. Last winter he had slept with Marie, and Richard had been alone. This winter it was Richard who had a woman and Jacques was alone. But he could not envy his friend. Jacques knew that with Marie he shared something on which to build the future. What they shared went beyond the physical. They talked, they had plans, they exchanged ideas and dreams. For all that Richard had a female in his furs, he was, in fact, still quite alone.

And, Jacques reminded himself ruefully, he really had nothing to complain of at all. They were exceedingly fortunate to have this shelter and the hospitality of these people. They could just as easily be frozen meat for the wolves out there somewhere in the frigid, gale driven snow.

The plump young Indian girl stirred beside Richard. She slipped out from under the furs, completely naked except for the long thick straight black hair which fell about her shoulders to her waist. Taking care that her hair did not fall into the fire, she stooped to put more peat within the circle of stones in the middle of the hut. Next, without inhibition, she squatted over a designated vessel and urinated, her gently rounded belly protruding slightly over the almost hairless pubis at the apex of her legs. Jacques saw her go to the entrance of the hut, her bronze skin blending into the shadows. She peeped through a flap in the skins and muttered something softly. Then, she took a long, thick fur robe and wrapped it around herself before grabbing up a large vessel. Opening the flap over the opening at a point low to the ground, she used the vessel to scoop snow from a white wall drifted up against the portal. In her other hand, she grabbed a large pile of snow. She promptly brought the snow back to the fire, emptying the contents of her hand into a cook pot and setting the vessel, now filled with snow, within the circle of heat created by the fire. Soon the snow would melt to water. The first added water to the stew pot which hung, always warming, by the fire; the second would provide drinking water. She went back with a second vessel, repeating her actions, and then a third. Each vessel took its place near the warmth of the fire. After assuring herself that the door flap was closed tightly again, she dropped the robe and returned to Richard's side, crawling back into the skins beside him.

The wind continued its relentless howling, shaking the top of the shelter and threatening to carry them all away. Jacques knew the snow which was building up around them actually had the effect of insulating and protecting them from the worst of the wind. They would stay in the small hut made of sapling limbs, bark, mud, and skins for the entire day. They would sleep late, eat dried meat and stew, drink the melted snow water in the form of a weak herbal or berry tea, and sleep some more. He and Richard would play cards as they puffed on pipes of tobacco or chewed upon licorice root. At some point each in turn would go out to a designated area which lent itself to the purpose and defecate. Undoubtedly today it would take many minutes to warm up again after that experience. And later, Jacques knew he would turn his back as he heard the quiet noises of Richard sporting with the girl whose belly appeared to already be swelling with his child.

There were a half dozen long houses located near them in which the rest of the community lived. Each was approximately fifty or sixty feet long and fifteen to twenty feet wide. Each a low structure with a large fire ring in the middle and several smaller ones with strategically placed holes in the roof to allow the smoke to rise upward and out. The roof openings were baffled by an over structure of woven branches designed to keep the wind and snow from having direct entrance from above. Jacques had only obtained the briefest glimpse into one of the buildings through an open doorway when they had first arrived in camp. They were strangers and had not been welcomed into these lodges where each family already had their own areas staked out. But as guests brought into the camp by the Indian Giles, they had been offered young maidens to serve them through the lonely winter and a shelter of their own nearby.

At the risk of offending his hosts, Jacques had declined the offer of a female. Giles had told the chief man that Jacques was "newly joined" and that seemed to have brought some measure of acceptance and understanding of his refusal which else wise could have been taken as an insult. The head of the tribe later sent Jacques a gift of the white man's playing cards, left behind by a past traveler. They understood that these helped white men to pass the time.

Richard, on the other hand, had accepted the offer of a maiden with great enthusiasm and chose the plumper of two graceful, dusky skinned sisters. She seemed very pleased with his almost nightly attentions to her. And he was pleased by her eager willingness.

The young girl was satisfied with the white man who had chosen her but she would have willingly gone to the yellow hair as well if he would have asked for her. The whites' unusual ways were not without excitement but she had a greater goal in mind. When her moon time came and went with no evidence of bleeding, she had said nothing but knew she would have a baby by late summer. If the child was born strong and healthy, proving her own fertility would increase her bride price. She would have a choice of suitors approaching her father with offers for her to mate before her sister. Meanwhile, the young girl, quiet, unassuming with a smooth round face and eyes like a doe, placidly cooked for both men.

Jacques thought of when Marie had cooked for them. In his mind he saw the wispy little curls at the nape of her neck when she wore her hair up on her head to keep it out of her way. Her neck was warm and tender and he liked to nibble the spot just below her ear where her blood pulsed and she smelled like sun on a summer wind. Then, working his way around to the tops of her full, round breasts he could inhale another magical scent there, like a cross between fresh hey and spices.

Jacques scowled to himself as he felt his loins tighten again and he forced his thoughts away from Marie and back to the previous summer and the events that had brought them here. How far had the French really gone? He wondered. Giles had said they held the fort, did that mean the town? That did not seem possible. It was maddening not to know. Were the Wingates and the Thompkins under French occupation? He could just see Mistress Van Hootenaug giving them a piece of her mind. He smiled at the thought. At least he knew Marie was in no danger on that account. She was an innocent civilian. But what must she be thinking now? He had promised to return in the autumn. He was a man of honor, a man of his word and he had not been able to keep his word to his beloved. Did she think he was dead? He wished he could get a message to her. To let her know he was safe, to let her know he would return, to let her know she was not a widow.

It was impossible, he realized, all his thoughts eventually led back to her, his wife, his darling. He couldn't get back to sleep and he couldn't stop thinking of Marie. While he lay there in relative comfort in an Erie Indian village as the snow fell upon a frozen landscape, how was she faring? Was she suffering from his absence? Was it possible that she might miss him as much as he missed her?

The wind had died down and the snow had ceased by the time Richard awoke and nudged the girl to get them food. She obediently got up and pulled a buckskin shift over her head, covering her full breasts and ample hips. By the dim light of the fire, the two men emptied their bladders into lidded containers designated for the purpose, then they dressed in their leather clothing. Jacques, like Richard, had ceased shaving when they had lost all their possessions but he ran a crude comb through his hair before sitting down cross-legged by the fire ring, dipping his fingers Indian style into the stew pot and sucking the contents off them.

"In a few days," Richard said cheerfully as he ate, "this storm system should pass, the sun will shine and we can go out again and check our traps, eh? Perhaps Giles and the others will arrange a hunting party. And if we are successful there is always a celebration and perhaps an invitation to the sweat lodge. We could stand the diversion of a party, *n'est-ce pas?*"

Jacques nodded silently, wishing, hoping, and praying for an early spring.

Chapter 25

Northwest of the river valley, two ridges over from the small bay, a proud brave stepped from his lodging into the bracing wind. His snowshoes made a light squeaking sound as he walked across the snowy landscape. He was unmindful of the biting chill as he progressed up to the crest of a knoll where he stood to look southeastward toward the sea. He saw no smoke. The thin trail of smoke, which day after day told him the *shëwanàkuxkwe* was there and alive, could not be seen. His keen eyes continued to search the sky. The storm had passed and the day was clear and still. He stood silently for many minutes stoic in his resolve. Pulling his buffalo skin robe closer, he walked back down to the fires of his village. Pausing at the doorway of his longhouse he called to his sister.

"She-Who-Laughs-In-Her-Sleep, I want you to come with me. Bring a travel packet, a sack of meal, and snow walkers." A grunt told him he had been heard. Satisfied, he went to the large fire at the center of the village to warm himself and wait. From here he could quietly survey the community activities around him.

After a few minutes, a stout little squaw dressed in thick fur-lined boots, heavy fur trimmed leggings, a long buckskin tunic, and a robe to match her brother's, appeared outside the hide covered doorway. It was not her place to question why or where they were going. She was the elder of the two but he was the undisputed authoritative head of their extended family and their clan. She had packed a bundle including basic necessities as well as travel cakes made of cold cooked meat, dried fruit, and rendered fat. She nodded to her brother handing him an empty clay pot and stooped to fasten lightweight, woven reed snowshoes upon her feet. He used a long wooden shovel designed for the purpose to load hot coals from the active fire into the pot. Together, they left their village and she followed quickly as he broke the trail and led the way carrying the pot full of coals dangling from rawhide roping.

§

Marie stirred in a languid fog of consciousness. Her bladder ached for relief but she was still so very sleepy. She wanted to sleep on, just a little longer. The pressure continued to mount. Her limbs felt like lead. If she could only sleep a little more, she thought muzzily, but the automatic functions of her body continued to demand attention. She didn't want to open her eyes but by now she was murkily aware that if she did not get up she would urinate right there in the bed. For a fleeting second her brain half formed a thought that it would be warm and warm would be good. With an immediate reaction of disgust, she forced herself to reject the idea of soiling her lovely feather bed. She blinked her eyes and began to become aware of just how cold the cabin was. Her limbs were stiff, oddly cold even under the furs. Was there a window open? She was beginning to shiver and she thought her bladder would burst. First, she must relieve herself, she thought, then, she must put more wood on the fire and discover the cause of the draft. With great discomfort, Marie rolled over swinging her feet out of the bed. The bear skin rug felt icy even through her thick woolen stockings. Suddenly, she realized with a jolt of alarm that there was no fire. It had gone completely out and the chimney was funneling frosty air into the cabin like an open door.

"*Mon Dieu!*" she cried aloud, her breath gushing forth steamy vapor. "I could freeze to death!" Her words hung in the paralyzing cold of the cabin as a flush of panic made her heart beat faster.

The instinct to survive is strong. When faced very tangibly with the alternative, Marie definitely wanted to live. But first things must come first. Freezing cold as it was, she had to use the slop pail or urinate upon the cabin floor. Vapor steamed up from the pail just as her breath steamed in the air of the cabin. It was so very cold, she thought, shivering so violently she could barely control her stream. She pulled her boots on as quickly as she was able although they too were icy cold, and she wrapped herself in the long fur cloak Jacques had given to her. She set about finding kindling. Stomping her feet and rubbing her hands together, she looked for something with which to start a flame from the spark of the flint box. Normally, she kept a small cash of dried grasses but she had used it up and failed to replace it.

The hearth was full of snow. She swept it aside. It would surely put out any small fire if not wiped completely dry. She took a cloth and rubbed hard to rid the hearth stones of any trace of ice crystals or the slightest bit of moisture.

"How could I have been so stupid?! So, so stupid!!" she castigated herself aloud repeatedly. Everyone knew it was far easier to keep a fire going than to start one anew.

She recalled the terrible wet winter in France when so many had died. She remembered how wet the wood had been and how the fires had to be kept hot enough to dry out the next sticks to be burnt. But back in France, she told herself as she blew on her numb fingers and searched for one of the men's tools to make shavings from the wood blocks... back in France, if your fire went out and you had trouble, at least you had a neighbor nearby. There had been many hearths from which to beg hot embers. Here there was no one!

She found a plane and scraped at the wood block until she succeeded in making a small pile of shavings which she gingerly stacked on small sheets of birch bark placed upon the cold hearth stones. The shavings would burn quickly, she thought, she needed twigs. Twigs! And where was she to find twigs? She had to stand up again and jump up and down. As she did she sang a silly children's song in French and flayed her arms about. Anything to make herself warm. After a few minutes of exertion, she did feel warmer again but she knew she could not do that forever. She would become exhausted and to fall asleep again would be certain death. Marie had no means of measuring but she could tell the temperature had dropped significantly beyond mere freezing.

She must think and work quickly. Thinking was becoming more difficult. Twigs. That is right, she told herself, she needed twigs. Where? Perhaps she could cut twigs. Her eyes fell upon a log. No. Not from a log. Too difficult. It would take too long. Perhaps if she could make the smallest kindling even finer. No thicker than twigs. She took the head of the axe with both hands, trying to still her shivering, and sliced along the grain of the kindling wood creating huge slivers. It was exactly what she needed. Reducing several larger sticks of wood to large slivers, she considered her chances of progressing to the larger pieces. As long as it was dry, it should burn well. She felt it. Her fingers were so cold and numb she could not feel. But it should be dry. She was ready. Taking the flint box she struck and struck to get sparks. The sparks fell ineffectively upon the wood shavings. If only she had dry grass, straw... pine needles! She found her sewing scissors and opened the door to Richard's bedroom. To her surprise it actually felt a bit warmer in the second room. Opening one of the mattresses, she pulled a handful of needles out and rushed to the hearth adding them to the wood shavings and birch bark.

She needed a spark large enough to ignite the needles and prayed the birch would help. Once there was a steady flame she knew the birch bark would burn easily. Clumsily she struck the flint a half dozen times or more when a large spark hit the tinder, flared up and began to burn. As softly as her chattering teeth would allow, she breathed upon it to coax it into a flame. She saw the flame flicker when a gust of wind came down the chimney and scattered it out.

"Oh no!" she cried. "Please, God, please... help your stupid child!" She gathered the needles together again and continued striking the flint. "Please, please," she begged. By now her fingers were so stiff she could not feel the flint in her grip any longer. Another large spark hit the birch bark and she sought to protect it by cupping her hands around it. Her fingers were clumsy.

This time the spark ignited the needles and a tiny flame curled up. She coaxed it on, protectively sheltering it, gently blowing on it, adding more needles. The flame burst forth larger, igniting the birch. Marie nervously added the remaining needles, then the wood shavings. They burned. On top of the shavings, she began to lay the twig-like slivers. The flame grew larger still. As the twigs burnt, she tenderly added the wood sticks, the smallest at first, then a few larger.

The fire was now established and she thrilled to its first heat as she spread her hands close to it. Quickly she broke down more kindling into smaller twig-like pieces, nursing the precious flame. Adding some of the larger kindling, she let it take hold before attempting to put in more. When she thought it was burning hot enough she added one of the smallest chopped logs and then a second for two burning together always burnt the best.

It would take time before the cabin would be warm again. Without a bed of coals, she would have to watch over the fire very carefully. She huddled at the edge of the hearth and continued to whittle more tinder to add around the log.

It had taken all morning but, at last, Marie had a fire going on the hearth and she was able to think of other things, such as food. She was famished. She still had some smoked fish and pheasant on the table. They were brick hard and she brought them to the hearth to warm. She must remember to go to the smokehouse and bring more meat into the cabin so it could thaw, she told herself. She swung the stew pot over the flames to melt the cold fat and warm the leftover contents. Now she needed to get some fresh snow to melt for tea.

She opened the door and was visibly startled to find Looking Glass standing there holding snowshoes in his hands with a squaw behind him in the act of removing her own snowshoes. Marie let the door fall open and the tall brave strode passed her into the cabin. The squaw followed quickly and was drawn to the warmth of the fire where she immediately removed her fur mittens and extended her hands over the flames.

The brave's sharp, dark eyes took in everything including the tools Marie had left on the hearthstones, the hollow of the bed where she had been sleeping and the wood chips clinging to her cloak. He could picture what had happened.

Marie filled her large pot with snow and shut the door. She had no time to guess what he was doing there before he spoke to the squaw and she turned and spoke to Marie.

"My brother say... where you men?" she said in rough but understandable English.

"You speak English?!" Marie gasped in astonishment. "How...where...how do you know English?"

"I learn my man," she answered simply, her dark eyes placid as she pushed back her fur hood. Marie stared, observing that the woman had painted her eyelids, cheeks and the rims of her ears with the same vermilion color as her brother.

"A white man?"

The squaw nodded.

After a moment, Marie asked, "What is your name?"

The little squaw spoke something Marie could not pronounce or understand. Then she said, "You say... She-Who... mmm... Laughs-In-Her-Sleep."

"She-Who-Laughs-In-Her-Sleep," Marie repeated gravely. It was odd but she dare not laugh.

The squaw nodded.

"I welcome you, She-Who-Laughs-In-Her-Sleep and your brother."

"He call... Son-of-Sky-Hawk," the squaw said by way of belated introduction.

"Son-of-Sky-Hawk," Marie nodded and added graciously, "Come, please, sit by the fire."

The brave spoke again.

"Son-of-Sky-Hawk want know... why you men no here?" the squaw translated. "Why leave you alone?"

"I do not know," Marie answered quietly frowning slightly in worry.

The squaw spoke in her native tongue and the brave answered.

"My brother say, not good be alone in winter."

"Tell him I thank him for his concern," Marie tried to speak slowly. "Please, make yourself comfortable. I am so pleased, so very happy to be able to speak with you. You must have some food with me and hot tea." Marie gestured as she spoke.

As the squaw tried to translate, Looking Glass grunted, laid his snowshoes aside and sat down before the fire. The squaw did the same. Marie tried to get them to sit on the chairs up off the cold ground but they refused. So, as she made tea, she drew up her small stool before the fire to join them. They all shared the comfort of the bearskin rug.

After she had passed out cups of the hot beverage and they had drunk, the brave spoke again and the squaw translated.

"My brother say, white men must be weak. You have two men but no children."

Marie had to smile at the assumption that she had two husbands. She dished up the food and shared it with them. They ate silently for a few minutes. Marie noticed that the Indian brave would not look directly at her although she had the distinct impression that he observed everything about her. This was not like his behavior when he came to trade. He spoke again.

"Son-of-Sky-Hawk say you much brave woman live alone. But wrong to be alone. He strong man, have many sons. Be your man. Give you many children."

Marie was conscious of not allowing her mouth to drop open as she sat stone still and was more than a little shocked by this... proposal. She kept her eyes on the little squaw as she thought for a few moments. She looked cautiously at the brave who sat stoically upon her cabin floor not looking at her. Finally she spoke.

"Tell your brother... I am... very honored by his offer. Very honored to call him, *friend*," she replied slowly using her hands to help illustrate her words. "But tell him my God says I can have only one husband and this I already have. We only just," she gestured by locking her little fingers together to indicate a joining, "became man and wife this spring. In time, I am sure we will have many children," she added valiantly.

The squaw turned to the brave and translated. As she finished Marie continued, "The second man is a friend, not my man. He is my husband's friend... like brother... for many, many years. They hunt and trap together. He has his own room." She gestured toward the additional room.

After the squaw finished, there was a short silence before Looking Glass spoke again.

"My brother say he think you man not come back this time."

Marie swallowed hard. It was a terrifying thing to hear voiced aloud. "I do not believe that," she said quickly. "I cannot believe that. My heart is with him," she gestured, "and he must come back. Do you know anything about the fighting to the north?" she asked the brave directly.

The squaw spoke and Looking Glass replied by shaking his head.

They had finished eating and Marie put more wood on the fire. "Where do you live?" she asked, wanting to change the subject.

"Two… mmm…." she chopped the air. "Long-hill over," gestured the squaw, pointing northwest behind the cabin.

"Do you have children?"

"Oh, yes, three son, big... hunt with Son-of-Sky-Hawk many time."

Marie had a sudden realization. If those were her sons that came with Looking Glass, no wonder one had green eyes. His father was evidently the white man who had taught the woman English. And now she understood the odd colored hair on several of the youths. They did not have Indian black hair and were able to add some form of coloring to it.

"Tell... Son-of-Sky-Hawk," Marie spoke again, "that I did not know his name before so I gave him a name myself. In my mind I called him *Looking Glass*."

When the squaw spoke to the brave this time, he reacted pleasantly, smiling and then replied.

"He say like name. You call him this. He say he give name for you, too."

"What is it?"

The brave said something and the squaw questioned it, the brave grunted, and the woman shrugged and spoke.

"He call you *Woman-Who-Make-Battle-On-Bread*."

Marie remembered when she had slapped his hand from her bread dough and she laughed lightly and nodded her head in amusement.

"Tell him, it is a good name," she smiled broadly, "but my Christian name is much shorter... it is Marie... he may call me that if he likes."

Marie gave them more hot tea and as they continued to sit before the warmth of the hearth, she began to reason to herself. Had Looking Glass been watching her cabin? Surely he could not see it from two ridges away but perhaps he could see her chimney smoke. That must be it; he saw no smoke and knew she had lost her fire. They had come all this way in the snow and icy temperatures to save her from freezing to death. Such a friendship was invaluable and she wanted to give them both a token of her gratitude. *It must be something dear to me,* she thought, *so they will know I prize this friendship.*

During her last year of working for the Wingates, she had taken a fancy to a little music box that had come in one of their shipments of merchandise from England. It was the only extravagance Marie had allowed herself as she struggled to save her pennies for the future. She took it out every once in a while just to hear something besides her own breathing and the crackle of the fire.

She went to the trunk, opened it, and took out the music box. She also found a small hand mirror with tiny painted flowers decorating its frame. She knelt down before the couple and presented Looking Glass with the music box. She opened the lid and it began to play. The brave looked startled at first and then smiled broadly.

"Please tell your brother that I wish him to have this gift with my many thanks for the honor he does me by being my friend," Marie said slowly allowing She-Who-Laughs-In-Her-Sleep to interpret. "How do you say *friend*?"

"*Win-ga'-leet,*" the squaw responded.

"*Win-ga'-leet,*" Marie repeated.

Looking Glass listened attentively, then he spoke, shaking his head.

"My brother say he cannot accept, he have nothing to give you," the squaw replied. "Gift giving must be... ahhh…" she gestured in frustration.

"An exchange?" Marie guessed.

"Yes. Exchange."

"No. He must accept," Marie said firmly. "Tell him I know he came here to save my life. Such a friendship is his gift to me. Tell him it is I who am in his debt, I who need to give him a gift in exchange. Please, tell him." She urged the squaw and waited for her to translate. Marie thrust the music box into the brave's hands with an expression that matched the words.

He accepted. Marie studied his face and he looked pleased. He spoke again.

"My brother say you give him much honor."

"And this is for you," Marie added and using both hands, she presented the mirror to the squaw. "I am happy to call you *win-ga'-leet* also, and give you this as a token of my friendship to you."

The squaw smiled for the first time. She was missing several teeth. She giggled as she looked at herself. Looking Glass was still staring fixedly at the music box. After the music ran down, Marie demonstrated how to wind it up again so the music would play on.

"Tell your brother he must not wind it too tightly or it will break," Marie warned and after the squaw finished speaking, Marie showed him how to make it start and stop by opening and closing the lid. He was fascinated.

It was growing dark outside and Marie did not expect her guests to leave anymore that day. It was difficult for her to reconcile the idea of trying to be a good hostess with allowing one's guests to sleep on the cold ground, even if it did have a bearskin rug, especially when there were two empty beds in the next room, but the two Indians would not leave the fireside. At last, she pulled the mattresses in from Richard's room and arranged them by the fire. Bidding her guests to make themselves comfortable, she said goodnight and slipped fully dressed into her own bed.

The next morning, Marie awoke to find the fire in the hearth burning brightly, fresh water boiling in the pot, and smoked fish warming by the hearth for her breakfast. She-Who-Laughs-In-Her-Sleep had baked cornbread from the meal she had with her and Looking Glass was not to be seen although a large supply of freshly chopped wood had been brought in and set by the fireplace.

"Good morning," Marie said sleepily and stretched.

"Food ready," the squaw said smiling a gaping grin.

Marie dippered out some of the hot water into a wash bowl, mixed it with some cold, and washed her face. She brushed and pinned back her hair. Then, making herself a cup of hot tea, she took some fish and sat down at the table to eat.

The squaw brought the cornmeal cakes to her.

"Eat... good," she encouraged Marie to take some.

Marie took one cake, brushed a trace of ash from it and gingerly broke off a bite. Putting it into her mouth, she considered the subtly sweet taste and decided it was good.

"What is this?" she asked.

"Mmmm...m-maize." the Indian woman strained to think of the white man's word. "Grow tall, have big stalk, dry, make meal... corn! You call corn," she finally remembered with satisfaction.

"It is good," Marie replied in surprise, she had eaten cornbread at the inn but it had not tasted like this. She ate in silence for a minute. She needed a cow, she thought, so she could have milk, cream and butter, and make cheese.

"Where is your brother?" she asked casually.

"He go back."

"Back?! Back where?" Marie asked quickly.

"Back to village."

"But he left you! Why did he leave you?" Marie asked in stunned surprise.

"I stay with you."

"But...." Marie sputtered, unsure what to make of that. "You have a home, family, children... do you not want to be with them?"

"My children big, they no need me. My family have each other. You have no one. I stay with you until your man come or snow go," she said matter-of-factly.

"Your brother is making you do this. He ordered you to stay with me."

"My brother right. No good be alone in winter. Much bad happen," she spoke casually.

"And your husband? Your mate?"

"No mate."
"Oh... I thought... I mean you said your man taught you English..."
"Many year ago. He gone now."
Marie was not certain what to say. She did not know if the man had died or had simply left the Indian woman. So she said nothing and dressed to go to the privy. When Marie returned she said "She-Who-Laughs-In-Her-Sleep...oh, my, I cannot keep saying that. I am going to call you *Sheehoo*. Do you understand? Sheehoo. This is my name for you, is this acceptable?"
The squaw looked at her and grinned.

As the days and weeks went on, Marie had to admit to herself that Sheehoo helped to keep her mind from dwelling on Jacques' absence. The squaw continued to sleep by the fire but each day she rolled up the mattress and stored it on the bed in the other room. She shared in the cooking tasks, watching and trying to do as Marie did things.

Shehoo was quiet and as unobtrusive as possible although more than willing to talk and laugh if she sensed that was what the white woman desired. This was an extraordinary experience for Marie. To have someone who was not a lover, live each day trying only to serve her was a very different and novel experience for the young woman sprung from peasantry.

The squaw's English grew better as she practiced it, but her thoughts remained simple and direct. At first, Marie thought the woman to be a little dull witted. But, she was quick to learn many things and wise in her own way. No, Marie finally concluded, the Indian squaw simply had such a different way of looking at life. Perhaps to her, Marie was the one who seemed dull witted.

The Indians appeared to put great store in family and a need for community. Marie learned that apparently they never did anything alone except for specific challenges, religious rituals, or punishments. Usually a lone brave did not go hunting; several braves formed a hunting party and went together. And they left their women behind... but together. From what Marie could understand, the supreme punishment in their society was ostracism, being cut off from the rest of the tribe. Well might they wonder what she was doing here in the wilderness, all alone, an ocean away from anyone she could legitimately call family. She was not even living within the greater community of white settlers. Did they think she was being punished and were too polite to ask?

And if, indeed, Jacques and Richard were never to return, what then, Marie asked herself? Would she continue to live alone, or go back to New York? And if she were to go back to New York, what could she do there besides become someone else's servant for a pittance? Well, she answered herself with bleak sarcasm, she could always take Looking Glass for her man and have many papooses.

No sooner had the thought passed through her mind when she reprimanded herself for it. She had known people far worse and more savage than these natives.

It was, in fact, a noble gesture on his part. He was offering to look after her, protect her, take care of her and provide her with the joy and security of family. Not so very savage an attitude. She was undoubtedly as alien to him as he was to her but he had had a white brother-in-law at one time. She supposed it was possible that he might even feel a kind of affection for her, in his own fashion.

And why not, she told herself less glumly. If Monsieur Jacques-Jean, the handsomest nobleman in France, could view her with affection then it was certainly possible that other men could as well, even a New World savage. She smiled to herself ruefully. But the sad reality was, she could never love anyone else, not as she loved her Jacques. He *must* come home to her, he simply must.

And so the days passed.

Chapter 26

Marie stood in the doorway of the cabin basking in the warmth of the early morning sun. She could hear the steady dripping of the melting icicles as their water fell to the ground off the edges of the roof tops on the various structures. It was good to see the snow melting into the earth and feel the tender, warming breezes float in on the air. She noticed wild bloodroot flowers pushing up in sunny spots away from the streaks of snow along the edge of the forest. Spring was coming early this year. That was good, she thought, she was hungry for fresh greens. But that also meant there would no longer be any reason for Jacques not to make his way back home... if he was alive. And if spring came and went and there was still no sign of him? What then?

She pulled her mind back from that avenue of thought and considered instead her food stocks. Some of her stores of harvested food remained but the purchased goods were seriously depleted. She had not been back to New York Towne since spring of the year before. Doubtless, if she had been cooking for two men all winter, she would have run out of all her staples. But as it was, she and her female companion had made it through the winter without much difficulty.

Turning back into the cabin, she watched with curiosity as Sheehoo began to gather up every pot or pail she could find around the cabin including the new ones Marie had in stock as trade goods. Taking the container her brother had carried hot coals in, the Indian woman filled it with fresh hot coals. Putting several of the pots into Marie's biggest cook kettle along with a mallet from the tool box and an awl, she beckoned to Marie.

"Come, we walk," she said simply and waited for Marie to bank the fire and put on her heavy boots and cloak. Giving her the remaining smaller containers to carry in the second largest pot, along with a food packet Sheehoo had prepared, the stout little woman led the way across the roughened ground.

Marie had no idea where they were going or why but she followed. The native woman led them up a hillside through the naked forest. Marie had never gone into the forest this far from the river for fear of losing her way but Sheehoo seemed to know exactly where she was. They climbed and while the southern exposures were clear and dry, snow still clung in deep patches in the hollows and on the northern sides of the hills.

They had walked perhaps three-quarters of an hour, perhaps more, and Marie was beginning to run out of patience with the burden she carried while lacking a reason for it. She still knew no purpose for this hike and she was about to say something when they came to a stand of sugar maple trees. Sheehoo halted with a smile of satisfaction and put down her load in the midst of a small clearing.

Marie watched as the Indian woman began systematically tapping into the trees with the awl and mallet in order to insert a small trough shaped tree branch into each hole. Before long, sap was dripping from the spout-shaped branch and into a pot strategically placed below to catch it. Sheehoo could tap only two dozen or so trees before the containers were all in use. With a final grunt of satisfaction, the woman began to pick up scattered tinder while beckoning Marie to join her. In a short time they had foraged a heap of dead-fall and with the coals they had carried, they started a small fire and sat down to have an early lunch.

They ate unhurried and enjoyed the warmth of the sun and mildness of the day. The wind came gently from the south and Marie could swear she smelled spring in it, a robust fecund scent laced with chlorophyll and sweet blossoms carried from some distant place already budding forth in fresh growth.

After lunch they checked all the pails. Marie was amazed at how quickly the sap flowed out of the trees. Sheehoo urged the continued gathering of firewood and so the pile grew until she decided it was time to pour all the sap drippings together in the largest kettle and commence to boil it down. The women continued to feed their fire.

The boiling sap gradually rendered down into a sweet syrup which Sheehoo poured into two equal smaller pots. She kept some back, and returned it to the fire to continue boiling. Now, she stirred the pot continuously, watching it closely. As drippings outside the kettle were licked by the flames, the smell of burnt sugar perfumed the air. After considerably more boiling, she took the kettle from the fire and set it into a deep patch of snow.

It was getting late in the day and the shadows were growing long. The women picked together their belongings and organized everything for their trek back to the cabin. Just before they left, the native took the cooled pot and poured its contents out upon an area of deep snow which she had prepared by scraping off the top layer and exposing a pristine surface beneath. The thickened liquid crystallized as it hit the cold snow and turned into hard maple sugar chunks. She handed a piece to Marie and gestured for her to eat. As Marie put it into her mouth, the older woman gave her a gaping grin.

Marie ate a small piece of the maple sugar and nodded her approval while exaggerating her sounds of pleasure. It was different, she thought to herself, a bit too sweet for her liking, at least to just eat by itself, but she did not want to offend her companion. It was obvious that Sheehoo thought this a very great treat indeed. Marie did not know that this syrup was a greatly prized trading commodity introduced by the northern tribes. Indians far and wide used the sweet syrup to flavor many of their dishes. Marie was not certain what she would do with the container of syrup she had been given. Jacques or Richard might like it, she thought, perhaps over pan bread and it would serve as a substitute for honey.

In the next days of early spring, Marie noticed the birds returning. Sheehoo showed her early greens which could be eaten and pointed out a number of plants that made passable teas. Others had medicinal qualities, the native woman told her. Some, however, could make one ill or even bring death and should not be touched. Marie took in all this information and made notes as best she could until she finally gathered the courage to ask the question burning within her.

"Can you tell me..." she began hesitantly, "is there something... do you know of anything that could help me have a baby?"

Sheehoo giggled profusely from behind her hand. At last, with appropriate sobriety she spoke. "Need man for that."

Marie smiled sadly and nodded. "I know... but after all winter together with my husband last year, I have no child."

"You make..." Sheehoo made a sign which Marie took to mean the act of sexual intercourse and she nodded.

"Many, many times."

"Not that many. He gone again in early spring."

Marie thought carefully. Sheehoo was right. They had said their vows just before Christmas and Jacques had left again in... was it really only three months? But still was that not enough? "I had a child, many years ago," Marie confessed "but I was very young and it died."

"Same man?"

"No, but we," she made the sign for intercourse, "only one time and I was pregnant."

"Maybe that one have stronger spirit."

Marie thought of the young boy from the traveling players whose face was now blurred into a blank and the idea that he was in anyway *stronger* than Jacques was absurd. But she nodded in agreement not wanting to debate. She knew from the medical book she had read that conception had to do with a female's eggs and something called *spermatozoa* from the male and had nothing to do with spirits. So the Indians were mistaken there. Perhaps she had somehow been damaged carrying a baby when she was so very young. Perhaps she should see a doctor. She shook off the thought as she told herself bitterly she did not even know if Jacques was still alive.

Game began to appear more frequently and the river was full of fish. Marie had learned how to set snares and fish nets and knew she would not starve but she could not do business without trading staples and supplies. She pondered on the plausibility of going to New York Towne alone. The boat was there where Jacques and Richard had left it. She was not overly fond of boats for she could not swim. The idea made her uneasy. To put off making a decision, she turned her attention to preparing her garden for planting.

She had plenty of seed from last year's harvest so she and Sheehoo worked to clear more land. Marie could clear brush and saplings but there wasn't much she could do to fell large trees, she thought. Sheehoo showed her there was. By cutting a deep ring completely around a tree and pulling the bark away for several inches, one essentially cut the tree's throat, the woman told her. Sap could not rise and the tree began to die. It was slow but it would work and had the added advantage of becoming dry wood for easy burning when it was chopped down. In the meanwhile, no foliage grew to shade the ground around it. Sheehoo wondered where Marie's corn was to go.

"We do not need any corn," Marie answered simply. "since we have no cows or pigs yet."

"Cows?"

"Yes, in France we feed corn to the cows and they give us milk and cheese."

The Indian woman said nothing. She was not certain what *cows* were and did not understand the meaning of *cheese.*

Marie was enjoying an early evening soak in her over-sized wash tub while Sheehoo sat quietly by the hearth tending the hot water for her. She had become used to seeing this *shëwanàkuxkwe* do strange things. When the air warmed, the squaw would go to the river to bathe. There she would find the soap root plant. By pounding its roots she would obtain a juice with which she would cleanse herself along with a handful of sand. Throughout the winter she had missed the regular visits to the tribe's sweat lodge but she could not imagine sitting in stagnant hot water like a vegetable in a stew pot.

"My brother will come soon," Sheehoo said matter-of-factly.

"To take you home?" Marie asked quietly as she languidly squeezed the water from her washing cloth, letting it run over her exposed flesh.

The squaw nodded. "Time to go."

Marie felt a rush of loss and small tremor of panic. "I have been very glad to have your company. I shall miss you." The squaw was silent but acknowledged Marie's words with a nod. "You must miss your family," Marie added after a moment, realizing she was thinking selfishly of only herself.

The squaw said nothing for a moment but watched Marie bathe her compara- tively pale skin. The sheen from the water made the white woman's skin reflect the fire light. Her shoulders and breasts sparkled. Sheehoo understood for the first time how her brother might be attracted to this person.

"My brother good man, very good provider," she said at last.

Marie nodded.

"He care much for you. Will treat you good. He make good husband. He have strong spirit to give you children. Have two wives now, plenty children. Never beat wives. Very patient. They share work. Raise children together. Have easy life."

Marie paused midway from wringing out her washing cloth. "I understand... but it cannot be. I wait for my husband."

"What if husband no come back?" the woman asked bluntly without emotion.

"Please do not say that. I cannot think like that." Tears welled in Marie's eyes and the squaw remained silent for a long time. Finally she spoke again.

"Not safe to be alone so long time... very bad in winter. No good for mind, no good for heart, no good for body," she asserted and emphasized her words with gestures.

Marie sat staring at the water in her tub.

"If he no return by time leaves fall again, you go back to your people. My son guide you to white men's village north, many days walk but he guide you," the In- dian woman said simply and as if there was nothing left to be said on the subject, she got up to add wood to the fire.

Marie understood the wisdom of what the other woman was saying. She had become dangerously melancholy in the lonely sameness of the close solitary con- finement of winter. The company of another human being had made all the differ- ence. Since the Indian woman's arrival Marie had not once thought of just giving up and dying. And she had not allowed herself to be haunted with doubts about Jacques.

Sleep did not come easily that night. Marie kept hearing Sheehoo's words and dwelling on what would become of her if indeed, Jacques and Richard never came back. They could be dead. They could have been attacked by an animal, become infected and died. They could have been attacked by natives, or by French sol- diers... or English soldiers. Had she not heard them say there was danger from both sides? Or might they have drowned? Or fallen off a precipice? Or become ill?

Her mind would not be quiet. Marie tossed and turned all through the night.

The next day at daybreak she was still thinking. If she had lost Jacques... her breath caught in her throat. She was not giving up hope. There might be any num- ber of things that had happened and he could appear again at anytime. But if she had lost him there was nothing she could do about it. But there was something she could do about not losing everything they had started here together. She would steel herself and continue on. She would fight to keep it. She would continue on here no matter what until the wilderness took her as well, if that was God's will.

Marie set her mind. As she finished her morning tea she resolved to ask the next person who arrived by boat or the first settlers who came to trade, to go with her back to New York Towne for fresh supplies. She had the pelts and furs which the Indians traded last year. It would doubtless be a difficult struggle but it was a chance for something. And was that not why she had sought coming to the New World in the first place, for a chance at something better? She had never expected it to be easy. If Jacques and Richard did not return, she would try to find someone to stay with her over the next winter. She now realized how deadly and dangerous solitude could become. Perhaps one of the older Indian children would like to learn English. Somehow she would continue on. She would not give up hope. Had not Anoui said we must never give up hope?

With determination Marie put on her oldest clothing. She wrapped small rags around her hands and taking the axe and sickle, she set about clearing a wider swath into the forest. She worked with a purpose. She worked to clear the under-brush and seek out any fallen trees which she could chop into firewood. The winter had used up her supply. The Indian woman joined her and together they toiled away until sunset, stopping only to eat and saying almost nothing. That evening Marie prayed. It was a simple prayer asking God for the wisdom to know what to do next. Physically exhausted, Marie slept soundly that night and woke up re-newed.

The next day the women set about burning the pile of underbrush they had created and a column of smoke rose high in the air announcing their existence to the world. After a time Marie thought she caught sight of a craft coming into their harbor. Immediately she felt her heart leap within her chest and begin beating rapidly with joyful anticipation. She raced to the cabin to wash her face, take off her apron, and comb her hair. She said nothing to Sheehoo but the squaw could guess from the huge smile upon Marie's face and Sheehoo returned to the cabin herself to wash her face.

Fairly flying back outdoors, Marie could no longer see the craft but awaited its reappearance upon the river. At last it emerged into view and Marie's happy joy suddenly disappeared. They were strangers! But strangers could take her to New York Towne. They saw her and steered towards her.

Suddenly Marie's instincts told her something was not right. Unlike previous visitors, there were no women with these men. She had a sudden awareness that she was more than halfway down the switchback and she had no weapon with her. She began to backup as inconspicuously as possible.

"Halloo!" one called as they moored their craft on the river bank below her.

She did not like the look of them. There was something about them that re-minded her of the men who had robbed her on her first day in New York Towne. And they had no skins to trade that she could see, nor did they carry trade goods.

"Hey there, little missy," one grinned wolfishly at her as he stepped out of the boat and onto the shore. Marie instinctively continued to backtrack up the switch-back. "C'mon now, no need to be afeared. Would your man be around?"

None of her former visitors had ever asked her such a question. She saw the way their eyes kept darting around as though they were assessing her vulnerability.

"What is it that you want, monsieur?" she called out, hoping she did not look as frightened as she felt.

"Well, did ya hear that, Jethro?" the first said to the second with forced jovial-ity, "looks like we found us a *ma-dam-mo-zell*."

"Yeah, Herk," the other nodded with a manic giggle and they both continued walking steadily up the path. The second man suddenly leaped from one level to the next putting himself within striking distance of Marie's feet and she bounded up to the top. "Now what's a pretty little Frenchie gal doin' down here all alone?" His eyes continued to dart, searching the cleared area for signs of anyone else.

"Maybe this here's a comfort house, Jethro," Herk chuckled slyly as he came up behind his partner. "Is that it, huh?" he asked Marie, "I hear-ed about them Frenchie comfort houses with the fancy Madams and the friendly young girls. Are you a friendly girl 'cause we sure could use a little... comfort?"

They both laughed maniacally.

"Stop right there!" she said in her best shopkeeper's voice. "You are not wel-come here. You are rude and insulting! I am a married woman and my husband who is very skilled with weapons has only stepped away to check on something and he shall return at any minute. Best you leave before he returns."

Her attempt to sound confident and bluff them was not working. She contin-ued to back up passing her oven and pressing toward the cabin. Suddenly the door flew open and Sheehoo darted out, musket in hand. The Indian woman passed the musket to Marie who checked the pan and held it steadfast toward the strangers. She had never fired upon another human and she remembered what Jacques had once told her – not to face another with a weapon unless she was prepared to use it. With lightning flash speed she remembered how Bouchet had violently raped her, how those wretched men in New York Towne had robbed and tried to rape her. She *was* prepared to use it. Marie's fear was replaced with confidence, she was prepared to kill if she must.

"I know how to use this, monsieurs, and I will. Now leave and do not come back!"

Startled for a moment, the pair stopped in their tracks to assess.

"Well, now, there ain't no need to get all uppity. We was only funnin' with ya and besides," the one called Jethro slowed his speech to a threat, "there be two of us and you ain't got but one shot."

Marie knew it was true and doubt showed on her face.

The men considered. They were far enough away that she might miss. The Indian woman flashed a knife but either one of them could take her down. The first one laughed as they once again began to inch their way forward.

"So what is it ya do way out here all alone?" asked the one called Herk.

"Stop! Come no closer! As I said, I am not alone. This is a trading post. People come all the time to trade but you have no skins so be on your way."

Trading post! It was a business! Business meant if not money or gold, at least supplies, furs, weapons perhaps, and all that stood between them and that kind of booty was this little slip of a gal and some dumb squaw. The two men looked at each other. In that moment they rushed the women. Marie did not hesitate; she fired and hit Jethro full in the chest while Herk wrenched the knife from Sheehoo and punched her unconscious.

"Jethro!" bellowed Herk, turning to his partner who was bleeding out on the ground. He looked at him in shock for a moment before he grabbed at the musket and screamed at Marie in rage mixed with anguish, "He's dead, you brainless cunt! You kilt him!! You done kilt him dead!!" Marie clung desperately to the weapon. After a brief struggle, he succeeded in wrenching it from her hands and using it as a club he knocked her in the head and only then realized he was bleeding himself from where the native woman had sliced him deeply in his side.

Marie felt his blow like an anvil and her legs crumpled under her. Everything was swimming around her, she barely heard her attacker's screams of anger nor was she aware that after inspecting his own wound he was swinging the musket up aiming another vicious blow at her head. Everything had gone black.

The next thing Marie knew hands were on her and she tried to push them away but arms lifted her and she was powerless. White hot bolts of pain shot through her eyes and her head throbbed while her limbs felt dead and weighted. Somehow her featherbed seemed to swallow her before she blacked out again.

§

Son-of-Sky-Hawk carried the wild turkey he had just killed on his way to the white woman's cabin. He planned to give it to her and escort his sister home. As he walked in silence with his nephews, he wrestled with the idea of asking She-Who-Battles-On-Bread once again to join his family. He would protect her and provide for her and he would not leave her all alone. He was a proud man and facing a woman's possible rejection was not an easy thing. But this time she had been abandon for over a year. In his culture this was considered breaking the union. After a year with no word, even if the husband came back he could not expect to find his wife still waiting. If this woman wanted a cabin to live in, he would build her a cabin rather than bring her into his long house. Was it not sometimes better to keep wives in separate dwellings from each other, he asked himself?

Musket fire rang out! At the sound, Son-of-Sky-Hawk dropped the bird and dashed out of the forest ahead of his three nephews. A man was shouting. He knew immediately what was happening when he saw the white man wrench the weapon from Marie's grip and deliver a blow to her with the end of the musket that dropped her to the ground. His sister already lay fallen. Grabbing his hunting knife from its sheath as he ran, Son-of-Sky-Hawk leapt upon their attacker before the offender knew what was happening. Throwing the full force of his solid body against the other with an enraged visceral need for violent retaliation, the large Indian knocked him to the ground and slit his throat in one swift continuous motion. The man was no good and the world would not miss him. Son-of-Sky-Hawk was no stranger to having to make such swift judgments.

As his nephews ran up, he said, "See to your mother." There was no need; her oldest son was already assessing his mother's injuries. All three sons carried She-Who-Laughs-In-Her-Sleep into the cabin and made her comfortable on one of the mattresses brought out onto the bearskin rug. The eldest produced a softly sueded piece of leather, dipped it into the water pail, and mopped his mother's face until she could think clearly.

Meanwhile, Son-of-Sky-Hawk picked up Marie and brought her in to her bed. There was no doubt that she was alive for she tried to fight and he admired her for it. She was only half conscious and did not recognize him but she was brave.

"This is what comes of a woman being left alone!" he stated rather forcefully as Marie still lay unconscious. "Sister, my heart is heavy that I put you in this position. It is because of my decisions that you have been injured. Forgive me. As leader of our clan, it is my responsibility to protect you, not put you into danger."

She-Who-Laughs-In-Her-Sleep touched her jaw and moved it gingerly; nothing felt broken. She could open and shut her mouth but her entire face ached as if she had been slammed against the log walls. "My brother," she spoke softly, "it has been a rare experience to live with the *shëwanàkuxkwe* and learn her ways. I must thank you for it. There is no cause for guilt or reason to apologize. But I am very glad you are now here. We both owe you our lives. The Great Spirit sent you at the right time; these men are evil."

"These men are no more, my mother," said her eldest son.

"Good. The world is better without them."

"Take the bodies to the far side of the clearing and burn them without ceremony," the older man instructed his nephews. "One of you stay to tend to your mother, the other two say the prayer to bind their spirits to the darkness. Strip the bodies and the injured shall have first choice of all their possessions. Anything they do not want you may keep."

"Yes, Uncle," they said almost in unison and worked out who would stay and who would see to the tasks.

"I intend to claim this woman," Son-of-Sky-Hawk said turning again to his sister. The youngest of her son's had chosen to stay with her and the youth respectfully did not listen to the conversation of his elders. "It has been over a year. She has been abandon by her men. It is not just and she is not safe."

She-Who-Laughs-In-Her-Sleep propped herself up against her son so she could look more easily into her brother's face. "My brother," she said sadly but evenly, "I would advise against this."

"I saved her life! It is my right to claim her!"

"Yes, it is your right… in *our* world but not in hers. She would hate you if you forced her to leave this place against her will. She would think herself nothing but a prisoner and slave. You cannot want to bring a woman into your family who feels only discontent."

Son-of-Sky-Hawk did not like the words he was hearing but he heard them all the same. She-Who-Laughs-In-Her-Sleep had lived with the *shëwanàkuxkwe* many months and possessed the greater knowledge of her. His sister's insight and advice were worthy of his hearing.

"Today has proved she should not live here alone," he persisted.

"I agree, my brother, and I have already told her this myself. I told her if she cannot accept you as her mate, she should go back to her own people. I think when she thinks on the events of today, she will know the wisdom of this. But *she* must decide. It must be her choice."

"To leave her more than a year," he scoffed unkindly, "they must be dead."

"Perhaps." The squaw tried to sit up on her own. Her head was throbbing. "I have need of willow bark tea," she said evenly.

"I will make it my mother," her son said and left the cabin in search of the nearest willow tree.

"She has much love for her mate," the Indian woman said quietly, looking over at Marie. "I do not believe he abandoned her. I think he is dead but it will take her a long time to accept her widowhood. Do you care so much for this woman, my brother?"

"No, no, of course not," replied the brave stoically, unwilling to share his true feelings. "I feel sorry for her; she is a pleasant person, a good human being. Have you not found this to be true?"

"Yes," she replied looking sadly at her brother, "yes, she is a pleasant person but she is not one of us."

The dead bodies were stripped, burned and eventually the ashes buried. The turkey was retrieved from the forest where it had been dropped. The sons of She-Who-Laughs-In-Her-Sleep next searched the strangers' craft and brought all they found to the cabin.

It was not seemly for Son-of-Sky-Hawk to tend a woman but in the absence of any other women he tended to Marie until his sister was recovered enough to take over. The gash on Marie's forehead bled profusely at first but it was not deep and it clotted over, leaving her hair matted and stuck to her scalp. More disturbing was the swelling and intense discoloration of her flesh. But it was the pain that was debilitating and all they could offer her was willow bark tea and a strange mushroom that took her to a land of oblivion.

It took days for Marie to be able to rise to her feet on her own. At first, her head hurt so fiercely she became nauseated and threw up. She did not want to talk and said little while the natives murmured around her. Sounds bothered her, light bothered her. She could not tolerate the sun. But in her mind as she lay quietly in the darkened cabin, she relived every detail of what had happened over and over, dozens of times.

She had killed a man!

She had killed a man and she did not know how she felt about that.

She had killed a man, taken a life. She knew nothing about the stranger but it was obvious he had been intent on doing no good. He and his partner would have most certainly raped her, undoubtedly hurt her, robbed them of what little they had and perhaps even enslaved them but would he have attempted to kill her if Shee-hoo had not produced a weapon? Perhaps. Marie would never know. She had learned to submit and survive in Bouchet's tavern. But Jacques was right, once the musket appeared, either he or his partner would most certainly have seen both her and Sheehoo dead. So, had she not acted in self-defense?

She had killed a man in self-defense. But that would not have saved her from his partner if Looking Glass had not come upon the scene. She owed the brave her life. She knew it and she knew he knew it. And for her this also made things... awkward.

She had killed another human and Looking Glass had been forced to kill as well and Sheehoo had been injured. Was it all because Jacques had not returned last autumn as he had promised? Was he somehow at fault? Or was he dead? No! No! She could not blame anyone but herself! Had he not told her it could be very dangerous? And had she not insisted on coming to the frontier anyway? Had she not begged to come no matter the dangers? And had Jacques not taught her how to shoot in order to defend herself from the dangers? But, in reality there was no way she could have won, she was no match against two, not when she had only one shot.

Finally the headaches lessened.

Marie rose from her bed, careful of her balance, and sat down at the table. For the first time she was aware of the pile of strange items setting there before her.

"What is all this?" she asked of no one in particular, yet knowing only Shee-hoo could answer her question.

"Belong to white strangers," the squaw explained quietly. "We are the wronged. It is just that they are now dead, they had evil in their hearts, and because they sought to do us harm, it is our right to take all that we want of what belonged to them."

Marie sat looking at the woman letting the meaning of her words sink it. It was so simple to these people. The men were evil, they sought to do harm, they deserved to die, so now they were dead. There was no second guessing, no recriminations, no guilt. It is justice. Marie nodded. It *is* just. The swift retribution of life.

She was about to say she wanted *nothing* that belonged to them, that the very thought of touching their possessions made her skin crawl when she noticed a box. She opened it and inside she found a pair of shiny, well-oiled flintlock pistols with accompanying cleaning and priming paraphernalia.

"This," said Marie quietly. "This I will keep. Everything else is yours to do with as you want."

"You sure?" Sheehoo asked in disbelief. "Many things here, other weapons, rope, traps, even some white man *moni*. And they bring white man boat."

Marie reached out and took hold of Sheehoo's hands. "I am very certain," Marie said softly, trying not to squint or frown in pain as she looked at the other woman. "You and your brother have been... I have not the right words. He saved my life, twice. Once by bringing you here to be my companion through the lonely winter and because of that your life was in danger. I know this and I am deeply sorry for it. The second time, he saved my life by killing the stranger. And I am so very, very grateful for everything you and he have done. Please tell him this. And tell him I owe him a debt I can never repay. But also tell him I must stay here and wait for my husband but if he does not return I must find a way to keep my trading post going on my own. It is the life I choose. And this," she gestured to the table top, "you deserve much more than I."

The pain in Marie's head grew less each day. The fog and distortion within her brain and vision was clearing and her appetite returned. After carefully examining the pistols, one day she finally decided to load them and see how they fired. That night She-Who-Laughs-In-Her-Sleep told her brother it was time for them to leave.

"I go now," the stout little woman said without ceremony early the next morning. Marie nodded. "You no much food. Need new supply. I tell second son to come back in this many days." She held up both hands, her fingers spread wide. "He spend time in white man boat." She gestured out to the harbor, moving her hand back and forth. "He learn fast, good. If no one come to take you to big village, he take you. You get new supply."

"What is his name?"

"Call him... color of eyes..." she faltered trying to think of the English.

"His eyes? Green eyes?" guessed Marie.

"Yes, Green Eyes."

Marie nodded again indicating her agreement to the plan. Once in New York Towne she could ask Master Wingate's assistance in making arrangements to return via a small packet boat and to request the boat's return on a semi-annual basis. She spontaneously embraced Sheehoo. It was a good plan.

Looking Glass stood patiently waiting. He gave Marie a silent nod good-bye and began walking into the forest. His sister dutifully followed behind.

"Good-bye, and thank you again, my friends, my *win-ga'-leet,*" Marie waved and called after them. She watched until they disappeared from view. She shivered despite the warmth of the sun. She was alone for the first time since mid-winter. And she felt afraid to be alone for the first time since she had arrived.

Marie quickly went back into the cabin in search of a belt. She had no leather belt so she tore a long length of fabric from her oldest skirt and wrapped it tightly around her waist. She shoved the two freshly reloaded pistols into it, one on each hip. Sweat broke out on the back of her neck as she grabbed the musket and forced herself to walk out to the point of the small bluff. She stood at the top of the switchback trail. It was the first time she had done this since the arrival of the strangers. Looking down she could see that the craft they had arrived in was indeed gone. Sheehoo's sons had taken it. Good riddance. The early morning mist off the sea was lifting as she searched the waters making certain she saw no craft. Then she turned her back on the water and stood for a few minutes surveying the cabin site.

When she, Jacques, and Richard had arrived here, there had been nothing but forest. Now, there was a reasonable clearing, a two room cabin set among the trees, an outdoor oven, outbuildings, a growing garden plot, and a widening trail leading into the forest where a band of friendly Indians lived and came through to trade. In addition, a half dozen white families had gone up the river to stakeout homesteads and could be expected to come back to buy goods. She was not going to abandon it all. They had worked hard for this. She had worked hard for this. It was her home and if she had lost Jacques, she was not going to lose this as well. She would conquer the terror she now felt at being alone. She would master it and not allow it to conquer her. She had never realized how vulnerable she really was.

Marie chided herself. She could not believe she had once thought Sheehoo to be dull witted. The native woman had come up with the perfect plan to help Marie get back to New York Towne for supplies. And she would not allow herself to become so melancholy again. That would solve nothing. She remembered again what Anoui had said, *you must learn to go on and never give up hope*.

And what about winter, she asked herself? She had thought of offering to take in one of the Indian children who would like to learn English. Or perhaps one of the homesteaders with one more mouth to feed than they could provide for would agree to allow her to keep an older child for the winter. Now that she knew the dangers, she could work something out.

Marie saw the ship sail into the harbor from the south. She was prepared to bargain with them to take her north up the coast to New York Towne if she could just make contact with them. She watched it drop anchor in the harbor and launch a small boat. She strained to make out the flag. She thought she recognized it as English. As the small boat drew closer coming up the river she saw figures on board; she thought she recognized something familiar about them although they were not close enough to make out clearly. As she continued to watch, an arm went up and began to wave at her in a most familiar way. Her heart skipped a beat within her breast and began thumping wildly. In an instant she knew beyond any doubt that it was Jacques.

Jacques!

He was alive!

Making her way down to the water's edge, Marie's heart was racing as she waited for the boat. She stood on the bank, then turned and began pacing up and down the footpath in agitation and excitement, trying to get a better view. Finally, the boat was in sight again, much closer now and she could see Jacques distinctly. She wanted to laugh for joy and yet she was on the verge of tears. He and Richard both looked so nonchalant, so fit, so healthy... as if staying away for an entire year was nothing to them at all.

Suddenly she wanted to slap him fiercely across his handsome face for driving her half insane with anxiety and despair. But she also wanted to throw herself at his feet and kiss them for bringing him back to her. She wanted to hear instantly everything that had happened to have kept him from her so long. She wanted to tell him instantly everything she had been through during the long, lonely year he had been gone. But more than anything else, she just wanted to touch him. She wanted to feel his arms around her, protecting her, his lips on hers, and to rest her head upon his neck.

Caught at the end of the footpath, Marie stood rooted to the spot. The craft hit the riverbank and Jacques and Richard leapt from it dressed in strange clothing. Motionless and speechless, with gaping mouth, she remained like a statue, watching them push the craft back out into the river so it could return to the ship from which it came. Jacques and Richard advanced toward her until Jacques was only a few feet away. It was impossible to read his face as he stared at her.

Before him stood Marie as still as a statue and it was obvious that something terrible had happened. Ugly bruises discolored her precious face. That they were fading into shades of yellow and green spoke to the fact that they had been far worse while a freshly healed scar marked her forehead. Two flintlocks he had never seen were stuck into a belt at her waist. He knew the smile on his face had been shocked away.

The statue moved. Her arms opened to him and she began to tremble violently as she softly cried out his name, over and over. He rushed to sweep her into his arms. Tears streamed uncontrollably down her cheeks as she clung to him fiercely. Soothingly he kissed her battered flesh and reassured her until she calmed.

"I thought I would never see you again," was all she could say, repeating herself over and over. She turned and gave Richard a hug as well which pleased him although he said little, trying to hide a frown as he looked at her. "They kept telling me you were dead," she sobbed as the tears kept flowing. "That you had to be dead to be gone so long."

"Who kept telling you?" Richard asked.

"The natives, they were certain you were..."

"Did they do this to you?" Jacques demanded fiercely.
"No, Jacques, no. *Mon Dieu*, no. They saved my life… twice!"

That evening Jacques and Richard hung on every word as Marie relayed in detail what had befallen her over the past winter and most recently with the strangers. She had taken to wearing the flintlocks, she said, because she realized the musket was not enough. She needed two shots, perhaps three, to have a fighting chance for she could not expect Looking Glass to be there next time.

"If it please God Almighty, there will be no next time," Jacques said quietly, hoarse with emotion. "Richard and I have been discussing things and have come to a decision. You should know I have no intention of going deeply into the wilderness again at least until the wars are over and we can know for certain which side of the line we are on. The borders between the French and English are too mercurial, constantly changing like the tide markings upon a shore. The interior is so unstable. There is a tug-of-war going on between these two powers of the Old World and it is almost impossible not to get caught up within it."

"But how will Richard avoid it?" Marie asked and looked to Richard.

"I am better at blending in with the natives and if I should encounter French troops, forget not, there is no price upon my head," he made himself smile broadly as if there were no marks upon Marie's face. "So, we have agreed and coming home to hear what has happened in our absence is proof that we make the right plan. I will travel the wilderness with guides while Jacques continues doing business much closer to home."

It was a plan that appealed to everyone and Marie's heart rejoiced.

Late that night the door to Richard's room was shut tightly and one candle still burned as Jacques and Marie held each other in their bed. Marie needed no words to express how very much she had missed Jacques. She was overwhelmed with the need to caress him, and feel his intimate touch. The reassurance, the comfort, the security of knowing he was there was heightened by all that had happened in a year that had grown much too long.

Jacques knew without any doubt that she had longed for him every bit as much as he for her. The pent up desires of the past year burst forth in a demanding fervor to find release in the voracity of their couplings.

Then, with less desperation they continued to savor the wonderment of being together again. He drank in the familiar clean smell of her skin, her hair, her flesh and savored the tastes of her, tenderly mindful of her bruises. He found himself silently thanking God repeatedly with an intensity fueled by the fearful realization of how very close she had come to being lost to him forever.

Jacques gently caressed Marie's face. It was a wonder she had not been hurt much more severely. The brute could have killed her or permanently maimed her; she could have lost an eye, her perfect nose could have been shattered, or bone driven into her brain. He was filled with recriminations for not being there as he gently kissed her brow, his lips soft and warm.

"It grieves me beyond words that you have suffered this, Marie, *ma chérie,* I should have been here."

"I am ugly now?"

"No-no, how can you ask that? The scar is so shallow, it will fade to nothing in a short time and even if it did not it would not matter to me. I am just sickened by the thought of what could have happened. I am your husband. I am supposed to protect you. I thank God that big Indian was around but I am certain he does not think much of me at the moment." He tried to smile as he stroked her tenderly. "I know Richard is not happy with me."

"But it was not your fault. You could not make it home. Could you have made it home sooner?"

"Impossible," he assured her. "Once we left the shelter after that storm, our fate was sealed. If only we had had the patience to wait another week before getting back onto the waters. We might have arrived as we planned. And in the far northwest, *mon Dieu,* you never saw so much snow. We were buried. Like animals forced into hibernation. Even after we arrived at Wilmington, we had to wait over a week before leaving on the ship that brought us here. But we will tell you all about it tomorrow."

She looked at him. "Jacques..." she whispered.

"Yes, my darling?"

"Have you ever had to kill... a person?"

"No..." he looked in her eyes, "but some day I might be forced to."

"I am afraid, Jacques."

"Oh, my dearest, be not afraid, I am here now." He pulled her closer.

"But I am afraid it has changed me."

"In what way?"

"I am not certain."

"Every day changes us, every experience, every trial. What can I do to help?" he asked earnestly. "What will ease your mind? Make you feel safe?"

"Hold me, when I am in your arms everything is right. Tell me... tell me I am not a bad person."

He raised up on his arm to look her in the face. "Marie, you are *not* a bad person, you are the very opposite. You are good, so good... oh, my darling, how can you even think such a thing? It was self-defense and it terrifies me to think I could have lost you. I need you. I need you desperately... the frustration of not being able to get back to you almost drove me mad!" He began to plant kisses on her again.

And so it continued, far into the night. They would doze, then awake with renewed disbelief at being in each other's arms only to reassure each other that it was true. And the hunger would return to seek pleasure in each other's caresses.

Morning came too quickly. Richard woke first, stretched, threw on his clothing and quietly tiptoed from his bedroom through the darkened main room and out to the privy. As soon as he left, Jacques woke Marie so she could dress.

When Richard returned, having passed Jacques on the path to the privy, he found the cabin bathed in the eastern sunlight with the window shutters and door wide open to the late spring.

"Ah, Marie, I cannot wait for one of your breakfasts. It has been much too long, a whole year in fact, *n'est-ce pas?*" he laughed. "I am hungry enough to eat anything."

"That is good, Richard, for I am afraid your choices are going to be somewhat limited. Would you fetch water while I go to the privy?" She handed him a bucket and took her own trip outdoors and catching Jacques exiting asked him to bring in fish from the smokehouse for their breakfast.

When Marie returned she pulled out the pot of beans she had shoved into the ashes the night before and created a bean mash to go with the smoked fish.

"Beans again? Oh, well. Where is the coffee?"

"I am sorry Richard, I have no coffee," Marie replied as she salted the beans sparingly.

"Allow me, I will make some."

She smiled. "I mean I have no coffee."

"Oh, well, if we must, I suppose we can have black tea."

"I have no black tea."

Jacques had returned with the fish.

"She is all out of coffee and tea," Richard said.

"The water is clean and cold, it will serve us fine. Here have a fish."

Richard took the fish and put it on his plate. "I have been dreaming of your hard crusted bread, please say you have some of that even if it is a day or two old."

"I ran out of flour several weeks ago," she replied as she served up the warm bean mash.

Jacques held her chair and Marie took her seat. It was then that he took a quick survey of her larder and realized she had almost no food at all. It was bad enough to think of Marie being frozen to death in the sheer mad loneliness of winter or being murdered by reprobates but now another horror was conjured.

There was still meat in the smokehouse. Obviously the Indians had kept her supplied on that score but she had run out of flour weeks ago she said and he saw no meal, barley, sugar, rice or oats. In fact aside from a couple jars of preserved vegetables and a half dozen jars of jam setting on her shelves, there was no food to be found in the cabin at all. The one sack of onions left in the root cellar had gone to sprout and begged to be replanted in the garden.

"Marie, how many days of beans have you left?" Jacques asked quietly.

"For the three of us?" she looked up to a sack hanging from the rafter. "I would say perhaps four."

"Good. Richard, do you think you can suffer beans, meat and water for three more days to give Marie a chance to continue healing before we go to New York Towne?

Instantly the dark haired man looked remorseful. "Of course. Marie, I am sorry I did not even notice that the cupboards were so bare. I complain like a child and you, on the brink of starvation."

"It is not so desperate as that, Richard," she smiled. "I would not starve, the Indians and I had a plan but, Jacques, we need not wait, not on my account unless," she gasped with the sudden thought and touched her face, "you are ashamed of me?"

"Ashamed of you?" Jacques looked startled at the thought and suddenly remorseful. "In truth, I am ashamed for me. What would your friends think of me? I return after a year's absence and having been unable to keep my wife from injury, they hear it was the natives who watched over you, cared for you, and saved your life."

"Oh, Jacques..." she leaned over to embrace him tenderly. "They will hear nothing on the subject." She looked over at Richard. "Is this not so?"

"It is not my story to tell," he shrugged.

"Besides," Jacques rallied, "I really do need to take a good look around, take stock, see what is needed for repair and so on. It has been a year," he smiled crookedly.

Throughout the next days, as the last signs of discoloration grew fainter on Marie's face, she heard how Jacques and Richard had been caught up and detoured by the war, lost everything in flood waters, took refuge within the Great Lakes region and were buried in snow and blocked by ice while impatiently awaiting the overly-long-in-coming spring. She heard of the wondrous furs they had acquired through their own trapping and the new contacts they had established with the Indians to whom they could return and trade again.

They even told her how they had been offered young women to cook for them and warm their furs.

"But Jacques refused. In fact, he risked offending the chief by refusing... indeed, I think he did offend until I told them Jacques was a newly wed," Richard laughed. Marie was sitting quietly watching Richard and then looked to Jacques.

"There was never a possibility," he said to her with quiet sincerity and then a smile. "No one could take your place in my furs."

Marie heard more than she really wanted to hear, it frightened her so until she heard Jacques tell how they had come eastward at last with their new treasures and down the Delaware River now guarded by English Forts. It was in the Delaware colony in a growing settlement, originally Swedish, then Dutch and now renamed "Wilmington" by the British, that they had sold their furs to a ship's captain and had been able to bathe, shave, get deloused and a hair cut, and purchase new clothing. They were most fortunate that the ship was there and heading to New York

Towne next and that the captain agreed to allow them to ride along as far as their harbor… for a price.

And now they were home with a new goal and plan.

To be continued in

The Huguenot II
Building the Dream

by
D.C. Force

visit the author's website at
www.DCFORCE.com

In *The Huguenot II: Building the Dream*, the adventure continues. **Jacques** and **Marie** build a Jersey frontier settlement on the "safe" side of the Atlantic Ocean, while **Richard** establishes a network of trading posts into the Great Lakes. The trio face new challenges in this powerful and sexy second book of the Huguenot series.

Greed, jealousy, sociopaths, opioid addiction, alternative medicine, self doubts, the challenges of business and parenting, secrets and lies in the marriage bed, the breakdown of communications, race riots, native people's resistance to losing land, teenage pregnancy… is it the 17th century or the 21st century?? Human problems are timeless!

Life is not easy in any century but LOVE can deal with everything… or can it? These three seek a path to succeed in building their dream in the New World.

Huguenot II: Building the Dream.

Author's Note

This is a story which has sprung forth from combining historical facts with family legends. Hopefully it entertains as well as sheds light on the often overlooked but brutal persecution of French Protestants during the 16th, 17th, and into the 18th century in France. While doing research, the stories unfolded themselves. The opening scene, for example, of the horrific "dead of night" visit and violent slaughter of a family comes directly from historical records as does the pitiful act of domestic terrorism visited upon the young Huguenot mother and her infant in their own bedroom. This was not France's finest hour.

The *Duc de la Force* was indeed thrown into the Bastille and it is recorded that King Louis XIV sent his personal confessor to discuss with the duke his "errant religious attitudes." La Force was a Huguenot but due to his high rank, his advanced age, and his very poor health, Louis allowed for la Force's release and return home after only a short incarceration. According to further research, when the old duke died, the next man "allowed" to receive his title was a staunch Catholic who is documented through firsthand accounts as being personally responsible for sending innocent Huguenots to the galleys.

That the Huguenot ducal heir eluded the pursuit of the *gen d'armes* during his escape from France by hiding under the skirts of his mistress is a story that has been passed down through the family for generations. It has also been alluded to in third party publications. And it was he, as the story goes, that ended up in America.

The French-Indian Wars were very precarious times for the people who lived them at the colonial frontiers and I have tried to depict the mood more than a chronological blow by blow of battles and raids. The lead up to the horrific massacre at Lachine on Montreal Island and the repercussions after it are accurate but I did take the liberty of bending the time by a year to fit the events to my characters' time table.

There was indeed a Huguenot Church in New York City which was lost to urban development. The last remaining Huguenot church still standing in the United States can be visited in Charleston, SC. Perhaps our most recognizable Huguenot founding father was Paul Revere, whose own father, *Apollos Rivoir*, escaped the French persecution and came to America in 1715 at age 13 where he settled in Boston, anglicized his name to Revere and subsequently married a colonial English girl.

Above all, *The Huguenot* is a love story depicting not only the love of humans for one another but also the love of man for his country and the love of the Huguenot immigrant for his home in America which has truly been and continues to be the land of enormous opportunity and freedom for so many millions who are "capable" and willing to apply themselves.

D.C. Force
Asheville, NC

Discussion Questions

Good, well-researched historical fiction can both entertain us as well as further our knowledge of history.

1. Before reading this book, were you aware of the Huguenot persecutions?

2. When Auguste Charte warns his grandson of dire things yet to come, why do you think the young man doesn't take it seriously?

3. It is sometimes said that the biggest lesson of history is that we do not learn from history. Do you agree? Do you think it is harder for young people to relate to history? Why?

4. How do we see Jacques, Richard, and Marie grow and change from the beginning of the story to the point where this book stops?

5. Do you think buying a horse immediately upon arrival in the New World was a wise purchase? What does it remind you of in today's society?

6. What was your first clue that Richard has serious feelings for Marie?

7. Discuss the need for swift justice.

8. Not all Native Americans were peaceful and friendly to the white settlers but not all were blood thirsty and war-like either. Discuss what you think Looking Glass found *fascinating* about Marie and if you think he could have accepted those same things if she had become his wife.

9. When Marie decides to accompany Jacques and Richard to the frontier, the Wingates are very concerned for her reputation. Why do you think Marie has no awareness of damaging her reputation?

10. Marie expresses the fear that the incident with the strangers may have changed her. What evidence do we see of just that the very next day?

CPSIA information can be obtained
at www.ICGtesting.com
Printed in the USA
FSHW011723010719
59616FS